Praise for Terry W. Ervin II and ~~~~

"Blood Sword is a tremendous installment in one of the most inventive and compelling fantasy sagas I have read in years!"
-Stephen Zimmer, author of the Fires in Eden Series and The Rising Dawn Saga.

"Blood Sword continues the adventures started in Flank Hawk, in which Ervin created a unique and detailed post apocalyptic world where magic works but ancient technologies from the First Civilization--our world--still exist. You'll cheer as they face off against griffins, fallen angels, gargoyles, and worse, in a fun, engaging adventure filled with wall to wall action."
-David Forbes, author of the Osserian Saga

"A worthy successor to the original novel, packed with action and entertainment."
-Jim Bernheimer, author of the Dead Eye series and Confessions of a D-List Supervillain

"A classic epic fantasy with plenty of original twists. You won't want to put it down, even when you've reached the end."
-David Debord, author of The Silver Serpent and Keeper of the Mists

"Grab hold! Ervin's got the magic!"
-C. Dean Andersson, author of the Bloodsong Trilogy

"A curious blend of epic fantasy, modern techno-thriller and non-stop action-adventure."
-Erica Hayes, author of the Shadowfae Chronicles

"Buy it or chalk it up on that long list of things you regret not doing!"
-Stephen Hines, author of Hocus Focus

Books by Terry W. Ervin II

First Civilization's Legacy
Flank Hawk
Blood Sword

FLANK
HAWK

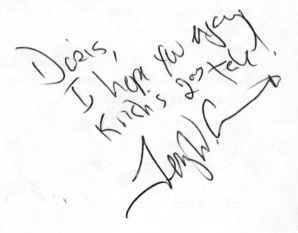

Terry W. Ervin II

Gryphonwood

Gryphonwood Press

BLOOD SWORD. Copyright 2011 by Terry W. Ervin II.

All rights reserved under International and Pan-American copyright conventions.

Published by Gryphonwood Press
www.gryphonwoodpress.com

Cover art by Christine Griffin

ISBN: 978-0-9837655-3-0

Printed in the United States of America

DEDICATION

This novel is dedicated to my daughters, Genevieve and Mira, who sometimes had to entertain themselves through summer mornings and afternoons while I typed away.

ACKNOWLEDGEMENTS

First, I would like to thank the members of Elysian Fields: Sandy, Bill, Jim, Rick, Cher and Jerry. Your crits and input helped keep Krish's story on track.

I would also like to express my appreciation to Marilyn Mitchell and Jeff Koleno for taking the time to read the manuscript, share their thoughts, and provide vital input. *Blood Sword* is a better novel because of your efforts. I shouldn't forget my wife, co-workers, family, and friends, all of whom encouraged, questioned, and prodded me along to get *Blood Sword* finished.

With respect to the awesome cover art, I am grateful for the opportunity to have worked with Christine Griffin a second time. You really captured Krish (Flank Hawk) and Grand Wizard Seelain, and the novel's tone.

As for Cloud Runner, know that Jim Coon devised the character's name, having had his name selected from the many who signed up for the chance to name a character in my second novel. It was a pleasure to work with him on that creative endeavor.

Finally, I'd like to thank David Wood and everyone at Gryphonwood Press for believing enough in my first novel to publish it, and for believing enough in Krish's second adventure to publish it as well.

That leaves you, the reader. You're the reason I wrote *Blood Sword*. Thank you for choosing my fantasy novel from the tens of thousands available. I truly hope you enjoy the story, and don't hesitate to let me know what you think.

CHAPTER 1

"They're coming," I said and handed the spyglass to Grand Wizard Seelain. Many officers and military tacticians had scoffed at Prince Reveron's prediction. They said it would be a waste of military assets to watch the passages through the Pyrenees Mountains. That was why Grand Wizard Seelain had volunteered, and brought me along.

Wizard Seelain crept to the outer line of stunted fir trees that hid us from the enemy below. She raised the brass telescopic device to her right eye and focused on the valley's narrow mouth. "Prince Reveron was indeed correct. They *are* coming."

We huddled in the secluded observation point a short distance from our camp. It was late afternoon, and the mountains would soon block the sun's light.

"They'll pass through to make camp further up the valley," I said, "where it broadens near the spring."

Grand Wizard Seelain returned the spyglass. "I agree, Flank Hawk." She opened her satchel and pulled out a small, leather-bound book and pencil. "We will depart soon after the sun sets. Until then, let us identify and count the forces which Fendra Jolain sends against us." Wizard Seelain didn't bother to conceal her hatred for the Goddess of Healing as she uttered the name.

The grand wizard wore a buckskin jacket and breeches over a sky-blue cotton blouse. Her white, almost translucent, hair hung in two long braids. I wasn't sure of her exact age, but she was at least thirty summers. And in our travels I'd discovered a few things about her many didn't know, like the surges of magic that coursed along her body when she got angry. As the assigned personal guard of the fiancé to Prince Reveron, I'd felt the prickling elemental energy more than once.

I avoided meeting her sky blue eyes. Partly because the left eye remained a shade darker than the right, ever reminding me of how I'd once nearly failed as her assigned guard. More so now, because they were narrowing. She was formulating a plan—without a doubt, plotting a way to dissuade the prince from again stepping forth to confront an enemy.

Words like 'dissuade' and 'plotting' weren't ones I normally used. They're what Prince Reveron said of Grand Wizard Seelain's objections when they openly discussed his leading military missions and campaigns.

In any case, I didn't want to be a part of the grand wizard's plan. Instead I stepped to the treeline and focused on looking through the spyglass into the valley, searching for something to say to that might distract the wizard from her anger.

"The scouts return," I said, pointing back along the wide trail leading toward the valley's broad eastern expanse. "Only half. I count three mounted on riding goats."

"Focus on the forces entering, Flank Hawk."

I nodded, knowing she held her pencil ready to scribe units and numbers. The truth was, I didn't really want to count. The numbers entering the valley were only advance forces, a small fraction what the Goddess of Healing sent to march against Keesee.

An armor-clad officer with a cape bearing red and white, the colors of Fendra Jolain, sat astride a gray warhorse. He pulled a map from a saddlebag and examined it before directing a group of foot soldiers toward a northern slope not far from the worn path. After marching over to an outcropping of granite boulders and engaging in a brief discussion, the soldiers stomped aside some brush before using spear shafts and shoulders to roll aside an oblong boulder.

"A cave," I said.

One soldier ducked inside the dark fissure, followed by a second. They emerged less than a minute later dragging a crate and two stuffed sacks.

"They've cached supplies along their route."

I shifted to my right as Wizard Seelain moved up next to me. "That is not good," she replied.

I agreed and voiced my concern. "They've been planning this march for at least a year, if not longer."

Wizard Seelain frowned at me. "They march for only one reason, Flank Hawk. Let us name it for what it is. An invasion."

I nodded. "Invasion. And that means they'd have thoroughly scouted this valley before stashing supplies."

"I agree," said Wizard Seelain. "A local inhabitant or guide familiar with the territory would have directed them to the cave." She shot a glance back to her bone-white staff resting against a dead limb. "Rare is a worthy mission that lacks some level of risk." She scanned the sky and distant mountainside. "The fact remains, my mercenary friend, we cannot depart unnoticed until after nightfall. Focus on our mission."

She was an air wizard—a powerful one, confident in her abilities. But I had been tasked to keep her safe. "Understood, Grand Wizard," I said and began counting troops and units.

She backed away and stood within reach of her staff and wrote as I spoke.

"An advance guard of twenty light horsemen followed by a company of light foot soldiers, mixed with maybe a dozen archers." A moment later I added, "Three beastmasters, each with an oversized pack of war dogs."

Fearless, muscled beasts, the canines had jaws that could clamp down on a man's leg, or throat, like an iron trap.

Then my heart sank. Coming into sight was the first of several company-sized mercenary tribes from the South Continent. They wore hardened leather armor adorned with exotic furs and colorful feathers. I'd heard about such mercenaries. They were both fierce and cunning. I kept my voice even. "Four companies of Malgerian mercenaries, different tribes," I guessed, based on feather color patterns and order of march, "carrying atlatls with javelins, and spiked maces."

I was counting additional light cavalry entering the valley when Grand Wizard Seelain sharply whispered, "Flank Hawk, remain still."

I froze, resisting the urge to look back, or up, or anywhere around. If Wizard Seelain issued an order, there was good reason. Still, I closed my right eye while opening my left to escape the spyglass' narrow scope.

Wizard Seelain whispered, "Above, from the east. Elemental beasts." She paused a moment. "Griffins."

The fir trees concealed us from eyes below and on the mountainsides, but we were visible among the trees from directly above. It could be that they were wild. But I doubted it, especially as they were approaching an army. And if the valley was a nesting ground, Grand Wizard Seelain would've detected them before now. Our mounts would have as well.

A hawk-like cry sounded from far above. Seconds later, a form shot past, just above the treeline. Not as large as a dragon, but big enough. A second griffin replied with a piercing call as it banked into a turn over the valley, back toward us.

Grand Wizard Seelain gripped her staff. "We are discovered."

CHAPTER 2

"Grand Wizard," I said, donning my steel helmet and readying my crossbow. "The mounts. Go and saddle them!" I glanced past Wizard Seelain to my boar spear lying under a ground pine's branches.

"Flank Hawk," she said, holding her staff and preparing a spell.

I stepped closer to the grand wizard. "Do as I say!" A third and fourth griffin announced their presence with piercing cries that echoed across the valley. War dogs barking, eager for blood, increased my urgency. "Your skill with wyverns surpasses mine." I selected one of my red-shafted quarrels and turned my back to the wizard as I scanned the sky. "I *will* follow."

Branches bent and snapped back as she sprinted through the trees, toward our camp a quarter mile away.

I was prepared to sacrifice myself to give Wizard Seelain time to escape, but only if necessary.

Six of the winged beasts formed up high above the valley's center. The smallest would put a prize bull to shame. A man—a beastmaster—sat astride the largest and pointed with his lance, giving our location to the enemy below.

I'd never seen a griffin before but knew of them. An eagle's head, wings and talonned feet with the muscled body of a lion. They were infused with the spirit of an air elemental, making them faster and more agile, and more dangerous than our wyvern mounts, which griffins preyed upon. On the ground the eagle-lion hybrids were said to be less nimble. Still, my breastplate and padded armor wouldn't stand to the power of a griffin's beak and talons. And five of them, directed by thought commands of their human master, were diving. Three angled toward me while two circled around beyond, to my right.

There was no reason to fret over the soldiers and war dogs seeking a path up the mountainside. They'd arrive well after this battle was decided. Wizard Seelain would escape, or we'd both lay dead.

I stepped beyond to the end of the treeline, four feet from the ledge's drop off, ensuring the distant beastmaster saw me.

The foremost firs at my back stood scarcely taller than me and offered little protection. The golden-feathered beasts knew this and came at me in a line, the mounted beastmaster observing from a distance.

The lead's green eyes locked on me. Front talons flexing. It leveled out and closed fast as any dragon. Only a lucky shot to an eye or artery along the neck would bring the beast down. Otherwise, my quarrel, although coated with fireweed resin, wouldn't be more than a nuisance.

I took several steps back into the trees, timing the lead griffin's approach. I had only seconds to act. The lead held its front talons closed with beak open to thrash as it passed. The second's tail dipped slightly with rear talon's flexed wide—to grasp. The third trailed fifty yards behind.

I screeched out my best guttural black dragon challenge. Road Toad, my mentor, would've laughed, but it had the desired effect. The lead griffin responded with its own call to my challenge. I called again, but instead of standing my ground I fell backwards before it reached me. Its wings clipped the tops of the trees and its beak snapped shut on air.

Just as I hit the ground I depressed my crossbow's trigger. The quarrel bit deep into the griffin's unprotected groin. It flew on, screeching in surprise, followed by pain. I tossed aside my crossbow and rolled to the right until my side struck the trunk of the nearest pine. I held tight to the roots. Branches cracked and shattered as the tree's trunk shuddered. Talons scraped across my backplate, but without force and failed to catch hold.

Crawling forward, I got to my knees and drew my broad-bladed short sword. Wings buffeting the air sounded behind me, ending in snapping branches and a *thump* as the third griffin landed. I turned and closed even as the griffin burst forward through the firs. The smell of carrion-soured breath hung in the air. I dodged right and thrust my sword into muscled flesh where the feathers met fur. The beast reared up before I could pull my sword free and slapped me aside, leaving grooves in my breastplate. I rolled with the blow, branches slowing my fall. With its beak the griffin pulled my sword from its shoulder. I scrambled through the trees toward my spear, avoiding both beak and talons as the griffin leapt after me.

I grabbed my spear on the run and shot through the trees. Griffins are pack animals. They work together to bring prey down even without a beastmaster's guidance. Two of the three hunting griffins were wounded. Not mortally but enough to slow them down. And to reach the overhang where our camp and mounts were, I'd have to survive an uphill dash through an expanse of tall white pines that offered little protection. Even so, I'd have to do what I could to distract and further cripple the griffins hunting me, and hope Seelain could take any that got past—not counting the two that'd already circled ahead.

I pressed on, up the steep grade through the trees while the sword-wounded griffin chased after me in squirrel-like bounds. It gained as the trees increased in size and also in the spread between them, leaving more room to maneuver. All to the beast's advantage.

A pair of griffin calls sounded in the distance. Another sounded above the trees and the one chasing me replied. No sound from the third in the group that had dived against me. I guessed it was lying in ambush with the sword-wounded one driving me to it.

I sounded a shrill black dragon call to keep the beastmaster focused on me and to let Seelain know I was still alive and fighting. I pushed off a tree and cut left. The sword-wounded griffin shot further left, then closed, trying to drive me back right. Near the camp we'd set a crude trip-cord trap that might further wound or even cripple one of my foes.

The sword-wounded griffin had closed to within fifteen yards. I angled right and slid through a stand of adult pines growing close together. That broke my pursuer's momentum. Instead of climbing toward the camp, I continued right and angled down toward a formation of trees growing in parallel lines eight feet apart. Five thick-trunked pines stretching ten yards, set across from a similar line of six.

My pursuer was again at full speed, gaining. But with luck I'd have time to enact my plan.

The sword-wounded griffin called out as I ran between the lined trees. It was less than ten yards behind. I spun and set the butt of my spear against the rocky ground and angled the steel tip, aiming to take my pursuer in the chest. The beast was coming on too fast to stop and the trees would block any attempt to maneuver left or right.

Despite its bloody shoulder and being unable to spread its wings, the griffin avoided my maneuver by leaping above my set boar spear's reach. Branches snagged and snapped against its folded wings. I thrust my spear upward--too slow to catch the griffin's vulnerable underside. It landed hard, favoring its wounded left shoulder. I charged as the griffin's claws gripped the root-ridden ground and the trunk of a sturdy pine. That allowed it to stop, spin and launch itself back at me through the shower of needles cascading down from the broken branches above.

I dodged left. Its talons caught my leg and tore through my armor. I knelt firm and slashed into flesh with my spear, the blade rattling across ribs as the beast shot past.

The wound my foe had inflicted sent sharp pain up my right leg. I stood and held my spear steady as the beast turned. It appeared surprised that I was standing my ground. My only other option was to run again. The wound would only slow me a bit, but I'd be heading into an ambush.

The griffin favored its injured shoulder, and the three-foot bleeding gash along its side made it wary of my bite. That was okay with me. The more time it took for the trio to take me down gave Grand Wizard Seelain a better chance to escape. And that was all that counted now. I couldn't fail. The king had scoffed at her choice of me over one of his elite infiltration soldiers. I'd prove she was right and he'd been wrong.

The needles stopped falling from above as I backed toward a narrow gap between two trees in the line of five. The smell of my sweat, the beast's hot sour breath and our blood filled the air. The griffin's eyes shifted between my gaze and the blood-stained tip of my spear while a trickle of my own blood began to fill my boot.

It stepped between the two close-set trees and feigned an attack. It clawed at my spear in an effort to knock it aside even as I pulled back. It paused before uttering a shrill staccato call. Summoning help.

A swirling disturbance in the branches above caught both mine and my foe's attention. The sound of wind, but not that made from flapping wings.

A dust devil-sized whirlwind gathered pine cones and needles as it descended through the trees and engulfed the griffin's head. The small elemental spirit began to dissipate the instant it made contact with the beast. Even so, the griffin was temporarily blinded and I took advantage of the aid sent by Wizard Seelain. While it bucked, beak snapping and talons slashing through the faltering elemental, I thrust my spear deep into the beast's throat, up to the crossbar before tugging back and releasing an arterial spout of blood.

I backed away from my mortally wounded foe as it fell to the ground in shock. I scanned the trees and game trail ahead for more griffins. Not spotting any, I looked down at my blood-soaked padded armor, trying to decide if I should tend my wound. The battle cry of another griffin racing toward me through the trees settled the question.

This foe stood several hands taller than the now dead griffin. A *thump* forty yards to my right announced the landing of another griffin—the one I'd shot with my crossbow. It moved across the mountainside slower but with determination equal to its pack mate now only thirty yards away.

Even without an injured leg, evading two griffins for more than a minute or two would've been impossible. I backed away, angling to put my back against an uprooted pine leaning against a smaller tree. Behind the conifers stood a small outcropping of granite boulders. No more aid would come from Grand Wizard Seelain, but my stand might buy her another thirty seconds.

"Come on!" I shouted. "How 'bout a taste of cold steel?"

They circled, the big one wide to my left, the crossbow-wounded one to my right, each daring me to turn my back to the other, or to make a foolhardy dash straight ahead between them. I knew my target, the crossbow-wounded one. It was smaller and stalked more hesitantly, the fireweed resin still stinging its groin. But I wouldn't commit until it was within striking range. I'd only get one thrust before being brought down from behind. And with a good measure of luck, maybe Wizard Seelain would have one less griffin to face.

I braced myself, shifting my gaze from one griffin to the other. I had to make my attack the instant before the griffin pair pounced. Suddenly they halted their approach—and retreated a step, then another. The larger looked up and sounded a guttural squawk.

Something was happening that I wasn't aware of. Both beasts backed away, ruffling their feathers and wings in a threat display before turning and bounding away. As soon as they reached a break in the canopy, they leapt into the air and took flight.

The beastmaster must've recalled them. Their focus had become Grand Wizard Seelain. Had she taken flight? Or was she on the ground, fending off the beastmaster and his other three griffins?

I made the quick decision to check my wounded leg. Pulling up the rent padded armor, I examined the shallow tear a talon had inflicted just below the knee. My armor and the sliced leather of my boot had absorbed most of the blow. There'd be a bruise, and it was still bleeding. I set aside the notion of casting the only healing spell I knew. I could probably stop most of the bleeding, but it'd start bleeding again once I began running. Still, if I kept bleeding, I'd be weakened even if I reached Wizard Seelain in time. I'd seen it happen, mercenaries neglecting a wound and regretting it later—if they survived.

I couldn't use my boot dirk—it was coated with fireweed resin. So I awkwardly cut away a strip of cloth by drawing the lining of my armor's left pant leg across the blade of my spearhead. The cotton was soaked with blood and slippery, but I managed to wrap it round the wound and tie a strong knot. It'd bleed upon moving my leg, but not very much.

The effort had taken a little more than a minute, an eternity in combat. I grabbed my spear and dashed uphill, along the game trail toward our camp. Above, through the trees, I caught glimpses of griffins overhead. Their echoing calls and the deep, rumbling screech—a wyvern's cry when threatened—sounded as well. From a ways downhill rose the sounds of war dogs on the hunt. I hoped Wizard Seelain had managed to saddle my mount. Wick responded well enough to my flight commands, but wasn't always cooperative on the ground. And with griffins overhead and dogs not far behind me, the wyvern would be frightened and on edge. That was, if Wick was still alive.

I raced uphill, wincing each time I pushed off my left leg. The trip-cord trap remained intact. Hopefully a war dog would take a hit from the spiked branch the crude trap would release.

We'd established our camp beneath a narrow overhang of rock and scraggly trees. Wick huddled low, pressing against the rock wall, his feather coat working to conceal him despite the presence of a polished leather saddle.

Wyverns are large beasts that most resemble a cross between a giant vulture and a black dragon. Except for their eyes, vulture-like beaks, and the females' barbed tales, a thin coat of feathers changes from deep greens to varying shades of brown and gray, all the way to black to conceal the nocturnal scavengers like a chameleon lizard.

The saddle straddling Wick's bat-like wings foiled his attempt to remain hidden to all but the most casual observer. Sprawled on the ground ten yards from my mount lay a griffin. Blood seeped from its glassy eyes, beaked nose and mouth, and where I guessed its ears would be found. The fallen beast was surely a victim of Grand Wizard Seelain's magic. Still, its chest weakly rose and fell.

"Easy, Wick," I said while approaching the griffin. With a quick spear thrust to the throat, I made sure the beast would never recover to fly against the forces of Keesee. I stared skyward while wiping blood from my spear's blade across the dead griffin's hide. "We must be swift, Wick." As with a faithful dog, I hoped the confident sound of my voice would instill confidence in my mount. I didn't explain Wizard Seelain's plight in the sky above. My anxiety might leak into my words. I secured my spear in its sheath before undoing the woven leather and steel wire tether looped from Wick's tail to one of his bluntly clawed feet. It was an odd but effective method to keep a male wyvern from taking flight when unattended, especially when spooked.

I kept my actions steady and deliberate to avoid exciting my mount any more than its wide eyes showed it to be. "Easy, Wick," I said while climbing into the saddle and fitting my boots into the stirrups before looping and pulling leather straps tight over my thighs. My mount's color shifted to a slate gray and he emitted a gurgling rumble from deep within his throat, telling me he remained unsettled. I urged him to step over the dead griffin to reach open ground.

Male wyverns aren't helpless. Sturdy with quick reflexes and a dangerous beak, they can take care of themselves. But unlike their domineering female counterparts armed with a poison barb on the end of their tails, males shy from combat whenever possible—and especially with griffins.

I leaned forward and dug the iron stud-lined stirrups into Wick's side. "Up," I urged.

Wick gazed into the sky above. They'd found reinforcements as five griffins circled Wizard Seelain on her mount, feigning attacks, testing her defenses while the beastmaster astride his mount circled a short distance above.

My mount craned his neck and looked back at me.

I kicked harder with the stirrups. The studs weren't long and not particularly sharp, but they sent the message nevertheless. "Up!"

My only remaining option was to pull my boot dirk, but I didn't want to play that card until absolutely necessary. Snarling barks from closing war dogs convinced Wick the ground wasn't a place to remain, so he spread his wings and leapt skyward. Wyverns can't match a dragon's grace. They have to work harder to get airborne, especially with a rider. But once in the air they can remain aloft for hours on end.

The aerial dance overhead drifted eastward as Grand Wizard Seelain sought an escape. Seelain's mount, Moon Ash, stalled and turned, climbed and dove, like a besieged duck trying to track and avoid a half dozen hawks— ones which dove and turned more like barn swallows than large birds of prey.

My objective was to get above the fray and use the advantage superior altitude provided to break up the aerial snare entrapping Wizard Seelain. The sun lowering in the west concealed me and my mount as we struggled for altitude. Enemy efforts focused on Wizard Seelain as she spun about with her staff, foiling attacks with wind blasts or undercutting air currents that'd send one griffin tumbling even as another swooped in to take its place. They never allowed her a chance to finish off any one of their number before it recovered, to climb and again come at her, beak open and talons ready.

Seelain and her mount worked as one, but both were quickly being worn down while Wick struggled to rise above the fray. Even worse, the beastmaster appeared to be a wizard of some ability as I watched him deflect at least two attacks Wizard Seelain directed his way.

My crossbow might've enabled me to wound or at least distract the beastmaster. It was gone along with my sword. My spear and dirk were my only weapons and neither was useful unless I got very close. Wick tugged back against the reins as I signaled him to turn about. We'd dive on the enemy. Maybe use my spear as a lance, even throw it, or ram one of the griffins if necessary.

Wick fought against me, unwilling to turn and dive. It was his instinct crying out for him to flee. I shifted both reins to my left hand, pulled my dirk, and drove its point a half inch into my unwilling mount's neck. Wick had other inborn fears, like that of a dominant female's barbed tale. The fireweed resin stung his flesh as would a female wyvern's poison.

My mount obeyed and winged over into a swooping dive. I sheathed my dirk before pulling my spear from its sheath. Not an easy thing with air buffeting past.

Wick aimed for the beastmaster and his griffin mount without my guidance. His instinct for ending the battle quickly was on target, just like his instinct to flee for survival had been. I gritted my teeth. Sacrificing myself was one thing, but sacrificing a loyal mount twisted my guts.

Two griffins came at Wizard Seelain at once. She summoned a wall of air and brought it down on the larger griffin, slapping the beast ten feet down, leaving it momentarily stunned. But neither Seelain nor Moon Ash was fast enough to foil the second attack. Eagle-like talons slashed into the wyvern's leg and tail. Moon Ash screeched in pain while turning on Seelain's command to face yet a third closing foe.

The beastmaster spotted us and pointed his white three-foot rod and began a spell. He was too far to hurl my spear. Wick's feather coat shifted to white, the color of aggression as he bellowed an attack cry, a sound caught between a crow's *caw* and a bear's growl. Whatever spell came our way, we'd have to bull through it.

The beastmaster's mount turned sharply and dove just after he released a spell. With a snapping sound like a sail struck by a sharp wind, a wall of air deflected us off course, away from our target. A smaller griffin came at us. Wick turned back into the aerial barrier and broke through to meet the new foe head on. This surprised but didn't deter the griffin who came with beak open and talons spread.

Wick's colors remained white—he was going to meet the griffin head-on. Although Wick was larger and could weather the impact better, it was risky. A wing could be broken or the griffin could latch onto Wick's vulnerable underside before tearing into it.

Spear ready, at the last second I kicked hard with the stirrups and ordered, "Down!" The same instant that I shouted, the griffin angled left to avoid a head-on impact and catch Wick's wing instead. Then the young griffin attempted to veer off even as Wick angled back toward our foe while diving.

I held tight as my spear lanced into the griffin's ribs up to the crossbar. The resulting jolt lifted me from the saddle. Luckily the leather straps held. My back and shoulder twisted as the griffin passed overhead, causing my grip to fail. The screeching beast fell, taking my imbedded spear along with it. Wick turned to chase the foundering griffin even as it snorted blood and erratically flapped its wings, struggling to maintain altitude.

I pulled up, searching for another target. I was out of weapons, except for my dirk, but Wick's blood was hot, ready to take on another griffin.

A thunderclap sounded nearby. Wizard Seelain had managed to work one of her devastating spells. She'd destroyed a sphere of air around the beastmaster and his mount. The surrounding air rushed in to fill the empty space, slamming the target like a hammer blow from all sides.

The beastmaster flopped to the side with leather straps the only thing keeping him in the saddle. His white rod slipped from his grasp, falling through the scattered puff of descending griffin feathers.

One screeching griffin dove at Wizard Seelain with reckless abandon. The others raced to their master's aid. I turned Wick to intercept the diving griffin while Wizard Seelain swooped toward the beastmaster's foundering mount. Her mount, Moon Ash, sensed the tide of battle changing and his color shifted to match his name.

The diving griffin angled away, avoiding a collision with Wick, but the maneuver threw him off, giving Moon Ash a chance to slide right. The griffin shot down past Wizard Seelain on her left, leaving her free to complete another spell. A rapid series of loud pops, like green logs on a hot fire, sounded around the unconscious beastmaster. His body shuddered even as a pair of griffins weathered the aerial concussions to hold the dying griffin mount aloft.

Wizard Seelain sagged in her saddle, weakened by her effort.

"We must make our escape now!" I shouted.

She nodded as I circled around and came up beside her. Wick and Moon Ash flapped their wings, straining for altitude.

I looked back. The griffins weren't giving chase. At least not yet. "You lead. I'll follow."

Wizard Seelain sat up straight, some of her strength apparently returning. She pointed to my blood-soaked armor.

"A shallow wound," I said and checked the sky behind us again. "Grand Wizard, take the lead."

She nodded and led the way out of the valley and through a pass to another valley filled with pines and stunted oaks whose roots gripped the rocky ledges. We raced along the northern slopes sixty feet above the trees as the shadows from the setting sun grew longer.

CHAPTER 3

Grand Wizard Seelain must've noticed my efforts to tighten the bandage on my leg. Or maybe it was a desire to examine Moon Ash's wounds. But after less than twenty minutes of flight, she led the way down into a thick stand of oaks.

During our short flight I'd been pondering what to do. My wound had continued to bleed and I couldn't get it to stop. I was preparing to signal Wizard Seelain to land so that I could tend to it as continued blood loss would weaken me, or worse. I'd already flown near Moon Ash to examine the talon wounds dug into his tail and leg. They were long but shallow and shedding only a trickle of blood. They were probably painful but not nearly bad enough to weaken a wyvern-sized beast.

Now, it was too dark to see clearly, especially concealed within the newly leafed trees. I dismounted Wick and tried to hide my limp as I hurried to take the reins of Wizard Seelain's mount. With the urgency of battle gone, pain coursed through my leg. Being a rogue healer—a neophyte—my wounds healed faster than other mercenaries, but I suffered pain like everyone else. I had the ability to cast a single, minor spell. That was all. Yet, if it was known, it was enough to cost me my freedom.

Wizard Seelain spoke as she dismounted. "You are injured."

I had to be honest, at least on this point. "I am, Grand Wizard. Possibly worse than I initially thought."

She pointed toward the base of a large oak tree. "Over there, Flank Hawk. Sit down and allow me to examine it."

"We should see to your mount's wounds first."

"Nonsense. You have already assessed Moon Ash's wounds. I will tether our mounts. You, remove your boot and leggings." She handed me a short candle and a metal case from her saddlebag. "We cannot risk a campfire, but we must be able to see."

"We must be on the move soon. The griffins may be seeking us."

"I slew their master, and you know griffins are diurnal sight hunters."

Healers and healing was already weighing heavily on my mind. I'd kept my ability a tightly held secret. Only a handful of people had *ever* known and, of those few, several were dead.

"Slaying the beastmaster rather than immediately escaping was a wise tactical move," I said while limping over to the tree. I grimaced and lowered myself to the ground with my back against the trunk. Its roots were uncomfortable but the branches and leaves directly above would block candlelight. I opened the tin which held wooden matches. They were rare, but Wizard Seelain was both wealthy and influential. I guessed she'd gotten them from a skilled alchemist as opposed to bartering for them with a Crusader.

I'd already cut the fabric of my padded armor so it was easy to roll it up to my knee. The beeswax coating had repelled most of the blood that soaked through my makeshift bandage and down into my boot. The warm sloshing of my sock at the bottom wasn't a good sign. I wasn't sure I had the spell strength to stop the bleeding, even with the white oak bark, a spell component hidden in the bottom of my saddlebag.

I gritted my teeth, preparing to pull my boot off but Wizard Seelain said, "Light the candle first."

I wanted to avoid lighting it as long as possible, just in case the enemy had a second griffin beastmaster on hand to search for us. I didn't argue and struck a match on the case's roughened bottom after screwing the cap back on. The candle lit quickly and Wizard Seelain maneuvered my hand to hold it where she could best view my wound located just below the knee.

I held my breath and gritted my teeth as she pulled my boot off and removed the bloody bandage. "I am not an expert in battle wounds," she said. "This one doesn't appear crippling, but you've lost a lot of blood and will continue to do so, leading to unconsciousness and death if you remount and ride."

I agreed. The deep gash bled, more when I moved or flexed my leg even slightly. Even a tight wrapping wouldn't stop it.

She cleaned my wound with a cloth and water from her canteen. I gripped a tree root with one hand while trying to hold the candle steady with the other. She held my leg still.

"I am quite sure that hurt, Flank Hawk," she said, handing me the canteen. "Drink."

"As usual, you're quite right," I said, trying to smile.

While she wrapped the wound with a fresh bandage, I said, "I'll rest until morning. You must continue as soon as you're finished here."

She met my eyes and I knew her words before she said them. "I will not abandon you, Flank Hawk."

"You must."

She shook her head while tying the final knot. "Travel under concealment of darkness is required with the enemy so close."

"Then I'll wait until nightfall tomorrow," I said, knowing if I could manage a strong enough spell, I could possibly leave several hours before dawn.

"And I will wait with you."

This was an argument I couldn't lose. Remaining in place a full day invited capture, or death. "Grand Wizard, I am *your* bodyguard." It was difficult to keep my voice close to a whisper. Red already showed through the bandage. "You are *not* mine."

"Keep your leg still."

"You must go and warn the prince. Warn Keesee."

"I have the split crystals, and will use them shortly."

"With them you can only signal an invasion, not numbers." It was a weak argument but it set up my next point.

"The intelligence on numbers we gathered is militarily insignificant."

"But the enemy is sure to have enchanters. They will detect the crystals being used."

"If I use them quickly, the mountains will still be between us and them. They will hinder identifying our location, other than direction, which they should logically have surmised."

I wasn't sure if what Wizard Seelain said was true. She wasn't an enchanter, but she knew far more about magic that me. Far more attuned to it than me. "Still, it's a risk which you needn't take." I had a sinking feeling that no matter what I said, she would remain with me. "What will the prince say? You risking your life to stay with me?"

"After all you have done for the Kingdom of Keesee?" She took the candle from my hand. Hot wax dripped on her wrist. She ignored it. "*You* completed the *prince's* quest to trade the Blood Sword. Besides, when we return safely, it will be a moot point." She stood. "And if your unlikely fear comes to pass and we are captured? It will not matter. I am confident you will sacrifice yourself to secure any measure of hope for my escape. So you won't be around to face his, or the king's disapproval."

"It will be far more than disapproval." She knew as well as I did that, by remaining in place a full day, the chances of being discovered were high— especially after using the crystals.

I was losing the argument and facing an action I dreaded. "I am without weapons beyond a dirk to defend you. I have fought and done all I can. Don't spit upon my duty and honor and shame me. Think of Keesee, your home and people. Even the small amount of intelligence collected is more important than me."

She looked away, knowing I was right.

"You're a Grand Wizard, powerful. Both skilled and knowledgeable. And fiancé to Prince Reveron. He loves you." I leaned against the tree while getting to my feet. "Your survival to defend the kingdom and its people outweighs the life of one mercenary, no matter his past service."

"We have yet to cross the lands of the Faxtinian Coalition and the Doran Confederacy. How dangerous is it for one to travel alone while remnants of the Necromancer King's forces wander those the lands?"

She had a point. We'd seen but avoided several mixed bands of goblins and ogres. "But there are friendly forces as well. You could join with one of them, find another escort."

"True, Flank Hawk. Healers of some ability would also be attached to the larger parties clearing the roving bands of goblins and ogres, and worse." The flickering candlelight revealed a tight smile. "And they would most certainly have a spear or crossbow to spare."

I frowned.

"So it is settled then." She turned toward our mounts.

"Will they have healers?" I asked. "If they march against us, mightn't their goddess have recalled them?"

"All the more reason to rest your wound before *we* travel."

I hadn't practiced anything related to healing magic for well over eight months. Instead I'd focused on combat skills training, activities certain to diminish my already weak spellcasting ability. Just as oil and water can't be mixed, healing and combat were incompatible. Even so, healers were rare. Gold bounties have long been paid to anyone who discovered someone showing potential. And refusal to join the ranks of Fendra Jolain's healers was unheard of. Years ago it'd happened to my sister. Nazlan the shepherd got his bounty. Raina was gone. Our family always told others, "She left." When they came for her, there wasn't any choice. But for some reason my father never said, "They took her."

Now, a difficult choice stood before me. I didn't think Grand Wizard Seelain would leave me behind unless my eventual ability to travel wasn't possible. Or I was dead. I didn't think I could cast healing magic without the Grand Wizard's notice.

The paid bounty wouldn't mean anything to her. But obligation through long-held agreements between nobles and the healers demanded her turning me over. She was a grand wizard and soon to be married to a prince—Prince Reveron, one who despite all, held my secret.

The answer was obvious. I was assigned to keep Wizard Seelain from harm, at any cost. Whatever happened because of that would just have to be.

Wizard Seelain came back from tethering the wyverns and held the candle so she could better see my face. "You remain silent, Flank Hawk." She cocked her head a little to the side and frowned. "You relented on my abandonment of you more readily than I expected. What stratagem have you been pondering to effect my immediate departure?" The flickering light caught a hint of a grin.

I kept my voice low and steady. "Grand Wizard, please go to my saddlebag. At the bottom is a small leather pouch about half the size of my fist. Please bring it to me before you begin to signal Keesee with the split crystals."

She hesitated for a second, then moved as quickly as the candle's flame allowed. Maybe my voice's lack of inflection worried her, or maybe she was curious about the pouch's contents.

She knelt next to me and gave me the worn leather container. Her face betrayed little expression.

I untied the leather cord, opened the pouch and stared at its contents while I spoke. "Grand Wizard, if I succeed, we may be able to resume joint travel shortly after midnight." I no longer felt the throbbing pain in my leg, but noticed the sweat gathering on my brow. "This finely ground white oak bark is the spell component to the only spell I know." I took a deep breath. "It has been a long time. But if I retain the strength and skill, I may be able to stop the bleeding in my wound."

"You, Flank Hawk? A rogue healer?"

"A neophyte, at best. It may not even work."

"But you are a mercenary."

"That I am," I said. "Please, remove the bandage from my leg."

She set the candle on the ground and quickly went about the task. She hung it across a nearby branch, the candle light showing it was already stained with blood. "Is there any way I might assist?"

I looked around and listened for half a moment. No sound of dogs or wings overhead. "Wish me luck," I said.

She nodded but remained silent.

There was nothing else to do. I closed my eyes and began the only chant I knew, the only one Raina had taught me. It opened my mind to the maelstrom of energy that raged beyond the reach of normal senses. I edged closer, seeking a sliver of the swirling energy, a strand that my eight syllable chant helped me recognized. One that I could direct.

Energies buffeted my mind as I delved deeper. They all looked too broad and long, more than I could handle—manipulate. Finally, I selected the thinnest silvery one I could find and increased my chant's pace. The strand shot into the wound, combined with the powdered bark, and brought a spark of renewed vitality and strength to the blood vessels and surrounding muscle tissue.

The effort exhausted me. I had to continue the spell and try for more. If the effort destroyed my mind, Wizard Seelain would be free to abandon me. I *had* to draw enough healing magic to the wound to be fit for travel. I reached out again, took hold of a broader strand, and struggled to peel it away—to direct the silvery sliver. It zipped about wildly, causing flashes behind my eyes before passing into the wound.

Everything was turning gray, closing in like when a dragon turned too sharply in flight. A warning I was about to pass out. I slowed my chant, backed out of the maelstrom, freeing my mind before it became lost to, or within, the wild energies.

I felt Wizard Seelain's tight grip on my shoulder. Her hand on my face. The light of the candle crossed my vision, followed by icy blackness.

CHAPTER 4

I awoke to the sound of deep, steady breathing mixed with the background of chirping crickets. At first I thought the breathing came from a pair of serpent mounts, but dragons remind me more of great bulls inhaling and exhaling. These breaths, working simultaneously, carried a slight nasally whistle, and the tang-filled odor of a black dragon or the sulfury fumes of a red was missing. I struggled to organize my thoughts despite the terrible pain behind my eyes.

It'd been many long months since I'd shared a camp with a true serpent mount. Instead it was resting wyverns that I heard. The hint of carrion in the air, along with the pain in my leg, solidified my recollection of where I was.

I opened my eyes and looked around. It was dark. The crickets should've told me that. Still, the star and moonlit shadows were enough to reveal Grand Wizard Seelain sitting between me and our mounts. Her white braids stood out against the black hulks of our resting beasts.

My leg throbbed, but not as much as before…before I attempted a healing spell. My wound itched as well. That was good. I sat up slowly, pushing aside the canvas tarp that made up half of our A-frame tent.

"You are awake," said Grand Wizard Seelain.

I was too stiff to immediately stand, so I began folding the canvas blanket while sitting. "How much time has passed since…" I still found being a rogue healer difficult to admit, even to Wizard Seelain.

"Since you fell unconscious? Approximately two hours." She struck a match and lit the candle. "You were correct, Flank Hawk. They did send griffins to track us, even in darkness." Before I could fully form the same thought, she added, "That they had a second griffin beastmaster in reserve indicates a very large force."

"Ahhhumm, yes," I said, working to ignore the piercing ache in my head.

She stood and walked with the candle toward me. Behind her, four split crystals were spread upon a flat stone next to a small sand-filled hour glass, what looked to be a half minute-sized one. Next to the arrangement sat an oblong rock she'd use to crush the messaging crystals.

"Flank Hawk," she said, "you still do not look—you look uncertain."

"Confused," I replied, scratching my neck and then rubbing my face. "I'll be okay in a minute."

She knelt and held the candle close to my face, observing my eyes.

"Just exhausted and a bad headache," I said, looking down at my leg. She'd wrapped it with what was probably our last fresh bandage. No blood had leaked through, yet.

"I am not so certain. You have hidden your rogue ability well, disguised as a mercenary."

I looked up at her. "I am a mercenary."

"You must have considerable potential as a healer then."

"Why?" I asked, grabbing the folded tent half and struggling to get to my feet.

Wizard Seelain took my arm and helped me up. "Be careful. Your spell stopped the bleeding and appeared to have healed some of the tissue damage, but you remain far from ready to walk far on your leg."

"I am aware of my limitations, Grand Wizard. I'm going to ready the mounts while you send the message to Keesee through the split crystals."

She stepped in front of me, blocking my path. "You may sit down or, better yet, lie down while I prepare the mounts for travel, and then inform Keesee of the invasion. Your valiant effort will have been in vain if you reopen your leg wound."

She was right, so I leaned on her shoulder and limped back over to the tree.

"It wasn't valiant," I said.

"Casting such a spell, having trained and fought as a mercenary as you have for as long as you have?" She paused while helping me take a seat by the large oak tree's trunk. "It would be analogous to me trying to summon an air elemental while standing at the bottom of a deep, water-filled cave."

She handed me a canteen.

The grand wizard gave me too much credit. Then it occurred to me and asked, "Should the candle be lit while griffins search for us?"

"I can sense them," she replied. "They are many miles to the east."

My head was definitely clearing. "That's not good. They're along our direction of travel."

"The beastmaster leading them isn't an air wizard."

She set the candle down and began saddling our tethered mounts. They opened their eyes and looked about, but otherwise remained motionless until she directed them to move. Their coloration remained coal black, the camouflage color of both night roosting and night travel.

I said, "I will turn myself in, so that you do not have to report me as a rogue healer."

She tightened Moon Ash's back cinch while laughing and shaking her head. Then she looked back at me. "First, I would never do such a thing, especially to you, Flank Hawk. Second, we are soon to be at war. That nullifies all treaties and agreements."

I'm sure my eyes widened. The thought hadn't occurred to me. But what did occur to me was that the Goddess Fendra Jolain must have been planning to invade the Kingdom of Keesee and her allies long before the Necromancer King's invasion faltered.

"What do you believe is going on in Keesee?" I asked. "The priests and priestesses, all of the healers, they must know what their goddess has planned."

"That, I do not know, which is why I was preparing the split crystals before you awoke." Wizard Seelain signaled Wick to lie flat while she placed the saddle on his back. "My plan was to lash you to Wick if necessary and tie a rope between him and Moon Ash for travel. You still do not sound like yourself, so it may still come to that."

"I will be ready to ride by the time you've finished warning Keesee."

"Let us hope so."

I rested while Wizard Seelain continued to make ready for our departure. A small breeze kicked up, requiring her to still the air around the candle while she arranged the crystals.

I'd not been given any of the codes to relay proper messages, which were based on the sequence and time between each crystal being smashed. My orders simply instructed me to smash all of the crystals within fifteen seconds, the clear crystal first, if Grand Wizard Seelain was captured, the green first if she was severely injured, and the gray one if she had been slain.

Somewhere in the King's City, capital of the Kingdom of Keesee, deep within the king's palace, I imagined an apprentice enchanter sitting at a table, watching the corresponding halves of the crystals before Grand Wizard Seelain. Probably there were a number of tables with crystal sets being watched. When Wizard Seelain crushed the commencement crystal in front of her, the corresponding one in front of the apprentice enchanter would shatter as well. Then the apprentice would record the sequence as the other three crystals shattered, and the time between. He'd deliver the coded message to one of the king's intelligence officers, and King Tobias would be notified of the impending invasion.

It took over five minutes for Grand Wizard Seelain to crush the four crystals in the proper sequence with proper timing using the small hourglass. While she did that, I waited astride Wick, my thighs already lashed to the saddle.

Lines of communication between units in the field, deployed from the King's City to Paris-Imprimis and Sint Malo, and all the way to the Dead Expanse surrounding the Necromancer King's stronghold, proved tenuous and unreliable. Grand Wizard Seelain estimated word of the impending invasion would take a week to reach all Keeseean and allied commanders in the field, while followers loyal to Fendra Jolain enacted her orders within hours of each other. We learned this upon finding a small patrol after a long day's travel, and the next two we met during our return flight to the King's City confirmed it.

The result wasn't total chaos reigning within the friendly encampments and formations on the march that we encountered the second day into our six-day return flight. But there were signs of disarray among the ranks. Few things shatter troop morale more than healers abandoning their duties and disappearing in the dead of night, or an outright refusal to heal the dying and wounded, even at the point of a sword.

Added to that, personal bodyguards accompanied every healer. In the past I'd experienced a minor fray with one. It hadn't been pleasant. The guards are strong, highly skilled, and loyal to their protective duty, always to the death. When the healers weren't able to sneak away from the units they served, sometimes eight or nine Keeseean soldiers died for each healer detained.

Terrible as that was, it in no way prepared us for our predawn arrival at the King's City.

CHAPTER 5

The ongoing war against the Necromancer King had decimated the ranks of the once vaunted serpent cavalry, a force enemies of Keesee rightly feared. In the past a half dozen dragons might be in the air above the King's City, both warding it from danger and providing a watchful escort to important messengers and dignitaries. Serpent cavalry numbers were always a close-held secret, but I'd have been surprised if more than two dozen of the fire-breathing red dragons and half that many acid-spewing blacks remained alive and capable of combat duty.

Major Jadd once explained to me that dragons are long lived, but also slow to reproduce. They come into season once every eight winters, resulting in clutches of three or possibly four eggs. For their eventual size, dragons grow quickly, but even nine or ten summers to reach maturity is a long time when engaged in a war of attrition. That motivated King Tobias to trade his own serpent mount to a ruler far to the east. The royal serpent steed's departure brought eighty wyverns, along with skilled handlers to train messengers and scouts how to ride them, including Grand Wizard Seelain and myself.

I pondered that as we approached the King's City from over the Tyrrhenian Sea, having swung out several miles for the long final leg of our trip. Flares of orange and red, far larger than any torch or bonfire, came into view. They were partially obscured by a smoky haze. The sun was at our back and minutes from peeking over the horizon when Grand Wizard Seelain urged her weary mount to greater speed. No dragon intercepted our approach, nor did we spot any above the city.

An inferno raged in a section of the lower city. Flames rose from warehouses near the waterfront and flames engulfed a merchant ship docked in the harbor. Nearby vessels had taken to sail and oar to reach a safe distance. Within the upper city housed on the plateau above the Tyrrhenian's reach, over a dozen plumes of heavy smoke rose.

We approached to within a half mile without challenge. "This bodes ill," shouted Wizard Seelain. She apparently didn't expect an answer as she pulled Moon Ash into an arc to avoid flying over the main harbor. "There appears to be no effort by man or wizard to battle the flames, yet there are organized units of men moving about."

I nodded in agreement. "And no enemy forces are outside the city walls laying siege."

"We shall make for the palace," said Wizard Seelain. "Remain vigilant,

Flank Hawk."

"I will," I assured her. In giving an unnecessary order, I figured she must be deeply concerned. I knew I was.

We flew above the capital city's upper level toward the palace near its center. There were few people on the narrow streets. Only organized units moved about—soldiers bearing the broad sashes of purple and gold, the Kingdom of Keesee's colors. Even the marketplaces appeared abandoned when they should have been bustling with merchants preparing for a new day of trade.

The palace courtyard where dragons might land came into view. I'd been privileged to land there several times, the most memorable as Road Toad's aft-guard before he regained his formal re-commission as a serpent cavalryman and his former rank and name, Major Jadd.

From a distance I spotted a black dragon on the courtyard green. That wasn't a concern in and of itself. Dragons didn't bother wyverns unless given reason, similar to how a wolf feeding on a kill would ignore a gore crow unless it got too close and tried to steal a ribbon of flesh. Major Jadd said during my initial wyvern training that dragons won't eat a fresh or even a rotting carcass of the vulture-like beasts. They just taste awful, especially to dragons, which really says something. Dragons can, and in desperate times will, eat just about anything, including rotted logs. I wondered what that said about griffins.

All that didn't mean my mount was happy to be in the presence of a dragon. "Steady, Wick," I urged.

"We cannot land," said Wizard Seelain. "The serpent is wounded and down."

I looked more closely. The black dragon lay on its side with a rope anchored by a dozen men holding its free wing swept forward. A large spear, probably from a ballista, was stuck deep in its ribcage. Several handlers worked to extract the weapon while the serpent cavalryman and his aft-guard lay across the dragon's neck just below the head. As I expected, nobody wearing red and white, the colors of Fendra Jolain, was in sight.

"We cannot land here," said Wizard Seelain, pulling Ash Moon into a circling climb. "We shall land at the stables and make our way to the palace from there."

"Something has happened!" I shouted. "And may not be over yet." I pulled Wick alongside Wizard Seelain's mount. "Even if the stables are secure, the streets may not be safe."

The horse stables that had been converted to house roosting wyverns weren't far from the palace grounds. Wizard Seelain begin descending toward one of them. "That is why I am accompanied by a personal guard."

"Then you will remain aloft while I land," I said, shooting past the grand wizard.

She slowed her descent and circled as I brought Wick down. I selected the largest of three landing circles surrounded by a twenty-foot stone wall. Wick's wings stirred up a small cloud of debris before his feet hit the hard-packed dirt. Both he and I looked about. The sliding door leading into the barn-like roosting shelter remained closed.

Wick's color shifted from black to brown. I patted my mount on the neck and ordered, "Speak, Wick."

Wick's *caw* sounded more like a bear's growl.

"You, inside the roost," I shouted. "Open the door." I waited several seconds. "In the name of Prince Reveron, I charge you to do as ordered!"

The door began sliding open. With my left hand, I signaled Wizard Seelain to remain aloft. With my right, I began untying the leather strap that held my spear in its sheath. A boy's face peaked out. He looked along the top of the wall and then slid the door the rest of the way open. He couldn't have been more than twelve summers and had to put his shoulder into the effort.

"Hurry, sir! Inside."

Wick's color began shifting to a mottled pattern of brown and black.

"There's another rider waiting to land," I said. "Take the reins."

The boy looked up at me with dirt smudged across his freckled face. Sweat matted his short blond hair. I doubted he'd ever been trusted to such a duty before.

"Wick is spooked," I said, patting the wyvern's neck. "Just hold the reins when I toss them down to you. Stand firm until I dismount." If necessary, I could dismount holding the reins, but the flames and smoke, and the blood of the wounded dragon had gotten to Wick. My wounded leg was better, but still stiff and tender. I couldn't afford to reinjure it, and Wick might damage a wing or worse if he tried to take to flight—especially when Grand Wizard Seelain sent an air elemental to keep him on the ground. That, I was confident she would do.

"You've seen it done before," I told the boy. "Yes, it's a man's job. I trust you to it." I pointed where he should stand. "Hurry now."

I released the reins and he took hold of them. He spread his feet in case Wick took a notion to back away from the roost or attempt to take flight.

I dismounted and pulled my spear from its sheath. It was sturdy like a boar spear but lacked the crossbar just beyond the broad-bladed tip. A mercenary named Razor Heart who we'd shared a camp with on our return trip gave it to me after Wizard Seelain told how I'd lost mine. He preferred a sword anyway and had been using the spear as a walking stick until he could throw it at an enemy, or trade it.

"What's your name?" I asked the boy.

"Rin," he said.

I took the reins from Rin and signaled to Wizard Seelain. She was already spiraling downward. I tugged on the reins. "Come on, Wick." The boy fell in stride next to me, ahead of Wick and his awkward gait.

I wanted to know what was happening in the city, but figured Rin wouldn't know. And getting under cover was more important. "Is there anybody else inside?"

"Only Bodie, the night watchman, and Bodie. He's an apprentice handler. Nobody else showed up, and Slatter—he's the other watchman. He went t'get the stablemaster, but he didn't come back. There's six—"

I cut him off. "I'll stable Wick inside. You take the reins of the grand wizard's mount when she lands." I didn't want to lose sight of my ward, but there wasn't room for two wyverns in the landing area.

I'd never been in this roosting stable. It was smaller than Wick and Moon Ash's stable a half mile northwest of this one, right near one of the smoke plumes. My eyes adjusted quickly and I led Wick to the first wyvern stall on the right. It was like any other. A large half door, like in a horse stable, opened outward, hinged on the side opposite the nearest door which led to a landing circle. A stout wooden wall about five feet high formed the base of the thirty by thirty foot roost. Rope netting lined with five-inch wide strips of cotton fabric made up the rest of the walls and ceiling of the stall.

Wick hopped in and began gulping down the remains of a goat carcass set in a far corner. Being in a stable reminded me of my father who worked in the king's royal horse stable. Whatever was happening in the city, was my family in danger? I shut and set the door's two bolt locks before hurrying back toward the landing circle.

Wizard Seelain was already leading Moon Ash into the roost with Rin standing ready to slide the door shut. With Wizard Seelain inside, I quickly took in our surroundings. Narrow unshuttered windows set high above let in some of the morning sun, providing shadowy light to a cavernous building. All of the side windows remained shuttered and barred. The foul odor of wyvern droppings hung heavy in the air. The familiar buzzing of barn flies along with the grousing squawks of several wyverns on the other side of the roosting barn only emphasized how quiet it was in the nearby streets.

I opened the stall door across from Wick for Wizard Seelain. "What's happening in the city?" I asked Rin.

The stableboy shook his head. "Nobody knows for sure." He pointed toward the glow of two distant lanterns and then started walking toward them. "Ma'am, sir, please come help. There's no Lain Healers and Bodie's trying t'keep Lieutenant Ohler's mount alive."

Wizard Seelain signaled with her staff for me to follow. "What has happened?" she asked.

I looked back to make sure the sliding door was barred before hurrying to keep up with the now fast-talking stableboy.

"They've all gone or were arrested," he said, swinging his arms tightly up and down as he walked. "And a bunch of Long-Tooths were rounded up by the king's men, too. Pop says there ain't any Long-Tooths."

Grand Wizard Seelain grabbed the boy's shoulder and spun him around.

"The Brotherhood of the Long-Toothed Tiger *does* exist," she said sharply. "They are traitors to the crown and the entire kingdom."

The wide-eyed stableboy stared at her. His mouth hung open, surprised and not knowing what to say.

"The grand wizard speaks the truth." I avoided using her name. It was her choice to reveal her identity or not.

The stableboy regained some of his composure. His gaze shifted to me and then back to Wizard Seelain. "Right," he said, and stepped back from Grand Wizard Seelain as the prickling energy of elemental magic began emanating from her.

"Who you got there, Rin?" shouted a lanky man holding a glowing lantern above his head. He stood leaning out of a stall near one of the two distant sliding doors.

"Th-That's Bodie" said Rin. "He's with Marquan, trying t'stop Lieutenant Ohler's wyvern from bleeding t'death. They sewed him up but—"

"Flank Hawk," Wizard Seelain said and strode quickly toward the lantern-bearing guardsman.

"Come on," I whispered to Rin and tugged his arm as I passed to keep pace with Wizard Seelain.

Bodie stepped out of the stall and hung the lantern on a hook. "Rin?" he said, pulling his short sword from its scabbard.

"They're 'vern scouts," said Rin, then repeated it louder. "They're 'vern scouts! Just landed. She's a wizard. Maybe she can help Marquan."

Bodie was tall and thin. The wrinkles on his face said he was a good number of winters past his prime. He slid his sword back into its scabbard and shook his head.

A young man with curly red hair and covered in blood, sweat and bits of straw stepped out of the same stall the guardsman had. The haggard man appeared to be a little older than me, probably a few summers past twenty. He turned his face, dripping with tears and speckled with blood, away from us while he blew his nose into a rag. "It's too late," he said in a wavering voice.

"Who are you?" Bodie asked, eyeing us with suspicion. "You're not wearing the king's colors." His leather jerkin had rings sewn into it, and the wrapping on his sword's grip showed use, but he didn't carry himself like a mercenary or a soldier in the king's service. Maybe he was an auxiliary guard, supplementing regulars the stablemaster had drawn from some of the king's men. Rin said others had not reported for night duty.

Although I was confident Grand Wizard Seelain was in no danger from this guardsman and the others, I remained at her side, a step back, alert and ready to act.

"What has happened in the King's City," Wizard Seelain demanded.

"You're an air wizard. That I can see."

"I am a grand wizard, guardsman." Prickling energy again emanated from Grand Wizard Seelain. "Answer my question."

The man shuffled a half step back and averted his eyes to the floor. "Well, I'm not rightly sure, Grand Wizard."

"Inform me of what you *do* know."

"The Lain healers have quit and the king arrested them. The king's patrols are arresting anyone on the streets. He's trying to root out them that follows the Pride's Grand Prime. Least I think that's what he's called, but he ain't in the city. Just calls the shots for his guerilla group." Guardsman Bodie rubbed his nose. "I think the king and his generals thought they'd rounded up all the Long-Tooths. He supports the Sun-Foxes, and they're sworn enemies of the Long-Tooths, ya know."

Wizard Seelain nodded.

"My pop says," Rin started, then his voice faded when Wizard Seelain turned her gaze to him.

She slid her staff to the crook of her arm. "Continue, Stablehand."

"Ahh, my p-poppa says all the Long-Tooths were long dead, but that the Necromancer King brought them back. But those causing trouble ain't zombies so they're not really Long-Tooths."

"What happened last night?" Wizard Seelain asked.

"Likely what happened almost a week back when them Lain Healers that wasn't arrested by the king's troops, those that were in the city, tried to escape. Heard from a fella who's a sergeant that the Long-Tooths recruited a bunch of criminals and malcontents. Killed some important folks, rich merchants and started fires. Then, when water wizards showed up to help douse the flames, they shot'em with arrows and such. Ambushed them, and with no healers…"

"Air wizards too," added the red-headed apprentice handler.

"Continue," urged Wizard Seelain.

"Captain Ringan is an air wizard. I heard him telling another 'vern scout something about it. When they went to suck air from the fires burning in the Blue District."

That was one of the better parts of the city, I thought. Nothing like the Brown District, where it wasn't wise to be wandering alone at night—and sometimes during the day. And the war against the Necromancer King had already whittled the number of spellcasters, including wizards, down quite a bit.

"Care for our mounts," ordered Wizard Seelain. "Flank Hawk, with me. I must get to the palace without delay."

"Wait," I said.

Wizard Seelain stopped and turned. A look of anger spread across her face. Some of it might have been directed toward me, but that didn't matter. "Guardsman Bodie," I said, "are the streets safe for travel?"

"Flank Hawk?" the guardsman replied. "You're the—"

I cut him off. "Answer my question."

"Yes," said Wizard Seelain. "He is that mercenary. Honored by King Tobias for striking a critical blow against the Necromancer King." She shifted her staff from her left hand to her right. "And I am Grand Wizard Seelain, fiancé to Prince Reveron, so answer his question."

All three men immediately bowed to Wizard Seelain. It wasn't really required as she wasn't royalty yet. Beyond that, King Tobias didn't really think that highly of me.

"My apologies, Grand Wizard," the guardsman said. "Curfew starts one hour before sunset to one hour after sunrise. The streets may appear clear, Grand Wizard, but I believe they are not safe. Even if the streets were full, it would be better for one of your importance to fly your mounts directly to the palace."

"We cannot," I said. "A wounded dragon occupies where we might land. How often do patrols pass this roosting stable?" My plan was to attach to one of those for escort to the palace.

"Land on a roof," the apprentice handler suggested. "Or the palace must have gardens."

"No," Wizard Seelain said. "Not in this time of strife."

"The patrols, Guardsman?" I asked.

"They're not regular. Once an hour, sometimes two."

"I shan't wait that long," Wizard Seelain said.

I moved to stand closer to Wizard Seelain. "I can make my way to the palace," I said. "If I encounter a patrol—"

"Enough. We go now!"

I shook my head. "One personal guard on dangerous streets isn't enough."

"Do you forget? I am a Grand Wizard."

"Guardsman," I said.

"His duty is here, Flank Hawk." The wyvern stable cannot be left unguarded." She started walking.

"I can go with you," Rin offered.

"No." I didn't want to insult the boy's bravery but he'd be little help and would likely die if trouble did arise. "Your place is here," I said before hurrying to catch up with Wizard Seelain.

Bodie matched my stride while signaling the stablehand. "Mercenary Flank Hawk, I'll go out the side door and check for danger. Are you familiar with the way back to the palace?"

"Hagelbin the Armorer's shop. This stable is within sight of it. From there I know two routes."

Guardsman Bodie addressed me instead of Wizard Seelain. Like most of his station, he was intimidated by her stature, in addition to her building anger—certainly from frustration, knowing the city and kingdom she loved was being attacked from within. "Mercenary Flank Hawk, I believe the main streets are best patrolled and safest. Rin, lock the side door behind me, and open the street-side door when I signal."

Wizard Seelain stood by the street-side door, staring hard at us. But the guardsman's reasonable precaution couldn't be ignored.

Within two minutes Guardsman Bodie tapped on the street-side door. "All clear."

Rin lifted the bar and pulled the heavy wooden door open. Bodie looked about, checking the roof of the two-story tailor's shop across the cobblestone street. "Armorer's down the street to your right."

"I know the way," Wizard Seelain said, striding into the street. "Thank you, Guardsman."

"Left side," I said to Wizard Seelain. "In the shadows of the morning sun. I'll lead."

"Very well," she said. "Swift pace."

I nodded, bringing my step to just under a trot. My wounded leg protested, but I ignored it. "I'll watch ground level. You above."

Fast footsteps on the cobblestones behind caused me to spin around.

Rin, sprinting with a pitchfork in hand, caught up with us. We were on the street, which wasn't a place to stop and argue. My first loyalty was to Wizard Seelain. I met his gaze for a split second. I'd use his eyes. "I assign you to watch our back. Keep up."

We made it past the armorer's and turned right, onto a street lined with skilled-merchant shops, toward the palace in the distance when the *thwunk* of a crossbow firing intruded on the morning silence. With a sharp sweep of her hand, Wizard Seelain knocked the bolt off course, and a second that followed from the roof above a glassblower's shop. Both bolts stuck the cobblestones, short of us—their mark.

"Ambush!" I said as a door to my left swung open. I didn't wait to see who emerged and instead drove my spear's tip into the chest of the man coming out. He dropped his sword and clutched my spear buried in his chest. Another man with a battleaxe shoved his dying comrade aside, dislodging my spear's tip. I swung my spear, scoring a bloody gash across the axe man's chin before striking the doorframe with my spear's shaft.

"Run," I shouted even as Rin warned, "Three behind us!" Staying to fight in the pocket of an ambush played to the enemy's advantage, especially with crossbowmen reloading above.

Wizard Seelain took the lead as I broke away from candle maker's shop before the axe-wielding man emerged, possibly with reinforcements. Rin was right next to me. "They got swords," he said with a frightened look in his eyes.

A crossbow bolt, fired from behind, clattered off cobblestones to the right several feet ahead of me. Looking over my shoulder, the four men following were about twenty-five yards behind. They wore light leather armor. Three carried curved short swords and one, bleeding down his chin, led the way with his a battleaxe.

Three similarly armed men leapt off a porch and took up a position in the road ahead of us. Wizard Seelain brought up her staff and with quick-uttered spell words sent a wall of air against the ambushers facing her, knocking them to the ground. The effort only caused her to slow for a few strides, allowing Rin and me to gain on her.

Without slowing she struck one of the downed men across the face as he tried to rise. I thrust at the stomach with my spear of another, but struck high, catching the stunned ambusher in the shoulder as I passed. Rin drove his pitchfork into the thigh of the third downed ambusher. The man grabbed hold of Rin's weapon. The stablehand tugged but the man held firm, so Rin let go of his fork and ran to catch up with Wizard Seelain and to keep ahead of the four chasing axe and swordsmen. They trailed by only fifteen yards.

My bad leg wasn't going to allow me to keep up the pace. Grand Wizard Seelain must have realized this.

"Rin, Flank Hawk down!" she shouted as she spun about, pointing her staff.

I dove to the street. Rin ducked but didn't drop flat. I latched onto his ankle as a gale-force wind gust shot over us, carrying Rin with it for ten feet and dragging me behind as it passed. The axe wielder and three swordsmen caught it full force and were knocked ten yards back, hard and to the ground. The three ambushers beyond them, those stabbed and struck by us, were blown down again.

Then Wizard Seelain summoned an elemental sprit in the form of a twenty-foot whirlwind. It picked up debris from the street as it formed and caught up the downed axe and swordsmen. After spinning about for quarter of a minute, the whirlwind dashed the screaming, helpless men against the brick wall of a three-story apartment dwelling. They fell to the ground, broken.

"Up and ward the Grand Wizard," I told Rin. I scanned the streets and rooftops while Wizard Seelain focused on directing the air creature she had summoned.

Rin didn't move, watching in awe as the elemental sprit pursued and caught up the wounded ambushers. It carried them a hundred feet into the air before dissipating, leaving the men to fall, screaming until they broke upon the street.

I continued to watch for further enemies, especially the crossbowmen. Rin got to his feet, wide-eyed and duly impressed by Grand Wizard Seelain's spell power. It had sapped much strength from her, especially to summon such a powerful elemental spirit so quickly. But her stance showed she had something left in reserve.

Seconds later a patrol of the king's men came into view.

After a quick exchange between the patrol's captain and Grand Wizard Seelain, a third of them sought after the crossbowmen while several gathered the bodies of the dead ambushers. The remaining soldiers escorted us the rest of the way to the palace. Rin shadowed my stride, relieved and grinning the entire way.

CHAPTER 6

I led Rin from the royal kitchen's back exit toward the palace's North Garden. Rin carried a large loaf of fresh bread and a sizeable wedge of sharp cheese. I carried a crock filled with aged apple cider and a satchel holding three tin cups, each harboring a hardboiled egg. A servant had offered to carry our meal, but I declined.

Rin, looking almost as hungry as I was, asked, "You live in the palace?"

"As long as I serve as Grand Wizard Seelain's personal guard, I am allotted a small room. It isn't much." I shrugged. "A goose feather bed to lay my head. No windows."

"Your own room?" he asked.

"Sometimes I think the barracks would be better, but I'm not around much these days."

We worked our way down several tapestry-filled hallways to the North Garden's main entry. Two guards with halberds stood on either side of the oak door reinforced by iron bands. Both guards had been recalled from retirement. I knew better than to let the gray hair fool me. I'd sparred with those guards several times in the practice yard. They were beyond their prime but they could still hold their own, which was why they'd been recalled to free up younger men for the campaign against the Necromancer King.

I nodded to the guards. "Weaver. Forbin."

"What's the news, Flank Hawk?" Weaver asked.

They knew I was a wyvern scout. "Nothing that I am at liberty to discuss."

Both guards nodded and frowned. "Ol' Orich is in a feisty mood today," Forbin commented. He slid open the slat and checked outside before unbarring the door. "The enchanter that was supposed to spell-protect some of the flowers got called elsewhere again."

"Good to know. Thanks."

Rin and I exited into sunlight and onto a gray stone-paved walkway.

"There's lots a guards in there," Rin said. "Do ya know them all?"

I smiled. "No, just a few." We stopped under a wrought iron trellis covered in some type of flowering ivy. "You know what's going on in the city. It calls for extra security." Rin looked about as I led him along the walkway that wove between different types of shrubs and fragrant beds of flowers—most containing more blossom types and colors than I could count on both hands.

"Your friend Lilly works here?" Rin asked. "And she met the Colonel of the West too?"

I nodded. Just about everyone in the King's City knew at least pieces of the adventure where I traded the Royal Family's evil Blood Sword for a weapon to halt the Necromancer King's invasion. It only happened because Colonel Brizich had betrayed us, killing most of Prince Reveron's escort, and nearly the prince himself. The treachery was known in noble circles, but not to the average soldier or general population. Brizich was executed for treason shortly after the prince's return. Prince Reveron believed the traitorous serpent cavalryman was a Long-Tooth, sworn enemy of his Sun-Fox Brotherhood, but I'd never heard if it was proven before Brizich was put to death by fiery dragon breath. His death didn't bother me. If it hadn't been for the timely arrival of one of Major Jadd's Sun-Fox brothers, and reinforcements, Colonel Brizich and some of his men would have cut Jadd and me down on a rainy night a year ago. Even fewer knew of that incident.

Chief Gardener Orich dismissed one of her assistants and stepped away from the shade of a towering bush trimmed to the likeness of a sword stuck into the ground. Although Orich wore a green shirt and heavy trousers like all the gardening staff, hers rarely showed any spot of dirt or stain. It wasn't that she didn't get her hands dirty, but she was expected to greet all visitors, and thus her garments were protected by enchanter spells.

The wiry woman of at least fifty winters met Rin and myself along the walkway and smiled. "Mercenary Flank Hawk, what an unexpected surprise."

Lilly once told me the smile was only on display when visitors to the North Garden appeared. Not that the chief gardener was cruel or unfair, just humorless, stern and demanding of those under her. Despite her pleasant greeting and courteous attitude, I could tell that she hadn't softened on Lilly's presence in the palace garden. Rather than my friend being selected by the chief gardener, royal politics had thrust Lilly upon her.

"Greetings, Chief Gardener," I said.

She nodded. "And who is your companion that you have brought to visit the North Garden today?" Her voice and manner remained pleasant, but I didn't think she was much impressed by Rin. He'd washed but the smell of sweat and the wyvern roost still clung to his clothes. Even so, Rin smiled from ear to ear.

"This is Rin, stablehand who cares for the royal wyvern mounts."

Chief Gardener Orich again nodded. "Are you here to visit with Lilly?"

"We are," I said. "To lunch with her and to relay a task assigned by Grand Wizard Seelan."

"It is hardly mid-morning," she responded. "Nevertheless, I am certain Assistant Gardener Lilly will be most happy to see and share a meal with you gentlemen."

My service to the kingdom, in addition to serving Grand Wizard Seelain, insured any request I made overrode any desires or tasks the chief gardener might have for my friend. She was going to be even less happy when she learned that Lilly wouldn't be working in the garden after we ate. But long years of answering to the whims of arrogant nobles made my rare visits and Grand Wizard Seelain's assigned task for Lilly stand as minor inconveniences.

I'd already spotted Lilly working around one of several large rosebushes covered in pink blooms. I knew Lilly's keen hearing had already alerted her to my arrival.

The chief gardener met Rin's eyes with what I am sure he considered genuine mirth. "This way," she said and turned, leading us along a narrow walkway to where Lilly labored, plucking small beetles from the leaves, blooms and buds of the thorny plant she tended.

The chief gardener stepped off the rock path and onto the manicured lawn with her soft-soled leather shoes. I stayed on the path. My hard boots would only cause more work for the gardeners. Many nobles didn't care. I did.

Lilly was barefoot, reminding me of the first time I encountered her when she'd hidden me from pursuing ogres. Her action then and many times after had kept me alive.

"Lilly, dear," called Gardener Orich. "Your mercenary friend is here to visit and share a meal with you."

Lilly flicked one of the small beetles she'd been plucking into a small wooden bucket before wiping her hands on her dark green trousers.

The chief gardener pointed our direction. "You are dismissed from your task. Enjoy your meal and visit."

"Thank you, ma'am," Lilly said, bowing her head once before running toward us. She threw her arms around me in a hug as I struggled to catch her while holding onto the crock and satchel, and staying on the path. "Flank Hawk, I've missed you."

I returned her embrace as best I could. "I've missed you too."

"Sure you have," she teased. "Flying off with Grand Wizard Seelain. Like you'd have time." Lilly stepped back and looked at Rin, who was only a few inches shorter than she was. "Who is this?" Her dark brown eyes sparkled as she ran a hand through her short brown hair.

"This is Rin. A stablehand in one of the royal wyvern roosts. He helped me escort Grand Wizard Seelain back to the palace this morning."

Lilly looked a bit confused but extended her hand. "Anyone that backs up Flank Hawk is okay with me."

Rin tentatively shook Lilly's hand. "I—I'm, it's great t'meet you, Miss Lilly." He looked from Lilly to me, and back at her. "You're—you met the Colonel of the West too, right?"

Lilly laughed, which was a rare and pleasant thing to hear. "Yeah, I met him. And his gargoyle assistant."

Rin looked duly impressed.

"Come on," I said. "Let's have an early lunch."

"You mean late breakfast," Lilly said.

"I mean I'm hungry, have food, and Rin and I would like to share it and our company with you."

"Meet me at the bench over by the pond," Lilly said. "I'm going to get my friend Bubble her lunch."

I led Rin along the path toward the far end of garden where the fifteen-foot stone wall overlooked an oval pond. It wasn't large but fairly deep with lily pads and flowering water plants along its edge, and orange fish with black and white speckles that occasionally swam along the surface. There were five and Lilly had a name for each.

"I've never seen any place like this, Flank Hawk." Rin looked at me with concern on his face. "It's really okay if I'm here, isn't it?"

I pulled the cups and eggs out of the satchel before setting it on the grass in front of the bench. "You're with me," I assured Rin. "And I'm with Grand Wizard Seelain, and she's to be married to Prince Reveron. So it's okay."

"What if the king or queen wants t'sit here?"

I knew the king wouldn't be in the garden this morning and the queen was meeting with her assistants somewhere in the palace's southern wing. "If they arrive," I said, "then we'll bow low to them and take our leave." He handed me the bread and cheese. I laughed. "There isn't much room on the satchel, but it'll do for a short picnic."

Lilly arrived. She set the bucket near the pond and then sat on the grass with us. Rin slid away from Lilly and a little closer to me. I broke the bread into three parts and did the same with the wedge of cheese while Lilly peeled the hard-boiled eggs. I said to Rin, "Why don't you pour the cider?" He did with great care.

It would have been a perfect spring morning, with the sun and birds in the nearby trees, except for the lingering smell of smoke in the air. Lilly talked about her responsibilities, mainly the rosebushes, daylilies, and the pond. They'd brought in a colorful turtle with yellow and red stripes on its face and a line of nubby spines running down its shell. She'd named her Bubble. Rin talked about the picnic his dad and uncle had taken their families on before the war started over a year ago.

After we ate, Lilly showed Rin how to throw the beetles she'd picked off the roses into the pond where Bubble and the five pond fish ate them. Lilly came back to sit on the bench with me while Rin enjoyed himself, selecting beetles from the water in the bucket and trying to make sure the turtle and each fish got an equal number.

Just as he was finishing up, Chief Gardener Orich approached and offered to take Rin on a tour so that we'd have time alone. Rin was unsure for a moment, until the chief gardener began telling him about the hummingbirds, their nests and tiny eggs.

"Orich thinks the war isn't over and it's going to get worse," Lilly said. "She's right, isn't she?"

I nodded. "I'll tell you what I can in a few minutes. First, how are you doing?"

"Well, I'm learning the Crusader language pretty well. I think the tutor was right, that I needed to know the tongue before I could read it. She also thinks I need to know castle etiquette and we spend time on that too."

"Have you started to read yet?" I asked, recalling the ceremony before the king and queen and all the nobles. King Tobias had asked Lilly what boon she desired for her service to the Kingdom of Keesee. She'd responded that she wanted to learn to read what was in the book that her friend, Crusader Paul Jedidiah Roos, had carried with him and tried to live by. That was also the ceremony where King Tobias took a disliking to me.

But learning the language of the Reunited Kingdom was what Lilly wanted. Grand Wizard Seelain suggested a position in the North Garden. Wizard Seelain explained to me that the tutor said it would be counterproductive for Lilly to study language all day, every day, and that she didn't mingle well with the palace workers, let alone the nobles. It would give her a place and responsibility within the palace.

What had isolated Lilly was the court gossip. That was why nobody wanted anything to do with her.

"A few words only," Lilly said. "When I told Tutor Roeth why I wanted to learn to read the Crusader tongue, she taught me this passage first." Lilly took a steadying breath. "Greater love hath no man than this, that a man lay down his life for his friends." Then her eyes teared up. "Besides you, Roos is the only friend I ever had."

I'd' sent one of Grand Wizard Seelain's servants to deliver Lilly's spyglass to her room shortly after our return. It had been Crusader Roos's spyglass. Lilly had found in his jacket shortly after his death and our escape. I knew it was something she cherished, and also it let her know that I'd returned safely.

"You got the Crusader's spyglass?"

Lilly nodded.

I put my arm around her as we sat on the bench and leaned close. In the midst of our escape from the Necromancer King's stronghold, the Crusader had turned back against our pursuers. Sacrificed himself so that I might carry Lilly to safety.

"And Road Toad," she began after a few sniffles. "I know he's Major Jadd now, but I'll always think of him as Road Toad. He's visited me here twice, even brought lunch like you. But he's gone to war like you. Your family invited me to dinner twice. I went once, but your mom doesn't like me and kept your sister Katchia away from me."

"I'll talk to her," I said.

"No, your dad already did that. It's what I am. Chief Gardner Orich doesn't mind me though. I work hard for her."

"What about you?" she asked.

Reflexively, my voice dropped to a whisper. "Grand Wizard Seelain knows I'm a healer."

"That doesn't matter anymore. I heard that there's trouble with the healers and that's what's causing all the trouble in the city. *Now* maybe the king will understand why you turned down his offer to be an officer in *his* army."

That was only part of the reason he was angry with me. He found out that after the ceremony, I felt he'd overlooked all that Lilly did, and I gave her the medal he'd bestowed upon me.

The chief gardener was nearly finished giving Rin his tour. "I'm sorry, Lilly, but I have to go. I've been debriefed, but I have to accompany Grand Wizard Seelain when she speaks before the King's War Council. I'll see you again, if I can."

"It's not over," she said. "And it's going to get worse."

"I think so, Lilly. It's a new enemy."

When I didn't say more she hugged me. "I'll return the cups to the kitchen."

"I'll do that," I said. "Wizard Seelain would like you to escort Rin back to the Wyvern Roost where he works." I handed her two gold coins. "And along the way, pick him up a dagger. I know you'll get him a decent one."

She looked a little puzzled but agreed. "I'll do that."

I stood and signaled Rin over. "The day may soon come when he'll be in need of it." I bumped my shoulder into hers. "You know a bit of dagger play yourself. You might offer to train him in its use."

She smiled. "First Mate did show me a few things."

Rin ran along the path up to us.

"Rin," I said, "I have to return to my duty with Grand Wizard Seelain. She assigned Lilly to escort you back to the roost where we met this morning. And she has something to obtain for you along the way."

He looked from me to her and back, and then over his shoulder toward the chief gardener.

I asked, "What is it, Rin?"

"The grand wizard assigned Lilly to take me?"

I nodded. "She did."

"I don't know," Rin said, looking at the ground. "I—I might get in trouble."

"For what? You shouldn't have left the roost, but you did. Guardsman Bodie will vouch for your absence to the stablemaster."

"Well, it—it's not that." He looked over his shoulder at the chief gardener again. "I asked her but she said she didn't know. She said it wasn't any of my business anyway."

"What?" I asked.

"The stablemaster, and maybe my pop would think it is, especially if I go t'the stable with her. Y-your friend, Lilly." He looked like a mouse trapped between two hungry cats.

He slid a half step closer to me. "Is s-she a werewolf?"

Lilly stiffened at his question but maintained her neutral expression.

"No, Rin," I said. "My friend Lilly isn't a werewolf."

"Them songs are all wrong then?"

"They are. And I should know."

A huge grin broke out across the young stablehand's face.

It hadn't taken two days after our return before someone had whispered to the royal court that Lilly was a werewolf. She was a lycanthrope, but *not* a werewolf. That mistake was incorporated into the court minstrel's ballad of our journey with the Blood Sword to find the Colonel of the West. He sang it not only in the royal court but for weeks after in dozens of taverns within the King's City.

Some day I'd find out the person who shared Lilly's secret. I knew the one person who could tell me, if the opportunity ever presented itself. Nobody could hide something like that from Imperial Seer Lochelle.

CHAPTER 7

It wasn't the first time I'd been in the octagonal chamber where Imperial Seer Lochelle, Prime Counselor to the King, conjured visions and cast her most powerful spells. This day nine lanterns hung from the domed ceiling, providing light enough to reveal the intricate runes etched into the walls and support columns.

Imperial Seer Lochelle sat on a tall stool at the head of the oval table stationed in the room's center. She looked down at the table, allowing the long strands of her stringy brown hair to conceal her face. Jeweled rings adorned her youthful-looking hands, but I remembered how they stood in stark contrast to her gaunt, lined face. She was a seer, and the more powerful a seer became, the further that seer's physical vision retreated. Lesser Seer B'down stood along the wall, to my left. He wore gray robes, lacking the intricate stitching that lined the imperial seer's. His eyes showed the milky beginnings of cataracts. Imperial Seer Lochelle, who'd reached the highest rank, denoting supreme and unsurpassed skill in the magical arts, her eyes had become sightless white orbs.

On occasion, I wondered if it was worth the trade. Knowledge and ability acquired in any of the magical arts left a mark upon the wielder, even healers. I couldn't imagine why anyone would be a necromancer. I'd seen some of the effects. In comparison, the imperial seer's sacrifice was nothing.

I stood, attending Grand Wizard Seelain, who sat to the right of Prince Reveron. Both he and Major Jadd, who was attending him, were dressed in high boots, leather leggings and jerkin over a cotton shirt, and riding gloves folded into their wide belt. Major Jadd stood to the left of Seer B'down, who was Prince Reveron's chief advisor. The other Council members seated at the table were General Riverton, First Military Advisor to King Tobias, Colonel Isar, Commander of Keesee's m'unicorn cavalry, and Supreme Enchantress Thulease. The graying general wasn't attended by anyone. Colonel Isar faced away from the table, conferring with a fellow cavalrywoman. Supreme Enchantress Thulease was a tall, thin woman--the tallest woman I'd ever encountered, until I saw her attending enchantress. Both wore the customary black mask covering their faces from just below the eyes, but I suspected anyone could pick them out of a crowd if they weren't wearing their masks. Being an enchanter made the individual more susceptible to magic worked against them, but I guessed when you became as powerful as Enchantress Thulease, the mask was a formality rather than a necessity to protect her identity. Both wore similar pale green robes and had their hair rolled into a flattened ball on top of their heads.

There were other men and women standing along the chamber's walls. Some were scribes with quills, ink and paper placed on tall tables next to their stools, ready to record. Others were soldiers. One man's red hair, beard, eyes, and ruddy complexion identified him as a fire wizard, at least a greater one. Not one of them I recognized.

Missing was Prince Halgadin. Major Jadd said he was in the field. I was pretty sure my friend and mentor didn't mind the crown prince's absence. We were all waiting for King Tobias to arrive. Having met the king twice and having heard others speak of him, I guessed this meeting was a formality. He'd already made up his mind as to a course of action.

Imperial Seer Lochelle raised her head, revealing her sightless eyes. A tingle of magical energy coursed over my body. With her magical sight and advice, maybe things *weren't* settled.

All stood and bowed as King Tobias entered. The enchantresses removed their masks. The king's stern, bearded face looked weary, yet regal. His piercing blue eyes scanned the chamber. An attending manservant removed the king's red cape, more clearly revealing the royal purple and gold colors of King Tobias's silk garments. The only jewelry he wore was the gold signet ring on his right hand. That hand rested on the pommel of his sheathed broadsword.

King Tobias strode around the table and took his place next to Imperial Seer Lochelle. "Seal the chamber," he said in a booming voice.

Lesser Seer B'down hurried to close the rune-carved iron door and set a similarly rune-covered wooden bar in place.

Imperial Seer Lochelle muttered an incantation. Suddenly the chamber felt stuffy, everything muffled—warded from spying through magical means.

King Tobias sat, then signaled for all to be seated. Prince Reveron sat next, followed by the rest around the table. Only after they were settled did I and the other attendants climb onto the tall stools placed three steps behind those we served.

King Tobias made eye contact with each of his Council. "As some of you know, Lochelle has withdrawn her efforts elsewhere and focused on the concern within the city. Many traitor contingents have been killed or captured.

"My apologies, Seelain, and my gratitude. You eliminated the core of one group that eluded our sweeps. It appears Jolain has a seer and enchanter, both of notable skill, within the city and opposing our efforts. A futile gesture now that Thulease and Lochelle have made securing the city a primary concern."

General Riverton placed his right hand on the table and slid it forward.

"General," said the king

The general stood. "Those of which you speak have been under pursuit and are hiding in the northeastern part of Green District." He looked at Imperial Seer Lochelle before making eye contact with Supreme Enchanter Thulease. "Without support of their now shattered Long-Tooth network. Those captured are under interrogation even as we meet."

The king nodded. "Turning our attention away from the approaching threat will weaken our response, but it is early in the new defensive campaign. I suspected Jolain's offensive when my emissaries failed to recruit more than a scattered few Malgerian mercenaries, even as the Ancient Dictator waged war upon us." He looked to his son. "Reveron was even more convinced than I."

In the past, Grand Wizard Seelain named the Necromancer King as the 'Ancient Dictator,' whom the Colonel of the West named General Mzali, one of *his* ancient foes. And the Colonel also hadn't appeared fond of the goddess Fendra Jolain, whom he suggested *wasn't* really a goddess.

I was momentarily distracted by the enchantress seated behind Supreme Enchanter Thulease. Her gaze had fallen upon me several times, as it did even now. I met it for a second and then looked back to King Tobias as he spoke.

"Reveron, report on our serpent cavalry forces."

Prince Reveron remained seated as he spoke with quiet authority. "The number of serpent steeds is down ninety percent from what we placed in the field at the beginning of the war against the Necromancer King. Without support of healers, it will take much longer to put those that are wounded back into action. We have captured two white dragons and have two experienced cavalrymen working to master them."

The prince nodded slightly to Wizard Seelain next to him. "The wyvern steeds are proving adequate mounts for our scouts, but they will not stand up to the griffins favored by the forces under Fendra Jolain. Latest reports indicate that of the original eighty, sixty-five remain in service, with three wounded soon to be back in the field.

"As Major Jadd has reported to you, we also are short of experienced serpent cavalrymen, both for dragon and wyvern."

"Yes," said King Tobias. "As are we short of experienced officers, and young men to replace those lost in battle. Isar, what of the cavalry, including the heavy cavalry?"

Colonel Isar stood. "We have lost far more cavalrywomen than m'unicorn mounts, and training new recruits is a long process. We remain at sixty percent pre-war strength. The heavy cavalry is at forty."

That the mule-unicorn cross had a better survival rate than the horses of heavy cavalry didn't surprise me. Although a m'unicorn retained only a fraction of its sire's fleetness and grace, its speed and maneuverability, not to mention its resilience, far surpassed that of even the best stallion in the royal herd.

The king nodded. "My navy is still largely intact. You have noted the absence of Lazney? The admiral is recovering from his burns and will soon be back to actively organizing defense of the Tyrrhenian and Adriatic. He owes his life to one of the rogues we've sheltered over the years."

The king's last comment caught my attention. He'd sheltered rogue healers? My head's sharp movement caught Major Jadd's notice, as it did the tall enchantress. Again, her gaze lingered on me from across the chamber, but I refused to acknowledge it and become distracted.

The king looked toward the supreme enchantress. "Thulease, what of the healers?"

The enchantress stood and bowed slightly. "Two-hundred and ten remain in custody. Three were discovered to have committed suicide this morning, bringing that total to sixty-three. The military sweeps discussed may have brought in a few more. My assistants will interview those suspected of having such abilities and will report to your liaison by sunset.

"Fifty-one, mainly those of moderate to minimal ability have pledged loyalty to the Kingdom of Keesee. Their sincerity has been verified through both seer and enchanter incantations. They supplement the seventy-five rogue healers you spoke of. Of those, all but ten have been sent into the field, each with two personal guards to insure their safety. General Riverton indicated their appearance and presence, even though inadequate in numbers, will improve troop morale.

"Unknown numbers of healers remain in hiding throughout the countryside, attempting to return to the Vinchie Empire or await the forces they must know are on the march. Commoners continue to think highly of healers, and readily shelter them."

King Tobias nodded, and the enchantress sat. A scowl crossed his face. "The refugees remain a concern. We have driven the Necromancer King's forces from northern Keesee and the Doran Confederacy, except for scattered bands of goblins and souled zombies. I provided wagons and escort to those willing to return to their farms, as we will be in need of the harvest come the fall. Providing garrisons and patrols will continue to drain our already depleted strength. Especially in the Confederacy. Most of the lords are slain, along with their heirs and trusted men. Their keeps and estates are largely destroyed. The Lesser Kingdoms are no better off.

"Lawlessness and strife plagues the Faxtinian Coalition, except its capital, Paris–Imprimis, which is struggling to rebuild and cannot exert influence beyond a day's ride. It will be the first to be conquered by Jolain's advance. An easy prize."

King Tobias paused. "Lochelle?"

Imperial Seer Lochelle nodded, but didn't stand. Instead, her sightless gaze fell upon her table, into the empty bowl set into its center. "Whether you ride out to meet her forces, or if you defend and await her assault, a weakened Keesee cannot withstand the tide."

Colonel Isar slid her right hand forward on the table. "All are welcome to speak their thoughts," King Tobias said.

"What if we send m'unicorn forces to raid the tribal lands of the Malgerian mercenaries?" suggested Colonel Isar. "Force at least some of their numbers to abandon Fendra Jolain and return."

"The Kraken has left its lair beneath the Gibraltar Rock," said Seer Lochelle.

King Tobias added, "And Jolain has sent elements of her fleet to patrol the Southern Continent's coast."

I knew tales of the Kraken from my childhood, a beast controlled by the sea goddess Uplersh. It was said to guard the straits, dragging down any ship that didn't pay proper tribute to the sea goddess. I'd been at sea when a sea serpent attacked our ship, and such beasts were said to be playthings compared to the Kraken.

"Uplersh has no love of the Reunited Kingdom," said Prince Reveron. "And she is allied with Fendra Jolain, is she not? The Kraken would be most effective in stopping a Crusader foray against the Vinchie Empire. We, with enchanters and water, fire and air wizards are better equipped to fend against such a beast."

"Better equipped," said Supreme Enchantress Thulease, "yet ill equipped. We may drive it off, but how many troop ships would be lost?"

General Riverton added, "The Crusaders are tenuous allies. They consider us the lesser of two evils when compared to the Necromancer King, and only slightly better when compared to the Vinchie Empire and Fendra Jolain. Reports indicate they have landed a fresh division on the continent. Their objective is to lay siege to the Necromancer King's stronghold and bring him down."

Wizard Seelain interjected, "But the Crusaders despise Uplersh, who has for centuries harried their steam-driven vessels which dare to venture far from their shores."

"They are our solid allies against the Ancient Dictator," said King Tobias. "I have sent diplomats to seek aid against our new threat, but I do not hold out hope. I do not believe they have the troops to mount a serious offensive elsewhere."

There was a pause in the discussion, each council member deep in thought.

"We have no friends to the east," said General Riverton.

"And none on the Southern Continent," added Prince Reveron.

Wizard Seelain gripped the table. "And of our gods? Algaan will not come to manifest for another seventeen years. And M'Kishmael, the god of farmers...?"

"Their presence *does* inhibit Fendra Jolain from advancing her cause directly," said Seer Lochelle.

"Is it certain that it is Fendra Jolain's intention to invade and conquer

Keesee?" asked Colonel Isar.

"It is," said Seer Lochelle.

"Has any thought been given to diplomacy before it comes to arms," asked the supreme enchantress.

"Jolain knows as clearly as we do that the forces of Keesee are too weak to withstand," said King Tobias through clenched teeth. "We must have some point of strength before we can consider such a course."

Prince Reveron said, "We need a wildcard."

"Mercenary," snapped the king. "What about the Colonel of the West?"

I was trying to think of a reason that might encourage the Reunited Kingdom to pull back against the largely defeated Necromancer King and ally with Keesee against the goddess Fendra Jolain. It took me a fraction of a second to realize King Tobias had addressed me!

I jumped from the stool and bowed. "Your Majesty," I said. "I do not believe the Colonel of the West will lend aid to us. Unless…unless there is a…"

All had turned to face me as I worked to recall the details of my meeting with the Colonel of the West—why he traded what he called a small nuclear device for the king's malevolent Blood Sword. Prince Reveron made eye contact and nodded slightly, urging me to continue with confidence.

"As I explained upon my return," I said, "there is some sort of ancient pact that the gods, or as the Crusaders call them, immortal bloods, have. The Colonel felt that the Necromancer King, who he named General Mzali and blamed for the First Civilization's fall, had broken that agreement. So he felt it right to counter what the Necromancer King had done through summoning damned souls to build weaponry from before the First Civilization's end."

I didn't want to continue my line of thought, but the king had asked, and I had already told it to Imperial Seer Lochelle, who certainly had relayed it to him. "Until that realization, the Colonel of the West stated his belief that the Necromancer King had out maneuvered his enemies militarily and diplomatically and it was not his concern.

"He hinted that another, future, enemy was awaiting to bring Keesee's downfall. I guess the goddess Fendra Jolain is it. Unless there is evidence that the goddess has in some way broken their ancient pact, he will not do anything on our behalf."

The king nodded and I returned to my stool. He rubbed his bearded chin in thought before lifting from one of his pockets a silver watch held by a chain. Etched upon its cover was a pair of ducks taking wing above a reed-filled marsh. I immediately recognized it as the pocket watch given to me by the Colonel of the West.

"Lochelle," said the king. "What did the mercenary say Colonel Ibrahim, the Colonel of the West, promised?"

Imperial Seer Lochelle repeated the exact words the Colonel of the West had spoken to me upon trading the Blood Sword: "Mercenary Flank Hawk, you may have guessed Dr. Mindebee objects to my decision to deliver into your hands a nuclear device for the sword. The ramifications whether you fail or succeed may be great. Nevertheless, I will retain this sword for you and your king. If you succeed in your mission and General Mzali's conquest is thwarted, the day may come when you will have need of it once again. I will be willing to lend it if retrieved by you, your prince, or anyone bearing my pocket watch."

It was eerie, the way Imperial Seer Lochelle said it. The voice was hers, but the tone, pace and inflections were those of the Colonel.

"I believe," said the king, "that Mzali and Jolain have been in league against us for years. The failed attempts by the Reunited Kingdom delayed their plans. What Mzali lacked in seers and enchanters he made up for through healers, spies traveling with our forces and reporting as best they could. Without the destruction of Mzali's souled zombie engineers he summoned from the depths of hell, along with the production facilities they built using technology from before First Civilization's fall." He paused and pointed a finger on the table. "By now his zombies, goblins and ogres, backed by panzers and Stukas would be laying siege to this city.

"As it is, driving him back has severely weakened us and our allies, the Faxtinian Coalition, the Doran Confederacy, the Lesser Kingdoms, and the Reunited Kingdom. That is what happens when one opposes forces backed by gods."

He looked around the table for consensus.

"What about Uplersh?" asked Colonel Isar.

The king scoffed. "What Uplersh has forever done. Whatever direction the wind favors, she goes. This century it is with Jolain and the Ancient Dictator."

King Tobias stood and walked around the table as he spoke. "What has kept Jolain in check has been the Blood Sword. She must have learned I no longer possess it, and this emboldens her. Her original target with the Long-Tooths reconstituted and the Malgerian mercenaries was the Reunited Kingdom. The numbers of war galleys and troop ships on her northern coast, reported by the Crusaders at the onset of the Ancient Dictator's invasion, could mean little else. She planned they would be broken fighting the panzer battlewagons and aerial dive bombers. Even now the Crusaders are proving more resilient and resourceful than even I anticipated."

He'd completed one circuit of the table and stopped. "She will settle for her ally Mzali falling to the Crusaders. And while they're occupied, she will sweep in, extend her holdings. Build and confront the Crusaders in the future." His fist slammed down on the table. "A future where Keesee will have been subjugated!"

He held up the watch. "This, Reveron, is your wildcard. We will bring the

Blood Sword back into the game. Centuries past, sages debated and scholars recorded that it was forged with god slaying in mind." He looked from Imperial Seer Lochelle to Supreme Enchanter Thulease. "Present company believes, whether or not bringing a god to his or her end was its intended purpose, such a feat is beyond the sword's power."

King Tobias moved to stand behind Prince Reveron. "I will settle for it stemming the enemy tide." He observed the silver pocket watch in his right hand, then placed it on the table in front of his son. "Reveron, I task you to see that it happens. Return the sword to my hand."

CHAPTER 8

Prince Reveron and Major Jadd remained in Imperial Seer Lochelle's chamber to discuss plans with the king and General Riverton. Grand Wizard Seelain and Supreme Enchantress Thulease had exchanged pleasantries outside of the rune-scribed chamber before making their way to Wizard Seelain's suite in the palace's White Wing.

I followed several paces to the left and behind Wizard Seelain. The young enchantress walked next to Supreme Enchanter Thulease on the right. Even so, several times she glanced back over her shoulder at me while listening to the two powerful spellcasters discuss whether Prince Reveron would journey to accomplish what the king desired, and if not, who would be sent bearing the ancient trinket. Their conversation outside of the imperial seer's chamber made sense to me only because I'd been in the chamber with them.

Both believed the prince would go. Wizard Seelain hoped to accompany him, and if the prince didn't undertake the journey for King Tobias, she discussed the possibility of leading the journey.

I had my doubts about Prince Reveron taking his fiancé with him, or tasking her to retrieve the Blood Sword, but his decisions had surprised me in the past.

We reached the pearly white double doors leading up to the White Wing. Two veteran guards stood at attention while an elderly servant hurried ahead of us to open the doors.

Wizard Seelain turned to me. "Flank Hawk, you are dismissed." She placed a hand on my shoulder. "I know you hope to visit your family, but King Tobias has not lifted the curfew. I could request Reveron to provide a writ enabling unfettered travel, but getting word to you should your counsel be requested would be both time consuming and difficult." She stepped back and clasped her hands together. "You and your friend Lilly are the only ones who have had recent contact with the individual."

"Understood, Grand Wizard," I said, knowing she meant the Colonel of the West.

"If I am one of those selected to undertake or participate in the journey, I hope to have you at my side."

"I appreciate your confidence."

She smiled at me then turned to Enchantress Thulease who was speaking to her attendant.

"Thereese, if you leave now, you may take the carriage back to the tower and arrive before the curfew. If you wish to stay, King Tobias has offered us rooms in the Purple Wing."

The younger enchantress said, "I would like to remain with you in the palace, Mother. Should a magical need arise, I may be of some assistance."

"Unlikely," said Enchantress Thulease. There was more amusement than rebuke in her voice. "Nevertheless, send the carriage and guards back to your father and inform him of our stay. Instruct them to return by noon tomorrow." She looked down at Wizard Seelain who nodded approval.

Enchantress Thulease glanced at the elderly servant standing ready to pull open the doors to the White Wing, then turned to me. "Mercenary Flank Hawk, you know your way around the palace?"

"I do, Supreme Enchantress."

"Our carriage is at the Western Gate. Would you see that my daughter is able to deliver the message to the driver and then see that she finds our rooms in the Purple Wing?"

The young enchantress's eyes showing above her mask widened as if she were mortified. After the initial response, I guessed she might have been blushing as her ears had turned red. The supreme enchantress took her daughter's hand. "This mercenary will assist you," she said. "Remember, he is weary from his travels."

"I will, Mother." Enchantress Thereese bent slightly to give her mother a kiss on the cheek. It seemed an odd thing to do with both wearing their enchanter masks, but the action allowed the girl a sharp whisper into her mother's ear.

The supreme enchantress appeared to ignore whatever her daughter said and turned back to Wizard Seelain. "I have brought with me a map crystal that may be of interest to you, Seelain." Together they turned and entered the White Wing.

Before an awkward silence could settle in, I glanced up at the young enchantress who stood well over a head taller than me. "We should get to the West Gate to give your drivers plenty of time."

"Our tower isn't far, but...lead the way."

I escorted her down the hall. "You gathered I am Flank Hawk, a mercenary serving Grand Wizard Seelain. You're an enchanter?"

"I am. An apprentice enchanter—but I'm nearly ready to test for the rank of journeyman."

"May I address you as Apprentice Enchanter?"

After several strides she said, "I'd prefer Enchanter Thereese."

We walked several moments in silence, passing a few nobles, servants and guards. I knew that underneath their strength, training and outward appearances, even powerful spellcasters were people. But I never thought of them as mothers. I tried but I couldn't picture Imperial Seer Lochelle as some child's mother.

I wasn't sure how old Enchanter Thereese was; her height, the form-concealing robes, and the mask covering her face just below the eyes made it difficult. The lighting beyond the table in the imperial seer's chamber had been more shadowy than illuminating, so all I had to estimate was her green eyes, unsure voice and her demeanor. I guessed between thirteen and sixteen summers, maybe seventeen. She seemed pretty young to be an enchanter, but then again, her mother was arguably the most powerful one in the kingdom.

"How does one advance from one rank to another?" I asked. "From apprentice to journeyman?"

"Knowledge of the art, strength and skill employing it."

"Are there certain spells you have to be able to cast?"

"No," she said, amusement in her voice.

"Do you compete against someone, to demonstrate strength and skill?"

"No," she said again. "Elders in the craft evaluate you."

"So it's a test of sorts?"

"It could be called that, but it's never the same. The trial is different for each enchanter wishing to advance. And different, should the disciple of the discipline fail and later be deemed worthy to attempt again." Frustration crept into her voice. "And I know they're going to hold me to a higher standard."

"I believe you'll do well and attain the next title rank."

"It is more than a title, Mercenary," she snapped. "Success means the elders will provide access and instruction to...I apologize, Flank Hawk. My mother has such high standards and expectations. It's stressful."

"No offense taken, Enchantress Thereese." I stopped at a cross hall. "Is this your first time in the palace?"

"Yes, it is," she said. Hesitance hung in her voice. "Why?"

"Because I am better at finding my way in the woods than the king's palace. Even in the city, you have the sun as a guide post."

"Oh," she said, her shoulders relaxing.

"This way," I said, turning to the right. "I believe we're almost there."

"I believe you are correct," she said. "Your right leg. You are favoring it. Were you wounded this morning, defending Grand Wizard Seelain? The renegades that King Tobias alluded to?"

"No," I said, not wanting to get into what had happened.

"Certainly not a lingering injury from your quest to trade the Blood Sword. King Tobias would have seen that was healed—before the healers abandoned us to become enemies."

"Oh, certainly. King Tobias would have seen to it. This is recent, mostly healed already on its own."

The hall was widening, with more people and activity apparent. I spotted the line of arrow slits in the distant dead-end wall and the metal floor plates with three barrels of oil set near them.

"It was a griffin," I said quickly. "I got him. But really, Wizard Seelain did most of the work." Before Enchanter Thereese could ask anything else, I nodded to the guard, who lifted the bar locking the door leading to the gate area below. "This way," I said, taking the first few narrow steps down. They way was steep and spiraling, and lit only by what filtered down from the entry door, requiring the young enchantress to concentrate, and to watch her head.

I recruited a servant to carry the two traveling bags from the enchantress's carriage. Conversation shifted to the more mundane, focusing on the weather. Enchanter Thereese knew as well as I to avoid discussions in front of servants that might lead to gossip, or worse.

We made it to the Purple Wing and the pair of elegant rooms prepared for the two enchantresses. After the servant set the bags inside the room I sent him to find the wing's chief maid.

"Would you care to dine with me?" asked Enchantress Thereese.

With possible travel in the near future, my leg's ache was a concern. I'd determined to try healing it myself before going to sleep. It wasn't something I looked forward to.

"Thank you very much for the invitation," I said. "But I am exhausted, not only from today's events, but a week of hard travel."

The enchantress's eyes sparkled just a bit as she spoke. "I brought little to entertain myself and it may be many long hours before my mother returns."

My leg didn't seem to hurt as much, and I thought I wouldn't mind putting off my attempt at healing for an hour or two. "There is certain to be spare tables in the noble's dining hall," I said.

"You would not be comfortable there and neither would I." The young girl's brown hair seemed to have more luster than I remembered, and the room rushed with the fragrance that reminded me of the North Garden.

Something didn't seem right. I'd had magic worked on me before, but not subtle like this—I was being distracted, mind-fogged.

I stepped back, and twisted my right leg, focusing on the pain. "I wish you a quiet and enjoyable evening," I said, trying not to sound harsh. "I hear the chief maid coming down the hall."

The enamor spell faded, and a look of sadness and desperation filled Enchanter Thereese's eyes. "I'm sorry, Flank Hawk." She took a hesitant step forward and then backed away, looking around the room. "I'm frightened," she said with sudden timidity. "I know, it sounds silly. Childish."

There was truth in her words, but I wasn't sure. I thought about asking her to meet me for breakfast tomorrow in the North Garden. She could meet Lilly, and I could see how things worked out with Rin, but I also recalled what the stablehand had thought about Lilly. And being an enchantress, even if only an apprentice, she might recognize something about Lilly. Matching that to the rumors of Lilly being a werewolf, it didn't seem like a good idea. And her mother might not approve.

"No," I said. "It's not childish. I remember *my* first night in the palace. You'll be okay." I pointed and smiled. "At least your room has windows."

I sat with my injured leg outstretched on my bed. Sweat beaded on my forehead as I concentrated and began to chant. I'd done it before—healed damaged tissue like when one of the Necromancer King's sorcerers had wounded my heart.

I focused and chanted, ignoring the flickering oil lamp on the nearby table. The ribbons of energy eluded my grasp. I dug deeper for courage and resolve until I separated one of the ribbons and directed it into my leg. An itching warmth ran through my leg just below the knee and faded, taking most of the ache with it.

I fell back on my pillow, panting and exhausted. I didn't even bother to turn down the lamp's wick or even crawl under the covers.

Sleep came easy. The dreams, they were difficult.

CHAPTER 9

The oil lamp's flickering light still lit the room when a knock at the door awoke me.

I stood, stretched and opened the door a crack. Outside stood two servants with a small tub of steaming water.

The older servant bowed his head quickly. "Mercenary Flank Hawk, Supreme Enchantress Thulease requests your company for breakfast in the Stickley Dining Hall."

That was where nobles, dignitaries and influential merchants dined, just off the Grand Ballroom.

I opened the door wider. "When?"

"One hour from now."

"Did *she* send the wash tub?"

"No, Mercenary Flank Hawk. Grand Wizard Seelain had it scheduled to be delivered an hour from now, but the Blue Wing's chief maid instructed us to prepare it for you early."

"My armor. Has it been mended and cleaned?"

"Chief Maid Rah-haba is personally seeing to it. She sends her assurance that it will be ready."

I stood aside and let them roll the tub in. They were careful not to allow any water to slosh over the side. The older servant hung a faded blue towel and washing cloth over my chair and a cake of lye soap on my desk. "Do you require assistance?"

"No," I said.

"We will return in fifteen minutes. I apologize for the brief time, but another visitor is scheduled."

"Fifteen minutes will be fine. Ten minutes if it will help you keep your schedule."

The younger servant nodded, but the older one scowled at him. "Fifteen minutes. We will have enough time, kind sir."

I lacked formal clothing so, in my armor, including my breastplate and backplate showing wear but polished—the same as my boots—I reached Stickley Hall several minutes before the hour had passed. Even though the sun had just risen and was beginning to cast its light through the high rectangular windows, nearly half of the hall's round tables were filled with diners. A few military officers were among the crowd, but mainly visiting merchants and nobles ate and quietly conversed.

A waiter wearing a lavender tunic that matched the tablecloths approached me as I nodded to the guard before peering through the arched entryway. "Sir, you would be the mercenary, Flank Hawk?"

"I am," I said.

"It is my pleasure to announce that Supreme Enchantress Thulease and Apprentice Enchantress Thereese await your company. If you will follow me."

The tables were well spaced, larger ones with six or eight high-backed chairs, and smaller ones with two to four. The smell of fresh bread mingled with that of ham and sausage. It reminded me how hungry I was. The enchantresses were seated near the center of the room. They wore matching lime-colored dresses with wide sleeves and high upturned collars. Circular hats bearing small emeralds set in gold studs demonstrated their wealth to the other diners, and their place among them.

"Good morning, Mercenary Flank Hawk," said Enchantress Thulease. Her eyes showed she was smiling beneath her mask, but even makeup couldn't hide the dark circles that hung beneath them. I guessed she'd had a long night working with Imperial Seer Lochelle to locate and root out the king's enemies.

"Good morning to you, Supreme Enchantress," I said. "And to you as well, Apprentice Enchantress."

Enchantress Thereese stared down at the glass vase holding a fresh pink rose. "Thank you. Good morning to you as well."

A few diners, mainly merchants in colorful silks and capes, discreetly glanced my direction as the senior enchantress asked, "Please, join as our guest for breakfast."

The waiter pulled out the remaining chair at the table. I nodded to him. "Thank you."

"Would you care for white grape juice?" he asked, indicating what the glasses in front of the enchantresses held.

"Apple cider, will do."

He smiled and hurried away.

"I believe you may have a busy day, so I took the liberty of ordering ham and pan fried cakes with strawberry jam for the three of us. I hope that will do."

"That was very kind of you," I said to Enchantress Thulease. I wasn't fond of strawberries, but I was too hungry to care.

A stern motherly look fell upon the young enchantress. "Thereese, dear, you have something to say about last night's impropriety?"

The young girl looked from her mother to me. "I am sorry for attempting an enchantment upon you last night. I fully apologize." Her voice broke as she finished. "It shall never happen again."

"I accept your apology," I said, a little surprised.

"My daughter's guilt weighed heavily upon her. Upon my return three hours past midnight, she confessed her misdeed. I appreciate your integrity and, as a mother, I am thankful my instincts about your character were correct." She laughed merrily. "Seelain speaks highly of you, but my daughter is young and innocent. Anything but worldly. I fear that her father and I have erred in the degree we have sheltered her."

"Mother, please," the young enchantress whispered.

Beyond the supreme enchantress's shoulder, I spotted our waiter with my glass of cider. A cook with hands wrapped in his white apron had followed him out of the kitchen.

All mirth disappeared from Supreme Enchantress Thulease's eyes. "Something is wrong," she said, looking about. "A latent enchantment has been triggered."

I stood and moved around the table next to the supreme enchantress, my hand on my sword's grip. "Danger?" I asked quietly.

"A charm spell. A compulsion variety of great strength."

I trusted Enchantress Thulease's instincts. "Guards!" If there was a dangerous enchanter or a charmed assassin in the room, it'd be harder for them to succeed with everyone alerted.

Before the guard near the entrance could respond, the cook pulled a butcher knife from beneath his apron, shoved past our waiter, and ran towards us, screaming.

I drew my sword and stepped between him and the supreme enchantress. She stood and mumbled an incantation and flicked her right hand upward. The cook's apron shot up, breaking its ties and covered his head, blinding him and muffling his scream.

Quick movement two tables away to the enchantress's left caught my attention. A blue-shirted merchant with black gloves and cape stood with a throwing knife cocked back—his arm already in motion.

I slammed into Thulease, knocking her against the table and onto the ground. The knife clanged off my backplate as I fell with her.

"Mother!" shouted Thereese, jumping to her feet.

"Get DOWN!" I yelled. The merchant had another knife ready in hand. An officer threw a table aside and charged the knife assassin, but he wouldn't get there in time. I kicked the girl in the leg, striking just below her knee. She dropped to the floor in pain as the spinning blade flew through the air where she'd stood.

With unexpected strength, Thulease shoved me off of her as the officer tackled the merchant from behind. Everyone but two guards and three officers lay on the ground or hid crouched by their table. One officer knocked the cook unconscious. I got to my feet with sword held ready while the guards helped subdue the knife-throwing assassin.

I looked around while more guards rushed into the dining hall.

Enchantress Thulease stood next to me. "Everything okay?" I asked.

The assassin spewed curses at the Supreme Enchantress until the tackling officer slammed a fist into his groin.

"It is now," she said. "Except for the poison I think you will find on those knife blades and the almost certain fact that you broke my daughter's leg."

I'd heard it but didn't pay attention to the *snap* when my boot connected. I knelt down next to the young enchantress, lying with her face twisted in tears and pain as she clutched her knee through the grape juice-soaked dress.

Word about the assassination attempt spread quickly throughout the palace. Few nobles and other visitors walked the halls without a personal or palace guard. Even then, they eyed the servants cleaning tapestries or scrubbing floors with suspicion.

Major Jadd and I stood within sight of the White Wing's guarded double doors and waited for Prince Reveron and Wizard Seelain to emerge.

As I told my friend what happened in the dining hall, a grin spread across his usually solemn, pock-marked face. Life as a mercenary had been more difficult for him in some ways, but the pressures of war and leading the diminishing serpent cavalry was proving more stressful. Despite his valor and shouldered responsibility, court politics had barred his promotion to colonel. The crown prince only half forgave my mentor's long-past transgression.

"So," Jadd said when I finished talking, "you weren't distracted by the diversion."

"I was for a second or two."

He slapped me on the shoulder. "I think you can count yourself a seasoned bodyguard, now."

"Maybe," I said, "but I still have a lot to learn."

"I see you're carrying your spear."

"That's part of my point. You know firsthand my sword skills."

"One cannot be everything," he said and laughed. "But you appear to be the *one* person who can break the leg of the daughter of a supreme enchantress and master alchemist and *not* be arrested, or worse."

"Supreme Enchantress Thulease didn't appear happy with me."

"If you're not turned into a newt by this evening, you'll know she's forgiven you." He rubbed his nose and glanced at the ceiling for a second. "You helped preserve her life and that of her daughter."

I wasn't so sure that Jadd was joking about the newt thing.

"The real question is, were you served breakfast?"

"I was," I said. "A cold slice of ham on bread while recounting the assassin's attempt to the Captain of the Guard. If it weren't for the enchantress's warning, the assassin might've succeeded."

"Speaking of food," said Jadd. "You'll be happy to know that the One-

Eyed Pelican is still standing despite fires at the docks. I'll see that you get a good meal there as soon as we get the chance."

"Thanks," I said, recalling the rat-infested tavern and its greasy fish soup and cheap ale. What he saw in the place, I'd never understand. I was about to comment on that thought when Prince Reveron and Grand Wizard Seelain strode through the double doors.

Jadd and I bowed to the prince as he and Wizard Seelain approached. He dismissed one of the palace's elite guards that accompanied the pair.

"Major Jadd, you will see to our safety?" A smile spread between the prince's wispy white mustache and beard, a harbinger of what would happen to the rest of his hair as his air wizard abilities increased. I'd never heard him addressed by his wizardly rank. I guessed he was at least a journeyman but no more than a lesser wizard. He was an accomplished serpent cavalryman and the sword at his side was far more than ornamental. I'd witnessed him both in battle and in the practice yard. He was more than Major Jadd's equal, and my mentor's skill with a sword was considered exceptional.

"Flank Hawk, accompany us as well," invited the prince. "Seelain and I understand you have already experienced an exciting morning."

"That could be said, Prince."

"Let us hope it was part of the final throes of the traitorous gangs working to spread mayhem and death." He paused and met Wizard Seelain's gaze. "Through last night's efforts, Seer Lochelle and Enchanter Thulease facilitated the cornering and capture of the enemy seer. I suspect that the enchantress shan't be lacking in additional motivation to track down the enemy enchanter."

Wizard Seelain added, "Being the enchanter who orchestrated the attempt upon not only the enchantress herself, but also upon her daughter? It can only end badly."

"Speaking of things ending badly for our enemies," Prince Reveron said, picking up the pace as he led us down a guarded stairwell, "General Riverton and my advisor, Seer B'down, are awaiting us to finalize a plan to bring about my father's desire."

"So, we are in agreement then," Prince Reveron said to General Riverton and Grand Wizard Seelain. "One red dragon and three wyverns."

We sat at the table, sealed within the imperial seer's magically warded chamber. Nobody sat on Imperial Seer Lochelle's stool, and I sat furthest from it.

I was still taken aback that Prince Reveron decided upon Grand Wizard Seelain to lead the team to retrieve the Blood Sword. It made sense. He was needed in the field against the new threat. Assets, as he called them, were tight and the number of aerial mounts, even for this important mission, was extremely limited. Having an air wizard as part of the team only made sense, and having a grand wizard lead it filled two slots with one person.

I was the next one selected. Grand Wizard Seelain stated I would provide security, plus I knew the lay of the land better than anyone else. But there were crystal maps and there were numerous soldiers with more experience in wild lands and skill in combat. I knew why I was going. The Colonel of the West identified me as one of three options to obtain the sword from him. Prince Reveron wasn't going and King Tobias deemed it wise to hold the watch against future need, especially should this first mission fail. Seer B'down suggested the possibility that decades or centuries down the road, the Kingdom of Keesee might have need to retrieve the Blood Sword. With near certain doom facing Keesee, the seer's reasoning rang hollow.

"You'll need an enchanter to call up images from the map crystals," said General Reverton to Grand Wizard Seelain. "Any preferences?"

"Lesser Seer Jonas," said Wizard Seelain. "He was part our infiltration team that scouted the fortified town where the Ancient Dictator built his resurrected war machines."

General Riverton sat up straight and rubbed his beard a moment in thought. "I know the fellow. He's a capable spellcaster and loyal to the king. But he never struck me as a rugged outdoorsman or handy in a fight."

"Enchanter Jonas stood against a powerful sorcerer for a time," said Wizard Seelain. "One that was in the process of slaying me until Flank Hawk drove him off. Even deeply wounded by sorcery, Enchanter Jonas wove spells that concealed the location of the souled zombie captured for interrogation.

"Flank Hawk," said Wizard Seelain. "You spent time with him. What are your thoughts?"

"General Riverton is correct. He's not an outdoorsman. But he didn't shirk his camp responsibilities, and listened and learned. And he *is* handy with a rapier," I said. "He slew three or four goblins and helped me bring down an ogre before the sorcerer's magic fell upon him."

I didn't think I needed to explain how susceptible an enchanter was to a sorcerer's attack. And the dark, twisted spellcaster had brought me down, nearly killing me with one spell.

"There was a giant and bands of souled zombies sent against us, General, sir. But he kept his wits and didn't run where others might have."

"You have an enchanter, then," Prince Reveron said to Wizard Seelain. "Major Jadd, recommendations for a serpent cavalryman and mount?"

"Captain Bray," suggested Major Jadd. "He recently lost his aft-guard, and his red has just been healed of her wounds."

General Riverton looked to Prince Reveron, who said, "Bray's a good officer, handles his mount well, and steady in combat. Came out on the winning end against a Stuka—on three occasions."

Stukas were the main cause of the devastation wrought upon serpent cavalry. Surviving a single encounter, let alone winning was a major accomplishment.

"Okay," said General Riverton. "I know of an infiltration soldier that can handle a wyvern. Jonas will be on the dragon, but with no aft-guard. That leaves a slot. Healer or another of the king's elites? Although we're tight on both, and even then it'd have to be a rogue. Wouldn't trust one recently loyal to the goddess on such an important mission."

At the mention of healer, Wizard Seelain, Major Jadd and Prince Reveron sent quick glances my way, but didn't say anything.

The general asked Wizard Seelain, "What do you think?"

"As you indicated, General, both healers and the king's elite troops are in short supply. I believe they will be needed here more than on the mission."

Wizard Seelain didn't care for the king's elite troops. As to why, I wasn't sure. I had nothing against them. Some were on the arrogant side, but they were also ten times better than I was, both with sword and survival skills. Wizard Seelain must've figured I'd suffice as a healer when she said, "A competent non-commissioned officer will do. Or, possibly no one, to keep the carrying weight down. We will be traveling long distances over water."

Major Jadd said, "Bray's mount, Flint Spitter, won't have a problem with three plus standard gear."

"Flank Hawk," Wizard Seelain said. "You desire input on this issue?"

I didn't realize it showed, but I did have a suggestion. "Grand Wizard, I believe Lilly would be a good choice."

"The werecreature?" asked General Riverton.

"Yes, General," I said, and continued before anyone could interrupt me. "We might only have one of the king's elite soldiers should it come to battle, but we'll also have a red dragon and an air wizard. Captain Bray is good with an axe, and Enchanter Jonas and I can fight should the need arise. Lilly can too."

I looked from the general to Prince Reveron. "The mission's success might depend on avoiding trouble. A second infiltration soldier would help in that area. But Lilly's senses are keener than any pure human's."

Everybody was listening, so I continued. "We'll be laying over in the Reunited Kingdom, and she speaks their tongue. And she's been to the Colonel of the West's mountain stronghold, same as me. Should something happen to me, it's possible that since he knows her as a scout who served me, and Wizard Seelain, fiancé to the prince who he said he'd trade the sword to, he might give it to one of them."

I wasn't really sure of the last statement, but it just popped into my head as I spoke. It sounded reasonable, even if unlikely. I met Wizard Seelain's gaze. "And she's lighter than most of the king's elite soldiers."

Prince Reveron stroked his lightly bearded chin. "I hadn't considered her."

"But is she loyal to the king, and to Keesee?" asked General Riverton.

"And how well will the Crusaders take to a lycanthrope?" asked Major Jadd.

Wizard Seelain said, "We should not allow the Crusaders' views to dissuade us from choosing one who may be a vital component to not only reaching the Colonel, but also returning."

General Riverton leaned on the table. "I ask again, where is her loyalty? And will she follow orders?"

"She is an honest creature," said Jadd. "And she does not enjoy living in the palace."

"To my understanding, she has mastered her beast," said Wizard Seelain. "And even when it is a full moon and the beast emerges, she retains some control."

"What kind of beast is she?" asked the general.

"A were-muskrat," I said.

"Quite rare," said Wizard Seelain. "I have heard some of the stories of your adventure, Flank Hawk, and Lilly's part in it."

"A witch with a familiar would offer some spell capability and animal senses equal to that of a werebeast," said the general.

Lesser Seer B'down spoke up. "This werebeast may be an element that the Goddess of Healing and her allies have not foreseen, should they move to thwart the king's mission."

"Mercenary, is she loyal to Keesee?"

"Honestly, General, I don't believe she has sworn her loyalty to Keesee, or ever would."

"Most lycanthropes are solitary," Prince Reveron said. "So one would not expect one to swear fealty to a kingdom and people who, if they knew she were a werecreature, would fear and be certain to reject her."

"They already know," I said.

"The minstrel's song," agreed Jadd. "The one which misnames her as a werewolf."

"Would she commit herself to this mission?" asked the prince. "For if she would, my gut says it may be a move, as my advisor has wisely pointed out, however small, that the enemy may not have planned for. Would you agree, dear Seelain?"

"It is your choice," General Riverton said to the prince.

"Yes, it is," said Wizard Seelain. "Flank Hawk, will you speak with your friend, Lilly, and see if she will join us?"

"And if she declines?" asked Jadd.

"Well, then," said Prince Reveron, "there is that young stablehand that my fiancé thinks highly of."

There were smiles and chuckles from around the table. It seemed so out of place in the shadowy chamber.

"Young Rin's heart is brave. But if not him," Wizard Seelain said with a broad smile, "then find an NCO with a heart that is equal."

"You're planning to go *where*?" asked Lilly. "Why?"

Interrupting Lilly's tutoring session had already annoyed her. Working in the garden was one thing. Learning to read the Crusader tongue was another. Fortunately, the private library where she met with her tutor was just down the hall from a meeting room that had security wardings which Lesser Seer B'down easily activated.

"To retrieve the Blood Sword," I said to her.

Lilly's eyes opened wider than her mouth. "That evil thing? It possessed you, remember?" She pushed her chair away from the room's polished oak table. "Why would that colonel even want to give it back to you?"

"I won't be going alone, and I want you to go with us."

"With who?" she asked, standing and putting her hands on her hips. "And you still haven't answered why."

I remained seated and waited while Lilly paced and relaxed. "Sit down," I said quietly, "and I'll explain."

"Okay," she said. "But I'm guessing someone thinks it's big since that seer spelled the walls, floor and ceiling." She avoided looking at Seer B'down who sat silently in a padded reading chair situated next to a narrow stained-glass window.

"It is important," I said. "The Necromancer King's been driven back, but a new enemy is on the march."

That got her attention. "The evil conjurer in Sint Malo?"

"No," I said. "The goddess Fendra Jolain. She's got the backing of the resurrected Brotherhood of the Long-Tooth Tiger and has thousands of mercenaries from the Southern Continent."

"What about the Crusaders? Are they going to help Keesee?"

I shook my head. "No, they're focused on wiping out the Necromancer King."

"I thought you said he was beat?"

"He's defeated. They want to utterly destroy him."

"Good," she said. "Will they help after the Necromancer King is destroyed?"

"Even if they would, I'm not sure if Keesee will last that long. The Faxtinian Coalition, well, you're from there. You know what the Necromancer King's forces did. The Doran Confederacy and the Lesser Kingdoms are all weak. They can't field an army, let alone resist Fendra Jolain's invasion."

"She's the Goddess of Healing, right?"

"She is," I said.

Lilly glanced at Seer B'down before saying, "What's the difference? I mean, I know Prince Reveron likes you, and Grand Wizard Seelain does too. But the king doesn't. Does he? And Prince Halgadin will be king some day, not Prince Reveron. That prince hates Road Toad, so he'll hate you too."

She leaned close. "I've not been around like you, but I've never heard tell that the Goddess of Healing mistreats her people."

"She took my sister. *Took* her. Like all healers."

"By now, if your sister really wanted, she could've returned home."

"If she really wanted to?" I asked.

"I would've. You would've. Why wouldn't she?"

I didn't have an answer for that, other than Fendra Jolain was a goddess.

"Did the king get your sister in his roundup?"

I shook my head. "Major Jadd checked for me."

"Then, if she's still alive, she'll fight for the goddess."

I hadn't really thought of that possibility. "Healers don't fight."

"She'll be there. Are you willing to fight her? What if you bring back the Blood Sword and it gets her?"

"I won't kill her. She won't kill me."

"But you won't have the sword. And a war is a big place."

"It hasn't been said, but I don't think the battlefield is where the Blood Sword is to be used."

She thought about that a moment. "Well, that's probably reason enough for that Colonel of the West and his gargoyle friend to give the sword back to you. What does Road Toad think?"

"He's for it," I said.

"If I go, will he be going with us?"

"Part of the way. As far as the Reunited Kingdom."

Lilly was quiet for another minute. "Does your dad know about the war?"

"No," I said. "And like you agreed, you can't share that or anything we've discussed with him, or anyone."

"I know better than that. The king might want an excuse to lock me up." Lilly laughed, but I knew she was only half joking. She ran her fingers along the table's beveled edge. "Who's in charge of getting the sword back?"

"Grand Wizard Seelain," I said.

"And, if that immortal colonel will give it to us, you think getting the Blood Sword back is the right thing to do?"

"Yes, I do."

"Okay then," Lilly said. "I'll go." She turned to Lesser Seer B'down. "You can see the future, right?"

"I can," he replied. "In a limited fashion."

"You know, this is my second mission for Keesee. And this time, if we return with the Blood Sword, will the king give me my *own* golden medal?"

CHAPTER 10

Rin's face held the biggest grin I'd seen in at least a year.
Grand Wizard Seelain continued to check the work the young
stablehand had done in preparing her mount. "Excellent, Stablehand
Rin," she said, finishing her inspection of the cinches and straps. "In
addition, Moon Ash appears well fed and groomed."

Rin nodded. "Thank you, Grand Wizard." Then he pointed at the
assistant handler standing next to me and Wick. "Marquan's been teaching
me t'do more than clean stalls. You should thank him some 'cause he
deserves it more than me."

Grand Wizard Seelain, dressed in her buckskin riding outfit, turned to
Marquan. "Thank you as well."

The red-headed handler bowed. "It was a pleasure to tend to and see to
the preparation of your mount for travel, ma'am."

While Marquan spoke, Rin stood at attention. He made eye contact with
me and rested his hand on the pommel of his curved dagger. I nodded and
he stood up even straighter.

Grand Wizard Seelain handed Moon Ash's reins to Rin so that he could
lead the wyvern out to the launch yard. "By your look, Flank Hawk, I can see
you're ready to be on our way."

I handed Wick's reins to Assistant Handler Marquan. "We've another
scouting mission and a great distance to travel." It was a lie, but one meant to
throw off anyone too curious. The plan was to rendezvous with the rest of
the team and an escort that would accompany us at least as far as the
Reunited Kingdom.

Wizard Seelain said to one of the king's guards that had escorted us
through the late evening streets, "Return and inform Prince Reveron that we
left the city shortly after nightfall and will return upon completion of my
mission." She handed him an envelope sealed with wax. "And deliver this to
him."

With that, Marquan led Wick out of the roost. With a command my
mount leapt into flight. Grand Wizard Seelain followed on Moon Ash and we
raced out to sea to meet the rest of the team. We found them circling high
above a pair of boats bearing three lanterns each, the fishermen quietly
casting their bait for orange squid.

We sat huddled in a small tool shed that appeared to have doubled as a workshop for someone with blacksmithing skills. All valuables had been taken when the farm was abandoned, or stolen sometime after. Along with the shed, a barn remained intact, but the house and two other structures, probably barns, had burned to the ground. Private Zunnert estimated the home had burned last spring, and the two barns in late winter.

Major Jadd and Captain Bray were in the remaining barn tending to the two dragons and three wyverns. Jadd's aft-guard, Sergeant Drux, patrolled the abandoned farm's perimeter.

Lesser Seer Jonas set two green crystals the size of my thumbnail on the dirt floor while Grand Wizard Seelain spoke to me, Lilly and Zunnert. The diplomat, a stocky woman with a round face and clad in brown riding clothes like what nobles wore during stag chases, stayed back against wall. By her looks I guessed she wasn't one to smile much. The name, Grimsby, didn't help.

"This farm and the one we'll reach tomorrow morning will shelter us from curious eyes during daylight hours," Wizard Seelain said. "From then on we'll travel by day and establish camp in isolated areas. Serpent patrols, while uncommon, are not unheard of. In any case, once we are outside the Kingdom of Keesee, I should not be easily recognized and the king believes the sight of serpent cavalry by both friend and potential foe is a positive for morale."

Enchanter Jonas mumbled a few words and ran his right hand over one of the crystals. A map, scaled to show what I recognized as the western shore of our continent and the island nation of the Reunited Kingdom emerged from the crystal. Opaque, and the size of a barrel hoop, with colors of brown, green and blue.

He kept chanting quietly, working to sustain the crystal spell while Diplomat Grimsby stepped between Lilly and me. "We are going to land on the shore near the Thames River and await permission to enter New London." Her voice bore little inflection, yet carried a musical tone. "Grand Wizard Seelain and I, accompanied by Private Zunnert and Mercenary Flank Hawk, will meet with the prime minister, or his representative."

"Why?" asked Lilly.

The diplomat answered without hesitation. "While that is an astute question, I am not at liberty to explain. Grand Wizard Seelain may, if she deems it appropriate."

Lilly pushed up the sleeves of the dark blue wool coat Roos had wrapped around her just before his death, but didn't look to Wizard Seelain for an answer.

"Lilly," said Wizard Seelain. "Inhabitants of the Reunited Kingdom do not use magic and communication between our two peoples, except on the battlefield, is sporadic at best. We will be asking for a writ of permission to fly over and camp upon their lands, en route to the islands that Enchanter Jonas is about to show us. One of them, long ago named Iceland, you have been on before."

As the enchanter slowly drew his hand toward himself, the map shifted, like a paper sliding under a circle of candle light.

"These islands are along the route we will take," said Wizard Seelain, pointing, until we reach the Western Continent, until we reach where both Flank Hawk and Lilly have been before. The Colonel of the West's Outpost Four." Her finger stopped above a spot on the continent's east coast.

Lilly held her tongue. I wanted to question the reason for going there as well.

"We are aware of your encounter with the Warden of Outpost Four."

I recalled the fallen angel that now served the Colonel. Even though constrained by some apparent orders, still he tried to wrest the Blood Sword from me through one of his minions. It wasn't something I liked to think about.

"If we do not receive aid there, we will use the second crystal, which holds maps drawn from Flank Hawk's memory by Imperial Seer Lochelle. It was wise of you, my mercenary friend, to periodically view the terrain from aboard the Colonel's mechanical flying machine."

Birdcalls, three of them resembling a brown-jay, signaled there was potential trouble. I got to my feet, donned my helmet and grabbed my spear. Private Zunnert grabbed his helmet and opened the wooden door a crack to peek outside.

I stood next to him and looked back to Wizard Seelain. "We'll see what caught Drux's attention." She nodded approval.

Lilly moved a step closer to the grand wizard and for a split second her gaze met mine. She'd protect Wizard Seelain should it come to a fight.

Zunnert and I slipped out the door and made our way to the rock wall that encompassed the main buildings. Jadd met up with us as we climbed over the four-foot barrier and stepped into the thin line of trees where Drux crouched behind a large maple. He pointed with my loaded crossbow along the hardened path that served as a road leading up to the farm.

I wished I'd asked Lilly for her spyglass to better view the approaching wagon. From a distance the wagon appeared weathered. A team of four oxen pulled it. Once or twice a glint of sunlight reflected off what had to be glass windows built into the faded red sides. The two horsemen, armed with long spears and scimitars and leading the wagon and the five that trailed behind, spoke of importance, if not wealth. The water barrels on the wagon's side and the string of goats that trailed the wagon between the riders suggested self-reliance.

"I know that wagon," said Jadd. "A gypsy named Madame Creeanne. She's traveled far from Sint Malo."

"Is she one of the Conjurer's minions?" asked Drux.

"No," said Jadd. "But her family clan hails from that region. She's a member of their council, and those on horseback are likely her sons."

Zunnert said, "So far from home, maybe she's been exiled."

Jadd shook his head. "I don't know much about gypsy culture, but I think they put to death rather than exile."

"Wonder why she's *here*?" asked Drux as we slid deeper into the thin stand of trees. "Are you on good terms with her?"

"Her family came into conflict with a cult of demon worshippers. I was one of several mercenaries they hired. I fought well. Earned my pay."

"Do you want to be seen by her?" I asked.

Jadd rubbed his chin. "I was wondering that myself." Then he added, "Some say there's a sliver of nymph blood flowing in her veins."

"They're getting close," Zunnert commented.

"Private, you're the best at not being seen. Go make sure nobody is approaching the farm from another direction, and then get into position should trouble start." After the infiltration soldier slipped back over the wall, Jadd continued, "No sense letting them get any closer. Sergeant, stay here ready with the crossbow. Flank Hawk and I will go out a short bit and meet them."

"Seven on horseback against two, plus what's in the wagon," Drux said with a crooked smile that emphasized the deep scar on the right side of his chin. I'd seen that look before, one showing he was ready for a fight.

"I have you with a crossbow, brother," said Jadd, mirroring his aft-guard's smile. "And two dragons and an air wizard behind me."

"Yeah? Air wizards and dragons don't dig graves none too well."

Jadd adjusted his sword in its scabbard. "If it comes to that. But with Flank Hawk at my side it'll only be gypsy graves. Come on," he said to me.

I followed my friend out, wondering about his decision. I was a better shot with a crossbow, and Drux had served for years in the royal guard in the roughest areas of the King's City. He reminded me of an experienced bouncer from one of the Brown District taverns. With his chainmail shirt and well-used broadsword, Drux was far more intimidating than me.

As we emerged from the treeline, Jadd said, "I see you finally replaced that rust-bucket helmet."

"Yeah, I did," I said, wondering why he made that comment now. "I figured I should at least look the part when guarding...you know."

He laughed and I shook my head. The lead riders brought their horses to a stop. A young girl next to the wagon driver stood on the bench seat and appeared to say something through a long rectangular window.

After a few more strides Jadd whispered, "I don't anticipate any trouble. Still, look sharp."

All but one of the rear horsemen joined the front two, blocking our view of the wagon. They remained mounted as we approached.

Jadd and I stopped about twenty feet from them. "Gerard," said Jadd. "I never expected to see you in the Kingdom of Keesee."

The gypsy rider on the far left answered, "Road Toad, I see you've traded your mercenary sword for allegiance to King Tobias." His reply came in Sea Spittle, language of traders, especially used among sailors. While Lilly had studied the complex Crusader tongue, I'd managed to pick up the basics of the straight forward trade tongue, sometimes through fellow wyvern scouts and other times through a tea merchant that I'd met and befriended.

What concerned me was that the rider's reply didn't reflect the light tone that Jadd had used.

Jadd shrugged, refusing to shift to Sea Spittle. "Times change. What brings you this far east?"

"A gypsy's travel recognizes no limits," Gerard said in the sea trader's tongue.

"And how many travel the Shadow Forest?"

"What reason would there be for us to travel within the Necromancer King's domain?"

"I don't know," said Jadd. "What reason do you travel within the domain of King Tobias?"

The question brought no response other than a scowl. The other riders, while listening to the exchange, betrayed no emotion. I had little experience with gypsies. They were rare around my home in Pine Ridge, and even rarer within the Kingdom of Keesee. Some said they were less than honest traders but, unless crossed, they were also said to be a friendly people.

Movement behind the horsemen soon revealed that the final horseman who hadn't joined the line had dismounted and was escorting a woman dressed in a colorful skirt and blouse. Patterns of red, blue, purple and green matched her gemstone rings, earrings and necklace. She appeared only a few summers past middle age and not in need of the gnarled walking stick she used.

"None of my sons know why we've travelled east," said the woman, stopping in front of the horsemen. She matched Jadd's use of the Mainland tongue.

Her focus shifted from Jadd to me, and she examined me with a penetrating gaze. I did my best to ignore her scrutiny while remaining alert to her sons and other potential danger.

"Road Toad," she continued, "you have been elevated to one of the king's dragon riders. This mercenary is your partner?"

"I once was a serpent cavalryman, and am one again."

"And the young mercenary?"

"He is not my aft-guard."

She asked me, "Are you a fellow dragon rider?"

"No," was all I answered. If there was some game, political, intelligence gathering, or otherwise, it wasn't my place to get involved.

"Would you gentlemen care to join me in my wagon? Share our tales of travel over tea?"

Jadd said, "We must decline, Madam Creeanne. Our mounts need tended to."

Her eyes narrowed and turned back to me. "You, mercenary, would lie to me?" The accusation stirred the interest of the horsemen.

I shifted my spear enough to be noticed. "I have not, and have no reason to lie to you, or to any of your sons." One of the rules among mercenaries was never to let an insult pass unchallenged. I was sure she knew that, although she hadn't fully named me a liar.

"It is odd. Dragon riders of the king traveling at night. May we camp and share the farm's well with you?"

"It is odd that you should keep a cold camp, without a fire to light the night," said Jadd. "You may take water from the well, if you desire, but then continue your journey."

"What makes you believe we have not traveled the night?" she asked.

Jadd glanced at the riders and their mounts. "I know horses almost as well as serpents."

"Very well then, Road Toad, or whatever name you now choose to go by. In truth, it is an unexpected turn that our paths have once again crossed. Yet I am pleased to learn that war has elevated you to your former station. However, I have not travelled east to exchange chary words with you."

She stepped closer and said to me, "You would be the mercenary given the name Flank Hawk."

I did my best to hide my surprise that she knew my name. "I am," I said, wondering what else the gypsy elder knew about me.

"Then the one you would name Belinda the Cursed is indeed correct. The King of Keesee has indeed set a favored pawn again upon the board. Does your lycanthrope scout travel with you, young mercenary?" She smiled, her left eye half closing. "Ahh, I can see by your reaction that she does."

Lilly and I met Belinda the Cursed over a year ago in the dark city of Sint Malo and bartered with her for passage across the Western Ocean. During the journey I learned that the woman many named the Eternal Hag was daughter to the immortal Colonel of the West. She was the gypsy's source and I saw no reason to lie. "My scout is nearby."

"Since you will not avail yourself of my hospitality, would you walk with me?"

Jadd turned to me and said, "I'll just stay here and continue my conversation with Gerard."

"You were not invited," said Madame Creeanne, before dismissing the son standing next to her.

"But I might have invited him," I said, handing Jadd my spear. He'd have a better chance with my spear against the mounted gypsies, while giving it up served as a gesture of trust. I still had my sword and dirk.

Bees and other insects took to flight from the yellow flowering weeds covering the untilled field as we slowly walked through it. I stayed to her right, interposing myself between her and the farm.

She shifted her walking stick to her left hand. "You smell of reptile. If not dragon, what beast do you ride?"

"Wyvern," I said.

"Iceheart told me of your cautious nature, and of your loyalty. Tell me, are you loyal to King Tobias?"

Iceheart was the name that Warden of Outpost 4 used when he spoke to Belinda the Cursed. Roos believed the warden was a fallen angel. "Are you Iceheart's servant?" I asked.

"I will take your question, instead of answering, as no, Mercenary."

"I will take your evasion as a yes, Madame."

"You would be wrong," she said.

It was my turn to smile. "I know Iceheart. Just as I'm not a true serpent cavalryman, you're not a *true* servant."

She stopped and turned to face me. "You, Mercenary, don't know me, and who I am."

"No, I do not." I squared up to face the gypsy. "But I do know Iceheart, as much a man might."

At that, she laughed. "What do you know of Iceheart?"

"I have fought by her side," I said. "Have you?" She continued to laugh but the mirth left her eyes. "I have faced a fallen angel with her at my back. Have you?"

"I have known Iceheart more seasons than you and Road Toad combined have walked the earth."

"Although you may not be such, I understand that a servant may know her master. I will take your response to mean you have not fought at her side."

Anger laced the gypsy's voice as she said, "You know nothing."

I had nothing to gain by angering Madame Creeanne further, and whatever her intent, anger was the conversation's path. I took a step back. "I will escort you back to your sons or, if you prefer, take my immediate leave. Where we are going can only lead to blood."

"It would be your blood, and that of your friend, young mercenary."

I shrugged. "Maybe, for a start. Maybe not."

"Fool, you cannot slay me."

"If my death is your purpose, I shall put your belief to the test." If I went for my sword, I'd put Major Jadd's life in danger, so I pulled my dirk from its sheath and held it down along my side, hidden from her sons' view. If the gypsy madame didn't recognize the smell of fire-weed resin coating my silver blade, she might wonder at the stain upon it. "I've stood to worse than you," I said quietly.

She glanced at her sons and then beyond my shoulder. Then I met her gaze, matching its intensity. "If it comes to my blood," I said, "you and your sons will join me well before witnessing today's noon sun."

Her face broke into a toothy grin. "As Iceheart said, King Tobias has placed a pawn upon the board. One that fears not sacrifice."

I still stood ready. "Iceheart knows that."

"And now I do. You may put your blade away and escort me back to my sons."

I hesitated then slowly slid my dirk back into its sheath in my boot.

"Good," she said. "I believe your lycanthrope scout watching from beyond the wall may now relax." She turned and walked back toward the wagon. "Road Toad was your mentor. Does he approve of poison upon your blades?"

Grand Wizard Seelain must have sent Lilly to see what was happening. Without looking her way, I signaled Lilly things were okay. "What's on my blade has its uses."

"Enough of the chary words between us as well," Madame Creeanne said, motioning to her dismounted son. He turned and hurried to the back of the wagon, disturbing the line of goats enjoying a meal of the flowering weeds. He high-stepped over the tether line to reach the steps and entered the wagon.

We stood in silence. I caught another glimpse of the gypsy madame's eyes. They had much the same cobalt blue color that Belinda the Cursed's eyes had, but the gypsy's didn't glow, especially when she'd been angry. I wondered if it was all an act, and that she hadn't been angry with me.

The youngest son, probably several summers younger than me, strode with purpose, carefully carrying a sturdy wooden chest reinforced by steel bands. He set it at his mother's feet.

The gypsy adjusted her skirt and knelt before placing an index finger upon the latch. She opened the lid and lifted a small wooden box and a narrow leather sheath from the chest and set them on the ground.

"Edmund, return this to its place," Madame Creeanne said, closing the chest. "And then remind Gerard that I will be most displeased if he allows the former mercenary to provoke him to violence."

Once Edmund left, the gypsy elder moved her walking stick to the side and invited me to sit with her.

I wasn't comfortable with the idea of sitting, so I knelt in front of her, with one knee on the ground and rested a forearm on the other.

She gave a frown of disappointment and picked up the small wooden box that had images of feathers lightly carved into it. She flicked a latch and slid the lid open to reveal a crystal the size of an acorn. It was attached to a sturdy necklace formed from paired silver links. "This is why I travelled east. To deliver a gift to you."

She lifted the necklace from the box and held it up for me to examine. "If you know Iceheart as much as you suggest, you know that she despises

Tyegerial."

The crystal dangled in the sun, capturing and reflecting a rainbow of colors. A dark blue spot in the center of the crystal marred its iridescence.

"Tyegerial?" I asked.

She looked at me as if assessing my question. "You might know him as the Warden of Outpost Four?"

"Yes. I am not fond of him either."

"This," she said, "contains a drop of the angel's blood."

I imagine my eyes widened at what she said. "How did she get that?"

"You would have to ask Iceheart."

"Why is she giving it to me?"

"You foiled and embarrassed the warden, and I imagine that pleased Iceheart. She said you'd lost a charm in the process. This repays you."

"The daughter of the Colonel of the West is giving me the blood of a living fallen angel to replace a charm that held the blood of a dead mercenary?" I looked at the crystal, but not too closely, wondering what power it might contain.

Madame Creeanne shrugged and lowered the crystal and silver chain back upon the cotton padding within the box. "I and my sons traveled through dangerous lands to deliver it for her."

"What is its purpose?"

She closed the lid and slid the latch back in place. "I do not know."

I wondered if it was a good idea to accept Belinda the Cursed's gift. Or if it might be a ploy to bring me to her. "How did you know I would be here, at this farm on this day?"

"That, she did not share with me. However, I will say that we have been here a week, awaiting your arrival. The advanced guard that scouted the farm yesterday helped me identify the correct place."

It worried me when I realized the length of time it took Madame Creeanne's wagon to travel from Sint Malo along the Western Ocean's coast to northern Keesee. If Belinda the Cursed could guess my movements, did she know what mission I was a part of? And if her blood was only half immortal, what about Fendra Jolain, who was an immortal goddess?

She held out the box for me to take. "Here, Mercenary Flank Hawk. There is something else."

I took the box with my left hand but didn't hold it close. The gypsy madame picked up the finely crafted sheath and withdrew a six inch rod the width of a rose stem. It appeared to be brass with tiny runes etched upon it in a spiraling pattern. "This is from Colonel Ibrahim for your scout."

"What is it for?"

"I see now that you are full of questions and glad of my answers."

"That I am," I agreed. "If you were me, wouldn't you be?"

The gypsy laughed again, but this time her eyes were filled with mirth. "If your scout drops it, the rounded end will point to her destination." She demonstrated before putting the rod back in its sheath and handing it to me. "It will work for her hand alone. None other."

She looked past me, over my shoulder to her sons. "It is time we return to Sint Malo."

I stood, holding the gifts in one hand and helped her to her feet with the other. It was a polite gesture that wasn't necessary, just like the walking stick.

When we got close enough to hear Jadd conversing with Gerard, I said to Madame Creeanne, "The Colonel and Belinda the Cursed consider me their pawn as well."

"You would have to ask them that," she replied.

"It wasn't a question."

"The prince is not leading your mission."

"He is not," I said, after a second's thought. Part of Prince Reveron's plan to keep our mission hidden was to make sure his presence was known within the city.

"That wasn't a question," she said, then laughed. "My chance to remind Iceheart she's not infallible." Madame Creeanne frowned. "Just like my eldest son, whom your friend Road Toad managed to distract while you drew a blade against me. He's just like his father was."

Lilly caught up with me as I went to join Major Jadd along the side of the barn to eat our evening meal. "How'd your shortbow lesson with Private Zunnert go?"

"Okay, I guess," Lilly said. "I'm still better with my sling."

She must have caught my expression and said, "I know what you're gonna say. I know, I'm sitting aft-guard for Captain Bray, and a sling won't work."

"You'll get better," I said and rounded the corner of the barn. I sat down in the shade next to Jadd and handed him his share of dried turkey and a raw potato. Lilly sat next to me and I shared what I had with her. I sighed and bit into my potato. I didn't care for them, especially raw, but they travelled well. Both Lilly and Jadd laughed under their breath and pretended to look away as I chewed and swallowed.

"Don't blame me," Jadd said. "Private Zunnert selected our travel menu."

I licked my teeth and decided to change subjects. I asked Jadd, "Why'd you take me out with you to meet Madame Creeanne instead of taking Sergeant Drux?"

"Why wouldn't I?"

"He's your aft-guard. Part of your brotherhood. He fights better and looks more like someone a gypsy wouldn't want to mess with. More than me."

He took a bite of turkey and chewed for a few seconds. "I trust Drux, same as you. We've been in some tough scrapes." He leaned forward. "When it comes to life and death, you're his equal.

"Beyond that, it was better to leave the gypsies uncertain. My armor and insignia mark me as a serpent cavalryman. Your mix of armor and arms, not wearing any purple and gold. That obviously marks you as a mercenary. It gave them something to consider, to be unsure about, and leave the notion my aft-guard might bring Flame Lance into the dispute should one arise."

"Everyone's afraid of dragons," Lilly said. "What're you gonna do with your magical pendant?"

"I don't know if it's magical," I said. "Enchanter Jonas detected enchantment in your rod. He didn't sense anything in the crystal."

Lilly sat up, ready to argue. "But you've seen it just like me. Crusaders aren't affected by magic." She pointed to Jadd. "Road Toad and Wizard Seelain said faith in their God blocks it. And that warding angel once served their God, and it's his blood."

"But remember the blessed saber Roos carried? When he drew it you sensed it, even saw an aura around it, right?"

She nodded. "Yeah, so?"

"You don't see anything with the pendant."

She shrugged. "Maybe blessing ain't the same thing as an angel's blood. Plus, there's lots of enchanters better than him, right Road Toad?"

"Enchanter Jonas is competent," Jadd answered. "He deciphered most of the runes on your rod."

"Yeah," said Lilly. "Wizard Seelain said we'd land tonight so I can try it. See if it points the same direction." She pulled the rod from a pocket and dropped it. As always, it pointed west.

"Either the Colonel's mountain fortress or Outpost Four," I said. "That's what I'd bet on."

"But look how far that Colonel's seeing ahead," said Lilly. "Wizard Seelain said it's like playing chess. I don't know how but I've seen people play it. She says seers, like the king's seer, see into the future, what the board will look like two turns ahead. And the Colonel of the West might be able to see three turns."

That bothered me, because Fendra Jolain was immortal like the Colonel of the West. Imperial Seer Lochelle was the most powerful seer in Keesee, maybe on the continent. But I recalled when Belinda the Cursed battled a high priestess of the sea goddess Uplersh. Belinda was half immortal, but couldn't defeat a high priestess channeling energy from her goddess. Even if Fendra Jolain wasn't a seer, she might be able work through one to outdo Seer Lochelle.

"You've stopped chewing and haven't even swallowed the potato in your mouth," Lilly said to me. "And you haven't looked this worried since you were getting ready to go into Sint Malo alone."

I explained my concern to her and Jadd.

"Yeah," said Lilly. "And if you're right on where my direction rod points, that means we don't need Enchanter Jonas."

Major Jadd drew his sword and examined it. "I thought of that too, Lilly. Maybe they didn't anticipate us having him and the map crystals. Belinda the Cursed thought Prince Reveron would be leading our mission."

"Or he's gonna die and we'll need the rod." Lilly's eyes became wide. "You think he's thought of that, Flank Hawk?"

"I'm sure Enchanter Jonas has," I said.

"I feel bad for him," said Lilly

Jadd nodded in agreement. "We'll cross that bridge if it comes. The question now is, what are you going to do about the crystal, Flank Hawk?"

"You gonna wear it?" asked Lilly. "You're not gonna leave it or bury it or something, are you?"

"I don't know," I said, thinking about the box stowed in my saddle bag. I asked Jadd, "What do you think?"

"I really don't know, Flank Hawk. You know Belinda the Cursed far better than me. You and Lilly met the Colonel of the West."

Lilly said, "They wouldn't give you something that'd hurt you."

"Maybe, but they've got their own objectives," I said. "How much do theirs match ours?"

CHAPTER 11

We made good time traveling by day, flying low enough for men to recognize the serpents but not close enough for the riders to be identified. The Faxtinian Coalition was truly in ruin. I recalled fleeing across it, chased by hound and ogre, seeing burned villages and battlefield carnage. The Necromancer King's forces destroyed all they could before fleeing north and east. Hardly a town or farm had emerged unscathed by the hand of war.

Major Jadd commented that walls and fortifications were being rebuilt before homes. They knew war was coming. I'd some experience of war, but even Lilly's untrained eyes could tell they weren't ready. Ragged lines of men, many maimed or crippled, toiled alongside women and children, and a few of the gray-haired elderly that had managed to survive. At least some would stand and fight, and crumble before Fendra Jolain's Long-Tooths and mercenaries and beasts of war.

Captain Bray's Flint Spitter and Major Jadd's Flame Lance traded taking point in our V formation every few hours. As we approached the channel that divided the lands of the Faxtinian Coalition from the Reunited Kingdom, Major Jadd took over the lead. Grand Wizard Seelain on Moon Ash drafted behind on Jadd's right with me trailing her on Wick. Private Zunnert flew his wyvern named Coils on the left, trailing Captain Bray.

Lilly always appeared alert, diligently searching the sky for danger. Sergeant Drux did the same, but in a more relaxed and methodical manner. Zunnert and I, the wyvern scouts, kept a watch below, occasionally tipping wings left and right as best we could manage while keeping pace with the stronger dragons. The Necromancer King's Stukas, along with his frost-breathing white dragons, had been driven from the skies before mid-winter had set in. Our main concern was griffins—advance scouts of the armies on the march.

The channel had some fishing boats along the Faxtinian shore and even a two-masted merchant ship sailing through it. About midway across we spotted a smoke-belching, steam-driven Crusader ship on patrol. The men on deck pointed up at us. One near the rear paddle wheel that drove the vessel waved. None others did.

Closer to the Reunited Kingdom shore there were small fishing boats, some with sails and others with oars. There were a few large ships the size of a two-masted galley dragging huge nets through the water. These ships used steam-driven machinery to haul in the nets filled with fish. I imagined in the wider ocean they'd have larger ships. Steel-clad ones that could resist Uplersh's serpents as Crusader sailors were certain not to pay tribute to the Goddess of the Sea.

Diplomat Grimsby shouted instructions to Major Jadd. He turned Flame Lance slightly toward the north and flew until we reached the coast. We followed the rocky shoreline northward, flying past small villages, some laid out in an orderly manner, others arranged like toadstools sprouting from a rotting tree stump. Each had at least one building topped with a cross. Occasionally I spotted isolated cottages and even a few small mansions not far from the rocky beaches, and every settlement had piers from which to land and launch vessels.

And everywhere along the coast our serpents drew attention. Some below pointed fingers. Others warily pointed muzzle-loading rifles much like Roos had carried. Maybe they hunted a lot, I thought. Or maybe the Necromancer King's annual crop raids and his invasion hadn't been limited to the Faxtinian Coalition, Doran Confederacy, the Lesser Kingdoms and Keesee. Or they worried about local raiders and bandits.

Diplomat Grimsby shouted and signaled to Major Jadd a few seconds before I spotted the estuary. I was too busy watching as we passed over a steamship towing two barges a quarter mile from shore, one filled with logs and the second with crates. I waved back to one of the crew that initiated the gesture. Another sailor sent an elbow to the waving man's ribs.

We swung inland for about a mile before turning back toward the river. After a minute or two of flight we approached a large estate with a central mansion surrounded by orchards, barns, livestock pens, and a few cottages. The farmstead didn't appear all that different from plantations lords owned in the Doran Confederacy.

The sight of our dragons sent the cattle and sheep into a panic. We flew over a hillock away from the farm and Major Jadd landed in a meadow while we circled above. After Diplomat Grimsby climbed down Captain Bray brought Flint Spitter to ground. Lilly and Sergeant Drux scouted the meadow and signaled it was safe for Grand Wizard Seelain to land. Private Zunnert and I followed her down.

The diplomat directed us to tether our wyverns while Jadd and Bray forced their mounts to lie flat with their necks and heads resting on the meadow grass. It was a serpent's submissive position, but even then they looked intimidating. I knew what damage a Crusader's rifle could do, but it'd take a rifle company's volley to bring a dragon down. Or an expert shot through the eye and into the brain.

With my spear in hand I stood between Grand Wizard Seelain and Lesser Seer Jonas. She clutched her staff tightly, and he quietly shifted his weight from foot to foot.

Major Jadd noticed the spellcasters' discomfort as well. "They'll send someone along shortly," he commented while resting a hand on Flame

Lance's scaly muzzle.

Diplomat Grimsby scrunched up her nose and said, "Your input is appreciated, Major, but when a farm representative arrives, let me do the talking."

"If he is on the property," said Jadd, "the owner will come himself."

"If you know so much, why did our prince send me?"

Jadd was about to replay when Grand Wizard Seelain sent him a hard stare. He nodded and went about inspecting Flame Lance, dragging his hand along the serpent's body to let the beast know where he was. I had to do much the same when working with Wick, to avoid getting accidentally knocked to the ground or tail whipped.

Enchanter Jonas leaned close to me and whispered, "I'd say Jadd must be at his limit with Grimsby's self-important attitude."

I nodded, observing the apple orchard in the general direction of the mansion.

Wizard Seelain said, "Wait here, Flank Hawk," before walking up to the diplomat.

Enchanter Jonas leaned close again. "I wager that upon completing their part of our mission, Jadd will ride every bit of turbulence available on the way back to Keesee. Keep Grimsby busy focusing on controlling her stomach as opposed to pontificating on subtleties of language and etiquette."

"She doesn't seem that bad to me," I whispered back. The enchanter looked a little pale. "Are you okay?"

His reply ignored my question. "Corporal Drux mentioned that the friendly diplomat relayed the same lecture on customs and social etiquette with respect to inhabitants of the Reunited Kingdom into the major's ear several times each day while aloft on Flame Lance."

All I could say was, "Oh." I'd been so busy seeing to Wizard Seelain's needs, and caring for both Wick and Moon Ash, and taking my turn on guard duty that I hadn't noticed. And Jadd hadn't said anything to me. I glanced over at Lilly, standing by the wyverns with Private Zunnert, and wondered if Lilly knew.

"I don't know if it's the land, or the people," said Enchanter Jonas, straightening his leather jacket and adjusting his rapier, "but I believe the grand wizard is feeling it too."

"What?" I asked.

"It isn't much, but noticeable. Probably less so to her. She draws her power from the elements."

I looked from the enchanter to Wizard Seelain whispering to Diplomat Grimsby. "Weakening your magic, and hers?" I asked.

"Not weakening it, I don't think. Just harder to feel. How shall I explain it?" He looked up and rubbed his chin. "Like trying to touch, or feel something, but now through a silk glove."

I'd never worn a silk glove but got what he meant. It might not be the same, but the more I fought and practiced mercenary skills, the less aligned I felt with the energies that I drew upon to heal. "Let me know if it gets worse," I said, thinking Grand Wizard Seelain might not let me know if her spell abilities weakened. Her being more vulnerable meant I'd have to be doubly aware and cautious on her behalf.

I nodded to Lilly, and she caught my meaning. She knelt next to Wick. Like Moon Ash, his color was gray with mottled spots of brown. She reassured him with a rhythmic patting on his neck. I said to Enchanter Jonas, "Maybe you'd better say something to Zunnert."

When he moved to do so, I approached the diplomat and Grand Wizard Seelain. I ignored Grimsby's disapproving frown and stood ready ten feet away. The diplomat had warned against me carrying my crossbow. It'd look excessively hostile, and that seemed reasonable when I thought Wizard Seelain could enact her magic. Crusaders were immune to magic, but not to indirect effects of it. If she destroyed the air around a Crusader, he'd still suffer the concussive impact when surrounding air raced in to fill the emptiness.

After several more minutes of waiting, three horsemen and what looked like a two-wheeled cart approached through the apple orchard that covered and extended fifty yards beyond the nearby hillock, and stood between us and the farmstead's stables and mansion.

The horses were tall, sandy-colored, and well trained to approach dragons. The spotted mule pulling the cart didn't flinch either, and that impressed me. When they reached the meadow's edge, the three horsemen dismounted. One hurried to take the horses' reins and led them back a dozen yards. The cart's rider reached awkwardly across his body to set the brake and lifted a crutch before stepping off and to the ground. He wore a black eye patch and a straw hat with a brown feather, but what stuck out the most was his missing right leg above the knee and left arm above the elbow.

All were dressed in dark trousers tucked in their high black boots and wore black suspenders over their black and blue plaid shirts. I didn't know if the colors were significant. The eldest man with a short gray beard and wearing wire-framed glasses whispered something to the stocky red-haired man next to him while they waited for one-legged man, who appeared to be the youngest of the three. Each wore a holster holding what I guessed to be cap and ball revolvers.

The older Crusader smiled and said in the Mainland tongue, "I welcome thee to the Reunited Kingdom. I am Luke Cromwell. How might I be of service to thee?"

His accent and mannerisms reminded me of Roos.

Diplomat Grimsby bowed slightly and responded in the tongue of the Reunited Kingdom. I didn't know what she said, other than when she gestured to Grand Wizard Seelain and gave her name and title.

Although I didn't anticipate any trouble, I stood ready as the three men stepped forward, the older man extending his right hand. Grand Wizard Seelain shook it and they exchanged pleasantries.

"Looks like things have started off well enough," whispered Private Zunnert. I hadn't heard him approach.

The young Crusader leaned on his crutch and appeared to take a deep interest in Grand Wizard Seelain as he was introduced to her. I gathered his name was Thomas Cromwell, probably the older man's son. Then Thomas's good eye shifted to me. I met his gaze and he responded with a grin and a nod, as if he recognized me.

I studied his face. Scars radiated from beneath the eye patch around to his ear, and his grin showed several missing teeth. I guessed he was a war veteran, and lucky to have survived. I snapped my attention back to what was happening. Diplomat Grimsby had given the writ of request to Luke Cromwell.

Diplomat Grimsby and Grand Wizard Seelain continued their exchange in the Crusader tongue and came to some agreement.

Wizard Seelain turned to me and said, "Luke Cromwell, the estate owner, is an elder in this district's council. Diplomat Grimsby and I will accompany him to his home to make arrangements for travel to New London. Flank Hawk, you will remain here." I prepared to protest but she dismissed me with a stern glance. "Major Jadd," she called. "You will accompany us. Captain Bray, you will be in charge."

While I didn't think Wizard Seelain would come to any harm, it was my responsibility to see that she didn't. But Major Jadd would be with her. I trusted him with her safety more than anyone else.

Major Jadd must have sensed my unease. As he helped Grand Wizard Seelain onto Luke Cromwell's horse for the ride to the mansion, he gave me a quick nod. Diplomat Grimsby mounted a horse as well. Major Jadd was offered the third horse, but declined and walked among the men who led the way.

Thomas Cromwell said something to Luke and the older man smiled and patted Thomas on the shoulder. Then, with his crutch propped under his good arm, the one-legged man walked up to me. "You remain the wizardess's personal guard," he said in Mainland. His pronunciation was mushy and exaggerated due to his missing teeth, but he spoke my language with hardly an accent.

"My father will see to her safety," he continued. "As well as her fiancé's personal guard."

I studied the crippled man's face once again and didn't recognize him. I'd met only a handful of Crusaders, and had spent more than a few minutes in the company of only one. And he was dead.

Captain Bray called for Zunnert to see to the wyverns. He signaled for

Enchanter Jonas to assist as well, but left me to talk with the Crusader, Thomas.

"A shrewd maneuver that my father didn't recognize," Thomas said with a crooked smile.

"What do you mean?" I asked.

"He believes the major is a dragon rider, not a personal guard."

"He isn't a bodyguard," I said.

"He was, but is no more then?"

"I've only known one Crusader," I said. "Paul Jedidiah Roos. But you know me, and Major Jadd?"

"I was at the First Battle of the Skydivers." He paused. "I believe your people named it The Battle of Zeffan Fields."

"You were there?" I asked, not wanting to fully recall that day of slaughter and death.

"My rifle company, from the First Coventry Volunteers, served as an expeditionary force to the Kingdom of Keesee. You," he said, "and the major stood watch around the dragons at night." He shifted his stance, leaning more on his crutch. "I witnessed you stand against the goliathan bone demon in defense of your Prince Reveron, after he abandoned his dragon and fell from the sky. My rifle company broke the hell-spawn demon and stood against the onslaught..."

Images of the battle flooded out from the dark corners in my memory...Some were stark yet imprecise images: laying in the blood of dead and dying soldiers, looking over the defensive mound at the Necromancer King's forces regrouping, the cries of dying men and the shrill scream of diving Stukas accented by the barking chatter of machinegun bullets—their biting through armor and thudding into flesh. But what stood clear and precise was the towering bone golem's image, a titanous evil creature lashed together with dark magic and the sinews of a thousand men, and harboring the heart of a demon within. Its hellcry shattered the morale of man and beast. It grated at my courage, its searing cry worked as if to grind my bones to dust.

Something about the Crusader before me called the moments that followed to clarity and flashes of that day filled my mind's eye and ear...

...But I hadn't fled. About a dozen of the Keeseean soldiers and half that many mercenaries held their ground against the bone golem's hellcry. Every other man and horse had fled or fell to the ground, oblivious to all but the terror that gripped them.

The only thing that advanced was Wizard Golt's earth elemental—and far behind it, the company of Crusaders marching forward with shouldered rifles bearing bayonets that sparkled in the sunlight. In the middle of their line an orange flag bearing a white cross flew and, instead of a battle cry, they voiced what sounded like a unifying hymn sung in their foreign tongue.

The golem's long strides gave it the speed of a quarter horse. Road Toad shouted above the surrounding moans, "Prince! Retreat toward the elemental." He hurled one of his javelins at the golem. The *Algaan*-blessed javelin arced toward the creature and struck it in the hip. It bounced off, leaving only a small black mark. "The Blood Sword will not avail you against this foe!"

"Agreed, Major Jadd," said Prince Reveron, pulling Wizard Seelain back. But by then it was too late. I ran forward and stood on Road Toad's right, interposing myself between Prince Reveron and the giant golem. Each of the bone titan's closing steps reverberated through the ground.

"Run, Prince!" snapped Road Toad as if giving an order. "Flank Hawk, spread right. Give it two targets."

I did, and held my spear ready. I had no intention of attacking, but instead prepared to dodge its attacks. I prayed quickly to M'Kishmael that the golem didn't cry out again.

Road Toad and I gained a reprieve when a three hundred pound boulder crashed into the golem's ribs. Only then did it take notice of the earth elemental. The golem looked once more at us and ducked, causing a second hurled boulder to miss. It then turned its attention to the elemental who hurled a third boulder. Like the first, the third boulder struck with devastating force. The golem staggered back as some of its bones cracked under the impact.

The earth elemental, an ogre-sized creature of packed earth and stone, wrenched free a wrecked panzer's cannon muzzle. The bone golem let loose with another hellcry before the two clashed in a flurry of blows.

The force of the second hellcry staggered me, but I steadied myself. The bone golem dwarfed the earth elemental. "Wizard Golt's creature can't win," I said to Road Toad.

He put a hand on my shoulder. "No, it won't. We must act." We looked around. The prince struggled to sheath his weapon.

"The Blood Sword is feeding upon it," Prince Reveron said. He finally succeeded and, with the power of the Blood Sword stifled, I felt a fraction of the battlefield's dread lift. "We must reach the Crusaders," said the prince. "Seelain," he called to the wizard who'd retreated twenty yards. "This way."

"No, the battle is almost over." She ran toward a horse that fought madly against its bridle tangled in a dead ogre's grasp.

She was right. The earth elemental had shattered one of the bone golem's four arms. But it had lost one of its own in the process. Two deep gashes marked where an iron scimitar had cleaved deeply into its earthen body.

In a desperate bid, the elemental hurled the cannon muzzle at the golem and dove for one of its pillar-like legs. Grasping the leg with its remaining arm, the elemental began sinking into the ground, pulling the leg with it. The golem rained down scimitar blows, shredding any cohesive remains of its foe.

The prince retrieved the wizard. "Won't take it long to free its leg."

"Goaff," called the bone golem in a hollow, unearthly voice. It strained to free its buried foot. "Shez-an dub nye-ee!" It pointed one of its scimitars at the prince.

"Friend Prince, we shalt take the demon down!" shouted a distant voice. One hundred yards from the bone golem, the Crusaders had formed into two rows. The front knelt while the rear stood. Swinging downward with his saber and shouting in his native tongue, the Crusader captain ordered his men to open up. Gunfire crackled and smoke billowed from the front rank's rifles. Flashes of gold light marked where the bullets struck the golem. Shards and bits of bone flew away.

The Crusader soldiers sang on, their words dampening the evil emanating from the bone golem. Their captain signaled and shouted again and the rear rank fired. Again, flashes marked a dozen impacts, staggering the golem. I realized they must be using saint-blessed weapons.

The golem cried out, "Aff, neecha o ga grullta haw!"

The once cowering goblins climbed to their feet and the nearby ogres responded to the golem's call with bellows echoing their newfound boldness. The bone golem hurled one of its iron scimitars at the Crusader formation, but it fell short.

The eighteen mercenaries and soldiers joined Road Toad and me as we surrounded the prince and ran towards the Crusaders and our distant defensive line beyond.

The Crusader captain shouted to his men. They fired and this time the united blast nearly toppled the bone golem.

I found Pops Weasel next to me at the rear with the other mercenaries. He was limping. "That demon spawn just said it'd eat any that didn't rise to kill the prince."

"The Crusaders will take care of it," I said.

"But who'll take care of them?" he gestured with his sword. Already a growing mob of goblins backed by ogres were closing on our heels.

The bone golem, tattered and nearly broken, let out a grumbling howl and a sulfurous wall of flames leapt up from the ground. It stood between us and the Crusaders.

"The flames will endure until the Crusaders slay the demon-beast," called the prince. He drew the Blood Sword. "Turn about and hold until then."

Pops Weasel readied his sword as I did my spear. "That's one powerful demon to stand to them Crusader guns," he said, watching the enemy close.

"Forward to meet them," ordered the prince, "or they'll drive us into the flames." He led the charge with red sword held high. I hoped its emanating dread fell upon the goblins. Road Toad was on the prince's left and I shouldered my way to his right. Wizard Seelain was among us, shouting such encouragement that frothing spit flew from her lips. It was our twenty against a hundred. Even if help came, the enemy from the woods would still overwhelm us.

I ran the first goblin through, nearly losing my spear to its momentum. Pops took out another of the yellow-skinned enemy before it could stab me. Seelain wielded her staff, cracking skulls and blocking spear and dagger thrusts. Cries of agony arose around the prince. Whenever the red sword found its mark a goblin fell back. Soon after, blood oozed from the wounded's nose, mouth, ears and eyes. They fell to the ground with red splotches signaling massive hemorrhaging beneath their skin. Then the ogres crashed among us. A broad, squat one charged directly at Wizard Seelain. Fearless, she stood ready. I leapt in from the side and set the butt of my spear to the ground. Before the ogre could react I guided the stout tip into the brute's groin. It penetrated the chain-mesh armor skirt and drove deep. I let go and rolled to the side as the spear shaft snapped under the force.

I didn't look back to see what had happened. I drew my sword before a pair of spear-wielding goblins were on me. My sword skills were moderate at best and not up to two foes. I gave ground to their stabs and thrusts. A third joined them.

A blue-robed figure leapt to my aid, knocking aside a spear and smashing the goblin between its slanted eyes. Seelain spun around and caught another across the helmet, ringing its skull. Her distraction allowed me to get past the third goblin's guard. I sheared away the fingers on its left hand as it hastily parried. Seelain caught the maimed goblin in the throat and it stumbled back, gagging for air.

Seelain said before turning, "Flank Hawk, the fire has dropped."

We broke from the enemy and gained an initial lead. Road Toad was in the front with Prince Reveron. Seelain was faster than me and strove to catch up with them. Only eight of us remained. I caught up with Pops Weasel who was limping badly.

"Pops," I said, slowing to his pace.

"I'm done fer," he said and pushed me away. "Good knowin' ya. Save the prince." Wiping a sleeve across his nose, he stopped and spun with sword ready.

"Krish!" shouted Road Toad, "We ward the prince!"

"I'll remember you, Pops!" I said before abandoning him. Pops Weasel shouted a string of curses against the shrill goblin calls before falling silent. Deep down I was thankful he fell instead of me. That thought hurt. I didn't look back.

We made it to the Crusaders and circled behind their lines. They'd rallied around their flag bearer, still singing as they fired and reloaded. The prince and Wizard Seelain flinched but the Crusader's words poured a vibrating warmth across my skin. The Crusader captain continued using voice and saber motions to direct his men, and they cut down the ogres pursuing us. Their gunfire rang my ears nearly as much as a panzer's cannon.

Road Toad grabbed my shoulder and shouted into my ear, "The prince assigned Wizard Seelain's safety to you. We go."

Short Two Blades blocked my path. Blood ran from a gash under his left eye. He stuffed his talisman into my dangling salt pouch. "My debt and honor endures," he said before pushing me toward the prince and Wizard Seelain who'd already broken into a sprint for the mound.

The sound of hand-to-hand combat rose behind me. The Crusader song faltered, men called warnings, threats, and cries of pain. Goblins and ogres did the same.

We'd escaped. And the Crusaders' sacrifice enabled it...

Recalling the hellcry had sent me into a cold sweat normally brought on through its echoes in my nightmares. "You were in that Crusader company," I said, my voice sounding distant as I pushed the images aside.

He nodded once. "I think upon that battle every day." He gazed up at the sky. "I am sorry that I reminded you of it. An unnecessary cruelty which I should have thought better upon."

"You survived? How could anyone have?"

He shrugged. "Lesser imps took me down with their swords. Maimed as I was, they left me for dead. I tied tourniquets, pushed the bodies of dead friends aside as night fell and crawled to friendly lines. Not before a death rot set in." He lifted the stump of his right arm. "You see the result."

"I am sorry," I said, working to hold back tears. I looked away, unable to meet his remaining eye. Like Pops Weasel and Short Two Blades, I'd abandoned this Crusader to death as I fled.

"Sorry about what? That you survived?"

"That you stayed and fought," I said, shuffling my foot over the meadow grass.

"And you didn't?" He stepped closer and rested his hand on my shoulder. "The Lord's plan for you. And for me."

"What?" I asked. "What plan?"

"You're Flank Hawk, the mercenary that delivered the bomb which turned the war's tide. That was in the Lord's plan." When I met his single-eyed gaze, he explained. "I am only recently returned from your lands to my home. I recalled your face from that day of battle, and learned your name moments ago."

"Oh," I said, regaining my composure.

Thomas asked, "The demon's cry haunts you, the same as me?"

"It does." I wondered if it haunted Major Jadd, or Grand Wizard Seelain. Or even the prince. "But you and your company brought it down."

"We did," he said with pride. "You stood to it too. We all played a part."

He looked past me. "The girl with the gray aura. That's the scout, Lilly, who accompanied you?"

I nodded. "Roos, a Crusader saw it upon her too. Can all Crusaders?"

"Some will be able to, but not all."

"Will it be a problem?"

"I haven't recovered my stamina," he said, turning toward his mule and cart.

I walked next to him. "She's not a werewolf like the minstrel tales claim."

"No, she's not black."

He made it to his mule and leaned on the sturdy beast. I walked around him and waited while he caught his breath and then took his crutch before helping him onto cart's padded bench seat.

"Your party," Thomas said. "You're seeking to retrieve the Blood Sword?"

I handed him his crutch. "Why would you say that?"

"Just a hunch." He smiled his crooked smile. "I know it's not your place to say or deny, even if you know. But, if you are, many of my folk will not be anxious to have that evil weapon returned to the continent."

"Despite being allies, there are many things our peoples do not agree upon."

"That is true," he said. "Is that blue jacket your scout friend wears, that of your fallen friend, Paul Roos?"

I followed his gaze to Lilly who was watching us while talking to Enchanter Jonas. "It is."

"His sister visited me shortly after my return home," Thomas said. "I told her what I knew of her brother, Paul's death. I am sure she'd like to know more." He took up the reins to his mule. "She is a nun at the convent in New London."

CHAPTER 12

"Here ya go," Lilly said, tossing the slaughtered sheep to Wick. The Cromwells had sent two sheep for each wyvern and a steer for each dragon. The dragons had come first and it took Zunnert, Drux, me and Lilly to drag the hefty bovines off the flatbed wagon. Flint Spitter and Flame Lance took over after we moved the wagons away. Zunnert and Drux were tending to Moon Ash and Coils while Major Jadd and Enchanter Jonas were preparing a butchered beef shank for roasting. That was for those of us who were staying behind. Major Jadd and Enchanter Jonas were to attend a dinner at the Cromwell Estate with Diplomat Grimsby and Grand Wizard Seelain.

"You wish you were going to eat with the Grand Wizard?" asked Lilly.

"Major Jadd will ensure her safety," I said.

Lilly watched Wick step on the sheep carcass and tear it in half with his beak. "I meant the food and seeing what it's like in the mansion," she said.

"Not really," I said. "I wouldn't understand what everybody was saying."

"That Crusader, Thomas, would talk to you."

I shaded my eyes as I looked west. The sun was about an hour from setting. "Maybe," I said. "Depending on where he and I were seated."

"You think he's the reason the head Cromwell insisted me and you travel to New London with Road Toad, Grand Wizard Seelain and that diplomat?"

"Probably," I said. "Diplomat Grimsby isn't too happy about it."

"Yeah, I could tell. But I'm not so sure she isn't right—at least about me. Do you think the Crusaders like my kind less than your folks?"

Wick had finished his second bite and was squawking, looking for more.

"That's it, Wick," I said to my mount and shrugged before suggesting to Lilly, "Maybe we'll get to meet Roos's sister."

"And they can spot me for what I am."

"Not all of them."

Lilly said, "It'll only take one to cause trouble."

"I don't think Luke Cromwell would take you with us if he thought there'd be trouble."

"There's a reason those like me hide what we are," Lilly said. "And it seems just about every Crusader carries some sort of gun."

"I know," I said. "Even some of the women. I've been trying to figure out why."

"I speak their tongue good enough to be understood," she said. "I could ask one of the women."

That got my attention. "You think that'd be a good idea?"

"Who knows?"

I scratched my head, still trying to puzzle it out. "I think maybe they carry guns because the Necromancer King sends undead over, like he did to disrupt crop planting around Pine Ridge every year. What do you think?"

She stared at the ground in thought, then looked up. "Maybe they see a lot of werecreatures."

I stared at her, not knowing what to say.

She slugged me in the arm. "Got you there," she said, showing a sparkling grin.

I shook my head. Sometimes I just didn't get Lilly's sense of humor.

Lilly and I had already stowed our group's gear below deck. I watched as Grand Wizard Seelain stepped along the wide plank to board Luke Cromwell's steam-driven paddleboat. I knew her footing would be sure. It was nothing like watching Thomas make his way, one-legged, his single arm working his crutch, all guided by his remaining eye. The black hound speckled with tiny white spots, jumping and barking on the wave-rocking deck, made things even more iffy. Thomas had even turned to assure and assist Wizard Seelain.

Major Jadd followed Diplomat Grimsby, who was the last to board before some of Luke Cromwell's men lifted the plank and pushed us away from the pier.

Thomas signaled for Lilly and me to join him on an aft bench seat. Lilly stood by me, looking about nervous and unsure. I awaited a signal from Wizard Seelain that she was settled. She and the diplomat were renewing a conversation in the Crusader tongue with the estate owner while Major Jadd stood by, listening and comprehending as best he could.

I asked Lilly, "What are they talking about."

"About traffic on the river we can expect once the sun rises." She looked east, toward the lightening horizon. "I think they call it the Thames River."

"Guardsman Flank Hawk," said the diplomat. "The major will attend us."

I looked to Wizard Seelain who nodded agreement after answering one of Luke's questions.

The boat's sharp whistle blew, echoing across the water.

"You'd best sit," warned Thomas. "I had them affix a rack with a few leather cords along the backside of this bench to stow your spear."

"Could you see to it?" I asked Lilly and handed her my spear. I unslung my crossbow and set it on the far end of the bench from where Thomas sat, petting his black and white-spotted hound.

The dog's attention shifted from watching Grand Wizard Seelain to Lilly, and his hackles rose when she sat next to Thomas. I sensed that Lilly was tense and poised for action. I'd seen her in combat. Her reflexes surpassed just about every human I'd ever met. A snap of Thomas's fingers with a harsh word in the Crusader tongue and the dog quietly lay on the deck, near his master's booted foot.

Jadd told me privately upon our arrival that the dog accompanying Thomas was a starhound, and they're used to hunt magical creatures, including werewolves. But this hound, named Quick, had a bit of white around his muzzle and was obedient, so I didn't think he'd cause Lilly any trouble.

The flat-bottomed boat wasn't large, maybe thirty-five feet long and fifteen feet wide, a good part of it taken up by boilers and bins filled with coal. A canvas canopy covered part of the deck and a high, oak railing ran along the sides. Although there were eye-hooks set into the deck to lash down crates, it appeared to me to be more of a pleasure vessel than one dedicated to transporting goods. There was even a number of long fishing poles tied to hooks along a section of the railing.

The whistle sounded again, two quick toots, and the paddle began spinning, propelling the boat named *Grandma Sally's Sloop* against the current into the broad river. I wanted to ask why it was named a sloop. It didn't have a mast for a sail. Instead I asked Thomas, "Why are there six rifles and six cutlasses on racks below deck?" I looked down at my crossbow. "Should I be watching for anything?"

Thomas leaned over and scratched Quick behind his floppy ears. "Every able-bodied man and woman is trained in the basics of firearms use and safety. Every youth serves at least twelve months in a local militia, and each family sends at least one son to serve two years minimum in the Island Defense Forces."

Behind us a deckhand shoveled coal into a boiler furnace and another on an elevated platform steered the boat.

"Why?" asked Lilly. She watched Thomas's hound warily while listening to the Crusader's answer.

"We are few. Our enemies are many. We must be prepared to resist and defend."

Lilly asked, "The Necromancer King sends zombies against you?"

Thomas shook his head. "Nay. Even the mindless corpses fear the salt water."

I recalled Major Jadd telling of ogres in longships pursuing Crusaders. "He commands more than zombies," I said.

"That is true. Heathen brutes and lesser imps have raided our shores from time to time. To burn and plunder and take our young for slaves. But that is rare."

I remained standing and scanned the river and shore fifty feet away. Although Major Jadd was attending Wizard Seelain, her safety remained my responsibility.

"Because you are prepared?" I asked.

"Maybe. Who can know the Corpse Lord's mind?"

"What of Uplersh?" I asked.

Lilly nodded. "Have you ever seen one of her serpents?" Her hand wandered to the thin belt holding her sling. Lilly had left her bow behind, not yet comfortable using it. I was sure at that moment she regretted the decision.

Thomas shook his head. "Sometimes her minions harass our vessels that wander far from our shores. But we have ironclads and cannon, and depth charges.

Lilly and I both looked at him, unsure of what he meant.

"Like the Corpse Lord's panzer cannon shells," he explained. "But dropped over the side or stern to sink and explode.

"And then there's the forces of Lucifer," he added. "Ever looking for weakness among us to exploit."

I knew the name. Roos had mentioned it several times. "Like the bone golem?" I asked.

"Rarely something so daunting. The enemy of our Lord relies on subtlety. On our human nature and frailty."

"Fallen angels, right?" asked Lilly.

Thomas nodded. "They are some of his minions."

"You know anything about them?" Lilly asked Thomas.

"Not much more than what Scriptures say."

"Flank Hawk," said Lilly. "Show him your amulet."

Lilly's words surprised me. I was hesitant to do so—to let anyone know I carried it. I glared at her for an instant, wishing she hadn't said anything.

Thomas looked at me with a questioning eyebrow arched above his good eye.

I pondered a few seconds. Denying I had the talisman wasn't an option. Thomas seemed to an ally of sorts, one we might need once we reached New London. He had some ability to sense magical auras, like Roos could. Upon first sight Roos identified Lilly as a werecreature. He named the Warden of Outpost 4 as a fallen angel, he saw the Colonel of the West as what he called an immortal blood, and Belinda the Cursed as a half-blood. Would Thomas recognize the crystal contained a fallen angel's blood? Would it matter?

I reached under my armor and lifted the silver chain holding the crystal from around my neck and gave it to Lilly to hand to Thomas.

Lilly must have caught that she'd overstepped and shouldn't have mentioned Belinda the Cursed's gift to me. She maintained an unusually meek look on her face as she cupped the talisman in her hand and held it out for Thomas to take and examine.

Her action caught Quick's attention. The dog sat up and observed her with interest.

Thomas said to Lilly, "Wait. Hand it back to your friend, Flank Hawk."

Lilly looked puzzled but did. I took it and asked, "What do you see?"

Thomas stared at Lilly with his single eye and then to my hand holding the talisman. "It's what I don't see," he said. "If you would, please give the amulet back to Lilly."

The starhound let out a quiet moan, his eyes remaining on Lilly.

"Quick sees it too," said Thomas, his eye once again studying Lilly. "The amulet mutes the gray aura of your inner beast." He looked to the dog and to me, and then back to Lilly. "I say mutes because what I see, starhounds both see and smell. That it hides or shields might be more accurate.

"You didn't know it did that?" Thomas asked.

"No," I said. "It was only recently given to me."

The Crusader held the chain and lifted it so that he could examine the dangling crystal. "It is quite beautiful," he said. "What is this liquid bead of blue inside the crystal?"

Lilly opened her mouth to speak but then looked back to me.

"I was told it's the blood of a fallen angel," I said.

As if on instinct, Thomas extended his arm, holding it at a distance. "Fallen?"

Lilly sat up erect and more alert. "That's what Roos said."

Thomas looked confused.

I explained, "I was told the blood in the crystal is from a powerful guardian we encountered across the Western Ocean. Roos named the guardian a fallen angel."

Thomas gave the talisman back to Lilly, being careful not to touch the crystal. He cleared his throat. "As I said, I don't know anything about angels other than from Scripture."

"But it appears to hide certain things. We'll have to ask Enchanter Jonas about this," I said to Lilly as she handed the crystal back to me. Then I thought a second. "Maybe you should wear it, Lilly. At least in New London."

"Why?" she asked.

"Thomas, you said others—at least some would see her as a lycanthrope, right?"

He nodded.

"Couldn't that cause trouble for Lilly? Roos didn't trust her the first time they met because of what he saw. He warned me that she wasn't what she appeared to be."

Lilly bit her lower lip while staring intently at the deck.

"There are those whose sight surpasses mine," said Thomas. "Would it be worse to hide what Lilly is? Only to be discovered at a crucial moment?"

"Crucial moment?" Lilly asked.

"Your grand wizard and diplomat are here to negotiate for passage and assistance of my people." Thomas rubbed the side of his face, just beneath his eye patch. "It could be someone might see the amulet that you carry, what it holds. Maybe for what it is."

I thought about that. Roos wasn't impressed with the Warden of Outpost 4, despite his power. He didn't respect the fallen angel. What deeper game had Belinda the Cursed involved me in—if there was one?

I scanned the river and caught Major Jadd's gaze as he watched Grand Wizard Seelain, seated and talking to Luke Cromwell. Had Jadd overheard our discussion? It didn't matter. I'd keep, and continue carrying, the talisman.

CHAPTER 13

The sun was two hours past noon when *Grandma Sally's Sloop* approached the outskirts of New London. Thomas said earlier that in winter a smoky haze from coal stoves hung above the city and that he was glad spring had come. While nearing the city Lilly commented things didn't look much different from the outer reaches of the King's City. Small fishing villages and towns dotted the shorelines. The people's garb differed, as did the occasional steam-driven boat and the metal-wheeled tractor on one farm that plowed a hillside field. All of the other farms used mules or oxen.

The homes and buildings were mainly brick with wooden-shingled roofs, different from the wood and stone construction I'd become used to seeing. What stood out as we neared the city were the groups scattered along the shoreline and small fishing docks filled with people, watching and pointing as our boat passed. Even some of the crews aboard the scattered fishing, cargo, and pleasure vessels stopped what they were doing and looked our way.

I asked Thomas if there was something special about *Grandma Sally's Sloop* or if our arrival had been announced. He said he didn't believe so. I walked to the foredeck. Major Jadd had also noticed the attention on us. Pointing and using his limited Crusader tongue, he said something about it to Luke Cromwell.

Several fishing boats and two pleasure vessels turned toward us, working their way closer. Luke Cromwell gave orders to the crew who went below deck and returned with rifles and cutlasses.

I stepped between Grand Wizard Seelain and the prow of the boat even as Lilly rushed up to me, bringing my spear and crossbow.

"What going on?" Lilly asked me.

"I'm not sure," I said to Lilly. "Grand Wizard, stay seated, behind me. Lilly, stand to her right." Major Jadd was already to Seelain's left, discussing the situation with Cromwell. All of the crew but the steersman stood along the port and aft sides, listening to Thomas's orders. They loaded their muzzleloaders. Quick barked twice, then stood alert at the bow.

A pair of steam-driven gunboats from upstream approached. Their hulls were lined with metal plates and they bristled with men and cannons. While both sounded their deep steam whistles, one sent signals using some sort of light flashing from behind slatted blinds. It was apparently directed at our boat.

Luke Cromwell removed his hat and waved it back and forth over his head and then said something to Grand Wizard Seelain and Diplomat

Grimsby in the Crusader tongue.

Lilly said to me, "He says they're gonna escort us in."

That was some relief, but the gunboats appeared faster than *Grandma Sally's Sloop*. And cannons were faster than any boat. Although their presence made me nervous, I saw no reason for them to open fire on us.

I began to wonder and worry. If New London was as big as the King's City, and the citizens were as interested in seeing us as those on the shores had been…with so many of the Reunited Kingdom's citizenry armed, and the fact that they'd invaded the Main Continent in the past with the intent of conquering to spread their morals and beliefs—those which left no room for magic such as Grand Wizard Seelain wielded. How could I keep Grand Wizard Seelain safe?

Lilly looked through her spyglass before handing it to Grand Wizard Seelain.

The gunboats continued to sound their whistles and the smaller boats turned to give them and us a wide berth.

Grand Wizard Seelain stepped forward, next to me. "All is in order, Flank Hawk," she said. "The military vessels are to escort us to port."

"If everything was safe," I said, "would the crew be armed?"

"That was before Luke Cromwell knew of the escorting ships."

Lilly said, "A lot of them carry guns, Grand Wizard."

"We are on a diplomatic mission," said Diplomat Grimsby from behind us. "They will not harm us."

Luke Cromwell was saying something to us. I couldn't understand what he said, so I spoke over him. "Lilly is referring to the citizens, Diplomat. Not the military escort. My responsibility is to see Grand Wizard Seelain remains safe."

Luke Cromwell shifted to our tongue and addressed Wizard Seelain. "Rest assured, ye will be safe. A military escort will take us safely to the House of Parliament."

I said, "It only takes one gunshot. Can your diplomats meet us somewhere else? Back at your estate?"

Cromwell said, "Now that many of my people know ye are here, if ye do believe there is a threat to Grand Wizard Seelain, the House of Parliament is the most secure place."

Thomas spoke up from behind us. "My father's people sent ahead would *not* have revealed your presence. Some politician must have."

"To what purpose?" asked Jadd.

Thomas shrugged as did his father. "My countrymen are curious about your people, Major. They will want to see you. Wizards and warriors from the Kingdom of Keesee."

"I am sure that is the extent of it," said Luke Cromwell. Diplomat Grimsby nodded in agreement.

"It only takes one gun," said Lilly.

Cromwell called out something in his native tongue to his crew. Then all nodded and said something I guessed to be a 'Yes.'

"My men will stand close around ye," Cromwell said. "Shield ye from any possible harm. As will I."

"If an escort is waiting for us at the pier as you say they will be," said Jadd, "professional soldiers would serve better."

"Unless they want to take us prisoner," Lilly said just loud enough for me, Grand Wizard Seelain and Diplomat Grimsby to hear.

Diplomat Grimsby turned red-faced, but a stern look from Grand Wizard Seelain stopped her from saying anything.

Major Jadd helped with the buckles to my breast and backplate while saying, "Guess our diplomat's firm belief that bringing our armor, even if stowed below deck, wasn't bad form."

"It won't stop a Crusader bullet," I said.

"Not a direct on shot," Jadd replied. He slid on his serpent cavalryman's helmet with its red plumes flaring across the top and dangling down his back. "But I bet you feel better nevertheless."

I put on my helmet and buckled the strap.

He laughed. "Flank Hawk, you've never taken to helmets."

"I'm thankful more than once that I've worn one, but you'd think I'd be used to the nose guard by now."

The crew still stood protectively on the deck of *Grandma Sally's Sloop* even though the two gunboats had taken up station on either side of us. Lilly stood near the prow with her spyglass, talking to Thomas. Grand Wizard Seelain sat between Cromwell and Diplomat Grimsby on the back bench. Cromwell continued to exchange words over his shoulder with the steersman.

"Looks like we're going to disembark on a main pier," commented Jadd. "With this small boat, it'll probably require a ladder up or stairs up."

I nodded while slinging my crossbow over my shoulder so it hung across my back. I picked up and checked the head of my boar spear. Jadd looked from me to Wizard Seelain and back but remained silent. Her safety had been entrusted to me, but I wanted his advice. "What do you think?"

"You go up first," he said. "If it's a ladder, I'll hand up your spear. If everything is okay, the diplomat next, followed by me. Lilly will then follow up the grand wizard."

It sounded good to me. "Cromwell will probably go up first," I said after waiting for several soundings of the gunboat whistles to end. We went over to Grand Wizard Seelain and I explained the plan.

Lilly hurried back and said to me and Grand Wizard Seelain, "Only a couple hundred yards. Looks like they've got wooden stairs from the pier pretty close to the dock that reach down to about our level and there's a lot of people with soldiers holding them back. They have uniforms like mine," she said, referring to Roos's dark blue wool jacket that she wore. "Some have rifles, but no bayonets on them. Others have red jackets and long shields and clubs."

"To intervene themselves between us and curious crowds," said Diplomat Grimsby.

"Or riot stiflers," said Jadd.

"Useful for both, but only a precaution," said Cromwell. He met Thomas's gaze then added, "Let us hope."

There were no other ships near the pier. About two hundred soldiers held back three times their number of civilians. Using her spyglass, Lilly reported that she didn't see any regular folks carrying rifles, but that she saw two with revolver holsters. The red-clad soldiers were pressing the crowd back to a line of warehouses as our boat's paddles reversed direction and we slowed. Not far beyond where the pier met the dock area stood two carriages. Big and black and each pulled by six sturdy horses. A dozen horse-mounted soldiers formed a loose circle around them.

Jadd and I stood in front of Grand Wizard Seelain with Lilly directly behind her. A moment later we were too close to the dock to see over its lip.

Cromwell and two of his men strode up the wooden steps and onto the pier. Diplomat Grimsby tried to step around me to follow them, but I blocked her and Major Jadd put his leather-gauntleted hand on her shoulder. I followed Cromwell, carrying my spear. I studied the horsemen, soldiers and crowd beyond before searching the tops of the warehouses while Cromwell walked forward to confer with an approaching officer. Two men stood at attention atop each warehouse, dressed in the blue garb of soldiers. I signaled for Diplomat Grimsby to come up.

Cromwell finished his conversation and the officer said something to me. Diplomat Grimsby joined them and nodded while Cromwell translated, "All is secure for thy people. I, mine son and Diplomat Grimsby will ride in the first carriage, and ye, Major Jadd, Grand Wizard Seelain and Scout Lilly will ride inside the other."

I turned to see Quick bound up the steps, followed by Thomas working his way up the last two steps with the assistance of the oldest of *Grandma Sally's Sloop's* crewmen.

I strode back to the pier's steps. "Major, all looks in order," I said and then turned back and stepped onto the dock, watching the crowd. I wished we had Drux, giving us another set of eyes, his sword, and long experience as a city guard in the roughest parts of the King's City. He looked like someone not to mess with. But we didn't have him or, even better, the sword hand of Private Zunnert.

Thomas said to me, "There should be room enough for all of you in the rear carriage. They're made of sturdy wood. Able to absorb a .58 caliber bullet."

I shook my head. "No. We'll not all be shut up inside. I will replace one of the two soldiers standing on the back platform. Lilly will sit next to the driver."

Major Jadd came up next to me and surveyed the crowd while I continued. "I trust you and you're armed," I told Thomas. "I'd ask that you ride in the carriage with Grand Wizard Seelain, along with Major Jadd, and Quick."

The dog gave a sharp bark at the mention of his name.

A murmuring rose from the crowd as Grand Wizard Seelain and Lilly stepped onto the pier. Jadd said to me, "I will see your arrangements are put into action, if Thomas agrees to ride with Wizard Seelain."

Before Thomas finished his first nod, Jadd turned and marched toward the officer standing with Grimsby and Cromwell.

"I'll go on ahead," Thomas said, and whistled for Quick to follow him to the big-wheeled, fancy carriage waiting twenty yards away.

"Grand Wizard, you'll ride in the second carriage," I said. "Lilly, you'll ride next to the driver. I'll ride on the rail behind. Major Jadd and Thomas will accompany you inside. The diplomat and Cromwell will ride in the first carriage."

Grand Wizard Seelain stood tall with her white staff in hand. "One would certainly think the city leaders might have a larger carriage so that we need not be divided."

"They may not have large ones built like those," I said, meeting her eyes only fast enough to acknowledge her, and then returned my focus to the crowd. "Small windows. Thomas says the sides can stop bullets." Grand Wizard Seelain came up next to me as I spoke. Lilly moved to stand several steps in front of her.

It was obvious we were in a weak tactical position, and I knew that Grand Wizard Seelain's status would not allow her to cower or retreat. I didn't face Grand Wizard Seelain as I reminded her, "Many of them have guns. Do not expose yourself unnecessarily." The crowd was pressing forward to get a better view. It didn't seem to bother Grand Wizard Seelain. Maybe she was used to such attention in the King's City. But it made me increasingly nervous.

Major Jadd stepped between Diplomat Grimsby and the officer as he spoke using his command voice. Without turning to us he signaled to me.

"With me, Grand Wizard," I said. Gut instinct kicked in. "Hurry!"

Wizard Seelain placed a hand on my shoulder. "Flank Hawk, I believe you are being unduly cautious." That was when I spotted the first rock hurled from somewhere in the back of the crowd.

The oblong stone was the size of my fist. Before it reached the top of its arc two more joined it, thrown from the packed mass of onlookers a little to our left. Everyone—the crowd, the soldiers, and even the riverboats behind us fell silent as the first rock sailed over the horses, toward us.

I warned Grand Wizard Seelain, but she whispered, "I see them."

The first stone landed wide left, smacking into the dock's brick-paved surface before clattering into the river. The second rock flew short, slamming with a *thwack* against the far side of the lead carriage. The final stone flew at us with less of an arc. It barely cleared the heads of the lead carriage's team of horses and right between two horse-mounted soldiers. It was certain to fall a few yards short but a swift magical gesture by Grand Wizard Seelain sent a narrow wind-gust, stopping it from bouncing and skittering among us.

Shrill whistles sounded as the red-clad soldiers drove into the crowd toward the stone throwers. I didn't know if their goal was to capture them, club them, or drive them off. Chaos ensued, shouting and screaming. But, for the moment, no rocks flew. It was one of the few times I wished I carried a shield.

The cavalry mounts stood steady, but the carriage drivers worked to calm the six-horse teams. A soldier on the back of our carriage hopped down and pulled open the door facing us.

"Let's move," I said to Grand Wizard Seelain, striding forward at a measured pace—one that spoke of confidence, and one that she would not feel inappropriate to follow. I remembered Lilly saying some onlookers carried revolvers. That thought made me want to take Wizard Seelain by the arm and drag her as fast as I could.

I didn't understand what the crowd shouted, but it sounded like two, or maybe three, sides arguing. Grand Wizard Seelain stepped up into the carriage, followed by Major Jadd.

"Lilly," I said, "you don't need to ride outside."

She ignored me and nimbly climbed up to the driver's bench and sat on the anxious driver's right. I slid my spear into a slot meant for a rifle and tightened the leather strap to hold it in place. The soldier holding the door looked at me as I stepped up, taking his former station on the back of the carriage.

He started to protest, but the soldier standing on the back board to my right give him a sharp rebuke.

We were ready to go, but the crowd pushed forward, against the soldiers as they tried to wedge an opening so that the carriages could pass through. Punching fists and kicking boots met the red-clad soldiers' slamming shields and swinging clubs. Although better armed, the soldiers were outnumbered, especially as a rush of new citizens appeared to have joined the growing fray.

Quick barked as rocks once again flew our way. One came straight for Lilly. She calmly caught it with one hand—and surprised me by simply dropping it instead of hurling it back into the crowd as I expected her to do.

Thomas shouted something to the guard at the door waiting for the one-legged man to climb in. They argued for a second before Major Jadd climbed back out of the black carriage.

A stone struck one of the lead horses in the shoulder. It neighed and reared, and the diver spat curses as he struggled to control his team.

"Flank Hawk," shouted Jadd. "Help me boost Thomas atop the carriage." When I looked questioningly, Thomas had already handed his crutch to the door soldier.

"Are you sure?" I shouted to both Thomas and Jadd.

Thomas nodded while Jadd locked the fingers of his two hands together to create a step for Thomas. I helped him onto Jadd's hands and, with the help of the nearby soldier, boosted him onto the carriage roof.

Thomas, having only one leg and arm, struggled to stand, but Lilly leapt to his aid atop the rocking carriage. The horses threatening to bolt any second. Even so, Thomas stood steady, leaning on his crutch with Lilly at his side.

With an almost casual effort, he drew his revolver and fired it once, into the air. The carriage shot forward a few feet, but the driver pulled hard on the reins, halting them. Lilly kept Thomas from losing his balance and tumbling down.

Everyone turned toward the single *crack* of gunfire. The whistles and shouting ceased. The soldiers disengaged and took a step back from the crowd.

Thomas's voice boomed as he shouted out to everyone in his view. I glanced in the carriage and stood to block Grand Wizard Seelain from exiting. I couldn't understand what he said, but Grand Wizard Seelain translated for me.

She said, "Thomas says, he is ashamed. He says, 'These are friends of our country. They fight alongside us against the Corpse Lord, our enemy. They sacrifice and die for our mutual cause.'"

A woman's voice from the crowd shouted a response.

"She calls us pagans," Seelain said. "Wizards and beasts."

I didn't know what pagans were, but I could guess.

Wizard Seelain said, "Thomas says, we're gentiles and should be welcomed as his Lord the Savior welcomed them."

The woman replied and Wizard Seelain translated through clenched teeth, "She says we are evil!"

"'No,' says Thomas. 'Lieutenant Colonel Paul Jedidiah Roos. Many of you knew him. His faith. His judgment.'"

The crowd murmured amongst themselves.

"'He named two here Friend.'" As Wizard Seelain continued to translate, I decided I should be seen as Thomas spoke about me. So I moved around the carriage, into full view. Wizard Seelain followed me, but it wasn't the moment to argue. Major Jadd joined us.

"Lilly and Flank Hawk. They fought alongside Paul Roos. He died, sacrificed his life for them as they brought destruction to the Corpse Lord's war machine factories.'"

Thomas pointed down at me. Wizard Seelain said, "He says, 'This is the one you've heard about. The mercenary Flank Hawk, who turned the tide of the war. This is his scout, Lilly. They *are* our friends.'"

The woman shouted again, more shrill than before. "She says, 'We are not to take council from wizards. Scriptures say so.'"

Thomas replied evenly. "'Scripture also says to let he who is without sin cast the first stone.'" He reached his arm across to grasp the stump of his missing one. "'Stones have already been cast—'"

The woman interrupted Thomas. "'She is a beast, I can see and so can you!'"

"My hound Quick, purebred Starhound, sits quietly. Do hounds lie? She is not evil! She...she is gentile. Like Paul Roos, I name her Friend.'" He stood tall and scanned the crowed with his good eye. "If you know her heart, if you find me corrupted, cast your stones upon me as well.'"

In response a stone flew from the crowed, straight and true toward Thomas. Grand Wizard Seelain began a spell, but Jadd grabbed her arm and whispered harshly, "No."

There was nothing I could do but, like the silent crowd, watch it strike Thomas who did not move, did not duck. At the last second, Lilly leapt in front of Thomas, hugging him and took the fist-sized stone in the small of her back. I heard the *thud* and her grunt as she absorbed the painful blow. The rock clattered off the carriage's roof and onto the paved brick dock.

Quick growled and shot toward the stone throwers in the crowd. New shouts erupted in the mass of people, but now directed at the woman and her band of supporters.

Thomas called his hound back.

"With haste," said Wizard Seelain, "help him down."

We got Thomas into the carriage. Lilly remained next to the driver and I took my place on the back of the carriage as the onlookers gave way, opening a path through them and into the city.

The lead carriage moved forward and our driver snapped his reins to follow. We departed amid angry-fisted shouts matched by nearly as many waving cheers. Quick ran alongside, barking at no one in particular.

CHAPTER 14

Frustrated as a caged wildcat being poked with hot embers, I stood outside the thick oak door of the Prime Minister's office. I held the butt of my boar spear against the hardwood floor, certain my knuckles were white beneath my leather gauntlets, and stared at the painting of a large Crusader church, white cross emblazoned on the stained-glass windows above and on either side of its main entrance.

We'd passed many less grand churches than the one pictured as we raced through twists and turns, down both wide and narrow streets of New London. Not a direct route, but it avoided trouble. The hard-riding mounted soldiers ensured the way was clear.

The Central Parliament building wasn't nearly as impressive as the King's Palace in Keesee. Two and three story wooden apartment and office buildings encroached upon the ten-foot wrought iron fence that contained the small grounds and octagonal Central Parliament building. Ivy vines covered the four story brick structure, except where they'd been trimmed away from the main entrance and windows. Narrow and set into four rows equally spaced across each of the outer walls, all of the windows appeared dark and empty.

Hundreds of Crusaders, mostly women and children, had gathered along the rusty brown brick road that circled the Central Parliament. From inside the fence, Crusader guards observed their fellow citizens peering in at us through the black iron bars. No rocks flew when the carriages stopped and we entered the island nation's center of government.

Diplomat Grimsby and Grand Wizard Seelain remained confident as they prepared to formally request assistance from the Reunited Kingdom. Upon meeting Prime Minister Ursella, a thin-faced woman wearing a coal-black dress with gray buttons and rectangular metal-rimmed glasses set on the end of her long crooked nose, Diplomat Grimsby dismissed me. Grand Wizard Seelain silenced my objection and those of Jadd with a stern glance before we could a say word. Granted, Minister Ursella was an ally and, judging by her short gray hair and wrinkles, well beyond sixty winters. But, there might be a second entrance to her office. She—or someone opposed to wizards like at the dock—might carry a saint-blessed weapon. I'd witnessed Roos's blessed saber in action. It proved more lethal to magic and creatures than any Crusader gun.

Two Crusader soldiers stood at attention on the other side of the door to the prime minister's office while Lilly and Major Jadd stood opposite me, next to the church picture.

Jadd said to Lilly, "That bruise on your back must hurt."

"It'll heal," she said.

"You handled yourself well on the docks."

She shrugged.

"It could have gotten very bad out there," he said. "You did the right things at the right time."

Lilly glanced at me and then looked away. "Anybody could've done the same thing."

"No, I disagree. Only a very few." Major Jadd glanced down the hall to where Thomas and his father sat on a bench, speaking to a political representative they knew. "Catching the rock and dropping it. Shielding Thomas. You kept the violence from rising."

"I just did what I thought others would do. Just not as good."

"What do you mean?" asked Jadd.

"Roos would've caught the stone," she said. "But he'd have said good words while dropping it."

"I jumped between Thomas and the enemy when they were throwing rocks, just like Flank Hawk would do." She glanced across the hall at me, and met my eyes. "But he'd have done it better."

"How so?" asked Jadd.

"He'd have faced the enemy while taking the hit." She shifted her stance and stared at the floor. "I didn't."

Major Jadd rested a hand on Lilly's shoulder. "Look at me."

She did.

"We learn from others but we can *never* be them. Trust in your experience and instincts." He gripped her other shoulder. "You are who you are and will always be so. Be proud of that. You're Flank Hawk's chosen scout. You were there to do the right thing today because of his faith in you. He insisted that you be a part of this mission. Prince Reveron trusted his judgment in that, and you proved him right today. Not only in the eyes of Grand Wizard Seelain and Diplomat Grimsby, and mine, but in the eyes of those who stood against us as well."

He released her shoulders and took a step away. "If you were a mercenary in training, you'd have earned your name today."

She stood up straight, wincing at the pain from the bruise on her back. "I'm not a mercenary," she said. "I'm a scout—Flank Hawk's scout. And proud to be named so."

Jadd smiled, as did I.

Lilly reached back and rubbed her back just above the hip. "Scouting's easier than bodyguard."

Jadd nodded. "Wait until tomorrow morning with your back."

I wasn't sure Lilly's back would hurt that much the following day. As a neophyte healer, I recovered from injuries more quickly than most. But as a lycanthrope, she healed far faster than any warrior. Jadd certainly knew that.

"Flank Hawk," Lilly asked in a solemn voice. "If I *were* a mercenary, what name would *you* give me?"

"Quick Shield," I replied, knowing it was the right name.

She smiled and rolled her eyes before glancing down the hall at Thomas petting his starhound. "Good thing I am a scout and *not* a mercenary."

I looked at her, puzzled.

"My mercenary name. Half of it would come from a dog?" She held a straight face for several seconds, then broke into a huge grin. Major Jadd looked away, trying not to laugh, but he couldn't help himself.

I shook my head and smiled back. Maybe I'd eventually get Lilly's sense of humor.

I stood at attention while Major Jadd gave an inspection. "I believe they did a better job cleaning and polishing your armor than they did mine, Flank Hawk."

I shrugged. My breastplate still bore scrapes and dents from combat. My newest boar spear didn't. It leaned against the wall next to me while Diplomat Grimsby and Grand Wizard Seelain sat across the room on cushioned powder blue chairs, discussing the upcoming evening events.

"I believe we have the support of the prime minister," said Diplomat Grimsby to Wizard Seelain. "But the real challenge will be the cardinal and the bishop."

Major Jadd had explained the Constitutional Theocracy that directed how the Reunited Kingdom was governed. There were two voting houses whose decisions had to agree. The House of Lords was selected by the major land owners from districts across the Reunited Kingdom. Luke Cromwell was close friends with one of the ninety elected representatives. Then there was the House of the Commoners. Two-hundred seventy-five men and women elected by citizens across the Reunited Kingdom represented everyone else. In the House of Lords, the orange-robed bishop appointed ten priests of his religious order to serve as representatives, while the green-robed cardinal appointed fifteen priests and ten nuns to serve as voting representatives in the House of Commoners.

Then there was Prime Minster Ursella. She, Cardinal Johns and Bishop Dowlin had the power among them to overrule any decision the Houses of Parliament agreed upon. But depending on how many of the three voted against a parliament decision, a greater threshold of agreeing members in each house could overrule the three leaders' dissent.

It was confusing. A good king with wise counselors was more reasonable and effective, but I didn't voice that opinion. Or ask why it was called the Reunited Kingdom if it wasn't ruled by a king.

"It is a positive turn of events that the lycanthrope scout was invited to the convent to visit the deceased Lieutenant Colonel Paul Jedidiah Roos's sister."

Grand Wizard Seelain shot a glance my way before returning her attention to Grimsby as the diplomat continued. "It will keep her away from those with the vision to identify her and raise questions. At the same time it offers a chance to remind the representatives attending the dinner and concert to follow of the bond the lieutenant colonel had with her, and with your personal guard. And the sacrifices made to further our mutual cause, emphasizing our alliance."

In truth, I wanted to accompany Thomas and Lilly and visit Roos's sister. But my duty was to protect Grand Wizard Seelain. "Pawns," I mumbled, believing Jadd wasn't paying attention to me.

"What was that, Flank Hawk?" Jadd asked in a hushed tone.

"The diplomat speaks of me and Lilly as political pawns," I replied just above a whisper. "Madame Creeanne said I was King Tobias's pawn on the strategic battlefield."

Jadd moved to stand between me and the diplomat across the room, interested only in her discussion with Grand Wizard Seelain. "I know you're not fond of Diplomat Grimsby." He rubbed his mustache to hide a smile. "But she is knowledgeable and effective in her realm of expertise."

I nodded.

"Years ago I had the chance observe King Tobias playing chess. He even invited me to play once."

"Oh," I said quietly. I knew the basic rules and strategies, having watched others play and tried my hand once or twice. "I bet King Tobias is good."

"He is," said Jadd. "Much better than me. But beyond that, from what I observed." Jadd paused and looked over at the two ladies talking. "He does not like to sacrifice pawns unless he has to."

"Like to save a queen," I said, thinking of Wizard Seelain.

He nodded. "Or to defeat an opponent."

A knock at the door announced it was time for the formal meal.

"I'll relieve you so that you may dine," said Jadd.

"That's okay," I told him.

"It won't do to have your stomach growling during the music and events that follow."

"I'll eat fast."

"And smile," Jadd said. "And be open to conversation with those who speak our tongue. Your success against the Necromancer King's forces, at least for the diplomatic board set before us tonight, has elevated you from a pawn to a knight—at least."

I sat in the back of the candle-lit auditorium, getting a loft view of the stage below where reflected lanterns showered three musicians in amber light. Although I couldn't understand any words the harpist at center stage sang, to my ears she rivaled the best I'd ever heard, including several performances for the Keeseean Royal Court. From my upper-seating where several couples dined at small round tables, I observed Grand Wizard Seelain seated in the front row with Prime Minister Ursella on her left and Diplomat Grimsby on her right. Major Jadd stood along the wall, watching over her while I hurried to finish my meal.

A short man approached my table. He leaned close and asked, "Doth all Mainland mercenaries devour food with haste equal to thee?"

It was difficult to get a detailed look at the man until I allowed my eyes to adjust from the bright stage to the dim light shed by the stubby candle at my table's center. The oils used to hold the man's hair combed in curvy waves behind his ears reflected the candlelight. It almost masked the glint of his blue eyes set deep in his wide, meaty face.

He offered his hand. "Allow me to introduce mineself," he said in just above a whisper.

His accented dialect and odd usage of the Mainland tongue reminded me of the way Roos had spoken. But this man wasn't nearly as smooth or practiced, and nowhere near Thomas's proficiency.

As we shook he spoke into my ear, introducing himself as Sullivan Jones, Majority Whip in the House of Commoners. I nodded and replied in kind. "I am Flank Hawk, mercenary serving as Grand Wizard Seelain's personal guard." It felt odd saying such while someone else performed that duty.

I didn't know what a 'Majority Whip' was but I recalled Grimsby mentioning the name Sullivan Jones to Grand Wizard Seelain as someone important. The proud manner in which he used the title reinforced the diplomat's words, and put me on guard. "And I am finished with the fine meal your people provided," I said, wiping my mouth with a folded napkin. "And must return to my duty."

"I have indeed heard of ye, Flank Hawk, and I would ask ye to share a drink before returning to thine duty." He raised his hand and signaled to a server who nodded and strode with purpose toward the kitchen area.

The Majority Whip stood next to me and asked. "Doth ye enjoy the melody?"

I glanced down toward the silver-haired harpist accompanied on her left by an elderly man playing an oversized fiddle resting on the ground between his legs, and a young flutist on her right who swayed gently, causing her long blond braids to swing in rhythm. "They are the best I've ever heard."

He motioned with his hand to the curtained doorway that the server had used. "Please, I would ask that ye might join me so that we mightest speak."

I glanced down at Grand Wizard Seelain, and then to Major Jadd. Somehow he must've seen me and understood because he nodded to me and then refocused his attention on the auditorium and its occupants around

Grand Wizard Seelain. I turned and followed the representative out into a hallway lit by small chandeliers whose red candles matched the color of the painted walls.

We could still hear the music, but wouldn't disturb others' enjoyment by speaking above a whisper. Majority Whip Jones sighed and said, "They sing an ancient melody of a majestic tree and accompanying forest, felled to build great ships of war and conquest."

"I don't understand the words, but her voice rings of sorrow," I said.

The stocky man nodded. His attention continued to be drawn by the song. "It reminds us in the Reunited Kingdom of the balance we must keep, or risk the destruction of our Lord and Creator's gifts to us, and to our children to come." The arrogance in his voice and manner faded as he spoke, just as his command of the Mainland tongue improved.

He must have seen the observation in my eyes as he grinned and shook his head. "My friend mercenary, few have accused me of being a convincing gold-tongued politician, and the melody reminds me of many deeper truths."

I didn't know what a politician was, but I guessed it was similar to a diplomat.

He rubbed his hands along the front of his black formal jacket. "It is true, ye have met the Colonel of the West?"

"Yes, I have."

"Tell me about him," he said in a way that reminded me of a high noble speaking to one of lesser rank.

"Why?" I asked.

He stared at me a few seconds, his left eye squinting. "I will be against the wall honest. The main point of your visit to New London is to seek aid in seeing the Blood Sword returned to the hand of King Tobias. I am against such evil returning to the Mainland continent."

The hall was empty. Still, I kept my voice low. "I am a mercenary, serving to protect Grand Wizard Seelain, fiancé to Prince Reveron. It is not my place to—"

The representative raised a hand and cut me off. "Hear the truth of it," he said and gestured with his hand to the right. "Would you walk with me?"

I wondered what the servant would do upon returning with our drinks. The salty ham had made me thirsty and I'd anticipated either a dark wine or a hard cider. Water would do.

"For a few moments," I agreed. "Then I must return to my duty."

"You may know," he began, not looking at me but at the floor as we walked, "word of your arrival and subsequent request to address the full Parliament went out by telegraph. Even as we dine and enjoy the music, representatives race to New London aboard trains. All except for a few in the most outlying districts will be in attendance by late afternoon tomorrow."

I didn't know what telegraph was, but I knew that trains were steam-driven wagons that pulled carts along raised paths lined with steel rails. Diplomat Grimsby said they travelled faster than a quarter horse at full gallop.

"That is when your grand wizard and worthy diplomat are to address the Parliament, making their formal request, arguing their case and taking questions. Debate will follow, but as I said, the truth." He slowed his pace and looked up at me. "Even before the Parliament assembles, minds will have been set and the decision largely settled."

"How?" I asked.

"Politics." He thought a moment when I didn't respond. "My father and uncle were merchants and established a trade outpost with Mainlanders in the Village of Hommel, north of Sint Malo."

His mentioning of Hommel brought back the memory of the cold night waiting in the village's burned-out ruins for Belinda the Cursed's ship to arrive.

"You know of Hommel?" Majority Whip Jones asked.

"The Necromancer King's forces," I said. "Hommel's destroyed. It's people scattered or dead."

"I spent five years of my youth around Hommel," he said. "Decent people, whose souls I shall pray for tonight." He took a deep breath. "But, back to my point. My uncle petitioned the Parliament to establish a trading post on the Mainland. Even before he addressed the committee on foreign trade, the vote had already been decided. What he had to say *may* have swayed the vote of any on the fence, but most already knew. As I watched my father and uncle speak, I saw it in the committee members' eyes." He smiled. "Fortunately, they had decided favorably upon the outpost. And five years later, upon requesting a renewal of the permit, they'd already decided to deny it, despite what my father and uncle said."

"And what is the decision we should expect tomorrow?"

"It was politically astute, your king, sending Major Jadd—who'd suffered disgrace and exile for saving routed Crusaders fleeing the forces of the Necromancer King, against the orders of a crown prince. And you, the mercenary befriended by Lieutenant Colonel Paul Jedidiah Roos, who together with your scout—now conveniently visiting his sister—brought destruction down upon the Necromancer King and returned those summoned damned souls back to their doom."

The notion of me being a pawn returned to my thoughts. "It may be coincidence," I said. "I have served as Grand Wizard Seelain's personal guard long before this journey."

"Nevertheless," said Representative Jones, "those who are to vote will be arriving throughout the night and morning. And it is those such as me, the Majority Whip, who will be informing them of the details and consequences of the Blood Sword's return. Long before Diplomat Grimsby speaks before them."

We reached the end of the hall, where it formed a 'T'. We were still alone. I was beginning to think it was planned. Maybe the servant sent for drinks instead made sure we'd be alone. It also made me wonder what could be going on around Grand Wizard Seelain.

There were two cushioned seats in a small alcove to the left with a small table between them. And upon them rested two wooden mugs filled with ale. Representative Jones invited me to sit with him as he continued.

"And I want to know the details that form the truth of the matter. That will help me decide what is best for my people. And how I will use my influence."

"You've not made up your mind?" I asked, adjusting my sheathed sword and taking a seat. "You're on the fence?"

"No," he said, and took a drink from his mug. "I am against your mission."

I sat up straight. "As I said before, it is not my place to speak. I will not give you reason to deny my king's request of assistance." I stood and prepared to return to the concert.

"I spoke to Major Jadd," Representative Jones said. "Formerly Road Toad, your mercenary mentor. He said among your strongest traits is your loyalty."

If the Reunited Kingdom decided against aiding us, and if any blame fell to me, I was confident Diplomat Grimsby would place it all on me. What the king would do upon learning that? Major Jadd might already be at risk.

But the Reunited Kingdom didn't hold all the cards. I knew that even without their aid, we still could attempt the journey. The distance and danger faced would be greatly increased. The chance of success, and returning in time, if we did succeed...I didn't want to think about it. My words could mean punishment. Lashes, imprisonment, exile or execution. I could handle any justice if even part of the reason for failure rested upon my shoulders. But the entire kingdom, my family—everyone would suffer in defeat. That would be far worse.

"I will speak with you in the presence of either Grand Wizard Seelain or Diplomat Grimsby."

"Would their presence influence what you say, or don't say?" He paused. "I can see by your expression that it might."

He was right, but I'd thought I betrayed no expression. "Why should I tell you about the Colonel of the West? You've already made up your mind against my people."

"Yes, I have. I will never vote to bring the Blood Sword near." He held his mug tight. "For personal reasons," he said and took a long drink. "Every one of my colleagues in Parliament expects that. But, how *strongly* I speak against it. *That* is what is important to *your* cause."

I stood. "My cause is with King Tobias of Keesee. I am serving as guard for Grand Wizard Seelain, soon to be wed to the king's son. I will not betray my king. Nor will I betray her trust."

I took a step away, ready to return and relieve Major Jadd. The Majority Whip raised a hand and said, "Bide a moment, if you would." He reached into his coat and pulled out a folded paper. "You might want to read this."

I took the paper. The wax seal above my name written in flowing script bore Grand Wizard Seelain's mark. I broke the seal and read the paper's contents:

Flank Hawk,
You have my leave to speak with Majority Whip Sullivan Jones with respect to the Blood Sword and with respect to concerns of its return.
Seelain
Grand Wizard of Air

I struggled some to read her script, but I'd seen her signature many times before. It was hers. I reread the message and ran my thumb over the ink, discovering it was dry.

Majority Whip Jones held his hand out, gesturing for me to return to my seat. His smile was broad and reassuring. Or it was meant to be. I refolded the message and placed it behind my breastplate before sitting once again.

"I must commend you on your steadfast loyalty, my young mercenary. Now, I trust you will answer my questions?"

"No," I said, keeping my voice low and even.

"No?" Representative Jones sat up straight. "But the directive I just handed to you." He stared into my eyes. "What game are you and your master playing, Mercenary?"

"There is no game that I am playing. Grand Wizard Seelain did not compel me to answer your questions."

"Ahh," he said, sitting back and nodding to himself. "It would seem politics remain politics, whether they originate within the guise of parliament or royal court maneuvers." He took another drink of his ale. "I now begin to see why a mere mercenary has risen to such a trusted position."

There was silence between us until he asked, "Might you have a question for me?"

I hadn't really been thinking along that path, but one came to mind. "Why do you want to know about the Colonel of the West?"

He adjusted his jacket and cleared his throat. "Because, my young mercenary, it may lend understanding as to why he would relinquish the Blood Sword to you and your companions." The representative settled back into his chair. "I have no doubt that Grand Wizard Seelain is powerful. But not nearly enough to in any way force an immortal blood to do as she asks. While there is the possibility of a trade, I feel it more likely the immortal blood will, or will not do so, based on his own machinations. And not for the welfare of King Tobias or his kingdom."

Representative Jones drained the rest of his ale from the wooden mug. "You can confirm to me the Colonel is an immortal blood?"

"Roos identified him as an immortal blood."

"Lieutenant Colonel Paul Jedidiah Roos," Jones said in a correcting tone.

"Roos," I repeated, "did. And from what I witnessed, I have no reason to doubt his assessment."

Representative Jones smiled. "It has been said, the Colonel claimed not to be a god."

"That, he does not," I said. "I believe he disapproves of other immortals like himself doing so." After a breath, I decided to add, "Roos and the Colonel discussed what they called monotheism. Their beliefs on this sounded similar."

"Do you know what monotheism is?"

I shook my head even as Representative Jones nodded. "The Colonel of the West—can you describe the man?"

I wasn't sure the Colonel of the West was a man. "He dressed in a green uniform, very much like what he wore before First Civilization's fall."

"How do you know that?"

I wasn't going to explain everything to the Crusader politician. I'd been given glimpses of the world before the cataclysm that destroyed the First Civilization, and even parts of the conflict that brought it to pass. "You can choose not to believe what I say."

"Why did he give you the means to shatter the Corpse Lord's plans?"

I recalled the turning point in the negotiations with the Colonel. "Because of the Necromancer King's path to conquest. The souls he summoned, damned before the First Civilization's fall." The Reunited Kingdom's military leaders knew the origin of the Necromancer King's resurrected weapons of war, so I didn't explain further.

"Is this Colonel a Jew? Has he retained his faith over the centuries?"

I shrugged. "I do not know."

The representative leaned forward. "My understanding is that you have held the Blood Sword. Wielded it. Will you confirm that it is evil?"

I recalled being possessed by the malevolent soul contained within the sword and nodded.

"I can see by your expression, the extent of that belief."

I took a deep breath. It was a horrifying memory I tried to avoid. "It is a tool," I said. "One that my king needs."

"Representative Jones stood and offered his hand. "Thank you for your words and insight." As we shook hands he continued, "I'm sorry you did not avail yourself of the fine ale. You are welcome to take it with you."

I met the smiling eyes of Majority Whip Jones. "I do not know the history or reason behind your opposition to assist in the Blood Sword's retrieval. But, in a game of chess, a move that appears solid and defensive can form the foundation of collapse in the end game."

"You play chess, my young mercenary?"

"Enough to know," I said.

"You continue to surprise me." He put his arm on my shoulder as we walked back toward the auditorium. "To be honest, I expected you to ask why I am set to vote against the return of the Blood Sword."

I knew what I wanted to say, and worked out how Major Jadd would say it. "You said your opposition was based on a personal reason, and it appeared to be one based on deep sorrow. It is enough that those who will decide the issue, know. My knowledge of the reason would neither advance my king's cause, nor would it lessen whatever pain drives your decision."

A thoughtful expression quickly masked the Majority Whip's look of disappointment, and he dropped his hand from my shoulder.

We completed our journey back to the auditorium in silence.

I thought again about my conversation with Majority Whip Jones as we made our way through the tunnels beneath New London. It was the safest route from our well-secured hotel to the House of Parliament.

Major Jadd had listened while Diplomat Grimsby and Grand Wizard Seelain debriefed me in our hotel suite after the meeting. Grand Wizard Seelain said that I did well and Jadd told me I'd held my own. Even Grimsby grudgingly admitted that I said little that would hinder our cause. Even so, I didn't feel any better about the exchange and that my words would be twisted and used against us in the upcoming debate.

Traveling through the tunnels avoided a possible recurrence of the near riot at the landing dock. A stage-like platform with polished tile and an ancient sign with faded lettering framed behind glass suggested the current tunnel was a remnant of First Civilization construction. I'd glimpsed images of underground trains during my meeting with the Colonel of the West. The thought reminded me of the preserved skyscraper that served as the Colonel's Outpost 4.

This tunnel retained little of the fancy splendor. Even the iron gates that secured the entrances showed signs of rusting. Brick and wooden beam construction shored up where moisture and age worked to undo what had survived for over two thousand years. Our escort, a company of Crusader soldiers, carried several lanterns to light our way. Major Jadd insisted on having one himself.

Lilly kept with the squad of ten soldiers ahead of us, using her senses to detect any danger. Grand Wizard Seelain walked beside Diplomat Grimsby and the company's captain while Jadd and I followed, a dozen paces ahead of ten soldiers bringing up the rear.

Narrow channels filled with slow-flowing water ran along the walls. Cats hid among long stockpiles of barrels and crates. The first night Diplomat Grimsby slowed to translate some of the black letters painted on them: Water, salted beef, dried beans. Where they occurred, the stacked crates took up half the tunnel's width and ran for spans of three or four dozen yards. Wooden supports kept them off the moss-covered stone floor, probably in case of flooding. Security against famine, or against invasion? Was there a reason we were allowed to see them? It made me wonder what other preparations the Reunited Kingdom had made over the years, and possibly centuries.

The captain and some of the soldiers slowed in surprise when the cats stared and hissed at Lilly. She'd spent the first night in the convent with Roos's sister, so this was the first time the cats had encountered her. The first time Lilly stared back, but every other encounter after that, she pressed forward.

Diplomat Grimsby asked the captain a question in the Crusader tongue. Major Jadd translated for me. "She asked why there are cats down here and if they're feral. The captain said they're certainly not tame and are meant to keep the rats under control and out of the food."

I knew Lilly hated cats. I understood a little better why.

We finally reached the correct metal-framed stairwell. Our clomping boots sent echoes as we, with our escorts, climbed up to the holding room. A guard behind a reinforced steel door awaited a password, one that was different from the day before.

I noticed Grand Wizard Seelain's small sigh of relief after we emerged to a level above ground. Being underground weakened every air wizard's ability to summon elemental magic, but it was nothing compared to what she was soon to face. Diplomat Grimsby had twice warned about it but Grand Wizard Seelain insisted it was important to not show weakness. Arriving after the official opening of the Special Session of Parliament called on behalf of Keesee's need was one more thing opponents in the Crusader Parliament might exploit. Wizard Seelain twice replied to Diplomat Grimsby with confidence that she could endure the prayer ceremony that opened each session of Parliament.

I wasn't so sure. I'd witnessed a company of Crusaders in battle. Their unified voice broke a demon-beast's hellcry. Moments before, the towering bone golem's withering cry had stopped hardened soldiers and beasts alike, most of them fell trembling in place. Others had turned and fled the battlefield.

Grand Wizard Seelain had been there too, stood against the bone golem's might. Diplomat Grimsby hadn't.

CHAPTER 15

Major Jadd stared out the narrow window into the morning sun, hand resting on his sword's pommel. Diplomat Grimsby stood next to the plush chair where Grand Wizard Seelain sat erect, holding her white staff set across her knees. Lilly stood opposite the diplomat, dropping the thin brass rod given to her by Madame Creeanne. As always, it hit the floor and fell pointing west, now angled just a little south. I stood between Wizard Seelain and the door that led to the Parliament Chamber just down the hall.

Except for our breathing and the *thunk-clack* of Lilly's rod striking the pinewood floor every half minute or so, we waited in silence.

"Stop that this instant!" Diplomat Grimsby demanded.

I turned to see the diplomat and Lilly lock gazes.

Lilly said, "I want to know when it starts." She picked up the rod and dropped it again. "It'll fall random, just like it did in the convent."

Diplomat Grimsby gestured toward Grand Wizard Seelain who continued to sit with her eyes closed. "We will know when they start. You dare not interfere with the grand wizard's concentration."

Major Jadd tore a thick curtain down from the window, folded it over several times, and tossed it on the floor at Lilly's feet. He met the narrow-eyed stare of the diplomat. "We may need to know when the opening prayer and the recitation of their Nicene Creed ends."

Before anyone could say another word, a dampening wave snuffed out my spell potential like a candle washed over by a surging tide. Grand Wizard Seelain tensed as her elemental energy surged to protect her.

It was Grand Wizard Seelain's conscious choice to resist the loss of her magic. Me? I didn't have a choice. When mine would return, I had no idea. If Wizard Seelain failed in her effort? I wasn't sure she knew for how long. I only knew, based on Major Jadd's discussion of historical records from past battles against Crusaders, that no matter the anti-magical surge's strength, the effect on spellcasters was never permanent.

Strain spread across Grand Wizard Seelain's face as she mumbled incantations through clenched teeth. She stood and held her staff parallel to her body as elemental magic flared anew. Maybe I could feel the struggle better than the others in the room. It was like buckets of water being poured into a fire pit—the hot flame sizzling and crackling in its struggle to remain alive.

A minute passed. Grand Wizard Seelain's shoulders drooped even as her knuckles whitened to match the color of her staff. Another minute passed. I felt her magical energy surge in ever weakening pulses.

There was nothing any of us could do to aid Grand Wizard Seelain. Jadd had moved closer. Nervous sweat ran down Grimsby's forehead. Lilly bit her lower lip, arms held ready to catch Wizard Seelain if she fell. I turned away to watch the door, in case someone attempted entry. Anger tangled with helplessness as I considered the possibility that Grand Wizard Seelain's ego might have driven her to a bad decision.

It was too late to do anything about it.

I turned back just in time to see Grand Wizard Seelain collapse back into the chair. Her staff clattered on the floor. Lilly moved to catch it but pulled away at the last instant, unsure if she should touch it.

I knelt in front of Seelain as Grimsby took her hand. Wizard Seelain's shallow breath strengthened and faint color returned to her face. She wiped a small tear from the corner of her right eye, both still closed.

"Hand me…my staff," she said weakly.

I placed the staff in her open hands.

"Step back." Some regality and strength returned to her voice. "Provide me room."

We all did. After several deep breaths, she opened her eyes. Redness of blood filled the whites of her sky blue eyes.

"Can you stand?" Major Jadd asked as he knelt to examine her eyes.

"My strength is sapped." She looked about, apparently trying to gather her thoughts. "More magical that physical."

"The blood vessels in your eyes have hemorrhaged," Jadd said. He went to a satchel and returned with a short, twisted root that I recognized and presented it to Wizard Seelain. "Night Bugle. It'll keep a bone-weary mercenary alert through a full night's watch. Might it help you?"

"Fethorthium Root," Wizard Seelain said. "Yes, it will assist me."

"Are you sure?" asked Diplomat Grimsby.

Wizard Seelain nodded. "I have used it before. It will help me through what lies ahead."

A knock sounded through the door. "The special session of Parliament has begun," a soldier's voice announced. "Prime Minister Ursella has a five minute opening statement. The Sergeant-at-Arms will then announce you."

Diplomat Grimsby walked to the door and hesitated until Grand Wizard Seelain began chewing the root and nodded. Grimsby then opened the door a quarter of the way and said something in the Crusader tongue.

Lilly whispered in my ear, "She said we'll be ready to enter upon the speech's end."

"Flank Hawk," said Grand Wizard Seelain in a commanding tone. "You and your scout secure the hallway. Be prepared to stand to your assigned posts."

The Parliament met in a huge half-circle room. Curved rows of seats faced the speaker's podium set below three rows of west-facing windows. The most senior and important members sat nearest the podium, with each row elevated a step to the least influential members. The House of Lords occupied the right third of the chamber with the House of Commoners filling the remaining seats moving left. The prime minister, the bishop, and the cardinal had seats elevated to the right of the speaker's podium. To the left three short rows of benched seats with padded backing were for guests. All of the seating had a narrow line of tables to the front, for writing or holding books and short stacks of paper documents.

Grand Wizard Seelain sat in the center of the front guest row with Diplomat Grimsby sitting to her right and Major Jadd standing to her left.

I stood along the wall near the bottom row of House of Commoners representatives, observing and watching for danger. Lilly sat with Thomas and his father, Luke, in the gallery seating above. If there was a danger from the floor, it was my responsibility. If a threat arose in the gallery above, Lilly sat poised to move against it.

Prime Minister Ursella introduced Diplomat Grimsby first. Even though she was speaking in the Crusader tongue, I caught the diplomat's name, followed by her standing.

Not understanding what was being said aided in my ability to focus on dangers, from outside along the back wall below the gallery, and the doors and steps there. I also scanned the representatives, watching their facial features, especially any which paid attention to me or to Major Jadd.

Diplomat Grimsby spoke for less than ten minutes. Her voice carried strength and conviction. It filled the hall. The faces of some representatives were open, occasionally nodding. Others were neutral or looked up in between writing notes with fast-moving quills. A good portion sat with frowns, even with arms crossed. Most of them wore brown, jackets for the men and shawls for the women. All, however, were quiet and polite.

Grand Wizard Seelain spoke next. As she stood at the podium, Diplomat Grimsby and Major Jadd stood behind her to shield her from possible snipers through the windows. She spoke with authority as well, but her command of the Crusader tongue wasn't as smooth as the diplomat's. Even so, the grand wizard kept her voice low enough to require all in attendance to focus, listen to her words with care. She spoke twice as long as Diplomat Grimsby.

After Grand Wizard Seelain finished, the prime minister stood and pointed to representatives, who then asked questions. It appeared orderly. Maybe the questioners had already been selected, or Prime Minister Ursella used her authority to determine who questioned Grand Wizard Seelain. Sometimes Diplomat Grimsby stepped forward to answer. Twice Major Jadd stood at the podium and briefly answered questions.

It seemed that those in brown were more animated and cutting in their voice and tone, and interrupted Grimsby on occasion, while those in gray were more polite and supportive.

I caught a simultaneous two-finger gesture from both the bishop and cardinal to Prime Minister Ursella. After two more questions, our time in the meeting hall came to an end. First, the gallery above cleared. Then, we were escorted out and the large doors behind us closed.

"I believe it will be an interesting debate," Diplomat Grimsby said after our short walk down the hall. We entered the room we'd waited in before the Parliament session began. Lilly was already inside with Luke and Thomas. She was standing on a chair, hanging up the curtain Major Jadd had torn down.

I looked to Major Jadd. He nodded and I went over to help Lilly. She'd reset the wooden rod, so I held the curtain up while she set the hooks on it.

While we did that, Luke and Thomas Cromwell, Grand Wizard Seelain and Diplomat Grimsby discussed the opposition to the king's request. There was solid opposition against us, but a majority at least appeared open to assisting. Their conversation often shifted to the Crusader tongue, but I caught that having Prime Minister Ursella's support was helpful, and that it probably would come down to the bishop and cardinal.

A short time after we'd hung the curtain, Thomas and his father left.

Although there were two Crusader soldiers posted outside, I stood guard inside the door. Major Jadd stood with arms crossed while listening to the diplomat and Grand Wizard Seelain's quiet conversation. Lilly stood next to me. It offered the first chance she'd had to show me a gift she received from Roos's sister. It was a steel locket containing a detailed gray-tone painting of our fallen friend. Lilly said it was a photograph and tried to explain, but just talking about the picture and the visit caused her to tear up. I told her we'd have plenty of time to talk later and suggested that she teach me some words in the Crusader tongue.

Hours passed and a chef brought us lunch consisting of chicken soup, salted crackers and a dessert of preserved peaches topped with cream. I reminded Wizard Seelain we didn't have Enchanter Jonas to check the food for poison. Even so, she declined my offer to taste it. I knew poisoned food was unlikely, but some of the representatives were strongly set against us. Who knew for sure to what extent they'd go to see our mission fail? When I insisted, Diplomat Grimsby said my taste palate might not be sensitive enough, and quickly moved to do it before Grand Wizard Seelain could object.

After Lilly finished her lunch she rejoined me by the door. I was about to ask her if any of the representatives had commented on Grand Wizard Seelain's blood-filled eyes during the debate when booted footsteps approached our door, followed by a knock.

Wizard Seelain nodded and I opened the door. The Sergeant-at-Arms stood at attention in the doorway. "The Parliament requests the presence of

Mercenary Flank Hawk, to answer questions that have arisen during debate."

This surprised me. I looked from him to Grand Wizard Seelain. "Him alone?" she asked. "He is not fluent in your language."

The Sergeant-at-Arms continued to stand at attention. "An interpreter will be provided."

"I would request that Diplomat Grimsby accompany Flank Hawk as his interpreter."

"Prime Minister Ursella anticipated your concern," said the Sergeant-at-Arms. "The Parliament agreed for Mercenary Flank Hawk's scout to accompany him as she speaks our language."

Diplomat Grimsby stood. "Her skill is rudimentary. She lacks a broad vocabulary and the understanding of subtle nuances, along with their intent and meaning."

"Prime Minister Ursella has arranged for Thomas Cromwell to stand ready to assist Scout Lilly with any interpretive and translation difficulties."

Major Jadd interrupted. "They have heard from King Tobias's official delegation, and seek to delve for further truth and insight?" The question was directed at the Sergeant-at-Arms. He remained silent.

Grand Wizard Seelain stood and walked over to Lilly. "Will you accompany Flank Hawk and act as his interpreter?"

Wide-eyed, Lilly looked from the grand wizard to me. She nodded and stood at attention. "I will."

The Sergeant-at-Arms gave us a few moments before Lilly and I went with him to answer the Parliament's questions. During that time Diplomat Grimsby began issuing both of us a verbal list of instructions.

Grand Wizard Seelain interrupted and told me, "Be honest and direct."

Major Jadd rested an arm on my shoulder and said, "The grand wizard is correct. They're politicians and expect deceit."

I stood behind the podium, wondering why I was nervous. I'd stood before King Tobias, bartered with Belinda the Cursed, faced a fallen angel while challenging for passage to meet the Colonel of the West. I successfully bartered the Blood Sword for a First Civilization weapon to break the Necromancer King's invasion.

Certainly, if the Reunited Kingdom denied assistance to our mission, we could still go on. Find a way. Facing the Crusader Parliament was less daunting than standing against wave after wave of zombie hoards. Even if all 350 spoke against me, as I estimated their numbers, I'd emerge unharmed. That's what I told myself as I took a deep breath and rested my hand on the pommel of my sword.

Lilly stood to my right, stiff, attempting to hide her nervousness. Her eyes were wide, moving from face to face in the crowd. I had to be confident for her. "You'll do fine. We'll do fine," I said, and then whispered in her ear.

"We've faced much worse together."

Thomas, sitting on a tall stool several feet to her right echoed with assurance. "You will do fine."

"I am ready," I said to Prime Minister Ursella, who waited several paces to my left. She nodded and called upon a brown-clad woman, one of four members who'd been moved to the front row.

The representative spoke with harsh confidence, locking eyes with me. She reminded me of my great aunt when I was a kid, round face with gray hair pulled back in a tight round knot.

Lilly leaned close. At first her voice cracked. Then she took a breath and said in a low, steady voice. "She wants to know if you believe Keesee can win…prevail against the Vinchie Empire."

"No," I said in the Crusader tongue. I knew that word, and I knew what I'd seen in my recent journeys. It was interesting the way my answer echoed. I must've spoken louder than planned. My response must have also surprised the representative as she searched through her hand-written notes before looking up again. Her brown eyes were just as hard, but more searching.

She asked another question. I caught Major Jadd's name mentioned before Lilly translated: "She wants to know why you disagree with Major Jadd."

"I am not a part of King Tobias's War Council," I said and gave Lilly a chance to speak before I continued. It also gave me time to organize my answer. "I have never led more than a squad in combat. I have not seen as many battles and campaigns as Major Jadd has." I paused for Lilly to translate, then finished. "I'd value his battle judgment more than mine."

Lilly finished and glanced at Thomas, who nodded. She let out a small sigh.

The Prime Minister called upon the next individual, a tall man with what looked like a set of wooden false teeth. His voice was deep and reminded me of a bard who often visited Pine Ridge.

"He says you have used—wielded the Blood Sword," Lilly started, and waited for him to finish. "Is it evil?"

"No," I said, in the Crusader tongue, and finished while many in Parliament sat up or raised their eyebrows. A few gasped. "The soul it holds is." Lilly quickly translated, which made a few—those that I guessed supported our cause, smile.

Lilly translated the man's next question. "Why should we risk the return of the Blood Sword, which holds an evil soul?"

"King Tobias is an excellent chess player," I said. "The Blood Sword will give him another piece on the board to use against Fendra Jolain." I didn't use the term goddess because, if they were all like Roos, nobody in the Reunited Kingdom thought she was one. After having met the Colonel of the West, and hearing what he had to say, I was no longer sure she was either.

"An unexpected piece," I added after Lilly finished translating.

The representative with wooden teeth sat down. Another man stood, this one wearing gray and wobbly despite his cane. He had to be at least ninety winters, and his eyes held a faint milky cast. His voice shook as he spoke.

"He wants to know why, through no action, the Reunited Kingdom shouldn't support the Goddess of Healing?" Lilly glanced quickly to Thomas.

He whispered to us, "Inaction," and then nodded.

"When I was young," I said, at first looking at the old representative, and then focusing on as many representatives in the hall that I could, "healers took my sister because someone discovered she had the ability to cast minor healing spells. A bounty was paid for the information. My family, my sister had no choice. They took her. No one has a choice. That is how Fendra Jolain rules."

I waited for Lilly to finish, then continued. "Before it was known that Fendra Jolain would attack, King Tobias could have easily taken control of the weakened Doran Confederacy even as his forces drove out remnants of the Necromancer King's army." I paused for Lilly and took several deep breaths. "He didn't. Same with the Lesser Kingdoms and all who fought our enemy, formal allies or not."

After my answer the old representative said, "Thank you," and hobbled the short distance back to his seat. Anticipating the Prime Minister's acknowledgement, the fourth representative rose and stepped forward. She appeared younger than any of the other representatives in the hall, with wavy red hair and a deep, jagged scar along her jaw line. She spoke quickly with an aggressive tone.

Lilly listened carefully and then said, "She says Colonel Paul Jedidiah Roos traveled to your lands. He joined your cause. You must have come to know him, although not as good as many here in Parliament." Lilly looked to Thomas to see if she'd gotten it right. When he nodded, Lilly continued. "Concerning the possible return of the Blood Sword to the continent, what do you think Colonel Paul Jedidiah Roos would do? Would he stand for it? Would he stand against it? Would he remain…"

Lilly looked to Thomas who said, "Neutral. Would he remain neutral?"

The scar on the representative's jaw couldn't have been more than several months old. I thought on this while I answered. "I don't know what my friend Roos would choose." The representative appeared ready to speak, so I continued my answer just as Lilly ended the translation. "From what I know of my friend, he would've read from his book of scriptures, said his night prayers, and answered after a good night's sleep."

There was a hint of a tear, mixed with pride as Lilly told the Parliament my answer. When she finished, I added, "My scout, Lilly, knew Colonel Roos better than I. Ask her."

Lilly turned her head sharply toward me. I leaned close and whispered, "You knew Roos better than me. Who better to answer?"

"I don't want to answer," she said, once again wide-eyed as she glanced back at the waiting representatives. "I'm too scared."

The young representative asked a question. Thomas translated. "Representative Stillow desires to know if there is a problem."

I met Lilly's eyes with mine. "Like Grand Wizard Seelain said. Be direct and honest."

"I forgot what you said. Other than to ask me."

I asked Thomas, "Can you?"

He stood up from his stool, leaned on his crutch, and gave my reply.

From what I could understand, the representative asked Lilly what Roos would do.

After Lilly and I switched positions, she stood silent for a moment. Then an answer spilled out. Thomas whispered to me what she said. "Roos wouldn't be closed to what the grand wizard requests. I know this because when we first met, Roos didn't trust me. But he gave me a chance to prove myself. We became friends. The best friend I'll ever have. And he died. He got killed by..." Lilly wiped a tear from her eye. "Sacrificed his life for mine and Flank Hawk's. He did what only he could do."

Lilly's voice switched from emotion-filled to one of confidence. "Flank Hawk is asking you here to do what only you can do."

Representative Stillow smiled, and it wasn't a friendly smile. She asked another question. This time Thomas translated for me. "Representative Stillow wants to know if you are asking the Reunited Kingdom to sacrifice itself. To risk the ire of the Vinchie Empire, if not invite war with an empire, which you acknowledge will defeat Keesee and her allies. And to risk the return of the malevolent Blood Sword, which will surely fall into the hands of Fendra Jolain, an Immortal Blood."

"War is coming to my home," I said, with Thomas translating. I knew I was about to ignore part of Grand Wizard Seelain's advice. I'd be direct, but not brief.

Gripping the pommel of my sword, I said, "We and our allies, which, from the representative's words, the Reunited Kingdom does not number among them. We will battle the forces of Fendra Jolain, despite little hope of victory. King Tobias doesn't ask you to join us in battle. Just to grant us passage through your lands so that we might bring a weapon to the field and alter the odds. If Keesee doesn't prevail, we will weaken her.

"Greater Elves don't plan in days, months or even years. They plan in decades and centuries. Even a young mercenary like me can see that Fendra Jolain attacks so that Keesee must turn away from fighting alongside Crusader forces, stalling the campaign to finally defeat the Necromancer King, a Greater Elf—an Immortal Blood. Her ally.

"Can you alone defeat the Necromancer King, the Corpse Lord? At what cost? Then, the Vinchie Empire will spread across the continent. What chance will you have against her? A year from now. A decade from now. A century from now."

Representative Stillow's response was measured but forceful. Thomas prepared to translate, but Lilly spoke up. "She says you're saying nothing more than what your diplomat and wizard said. You underestimate the strength our Lord and our faith provide." Lilly paused, listened, and translated. "Do you know the history between the Kingdom of Keesee and the Reunited Kingdom regarding the Blood Sword?"

"No," I said in the Crusader tongue, and then allowed Lilly to translate the rest of my answer. "I do know that Roos's faith, backed by his saint-blessed saber, swiftly defeated the Blood Sword after it possessed me and turned against him."

I stood to attention and looked across the assembled representatives, and then to the prime minister, cardinal and bishop. When Lilly finished translating what I'd said, I added, "I saw the struggle through the soul within the Blood Sword, and know. You should not fear it. Not as Fendra Jolain should."

CHAPTER 16

A double line of Crusader soldiers kept the crowd back. Even though I watched the hundreds that arrived to see us off before sunset, I felt Wizard Seelain was more secure from hurled stones with Wick behind me, *and* the two fire-breathing dragons nearby on the dock finishing a meal of slaughtered sheep, devouring one whole with each bite at the pile.

I'd already said my farewell to Major Jadd. Lilly was with him saying goodbye. His wishes for luck, success and safe travel were more sincere than Diplomat Grimsby's.

Majority Whip Jones approached with a wide grin and hand extended. "I will say this," he said to Grand Wizard Seelain as they shook hands. "Although the vote was destined to go your way, your mercenary's words resonated enough even for me to abstain rather than vote against your cause." His grin widened a bit more when he commented, "I'd heard your eye vessels had ruptured because of our prayer. I and many regret to have caused you any pain, but I see you're healing up just fine."

I'd managed to work a healing spell, and only a hint of a yellowish pink cast remained in the whites of the grand wizard's eyes. Maybe Representative Jones knew that, or maybe he didn't. He didn't say. All he said to me while shaking my hand was, "May the Lord guide you in your duty in keeping your charge safe, and may He watch over you as well."

Representative Jones didn't wish us success in retrieving the Blood Sword, but whatever his reasoning, he'd met us half way. "Thank you," I said. "And may your God keep you safe and guide you in your service as Majority Whip."

We were just about ready to mount and depart when the lines of soldiers let through a wagon pulled by a team of mules. Lilly dashed toward it. Once there she all but dragged an elderly woman dressed in black and white robes with a matching head scarf off the wagon, toward us.

I sensed something, like I hadn't felt since standing next to Roos when he'd drawn his saint-blessed saber. It wasn't nearly as strong, but still there. Grand Wizard Seelain shifted the grip on her staff, so I guessed she felt it too.

"This is Sister Ruth," Lilly shouted as they approached. "She's Roos's sister. One of them—but she's called a sister too 'cause she's a nun."

Sister Ruth smiled and slowed Lilly's pace as the two held hands. The nun bore the same straight nose and the same eyes as my fallen friend. "I'll give you a moment before we must depart," said Wizard Seelain, stepping away to help Private Zunnert with a final check of our wyvern mounts.

Lilly could hardly contain her excitement. "Flank Hawk," she said and took my spear. "You need to at least hug her!"

I wasn't so sure, but when Roos's sister opened her arms to embrace me, I couldn't do otherwise. Beneath the robes she felt thin and frail.

"Lilly hath told much. What ye and Paul endured. Thank ye for befriending him." Her gaze shifted between Lilly and myself. "Thank ye both."

Her way of speaking our tongue sounded so much like Roos. "If Lilly told it right," I said, "it was your brother who befriended us."

"Right when the ogres and mudhounds had nearly caught us," Lilly added.

Sister Ruth nodded and smiled broadly. "I know, friend Lilly. Paul was always there when I was in need of him. And in truth, I am thankful that ye both were there when he needed ye too."

I signaled for Major Jadd to join us. When he did I said, "This is Major Jadd."

Jadd stood at attention and offered his hand. Sister Ruth swept it aside and hugged him as well. I heard her say into his ear, "Thank ye for thy sacrifice made all those years past that saved Paul."

"It was the right thing to do," Jadd said. "And I am glad I did it."

"Who would have thought Parliament might move with such speed?" Sister Ruth said to us. "Mine sister, Rita, travels by rail but shan't arrive till the morrow. I promise thee, friend Lilly, I wilt share with her all that ye have shared with me."

She stepped back. "And now, ye must depart, friend Lilly, friend Jadd and friend Hawk. Into peril. I shall pray for ye each." She turned and walked with measured steps back to the wagon. Lilly wiped tears from her eyes and watched her go.

In moments we'd all mounted our steeds and prepared to depart. I nodded to Thomas and his father, waved to the crowd as they watched, some cheering. I spotted the mule-drawn wagon departing down the cobbled street. The old nun turned and I waved to her as well, glad in my heart to have met her, even if only for a moment. To hear the words, 'friend Hawk.'

At sunset our flight took to the air, spiraling ever higher above New London. The stiff breeze promised a chilly night. Wick liked flying in cold weather less than me. Captain Bray on Flint Spitter took the lead with Enchanter Jonas seated behind him and Lilly as aft-guard. Grand Wizard Seelain on Moon Ash followed in their wake to the right with me trailing her. Private Zunnert on his wyvern mount, Coils, trailed Major Jadd on Flame Lance until full dark, where observation from the ground would be nearly impossible. Then Jadd shot ahead, shouted, "Fare well," along with Sergeant Drux. I didn't hear anything from the diplomat before they turned southeast, beginning their journey back to the King's City. We continued north. It hadn't been much of a deception, unlikely to fool discerning eyes and ears for long, but any measure of uncertainty might help.

We angled east until reaching the coast and then followed it. The Crusader telegraph proved faster than our winged mounts. As we neared our destination shortly before sunrise a red-streaking fireworks rocket spotted at a great distance helped Captain Bray locate the small fishing town. There we rested, hidden within a large barn, until nightfall before continuing north along the coast and cutting inland to reach our destination on the northern tip of the main island. Again, the telegraph prepared them for our arrival long before sunrise. Although Captain Bray proved an excellent navigator, using the stars and described landmarks as guideposts, a succeeding duo of red flares in the night sky aided us in navigating the final stretch.

This time we sheltered inside a warehouse that smelled of salty fish. The soldiers that brought food to us and our mounts seemed distrustful and had little to say.

After the lesser enchanter cast his spell to check the food for poison, Lilly said to Grand Wizard Seelain, "I'm sorry. I should've said something sooner—probably when we were in New London."

Captain Bray was tending to his serpent mount. Private Zunnert standing guard within the warehouse probably couldn't hear the conversation around the table as we prepared to eat the stew that Enchanter Jonas was ladling into wooden bowls.

He slowed as Lilly continued. "I'm pretty sensitive to food that isn't right. Unless it's got some spices I don't recognize."

Grand Wizard Seelain asked, "Would detecting poisons require you to change?"

Lilly looked down and away with squinted eyes before shaking her head. "No. It wouldn't."

Grand Wizard Seelain nodded. "We shall continue to trust in the abilities of Enchanter Jonas. Nevertheless, it is a useful thing to know, Scout Lilly."

Enchanter Jonas said, "I wouldn't expect it from Crusaders, but a very powerful enchanter *might* be able to mask a toxin beyond what my spell ability could detect. For your safety, Grand Wizard, having the scout check where there might be doubt would *not* insult me in the least."

Wizard Seelain smiled. "That is useful to know as well, Enchanter."

I wondered why Lilly hadn't said something about it when we were in New London. It brought another concern to mind—the moon last night. Exactly how close was it to full?

"You appear troubled in your thoughts, Flank Hawk," Grand Wizard Seelain said.

That was the grand wizard's polite way of asking me to tell her what I was thinking about. Probably, she figured about poison or her safety. I didn't want to bring the moon's phase into question as Lilly already looked embarrassed, so I brought up something else that I'd been wondering about. "Grand Wizard, if I may ask. Why are we working to remain secretive?"

"About what, Flank Hawk?"

"Our arrival in the Reunited Kingdom, let alone our presence in New London, was hardly kept secret. The decision to assist in the Blood Sword's return being debated and approved—what spy couldn't find out about that?"

"And," she said, knowing I wasn't finished.

"And, by their telegraph message," I said, "the Crusaders here knew of our arrival. Red flares before dawn? Even if they've kept our presence secret to the local people, animal and livestock are not used to dragon scent. Their reaction will've raised concern. Word of serpent cavalry having been in town will spread shortly after our departure."

"I understand your concerns, Flank Hawk," said Grand Wizard Seelain. "The Parliament's debate was held in closed session. Those seated in the gallery above the members were military or high-ranking officials. Thus, it may take some time for word to leak out."

"If I may add," Enchanter Jonas said. "My understanding is that any seer's prediction is clouded when Crusaders are brought into the mix."

Grand Wizard Seelain nodded. "We could have taken a more difficult route and avoided the Reunited Kingdom. But their assistance and the effect Enchanter Jonas stated weighed heavily on the king's decision."

She ate a small potato from the stew. "Did you know that upon Major Jadd's return, both you and I will be seen within the palace of the King Tobias?"

"How," I asked, suspecting enchanter magic.

"You are familiar with Maid Julia? Even you once commented that she could be mistaken for my sister. A soldier with similar build, and bearing close resemblance to you, will be equipped with armor and weapons identical to yours. Subtle assistance from Supreme Enchantress Thulease will be enough to establish our presence, for a brief time at least.

"It might work," I said after chewing and swallowing a gristly piece of lamb. "Our wyvern mounts have more than one stable they call home."

Enchanter Jonas said, "A day, a week, a month. The further along our mission is before the enemy becomes fully aware, can only benefit us."

We rested the day and well into the night before taking flight for the Siren Islands, what the Crusaders named the Faroes. I'd heard stories of the sirens that inhabited them. Bird women whose songs lured to their death, sailors that ventured too close to their islands. Some tales said they were beautiful creatures, others said gargoyles were a siren's prettier cousin. Captain Bray assured me before we left that red dragons had a keen taste for sirens.

Because of that, we'd not be bothered.

After hearing what Captain Bray had to say, Lilly took me aside. "Don't worry, Flank Hawk," she said. "Any that escape Flint Spitter's stomach, or get past Grand Wizard Seelain's staff and magic, will have to fight through me to take you."

Her grin that followed that made me wonder if she was serious, or if she was poking fun at me. Probably both.

It didn't matter what either of them said. I kept two balls of candle wax handy to stuff in my ears. Private Zunnert watched me, nodded, and showed he'd done the same.

CHAPTER 17

An hour before sunset we spotted the first of the Faroe Islands. Captain Bray did well navigating over open water, during both day and night. Although he carried a compass, the serpent cavalryman relied on the sun and stars to keep on course. Most of what I'd learned about navigation came through Major Jadd's example, and some from Grand Wizard Seelain. I was best at traveling over land using landmarks. Get lost? Follow a river, and you'll eventually find a town.

"Good to see land," I said to Wick, patting him on the neck. "If we'd been in the lead, half-chance we'd have missed our target."

Some of the islands were large and expansive. We selected a smaller, rocky one where rough waves crashed against its high cliff walls. Private Zunnert and I spiraled downward toward crumbling ruins of what must have been a walled fortress, remnants of the only structure on the grassy, rock-strewn plateau.

We hadn't even secured the area before the rest of our flight dove sharply from the sky. The dragon landed first.

"Lilly spotted a sea serpent a few hundred yards off shore," Enchanter Jonas said as he dismounted Flint Spitter.

Lilly followed him down while I took the reins from Captain Bray. "It wasn't surfaced," she said.

I knew serpents often served the sea goddess, Uplersh. Was its presence a coincidence? "Did it see us?" I asked Bray.

"I can't be sure. Even if it was below the water, it still might have seen my dragon's silhouette against the sky." He glanced over at Wick who'd already taken on a mottled gray and green tone that matched a nearby crumbled wall. "The low sun's angle would've made it nearly impossible to spot a wyvern."

I pointed to Grand Wizard Seelain who'd just landed her mount. "Enchanter, assist the grand wizard." I pointed toward a line of rocks and boulders that had once been a fortress wall. Lilly, there. Help Zunnert and me finish securing the area."

Long shadows already stretched from the fortress' west wall. It must have been the sturdiest since it was the only one was that had major sections still standing. The shadows were even longer when we finished our task.

"Nothing but a few fat-looking rats with no tails," I said to Zunnert, who stood next to Grand Wizard Seelain.

Lilly nodded in agreement. "And some nesting ground birds."

Enchanter Jonas sprinted around a pile of granite blocks. "There is a serpent down there," he said. "Mermaids and mermen too."

"How many," I asked.

"I only spotted five mermaids and three mermen."

"What about the serpent?" Lilly asked. "How big is it?"

"A hundred feet in length," the enchanter said. "I was employing a night vision spell to determine its size when I spotted dolphins. Then the mermaids and mermen."

"Serpents and mermaids. They are the eyes and ears of the sea goddess," said Grand Wizard Seelain. "The question is, were they expecting us?"

Lilly asked Grand Wizard Seelain, "Can you kill the serpent?"

Grand Wizard Seelain shook her head.

I'd faced a sea serpent once before. Mermaids and mermen too. As long as we remained on land the mermen were the only threat to us. Mermen, fishermen and sailors lured from their vessels into the depths by the beautiful fish-tailed maidens, kept their legs, enabling them to board ships and fight upon them, as well as upon land.

"Did they see us?" I asked. "Do they know we're here?"

"I believe they know someone is up here," said Enchanter Jonas. "One of the mermen attempted the cliff face, but it was too steep. I then observed three dolphins towing three men east, toward the lower end of the island."

Grand Wizard Seelain rubbed her neck. "This disturbs me greatly, that the sea goddess anticipated our arrival."

"Maybe not," said Jonas. "Could be just the possibility of our arrival. Who can say how long they've been here, or who they're watching for. Or if it is an unfortunate coincidence."

"Three mermen against us and a dragon?" I said, knowing they had no chance at killing us. "If they knew it was us...would they investigate?"

"They were submerged when we arrived," said Private Zunnert. "They may have only seen something in the air, large and winged like a dragon. Even of that they may not be sure. Sirens are said to have more than a ten-foot wingspan."

I stepped to my right and viewed the sun as it slid below the horizon.

Wizard Seelain gripped her staff. "It will take them some time to scale the lower cliff face. If they were aware of a sure ascent path, they would not have first attempted the western cliffs."

She looked to Private Zunnert, who nodded in agreement.

Wizard Seelain continued. "We then shall allow the allies of our enemy to observe something, which may work to our advantage. Private Zunnert, Flank Hawk, keep your wyvern mounts tethered. Establish a camp. The rest of us will depart."

Private Zunnert confirmed the plan I suspected. "Understood, Grand Wizard. We will allow the mermen to successfully recon two scouts."

"Enchanter," Wizard Seelain said, pointing at the ground. "Some light." She used the pale glow directed at the ground to highlight a crude map she made using several rocks. A small one she identified as our island, and then skipping over several rocks, she pointed to the island she intended to relocate to, one I recalled passing over. Broad and rocky, with several small stands of trees.

"What about sirens?" the enchanter asked. Lilly nodded.

Zunnert said, "We cannot leave the dragon, and the king does not normally use females for scouts, especially white-haired wizards."

Bray said, "The sirens, if they exist, are said to inhabit the more northerly islands."

Wizard Seelain looked from me to Private Zunnert. He placed a hand on my shoulder. "Flank Hawk and I are best suited for the task. We'll be fine."

"Do not make the mermen's task too easy," Wizard Seelain said. "You are, after all, soldiers of Keesee."

I helped everyone remount while Zunnert gathered dry tufts of grass and whatever else he could find to build a fire. As the king's elite soldier set spark to his pile with flint and steel, the dragon and wyvern departed, flying south. Our job was to allow the mermen to see us, and to report—without us or our mounts getting injured or killed.

While we waited I tended to Wick. Private Zunnert shot one of the many fat rodents with his bow and was skinning it to cook over the fire. I thought about the time I'd fought mermen. Brave and competent fighters, but they lacked armor and shields. A straight up fight would hold less risk for us.

"Something must've been wrong with those frost dragons," said Private Zunnert as he began slicing flesh from the rodent's bones and placing it on a flat rock set in the middle of the fire. "Sure could use some real wood."

Zunnert's mention of frost dragons meant he heard the mermen approaching.

"No trees on this little island," I said, trying to listen for any sign of the mermen. "Them dragons, they must've been near end of their strength when they spotted us."

Zunnert nodded. "Lucky thing."

"Wick here's worn down too," I said. My mount became alert, raising his head. I patted his neck to calm him. "How long you think before we can head back east?" I would've preferred to speak Sea Spittle. Every sailor spoke it. I hoped at least one of the mermen knew the Mainland tongue.

"Long flight," Zunnert said. "Same span of sea going back." He stopped cutting on the rat. "Hey!" he yelled and flung his knife through a gap in the wall behind Wick.

I caught movement on the wall above Wick. I picked up my boar spear and leapt back, toward the fire. A merman on the wall whirled a net over his head and flung it at me. I caught the hook-filled net on the head of my spear. The crossbar snagged it, and kept it from entangling me.

Zunnert dashed with sword drawn through the gap where he'd thrown his knife.

Wick snapped his neck upward, locking his vulture-like beak onto my foe's thigh before yanking him from atop the wall. The merman screamed and tried to draw his flint dagger as Wick slammed him to the rocky ground. The merman's only garment was a pair of tattered breeches held in place by a seashell-adorned belt. He was no match for a hungry wyvern.

My spear's head was entangled with the net so I tossed it aside and drew my sword. Despite being tethered, Coils hobbled forward and joined Wick in tearing apart the stunned merman.

I looked about and couldn't see any foes. Nor could I hear much except the screaming merman and squawking wyverns. It was a gruesome sight, but a spark of pride and satisfaction ran through me knowing my mount had acted to defend me. I decided to follow where Zunnert had gone.

I slowed after dashing through the gap in the wall, holding my sword ready while I let my eyes adjust to the sudden darkness. A clump of shadows shifted and toppled fifteen feet away. It was Zunnert wrestling one of the mermen to the ground.

"That way, toward the sea cliff!" Zunnert shouted.

I broke into a trot toward the high cliff's edge not far away. There were too many scattered stones to move much faster. Up ahead I saw a man-shaped form with arms pumping, moving away from me. I picked up my pace just as the merman stumbled over a half buried stone. He fell and came up limping, allowing me to gain but not before he reached the cliff's edge.

I charged forward. He looked over his shoulder before taking several quick steps and leapt from the cliff. I made it to the edge and looked down. There appeared to be a splash atop one of the swelling waves before it broke upon the rock face. I looked around for other danger before kneeling down, trying to see in the waters below. It was a clear night with a few stars showing. I thought I spotted movement. Maybe a mermaid or two, maybe a dolphin's dorsal fin. I watched a moment longer before hurrying back to our camp.

An unconscious merman lay bound and gagged near the fire. I ran to help Zunnert saddle Coils. "He got away," I said. "Jumped off the cliff into the sea."

"Good," Zunnert said, pulling the cinch tight. "Figured you couldn't catch him."

"Don't know if he made it," I said. "Saw the splash but the wave hit the rocks right afterwards."

Zunnert shrugged. "Weren't supposed to make it easy. At least our mounts are fed." Except for blood scattered on the rocky ground, there wasn't a trace of the net-throwing merman. "Get your saddle, Flank Hawk."

Zunnert tossed the skinned rat to our mounts. "No time to cook it. No sense wasting it."

I nodded. "Get my spear." Deep down it turned my gut, having seen the merman torn apart, and now eaten. And the captive. He'd soon be dead by our hands, unless Enchanter Jonas knew a spell to wipe his memory. Unlikely, I guessed. That'd be more what a seer could do.

But they were the enemy, bringing war to Keesee. To where my family was.

Zunnert cut the net away from my spear and slid it into the sheath after I'd placed the saddle and bags onto Wick's back. Then he helped me finish the job.

Zunnert said, "We'll tie him to my mount."

"Are you sure Coils can bear him and you?"

"Bray took most of the gear." Zunnert lifted the unconscious man. "And we're not going far. Give me a hand with the rope."

It wasn't long before we were aloft in the night sky, traveling south to rejoin our four comrades. The rising moon was nearing full. It lit a wall of gray clouds approaching from the west. Flashes of lightning warned of heavy rains coming with them.

Our wyverns' ability to blend into the night sky meant that the minions of Uplersh below wouldn't be able to spot us. Thinking on that brought to mind the mermaids below who, with their turquoise and sea green hair and large blue eyes, were quite beautiful. The vision brought to mind a hauntingly enchanting song, soft and secure like a lullaby, but sensual and alluring at the same time.

The melody echoed in my thoughts, distracting me from...I couldn't remember. It wasn't in my head, not from memory, but floating on the air. I removed my helmet and turned my head from side to side, searching its source—soft voices calling to me.

Something didn't seem right. Heading south, the approaching storm clouds should've been on my right. Wick was still following Zunnert on Coils. The song began tugging at my thoughts again, fraying them. It reminded me of the enamor spell Enchantress Thereese had attempted on me in the king's palace.

Sirens! I shook my head to break the song's spell. It was still there, tempting me. I reached for the balls of candle wax and stuffed them in my ears, muffling the melody's sound and weakening its grip.

I urged Wick forward and came up next to Zunnert on his mount. He stared ahead. The moonlight revealed a relaxed smile upon the soldier's face.

"Zunnert!" I shouted.

He didn't respond. I searched the sky. Ahead and above three winged forms were leading us south.

I brought Wick even closer. "Private Zunnert! Do not shirk your duty!"

My words must've had some effect as Zunnert looked about, then at me.

I leaned towards him. "Your duty!"

The elite soldier squinted, and then faced ahead and upward, the music drawing him back.

I took a chance and pulled Wick around and under Zunnert's mount while grabbing at his reins. The move startled Coils and the wyvern shot upward, taking the reins beyond my grasp. Even so, the wyvern's massive chest slammed into me, nearly knocking me from my saddle. Wick screeched in surprise and challenge. Coils responded, but turned away, north at Zunnert's direction.

I raced to catch up, searching the sky when one of the sirens dove upon me. She appeared to be a beautiful woman but with wings instead of arms—feathered wings beat by massive shoulders and a powerful chest. Her feathers may have been white, but the moon gave them a silvery cast, except for her forked, hawk-like tail, which looked ink black. I discovered her feet were talonned like a hawk's when they latched onto my shoulders, digging into my breastplate while trying to haul me from the saddle.

The talon bit painfully as it found purchase through the leather overlay protecting my upper arm. The siren yanked me upward, but the saddle's securing straps held. Wick twisted and turned, snapping his beak. I managed to reach my dirk sheathed in my boot and thrust it into the siren's leg. She let go and released a scream that started out as human but ended in the screech of an enraged seagull.

I blocked the other claw with my forearm as it grasped for my head. I ducked before stabbing upward, this time twisting the blade when it found flesh. The siren was a magical creature, but my dirk was silver and coated with fireweed resin.

The siren dove right. Wick turned to follow. I pulled him up and searched the sky for Zunnert. I couldn't see him but heard the siren song to my left.

From the darkness ahead a dragon's roar sounded just before a siren's scream that ended abruptly. A small thunderclap followed. Then silence, except for the wind. No song. I realized then that one of the wax balls had fallen from my left ear.

I turned Wick toward the where I'd heard the sounds of combat and spotted the shadowy form of a dragon coming about. The serpent cavalryman's long white braids whipped in the wind while the aft-guard pointed and waved at me. It was Grand Wizard Seelain and Lilly astride Flint Spitter. As I closed, I was able to see Private Zunnert on Coils trailing close behind them. I also noticed that sometime during the battle Zunnert had lost the merman tied to his saddle.

I formed up behind the elite soldier for the brief flight south and was the last to land. Enchanter Jonas took reins while I dismounted.

Lilly ran up to me. "Are you okay?"

"My shoulder's injured, but not bad."

"What happened?" she asked.

"Three sirens tried to lure us with their song," I said, leading Wick to be tethered with Coils near a jagged outcropping of rocks. "I was fending one off when you showed up on Flint Spitter."

"How did you manage that?" asked Enchanter Jonas. "To resist their song?"

"I don't know," I said. "Maybe it was the wax." I shook my head in thought. "It fell out of one ear, though. And I put it in after they'd started singing."

Enchanter Jonas helped me tether Wick while Lilly began to remove the saddle and saddlebags. "Grand Wizard Seelain is checking on Private Zunnert," he said. "He insists the effects have disappeared." Then the enchanter leaned close. "I believe he is embarrassed."

The wind continued to pick up while we set up three small A-frame tents. Rain was coming in from the east.

Lilly and Enchanter Jonas stood watch while Zunnert and I crouched in a tent with Captain Bray and Grand Wizard Seelain. We told our tale of battle and near enchantment. Captain Bray examined the puncture wound in my shoulder by candlelight. It hurt but wasn't too deep.

Zunnert explained his experience and believed he'd cut the captured merman loose to help ensure I'd not catch up to him.

Grand Wizard Seelain said, "It was Lilly who detected the sirens' song. Although I am not a proficient serpent rider, Enchanter Jonas suggested Lilly and I investigate. A fortunate thing we did."

Zunnert and I nodded in agreement. He had trouble meeting the grand wizard's eyes.

"Whether or not the merman survived his fall to the sea cannot be known," said Captain Bray. "But it's likely that the one Flank Hawk chased over the cliff may have believed the false information fed to him. And although a dragon's roar carries over the water for some distance, she did not breathe, which would most certainly have signaled her presence."

I asked, "Do you think the sirens and minions of the sea goddess are working together?"

Nobody responded. Nobody knew.

"You'd better attempt a healing spell on your arm," Captain Bray said to me. Then he said to Zunnert, "I can't say why Flank Hawk was able to resist the sirens." The wind continued to whip and rattle the small tent we huddled beneath. The serpent cavalryman rested a hand on the elite soldier's shoulder. "I'd have fallen under their spell too."

We sat silent for a moment. Both men peered out through tied tent flaps straining against the whipping wind. "I'll relieve the enchanter after a few hours," Bray said to Zunnert. "I'll awake you to relieve the scout shortly after that. Grand Wizard and Flank Hawk, you get last watch."

"Heavy rain coming," Zunnert warned. "It's going to be a miserable night." He dug at the ground with his finger. The wind and this rocky soil, by morning nothing and nobody will be dry."

"Our companion Jonas might," disagreed Captain Bray. "I have observed that he knows an enchantment to dry linens."

"Uh, huh," said Zunnert as the rain began lashing down in sheets. "He'd better know *a lot* of them."

CHAPTER 18

Contending with a stiff wind from the east made the flight to Iceland more difficult. While wyverns can glide for hours without tiring, constant flapping to make headway wears them down. The troublesome wind let up by early afternoon. Still, without drafting behind Flint Spitter, I'm not sure that my wyvern mount would have made it. We struck landfall two hours after sunset and continued inland for fifteen minutes so that we might have a fire-lit camp that couldn't be spotted from the sea.

I'd been to the large island named Iceland before, but where Bray led us wasn't like the flat tundra region where large furry beasts were said to wander. I didn't see any the first time and was counting on the scent of our red dragon to keep them away this time.

The ground was rocky and the soil seemed poor. Tough grasses led to thorny bushes that ran along the edge of a birch tree woods near to where Private Zunnert selected to set up camp. The night air was crisp and cold, but not to the point of frosting our breath. Normally Lilly would've been with me to gather wood for the fire. Instead, Enchanter Jonas accompanied me. The full moon was soon to rise. Nobody said anything, but we all understood that her beast would soon emerge.

Lilly was a true-blood, born to what most named a curse. I'd seen her beast. Even its emergence. I sometimes had difficulty believing that inside, in her blood, dwelt a man-sized muskrat, a rare lycanthrope breed, unlike werewolves. Those were evil, blood-thirsty creatures, rightfully feared and hunted. A werewolf pack fell upon Pine Ridge before I'd reached ten summers. They killed and ate most of three men and dozens of livestock. Lord Hingroar's men finally hunted the pack down and slew them with silver and fire.

Lilly wasn't like that—her beast wasn't like that. She had no family. Lilly was my friend, and I was one of her very few friends. She'd stood with me when she didn't have to. She'd saved my life, both as a human and in beast form. But, deep down, the rising moon reminded me that she wasn't like me. Not fully human. I told myself it didn't matter. Yet a dark corner of my heart refused to agree. That dark part of my heart I hid from her—buried it from everyone, even though I wondered if others felt like I did. A question that'd never cross my lips. The best I could do was to blame it on what I'd seen as a kid.

"Flank Hawk, what is wrong?"

I turned my attention to Jonas who stood ready to draw his rapier. "What?" I asked.

"Nothing," he said and smiled. "The way you were staring into the woods, I believed you might have seen or heard something."

I shook my head.

"How is your shoulder?"

The talon-wound from the siren had been shallow. "Just a little sore," I said.

He walked back to me. "Here, give me the torch. With your gauntlets, you can pull the fallen wood from that thicket safer than I."

He was right. My leather gauntlets, a gift from Grand Wizard Seelain, were thin but sturdy, and lined with small steel plates sewn into them. "Here," I said and handed him the torch and my spear.

After a few minutes of hacking with my sword, I tied a small rope between two stout fallen branches and dragged them back to camp. During the third trip Enchanter Jonas asked, "You are concerned about Lilly?"

I nodded while yanking a branch from the brush.

"She departed toward an open area," said Jonas. "With her keen senses she is certain to detect any approaching danger."

"I've been here once before, Enchanter. They said some large creatures inhabit this land."

It was his turn to nod before looking up. "Do you hear that? It resembles a large canine."

"Wolves," I said.

He grabbed the rope to help me drag two heavy limbs the fifty yards back to camp.

A second howl sounded, followed by a third. "They are coming from the open land east of camp," he said. "They are still distant. A mile, would you agree?"

"Closer," I said, realizing the baying that began sounded deeper than any wolf I'd ever heard.

"Not werewolves, I should hope."

"Pull harder," I said.

In camp, Captain Bray sat astride Flint Spitter. Grand Wizard Seelain stood with her back to the now blazing fire. Zunnert stood next to her. I took my spear back from Jonas and told him, "See to the wyvern mounts." The three were huddled together, black against the night and spitting throaty hissed threats into the darkness.

Grand Wizard Seelain shouted up to Captain Bray, "Can you see anything?"

"I cannot," he said. "Shall I go explore?"

I came up to stand next to Private Zunnert. "Listen," I said. "Sharp calls to one another."

He nodded. "They're coming closer. Closing in on their prey."

"Do you believe it is Lilly?" asked Grand Wizard Seelain.

"We'll know soon enough." The elite soldier drew his sword. "Enchanter, bring me a waxed torch from my saddle bag. Grand Wizard, remain here. Send Bray if things sound desperate."

"I should send the captain on Flint Spitter first," she responded.

Private Zunnert shook his head. "If it is Lilly in her beast form, it may be difficult to tell one from another."

I didn't know if I agreed with Zunnert's assessment. A dragon might succeed in scattering the pack. "We're wasting time," I said and donned my helmet. If it was Lilly they hunted, she needed my help.

Enchanter Jonas raced up to us and tied a small rope around Zunnert's left forearm. From it emanated a golden glow equal to a dim lantern. "The enchantment's intensity will increase for ten minutes and then fade and be gone by twenty."

The elite soldier looked to Grand Wizard Seelain. "Go," she said.

He nodded and the two of us trotted toward the sound of the hunting pack. With his free hand Zunnert drew his hunting knife to match his long sword. Even though he bore the glowing rope, I kept the lit torch to match my spear. Most wild animals feared fire.

The rising full moon further lit the landscape as we ran toward the deep barks and throaty snarls. We circled around what must have been a spring-fed pond and spotted a pack of wolves arrayed around a rock outcropping. Perched atop it, outlined by the moonlight, was a huge muskrat, spinning about to fend off the near pony-sized wolves that lunged at it—at Lilly.

Some of the thirty-strong pack sensed our approach and turned to face us.

"Dire wolves," said Zunnert. "More than we can handle."

"I won't abandon Lilly," I said.

"Neither will I," said Zunnert and whistled a sharp call that resembled a Keeseean bugle call, one that summoned reserves to the front line.

Our appearance had momentarily halted the pack's assault on Lilly until Zunnert's whistle. After a few growls and snarls, half of the pack turned and trotted toward us while the rest returned their attention to Lilly, leaping with snapping jaws to drag her down from her rocky perch.

Zunnert and I marched forward in unison as the dire wolves closed with hackles raised. I hurled my torch at the lead wolf as it and several others slowed and stalked towards us while the rest split and raced to encircle us.

Although the lead wolf dodged to the right of my flaming torch, my ploy broke the unison of their assault. Zunnert shouted a battle cry as he sidestepped a leaping wolf and slashed with his sword, carving flesh from throat to shoulder.

I set the butt of my boar spear and caught a charging black-furred brute in the chest. My spear's shaft held as the tip bit into the wolf's shoulder, tearing it open as I sidestepped and let beast's momentum carry it past me. Luckily my spearhead came free, allowing me to slam the butt end into the maw of another wolf, driving it back. I stabbed deep into the shoulder-wounded wolf's thigh as it struggled to rise, then I leapt around it to cover Zunnert's flank. He fended off one attacker with a knife thrust into its eye while hacking into the forepaw of a second as it pivoted to turn on him.

I stabbed at one with my spear and missed as it leapt out of range. Its distraction worked as another pack member shot in low and clamped its jaws down on my boot and knocked me to the ground. I slammed the blade of my spear into its head, but not hard enough. The snarling beast began shaking me like a dog angry with its sack toy. I jammed my spear's shaft into the maw of an attacking wolf while kicking the one shaking me in the snout hard enough to break its grip. I rolled away and, as luck would have it, staggered to my feet next to Zunnert with my sword drawn. He'd lost his knife and was covered in blood, how much of it was his own I couldn't tell.

"Thought they had you," he said.

"Me too," I replied, testing my leg's strength and drawing my dirk.

A dozen of the wolves closed in from all sides at once. Our initial tenacity had caught them off guard. It'd cost them and wouldn't happen again.

"Where the hell's Bray?" Zunnert snapped and whistled again.

The same question crossed my mind.

There wasn't time to do anything about it. Several things happened at once. A dire wolf finally got a hold of Lilly and dragged her down from her perch, the wolves encircling us attacked in unison, and a red dragon's guttural roar sounded from above.

Flint Spitter's appearance broke the pack's confidence, scattering most of them. But battle frenzy still held several and they came on. Zunnert and I dashed into them, toward Lilly.

Flame licked the ground to our right, raising yelps of pain and fear. I grazed a gray brute with an off balance sword slash as it dodged right. A second wolf crashed into me from the left before I could recover, knocking me to the ground. Hot feral breath fell on me as I slammed a backhand fist against its jaw. My sword clipped only fir on the follow through. My dirk pierced the wolf's neck as its tooth-filled maw caught my cheek while clamping down on my helmet.

Our blood mixed as I stabbed again and again with my dirk and hammered its head with my sword's pommel. All the while the huge, snarling wolf shook me, tearing my helmet loose. Luckily my neck wasn't snapped.

The wolf threw my helmet to the side. That gave me the room needed to drive my sword up and through its lower jaw. I twisted the blade as the wolf leapt back, spraying blood. Even as it did, jaws swooping from above locked onto my foe's hindquarters and dragged it a dozen yards before releasing.

Lingering flames from its initial breath attack lit the dragon's underside as she rose to come around and dive again. I climbed to my feet and steadied myself while I searched for Zunnert and Lilly. Blood flowed down my face and chin, adding to that already covering my breastplate.

Halfway between me and the rock perch I spotted Zunnert pulling his sword from the spine of a downed wolf. From beneath the fallen brute a brown-furred creature struggled to escape. I ran that direction and arrived to help Zunnert lift and roll what had to be the pack leader off of Lilly. Deep gashes riddled the dead pack leader's snout, neck and shoulders. The were-muskrat was in even worse shape.

She collapsed onto her side. Blood poured from a gaping stomach wound and from the tattered remains of the left side of Lilly's face. Her surviving brown eye looked around wildly.

"The blood. Is it safe to help her?" asked Zunnert.

"It's me, Lilly," I said kneeling down and facing her. "Flank Hawk."

Lilly's beast bared its teeth menacingly.

"Lilly!" I said again, trying to remain calm. "It's me, your friend."

Lilly's beast released a whimpering moan.

"I don't know much about weres," said Zunnert, "but those wounds…"

Bray brought Flint Spitter down about twenty yards away. "What do you need?" he shouted, unstrapping before climbing down from his mount.

"She's in a bad way!" said Zunnert. "It may not be long."

"Bring bandages and wraps," I said. "She's losing blood."

"Is it safe to touch her blood?" asked Zunnert.

"I have my gauntlets." The squealing whimper began to weaken. "She's going into shock."

Zunnert grabbed my shoulder as I leaned in. "You've seen enough battle wounds to know."

I knew Lilly was dying. "She only has to survive 'til sunrise." I pulled a pouch from my belt and opened it.

Captain Bray rushed in, knelt down, and began unfolding a cotton cloth the size used for a sling. "Use this on her face," he said, and removed his riding cloak. "You're injured as well."

The cloying smell of blood and death surrounded us. "I'll survive," I said. The burning sting across my face and rising pain in my leg hinted at what Lilly was feeling. I sprinkled some ground white oak bark on Lilly's face and scattered a handful over her stomach wound.

Bray cut a notch in his cloak before tearing a wide strip from it. He'd seen me heal Wizard Seelain's eyes, so he knew what the oak bark was for. "Zunnert," he said. "Lift her while I get this under so we can pull it tight. Flank Hawk, it's going to hurt so keep her calm. Then we can bind the wound shut for your spell to better work."

"Lilly. Lilly," I said, placing hands on her shoulders and looking into her good eye. "We have to lift you. It's going to hurt. Do you understand?" I couldn't tell if she did or not. She'd gone silent, but was still breathing. "Hurry!"

Bray draped the cloth over her wound. "On three," he said. We all nodded. "One, two, three."

Zunnert lifted her hindquarters. Lilly squealed and I held her shoulders in place. Bray got the ends underneath and Zunnert set her down.

"She's gone well into shock," I said. "Zunnert, bring your rope light closer. Bray, hold up the cloth while I fix things in place before you and Zunnert pull it tight."

Both men nodded. I slid her intestines back in place and pressed the wound closed, and slid my gauntleted hands out as the broad strip of cloak tightened over the wound. Some of the ground bark stuck to my blood and gore-covered gauntlets. The sight of it suddenly knotted my stomach. I couldn't lose it, not yet.

I moved Lilly's head and wrapped it. She was unconscious and her breathing was growing more shallow. I had to hurry, but hurrying too much would do her no good.

"Don't let anything disturb me," I said as I leaned close and began the only chant I knew—the one my older sister had taught me. To clot blood vessels, halt bleeding. I opened my mind to the maelstrom of energy that raged beyond the reach of normal senses. I continued to chant, edging closer, seeking slivers of the swirling energy, strands that I recognized. Ones that I could direct.

Energies buffeted my mind as I delved deeper, seeking to draw upon broad strands, maybe greater than I could survive. Ones that might mend Lilly's wounds. Not completely, but enough until the full moon set.

Somehow there was less confusion in the maelstrom of energies. With my mind I redirected a strand's path, a broad one down into my friend's stomach wound. The effort sparked a sharp pain behind my eyes. I pressed on, isolated another strand and directed it down to Lilly's face. I had enough strength for one more, a small one. I focused, kept chanting, directing the energy, back down into Lilly's bandaged stomach wound.

Bray's distant voice echoed in my head as everything went gray, circling and closing into black.

CHAPTER 19

I awoke to the smell of burning wood and the crackling sound of a campfire. Beyond that, voices and the sulfury odor of red dragon.

Sharp, stinging pain across the right half of my face and throbbing ache from my right hip down to the knee brought back the night's battle against the wolf pack.

I stared up at the canvas tent sheltering me as daylight filtered through the tied flaps. Lilly's voice, probably near the campfire, sent a sigh of relief through me. Gentle probing with my fingers across my cheek revealed that eight or ten stitches held my wound closed. I examined my hands. No cuts. Another sigh of relief. The blood of Lilly's beast hadn't mixed with mine.

Although my breast and backplate had been removed I was still in my padded armor beneath my wool blanket. My hand brushed against my sheathed sword lying alongside me. That meant someone believed lurking danger remained.

I heard Captain Bray greet Flint Spitter, slapping the dragon's scales, probably along the serpent's neck. Then he joined those talking around the fire.

"Captain," said Enchanter Jonas in his precise manner. "The water has boiled and tea is available."

"No, thank you."

Lilly said, "The enchanter even has some sugar for it." Her voice held a hint of mirth.

"Flank Hawk still asleep?" asked Bray. "The grand wizard will want to know if he can ride his wyvern or at least travel aboard Flint Spitter."

"He heals faster than anybody here," Lilly said.

Lilly was right. Even without spellcraft, my wounds healed faster than those of other soldiers. While I could only stop bleeding in others, I'd had some success in the past healing my injuries. But I didn't yet have the strength to try.

I lifted my right leg an inch off the ground and immediately set it back down, struggling not to cry out as a burst of intense pain erupted throughout my hip and leg. I bit down on my lip and tried to focus on the conversation as a distraction.

"You look recovered," Bray said.

In a matter-of-fact tone, Enchanter Jonas said, "The wounds were neither silver nor flame inflicted."

"When my form changes," Lilly added quickly," it fixes most things."

Jonas asked the serpent cavalryman, "Might I ask what Grand Wizard Seelain discussed with you?"

"Just my opinion," Bray replied.

"About?"

Bray hesitated a moment before answering. "Private Zunnert's tactical judgment. Same as she asked you earlier." A few seconds of silence passed before he continued. "After his failure with the sirens, she believes he felt the need to prove himself."

"Prove himself to who?" Lilly asked.

Enchanter Jonas answered, "Himself. Us."

Bray asked, "How did the wolves get the drop on you?"

Lilly paused before answering. "They masked their scent, I think." She seemed deep in thought. "My recollection isn't exact. It's kinda like a dream, or experiencing it through a window with only a voice to influence my other…"

They sat around the fire, again quiet.

"Rutting scent," Lilly finally said. "Some sorta wild cattle. It fooled my muskrat form enough that they got closer than they should've. I made it to the pond and dove for safety. A hot water spring must feed it. And its bottom is deep down. There's bones, along the side. I felt them—a lot of them.

"Then I felt movement through the water." Her voice became more intense. "There's a huge snapping turtle in there. Almost got me in its jaws. Made the dire wolves look like pups.

"It was face them or it." Lilly's voice rose in excitement, as if she were reliving the moment. "The wolves cut me off from camp—from the fire. So I ran to the highest place I could find."

There was silence around the campfire again.

"She should trust Flank Hawk, or you, more than him," Lilly said. "He's only a private. Flank Hawk's seen more fighting than him."

"Maybe. Maybe not," said Bray with little inflection. "An infiltration soldier has to have stood out for not only skill in combat but also tactical sense. Most were at least sergeants before becoming one of the king's elite. Undergoing advanced training—more than I believe I could endure. When they join the ranks of the infiltration elite, they start again at the bottom, as a private.

"The war against the Necromancer King has decimated their numbers. They're called upon to go where no one else could hope to survive. We're lucky to have him. Not only for his combat skills and knowledge, but for his survival skills."

"Not so lucky for Flank Hawk," said Lilly. "He should've let Grand Wizard Seelain send you on your dragon."

"Maybe, Lilly. Hindsight."

"You know I'm right."

"He didn't hesitate to risk his life for you, Lilly. After the wolves retreated he stood over you alone until I was able to return with Enchanter Jonas and a makeshift stretcher."

"Private Zunnert's plan wasn't flawed," Enchanter Jonas said, his voice trailing off. After a deep breath, he continued. "Private Zunnert called for help, but my inept handing of the wyverns delayed the captain's response. The mounts were panicking at the dire wolves' approach and I was unable to calm them. Flank Hawk's mount knocked me to the ground, to near unconsciousness. The grand wizard had to turn her back on the approaching wolves to assist. If she had not, one or more of the wyverns may have injured themselves struggling against their tethering lines.

"The blame should fall upon me for the delay, Lilly. For your peril and suffering, and for Flank Hawk's injuries."

"The grand wizard and Private Zunnert return," announced Captain Bray. "It's back to our duties."

"You shoulda tried some tea," Lilly said.

"Next time."

"Captain," said Grand Wizard Seelain, approaching, "you and I will take the mounts to feed on the slain wolves before the scavengers clean their bones. Private Zunnert and Enchanter Jonas, replenish our firewood supply. How much will depend on Flank Hawk's condition, but we will need some to keep a fire going even for a short time, until we can depart. Lilly, awaken and check on our mercenary friend."

A moment later Lilly began untying the tent flaps. "I know you're awake, Flank Hawk. Your breathing changed a while back—and I heard you grunt. Betcha tried to move your leg."

I propped myself up on my elbows to face Lilly as she flipped back the tent flaps and smiled. "How is it?" she asked.

I kept the weight on my left hip. "Not good," I said through clenched teeth and lay back down. It also hurt to move my mouth, but not too much if I was careful how I spoke.

Lilly crawled in the tent and sat hunched over next to me. "Can't walk, can ya?"

I shook my head. The heat of battle enables a man to do things injured that they couldn't attempt even ten minutes afterwards. I was lucky to have stood and fought after that wolf had gotten a hold of me. "In a couple hours I should be able to attempt a spell. I'll be able to ride." I spoke slowly and didn't say all of the words clearly as some of them hurt my stitched cheek to say. But Lilly seemed to understand me well enough.

"Zunnert said one of the wolves got a hold of your leg and shook you around like hell."

I nodded.

"Your boot's scarred up, but your armor and it saved your skin." She placed a hand over my leg, prepared to touch it, then had second thoughts. "Where's it hurt?"

"Knee and hip. I'll be able to ride. Maybe."

"Maybe like a bedroll slung over that dragon's back."

"Won't that be fun."

"Hey," said Lilly, "you'll get to listen to Bray recite the duties of an aft-guard every five minutes."

"You know what any soldier would give to fly aft-guard?"

"I know," said Lilly with a frown.

"Sorry," I said to Lilly. "Serpent cavalrymen take the honor of their duty very seriously."

"I know Road Toa—Major Jadd," she said. "So I know."

"That's why I said I'm sorry."

"Last night. Thanks for coming to save me."

"You'd have done the same for me—you have."

Lilly smiled. "The proper words are, 'You're welcome.'"

We both started to laugh, but I winced as the pain shooting through my hip cut my laughter short.

Although thankful, I was surprised my spell strength had been enough to sustain Lilly until her beast retreated. I buried the thought.

"Grand Wizard Seelain," said Lilly. "She's hiding it, but something's bothering her. She's worried about you. The enchanter said she sat next to you half the night, but it's more than that."

I thought a moment. Lilly knew I was thinking, so she didn't say anything. I'd spent a lot of time around the grand wizard, as her personal guard and scouting companion. A lot depended on this mission's success. We all knew it.

"She's a powerful wizard, and soon to be royalty," I finally said. "The night before the sirens almost cost Zunnert his life. Last night was another command decision. And it almost ended in the death of half her team."

Lilly nodded. "It was my fault. Having to go out there."

"Your fault, the grand wizard's fault, Zunnert's fault, Jonas's fault. We all have to live with our choices and consequences, even when there wasn't a good one to make." It was getting harder to ignore the pain as I talked. Lilly saw it too, but I wanted to end on a good note.

"That turtle you talked about, in the pond. Must've been like the one Roos told that story about, fishing with his sisters when they were kids. Remember?"

That made Lilly smile.

"When this is over," I said, "I'd like to go back to the Reunited Kingdom and visit his sisters."

Lilly frowned and turned away.

"You'd come too," I said.

"She has a cancer," Lilly blurted out. Tears formed in her eyes. "Sister Ruth asked me not to tell you—at least not right away."

I thought back, how frail and old she looked. So much older than her brother. It put a lump in my throat, too. A minor hope I'd harbored, once the war was won, gone.

"Because of their faith, they can't even call upon a healer," I said bitterly. "It would've saved her life."

"It'd take a powerful one to fix a cancer," said Lilly.

"She's important enough," I said. Then I pondered a moment.

Lilly must have read my thoughts. "We're fighting against the goddess of the healers. They're our enemies, now. Or most of them."

Lilly wiped the tears from her eyes. "You say you can try a healing spell on your leg in a little while?"

I nodded.

"I'll tell Grand Wizard Seelain that." She began to back out of the tent. "Hey, didn't you notice how clean your armor is?"

I'd noticed, but it only dawned me then. There weren't any bite wounds except on my face. They wouldn't have risked removing my armor if they suspected how hurt my leg was—not at least until they knew better. And my armor was dry, not damp from washing, even if it was oiled and waxed.

She smiled. "Thank Enchanter Jonas when you get the chance, but maybe not around Zunnert."

I knew Lilly wanted me to ask why, so I did.

"Because," she said, "Zunnert was giving the enchanter a hard time about how domestic he was."

I held my face, trying not to smile, imaging the elite soldier ribbing our enchanter after a life and death battle. For Zunnert, that meant he accepted the enchanter as part of the team, even after all that happened. Things were going to work out between everyone.

Somehow Lilly knew just what to say to put me at ease.

Lilly was right. I flew on the back of Flint Spitter like a bedroll while Wick flew secured by a line to Grand Wizard Seelain's mount. Even that position put pressure on my hip and knee, but less than any other way, including being carried, clutched in the dragon's powerful talons.

It hurt a lot. I couldn't even grit my teeth because that sparked pain in my wounded cheek. But even a day's delay meant one more day the forces of Fendra Jolain advanced on Keesee and her allies.

We set up camp near Iceland's western shore. I worked a healing spell on myself, more easily than I expected, and I fell asleep as soon as they'd pitched my tent, despite the throbbing pain.

We rested the whole day, preparing for an estimated twenty-four hour oversea flight to a land once called Greenland. It was supposed to be ice-filled and desolate. I wasn't ready, even after another effort at self-healing. Fortunately, Private Zunnert had found a root he said was far more potent than willow. He boiled it to release a pain-numbing medicine. Then he wrapped my leg and hip with cloths soaked in the medicated water and promised it'd last for six hours. After that I'd have to endure.

True to his word, shortly after the sun reached its peak height the pain returned, but there hadn't been another choice. We had to proceed, and my mount had to bear me, as neither Lilly, nor Enchanter Jonas had either the training or skill to guide a Wyvern on such a long flight.

I told Grand Wizard Seelain I would endure. And I did. Shortly before sunrise the next day, they pulled me down from Wick. I was closing on the point where my thoughts began to cloud and contemplated falling to the icy-cold waters below as a reasonable option to escape the relentless pain. Even Zunnert's boiled root remedy didn't fully deaden the pain, but enough for me to complete a spell and drop to sleep, wrapped in blankets against Greenland's bitter cold.

I rode as before aboard Flint Spitter during two half-day flights south along Greenland's coast. This allowed me to heal while enabling our mounts to regain their strength. I was more than glad to ride aboard the dragon; the previous twenty-four hour flight had sapped from me all reserves of strength.

CHAPTER 20

Crossing the ocean expanse to reach the northern reaches of the Western Continent, and the subsequent flight south to reach the Colonel of the West's Outpost 4 was cold but uneventful. We encountered large deer striped black and gray, with males that retained their forked antlers through the spring. Private Zunnert spotted prints and other signs of large bears. None, however, approached our camps.

My face had nearly healed. The stitches were out and the scar fading. My knee and hip ached a little but not enough it stop me from standing my full guard duty. That was good since the place we'd landed to camp gave me an uncomfortable feeling. Lilly and Jonas were uneasy too.

As had become our habit, we camped far enough from shore to build a campfire that'd go unnoticed by water-bound creatures that might serve Uplersh. But in doing so this evening, we were several stone throws from the small line of unnatural hillocks that resembled barrow mounds.

Jonas came to stand next to me as I eyed them and the larger ones beyond. "They trouble you too?" he asked.

"I've seen their like before, south of here," I said. "They're remnants of the First Civilization. Or so I was told."

The sun was setting in the west, falling behind the more distant large hillocks covered in stunted trees and shrubs.

"We stand where once stood the greatest of cities," said Jonas. "Or so the ancient texts say. A city called New York. Held tenfold more people than all of Keesee." He picked up a stone and tossed it into a small ground pine, causing a nesting bird to squawk. "Maybe more."

"That many?" I asked.

"You've been in the skyscraper that is Outpost Four," he said. "Those larger mounds are the crumbled ruins of such that dwarfed what you've seen. I suspect lamenting souls maintained them for a time, or the mounds of rubble that marks their demise would have been worn down by time further than they are."

Lamenting souls, I thought. Creatures of balled light. Spirits of those that had ages ago inhabited the ancient cities.

One had once tried to possess me in a bid to take the Blood Sword. They entered the bodies of troglodytes, used their physical bodies to work stone, and magic I guessed, to keep the ancient structures looking new as the day they were built. After dark I wondered if we'd see any of the blue-white spheres in the distance, flitting like fireflies. Better them than barrow wights.

"Scout Lilly and Private Zunnert have plucked the waterfowl they shot and are busy cooking them. Take your meal and rest."

"You and Captain Bray have first watch?"

Jonas nodded. "We shall awaken you before midnight."

I lifted my spear and rested it on my shoulder. "Enjoy your watch."

"Tomorrow," he said as I turned. "It holds many possibilities."

I thought about the fallen angel, the Warden of Outpost 4. I couldn't think of one reason he'd favor my presence any better than the first time—which had nearly cost me, Lilly and Roos our lives.

"Possibilities," I said. The prospect of facing a horde of barrow wights somehow didn't seem so bad.

We broke camp before sunrise. At a quick meeting, Grand Wizard Seelain announced that since I'd been to Outpost 4 before and successfully negotiated an audience with the Colonel of the West I'd speak for the king. Grand Wizard Seelain said she'd be right there to support and advise. The trust she placed in me gave me resolve. It also caused my stomach to churn, thinking the entire morning about confronting Tyegerial, a fallen angel, the Warden of Outpost 4.

Wizard Seelain was powerful, but not as powerful as Belinda the Cursed. I didn't think the Warden considered Belinda the Cursed his equal, but she did. Probably was. And what was I? A simple mercenary. A bodyguard. A neophyte healer.

Before we'd mounted our serpents, Lilly slapped me on the back. "That gray angel," she said, "you got the better of him last time. He won't dare bar us from seeing that Colonel, his master this time either."

Lilly could tell when I was worried and I got the point. The Warden wouldn't want to cross the Colonel. On the scale of things, if I had to wager, the Colonel of the West could face Tyegerial, Belinda the Cursed, and Grand Wizard Seelain all at once without fear of defeat.

What if he didn't want to return the Blood Sword to us? I thought about that as well during our flight. Patting Wick on the neck, I urged him on. "One problem at a time," I told my faithful mount. "One problem at a time."

Just after the sun reached its peak Captain Bray spotted a plume of thick smoke rising in the distance along the coast. After signaling, we dropped lower, to about 100 feet above the tallest oaks and swung west until we were an additional mile inland. The maneuver gave Lilly, Captain Bray's rear-facing aft-guard, a chance to turn and see the smoke.

The smoke looked like what comes from a damp thatch roof on fire, fed from a hot wood-fire below. Only this was a lot bigger, with the ocean breeze carrying it inland. It reminded me of the fires in the King's City.

The rising smoke remained steady and we angled back toward the coast as we neared it.

Coming within a quarter of a mile, I could see that flames rose from the ground not far behind the skyscraper that was Outpost 4. The magnificent building stood fifty yards from the ocean.

Bray had Lilly's spyglass. "An attack," he shouted. "But it appears to be over."

He led us closer to the Colonel's outpost. Whereas before the skyscraper's smooth walls of red and gray stone had been untarnished by weather or age, some corners and sections had broken off onto the courtyard below. Many of the reflective, blue-tinted windows were cracked or shattered. I saw what Bray had seen through the spyglass. The outpost had weathered a recent attack.

We circled around. The ground between the skyscraper and ocean appeared wet. The dock's sturdy wood backed by granite had crumbled in places, like a giant shovel had dug into it. Behind the skyscraper, on a lower flat roof platform rested a black metallic craft with glass ports. It looked like a cross between a bug and the head of an eagle. The machine bore a propeller like those I'd seen drive the Necromancer King's Stukas through the air, but this one's two thin blades sat atop. It had stubby wings, like a plucked chicken's held close. A second, smaller propeller was mounted along the end of its tail.

Whereas the Necromancer King had summoned back damned souls to engineer and build war machines from before First Civilization's fall, the Colonel of the West had somehow taken control of war machines during or just after First Civilization's fall and maintained them over the centuries. Or that's how it appeared to me.

Recalling the time when I witnessed the Colonel's men refuel one of his flying machines, I shouted, "The fire comes from underground fuel used to feed that flying machine!"

Several soldiers dressed in mottled green uniforms stood near the flying machine, observing the smoke and flames rising from the ground behind the outpost. They were men who served the Colonel of the West. Standing behind and towering over them by at least two feet were a dozen gray-skinned troglodytes holding pickaxes and shovels. The brutes wore little more than tattered breeches and appeared like a cross between a bald man and a hairless ape, standing slouched but upright with long, muscular arms and powerful hands.

First, one of the soldiers pointed up at us. Then all looked our way.

Bray pulled a streamer cloth, bearing purple and gold, the colors of Keesee. Upon seeing it the shortest soldier stepped away from the group and waved.

"We shall land," Grand Wizard Seelain shouted to Private Zunnert, "on the seaside of the outpost tower. Away from the smoke and flame."

"Is that wise?" Bray shouted back.

I looked toward the ocean. The wind drove waves against the damaged dock. The water wasn't clear enough to see into its depths despite the sun. A sea serpent could be lurking not ten feet below the surface.

I pointed. "Inland further!"

"We will be safe inside the tower," Seelain said. "We cannot approach through the smoke and flame.

"I may be able to smother the flame," she added.

Whatever had attacked—storm, magic, or beast—the outpost had weathered the assault.

Zunnert shouted, "Flank Hawk and I will land first."

Bray warned, "The longer we stay aloft the more we risk notice by the sea goddess or her minions."

"Then we'll be quick," said Zunnert, diving. I followed.

We landed midway between the outpost and the dock. The stone walkways were dry, but the grass and plants looked unhealthy and the soil was very damp, smelling of ocean water. From what I could see of the area between the dock and building, grooves and divots had been dug into the turf, flowering plants partially uprooted, crushed, or knocked to the side. About fifteen yards to my right as I faced the building, a dark area on the grass caught my attention. It looked like an ink spot on parchment. There was a second spot of darkened grass about twenty feet beyond the first. Both were roughly a man's height in diameter.

I held Wick's reins and Zunnert handed me the reins to his wyvern mount. "Keep watch. I'll speak with those inside," he said and sprinted up the main walkway toward the courtyard and double-door entrance.

I held the reins and attempted to walk toward the dark spots, but both Wick and Coils dug in and held their ground. I couldn't blame them. Something felt wrong, sour mixed with dread. A dread that reminded me of the bone golem's hellcry.

I looked up. Wizard Seelain was already descending in a tight spiral. Nothing appeared on the ocean surface, and Zunnert had only reached the courtyard. Flint Spitter swooped down more swiftly and landed about twenty yards away, between the building and the dark areas. Lilly climbed down first, followed by Jonas.

Lilly ran toward me. She stopped, eyes darting toward the dark areas, and stepped wide around them. "Captain Bray told me to hold your mounts so you could go inside with Private Zunnert. He'll watch over the grand wizard."

I guessed it wasn't his idea to land. Grand Wizard Seelain came down on the far side of Flint Spitter, nearer the outpost. I handed the reins to Lilly. "In a minute," I said. The sick feeling rising from the ground concerned me. "Enchanter!" I pointed. "What do you make of those?"

I fought an urge to back away and instead stepped toward them, spear held ready. The feeling of dread didn't increase much as I examined the nearest dark splotch. The grass was withered, and sooty gray. Not burned. Not coated with ash. Just discolored. Several damp feathers lay between the spots, nearer to Flint Spitter. They looked like seagull feathers, but broader and gray. Even as Enchanter Jonas bent to pick one up, I recognized them.

"Wick! Coils!" Lilly shouted. The mounts *cawed* and *squawked*, tugging at their reins. They'd shifted to black, their color of fear. Lilly kept her footing and held them tight. Wizard Seelain had tethered Moon Ash, and her wyvern cried out, biting at the leather cord wrapped with steel wiring.

The smell of ash and burnt sulfur rose from the spots. "It's the black grass," I shouted.

"No!" yelled Jonas, pointing toward the ocean just as Zunnert called from the wrecked courtyard, "Get to high ground!"

I spun around to see that it was already too late. A wall of water crashed over the dock. I took several steps toward my charge, but Grand Wizard Seelain was already summoning some sort of spell. I'd never make it to her in time and what I'd do if I made it, I had no idea. I ran and locked arms with Lilly, braced, and dug my spear tip into the ground. Jonas muttered some spell and grasped Lilly's other hand. The wave wasn't high but the solid swell washed over the dock and toward us.

There was no time to see if Wick made it aloft. Only enough time to hear Lilly shout, "What's that?" before the four-foot wall of water slammed into us and knocked me off my feet. I went under, holding my breath and realized that there was something following the wave in. I only caught a glimpse—a turquoise shell and crimson tentacles. Huge, rising from the water!

The wash separated us and the raging flow tossed and tumbled me beneath it, but I managed to keep hold of my spear and climb to my feet. I got my bearings as the wave that had crashed upon the skyscraper's base fell back. My boots and spear butt held fast as the knee-deep water rushed past to drain back into the ocean.

My attention fell on the titanic sea beast that held Flint Spitter in one of its massive claws. The monster appeared to be a cross between a lobster and a squid with its four flailing tentacles. Gouts of roaring dragon fire fell upon the shell-hardened monster to no effect as it crushed the serpent like a gauntleted man would a thrashing snake.

The monster had hauled itself only partially onto the dock, crumbling stone under its weight. Two whip-thin tentacles lashed about above its yellow-beaked maw. A second stout set of crimson tentacles sprouted like roots on its back behind the claws. It used one of them to grasp the broken dragon to feed upon.

The sea beast had to be the Kraken, Uplersh's greatest minion—or close brethren. Our only hope was to retreat inland. I turned to see Seelain had raised a whirlwind elemental to battle an unseen water wizard. An eight-foot cohesive mass of ocean water thrashed against the whirlwind, trying to get past. Between me and Seelain stood seven manlike creatures with dark scales the color of a sea bass, bulbous eyes and wide mouths filled with pointed teeth. A row of recurved spines ran down their backs and across their forearms, from wrist to elbow, and shell-like plates covered their torsos. They carried black, barbed spears and hook-filled nets like mermen.

Zunnert and Jonas moved to stand between them and Seelain. Her elemental spirit was stronger than the water spirit but, even if Zunnert and Jonas fended off the fishman warriors, she'd be next when the Kraken finished devouring the broken dragon.

"Flank Hawk," shouted Lilly. "Behind you!"

I pivoted, trying to keep my footing. I hadn't thought to look to my own safety as a hurled fishman's spear *thunked* against my breastplate, knocking me back a step. Over a dozen more must've come ashore in the wave that'd taken me under. They came at me with nets, knives and spears while a couple harassed Wick, backed with broken wing against the skyscraper, viciously snapping in defense.

Like a sword-wielding whirlwind, Zunnert charged among the seven fishmen off to my right. Jonas with rapier followed him into battle. They had to hold—give Seelain a chance. I'd slow and take as many of the fishman warriors charging me as possible before they could fall upon Seelain. If Zunnert and Jonas survived, they might slow those that got past me. There were just too many.

"Flee the Kraken, Seelain!" I shouted, parrying a spear thrust and dodging a flung net. Lilly leapt upon the back of one, slashing its throat with her dagger, but fell away screaming in pain from what had to be venom-filled spines.

I drove my spear into one's groin before a black spear shaft slammed down on my helmet, knocking me to my knees.

Then the sound of gunshots rang out, sharp and quick, dropping three of my foes just before club and pick-axe wielding troglodytes crashed among the fishmen with bellowing howls. It was a brief, fierce melee, but the trog's hammering strength and numbers overwhelmed our foe.

Even before it was over, I broke from the fight and raced the direction Seelain had been. A thundering *whump-whump-whumping* noise from the sky drowned out the sounds of battle. The Colonel of the West's flying machine swung around the skyscraper with fiery rockets lancing down from its stubby wings at the Kraken. They exploded across the monster's back. From the flying machine's chin a machine gun sounded, sending bullets into the Kraken's face and shell.

The beast reared back and, with its tentacles, hurled globs of sand and stone at the flying machine. The rocks and sand struck the machine, covering the glass and colliding with the fast-spinning propeller, damaging it—causing it to warp. Within seconds the flying machine began shuddering out of control as the spinning blade flew apart.

I didn't bother to watch it drop from the sky. I charged and drove my spear into the spine of the largest of two surviving fishman warriors driving Jonas back, his flashing rapier no match in parrying their heavier, barbed spears.

Grand Wizard Seelain was still standing, but backing away from the wounded Kraken. Although the flying machine was down, it had taken a toll on the titanic monster. At least a hundred holes seeping viscous blood showed where the machine gun had bitten, including one of the beasts two shield-sized eyes. From my angle I couldn't see what the lancing flames had done.

The hissing Kraken slammed one of its flailing tentacles down where I'd fought, crushing several troglodytes.

My attack from the rear slew the fishman and distracted the remaining one, allowing Jonas a quick rapier thrust into scaled warrior's bulbous eye. The enchanter withdrew a step, ducking a wild spear slash attack. I took advantage of our foe's unbalanced attack, whipping the butt end of my spear's shaft into his legs. He dropped stunned but wasn't finished.

"Flee, Seelain!" I shouted again. I didn't see Zunnert and with the Kraken still on the attack there wasn't time to look for Lilly. I figured Bray dead along with his serpent mount.

Before the fishman recovered, Jonas drove his rapier's tip through the warrior's remaining eye and into its brain. "Come on," I said to Jonas and raced across the spongy grass toward the grand wizard, watching the Kraken as it lifted its massive crimson tentacle for another strike.

More gunshots sounded from soldiers who served the Colonel of the West. Three green-clad ones with domed helmets and rifles stood near the skyscraper, taking aim and firing at the Kraken. They had to work a bolt lever between shots, but their gunshots got the monster's attention. Two other soldiers, one carrying a long tube that looked like a mini-cannon, moved toward us and knelt. The other shoved a long bullet with fins like an arrow's fletching into the tube.

"Its eye!" Wizard Seelain said, raising her staff to begin a spell. Enchanter Jonas whipped off his cloak and began a spell of his own. There was little for me to do but distract the beast, draw its attention away from the grand wizard. I picked up a fallen fishman's barbed spear and hurled it at the Kraken. "Here!" I yelled, waving my boar spear. "Here!"

It ignored me and crawled further onto the dock to get within reach of the riflemen. I backed away as the enchanter's cloak flew through the air toward the Kraken. It got past the whipping tentacles and landed flat over the monster's remaining eye.

At the same time the mini-cannon fired, its shell exploding against the Kraken's beaked mouth. Wizard Seelain's spell collapsed the air in front of the cloak-covered eye. Rifle fire continued as the Kraken raised its claws to protect its face.

"Reload," said the soldier with the mini-cannon resting on his shoulder. The second shoved another long bullet into the back of the cannon and tapped his partner on the helmet.

Even as the Kraken backed into the ocean, the soldier's mini-cannon shell exploded against one of the Kraken's massive claws, blowing a chunk of hardened shell from it.

The surviving trogs let out a deep cheer as the crimson and turquoise sea beast quickly disappeared beneath the ocean waves.

I couldn't believe it—we'd driven the Kraken off. I didn't do much, I realized. But I'd survived. "Grand Wizard," I shouted. "Are you okay?" She waved back. She was safe, and I'd survived. Jonas too. Then I spun about, searching for Lilly and for Zunnert.

I spotted Lilly, unsteady but on her feet, wading toward me through the troglodytes that'd been crushed by the Kraken's crimson tentacle.

Surviving trogs looked to their wounded kin. I ran past them to Lilly. "Are you okay?"

She nodded but didn't look so good. A line of red welts the size of acorns ran down her chin and neck, and along her left forearm, which she held away from her body. Blood seeped from each welt. "No, you're not okay."

She sank to the wet ground with tears running down her face. "Maybe I'm not," she said. "At first it hurt, but now my arm is losing feeling. My face too."

Her speech was slurred and the wounded side of her face hung slack.

Poison, I thought. From the fishman spines. Zunnert knew about poisons. He'd know what to do—if he was still alive.

Wizard Seelain, came up to where I knelt next to my friend. "Oh, Lilly," she said and knelt beside me.

"Poison," I said. "From them." I pointed to one of the dead fishman warriors. "Their spines. Where's Zunnert?" I flashed a glance toward the water, just in case the Kraken or more fishmen renewed their attack. An old troglodyte closer to the water leaning on a crooked staff watched seaward.

Wizard Seelain said, "I do not know."

One of the troglodytes a few feet away, arms twisted and chest crushed, opened its eyes, and then its mouth. Light emanated from its throat. I'd seen that once before, when a glowing lamenting soul had entered a troglodyte leader, healing it.

"Stay with Lilly," I said to Seelain. "I've got to find Zunnert."

The grand wizard spread her riding cloak on the ground and helped Lilly to lie upon it. "With haste," she said.

I spotted Jonas and ran toward him. He was kneeling, leaning close over Private Zunnert, who lay fallen. A barbed spear had been driven deep into his chest and welts like Lilly's lined his face and throat. Jonas had tied a tourniquet above Zunnert's knee to stem bleeding from a wound that had nearly severed our comrade's leg. Blood frothed from the infiltration soldier's mouth as he spoke weakly into the enchanter's ear.

I tried to remember what Major Jadd had told me about goblin spears and arrows that were sometimes barbed. We'd have to break the shaft and then push it all the way through. Zunnert'd never survive it. His wound was mortal, through the lung, near the heart. The barbs, even angled to push through without snagging, would tear more flesh. Arteries near the heart. Then there was Lilly—dying too.

I got up and ran to the nearest trog, helping one harboring a lamenting soul, one healing. "Lamenting souls," I said. "Can you do this for my friends—heal them?"

The healthy trog stared at me with a questioning look. The healing one spoke in a deep voice, with sparks of light rising from the depths of his throat. "We know you, Mercenary. I cannot do as you ask. We cannot."

One of the rifle soldiers was next to Grand Wizard Seelain, bending over Lilly with something he'd pulled from a satchel.

There wasn't time to argue. "Hold on, Zunnert," I said. "I'll be right back."

"He's already gone," said Jonas.

The enchanter was right. Zunnert's pierced chest no longer rose. His heart stopped, the bleeding slowed to a trickle. I couldn't do anything for him, but maybe I could for Lilly. I ran back to her.

She lay still, but her eyes were wide and wild—frightened. Wizard Seelain ran her fingers gently through Lilly's hair. "All will be well," she told Lilly as the soldier slid a needle attached to a tube into Lilly's good arm, into a blood vessel.

His thumb depressed a plunger. "Broad spectrum antivenom."

"Will it work?" I asked.

"We'll know in the next ten minutes," the soldier said. He grabbed his satchel. "I must move on."

Wizard Seelain said, "You have our thanks, Corpsman."

CHAPTER 21

The size of the troglodyte's shovel made it difficult to dig. Enchanter Jonas had helped dig some of the grave but it appeared to be the first time he'd handled a shovel. While we worked Grand Wizard Seelain and Lilly prepared Private Zunnert's body for burial.

Captain Bray sat leaning up against the trunk of an unusual sort of hickory tree with bark that appeared to be peeling off. Bray's right leg lay outstretched and splinted. He'd leapt from Flint Spitter after the Kraken's claw had crushed the life out of his mount. I'd helped the corpsman, holding Bray as the soldier pulled the serpent cavalryman's leg to realign and set the snapped bone that had nearly broken through the skin in his calf. Bray endured the grueling process, sweating and biting on a thick leather strap. We'd then had to pop his dislocated shoulder back into place, but that was nothing compared to the leg.

Even more amazing was that somehow Captain Bray had managed to fend off a fishman with his battle axe until a troglodyte took it from behind.

About thirty of the gray trogs were caring for their own dead close to where Grand Wizard Seelain had extinguished the fuel fire by taking away the air it fed upon. Instead of burying their dead, they laid each of their fallen on a pallet of split logs and then covered the fallen under heavy stones before covering all with dirt. They did this now next to recently built burial mounds.

I asked Enchanter Jones, "What did Private Zunnert tell you before he died?"

"To tell his wife he loved her. To see that his sword is placed in his son's hand, and his hunting knife in his daughter's."

I thought of the hours on watch Zunnert shared with me, sometimes talking, and all the meals and campfires. "I never knew he had a family."

"Neither did I," said Jonas.

"His wife left him," Captain Bray said. He struggled to keep his voice even as he spoke. He'd insisted on being present for Private Zunnert's burial. The pain-numbing herbs helped some but not nearly enough. "She threatened to leave him when he volunteered for the King's Infiltration Force. When he passed the training, something that most volunteers fail to do." He took a breath. "His wife took his children and moved back south to her family."

The future of our mission was in peril, but we had to get this duty past us before we looked forward. Talking helped me some. "Why would she do that?" I asked, climbing into the hole and continuing to dig. King Tobias housed and saw to the needs of the families of all the elite soldiers serving him. They were known to be a solid community living in apartments just north of the palace.

After a moment Bray answered. "Zunnert believed serving as an infiltration soldier was the best way to ensure his family's safety. She thought joining would get him killed."

I shook my head and cut a root with the shovel's blade before lifting another shovel full of dirt out of the hole. My mother thought the same thing about my service as a mercenary. "They were both right," I said.

Lilly carried the front of a stretcher bearing Private Zunnert's body. A green-clad soldier, one of the bazooka men, carried the rear end.

They'd washed Zunnert clean of dirt and blood, and folded his hands over his chest. They'd mended the armor over his chest wound but couldn't disguise where he'd been struck by the poison spines.

The antivenom had worked on Lilly and the injured trogs as well. The welts across her face and neck had shrunk to a third of their original size. The other bazooka man followed them carrying five broken barbed spears bundled in a fishman warrior's net.

They set Zunnert's body next to the open grave in the shadow of the oddly barked hickory tree. Captain Bray gritted his teeth and grunted as Jonas and I lifted him to his feet and helped him to stand around the grave with Lilly, Grand Wizard Seelain and the two soldiers.

As Grand Wizard Seelain watched us, I could see her holding back tears. Bray was leaning heavily on me and in no shape to speak. I doubted I could've withstood with the pain he must've felt.

Wizard Seelain took a deep, stuttering breath but, before she could begin, I said, "I'd like to say a few words," while trying to imagine what Major Jadd would say under these circumstances.

When Wizard Seelain nodded, I continued. "Private Zunnert, his bravery cannot be questioned. He stepped forward to serve King Tobias, defend the Kingdom of Keesee, and ensure the safety of his family. One day his son and daughter will know how and why he died facing the Kraken and other minions of the sea goddess, enemies of Keesee all."

I took a deep breath because the next words were going to be hard to speak. "He stood in my place, between Grand Wizard Seelain and the enemy. Faced impossible odds.

"But that is not to say we let him down. We all fought."

I made eye contact with everyone around the circle around the open grave as I named them. "Lesser Enchanter Jonas fought at Private Zunnert's side before directly confronting the Kraken. Captain Bray could have fled upon his serpent steed, but instead took the fight to the enemy. Grand Wizard Seelain battled an enemy wizard under the Kraken's long shadow, and

Lilly threw herself upon the enemy without concern for her safety.

"Our allies came to our aid, entered the fray and turned the tide. They fought like us, to the best of their skill and ability. And like Private Randall Zunnert, some of our allies fell. But we prevailed.

"His and their sacrifice will allow our mission to continue. Give us a chance to reach ultimate victory over those who threaten our king, Keesee, and Private Zunnert's wife and children."

I breathed deeply, taking in the scent of ocean and lingering sooty air. It reminded me of a few words Major Jadd had said over a long trench grave of fallen soldiers. It seemed right for this moment as well. "May our comrade in arms, our friend, rest in peace, knowing that we will carry on so that his honor, duty and sacrifice shall constitute a piece in the mosaic of our ultimate victory."

A short way off the troglodytes were finishing their burial rites. They'd gathered in a circle around the mounds, holding tools extended between them. Shovels, pickaxes, rakes, sledge hammers, from hand to hand while they hummed, so deeply that the notes rippled across my skin.

Enchanter Jonas knelt close to Private Zunnert and said just above a whisper, "I shall see to it your sword and knife are placed in the hands of your offspring, with the knowledge of how and why you fell."

Then Wizard Seelain knelt and said, "Your family shall be cared for and never lack shelter, or suffer hunger or want."

Lilly knelt and said, "Thank you for showing me how to fight better. And for saving me from the wolves."

The two soldiers helped me lower Zunnert into his grave and then assisted Captain Bray back to the skyscraper. Enchanter Jonas accompanied Grand Wizard Seelain. Lilly dropped the broken spears and net into the grave at Private Zunnert's feet before grabbing the shovel, ready to help me finish the job.

"Guard Grand Wizard Seelain for me," I said, "while I finish this."

CHAPTER 22

The skyscraper's entryway opened into the well-lit lobby, just the way I remembered it. Globes that didn't contain flame showered the polished stone floor and walls in white light. Recessed rays lit the long, arched ceiling. Triangular patterns of brown, white, and gold formed large squares on the marble floor. It appeared more for decoration than a pattern with magical intent. My boots clapped as I walked, the sound echoing lightly even as the troglodyte's flat bare feet slapped on the polished floor.

We walked down several hallways to a formed stone stairwell leading up several floors. The trog knocked twice on a metal door painted white with a steel handle. One of the rifle soldiers opened it, exchanged a few words in a tongue I didn't understand, and then let us pass. Down the narrow hall lined with doors, and whose floor was covered by a sturdy tapestry, stood Lilly. Her alertness showed she was guarding the room to where Grand Wizard Seelain had summoned me.

I'd been on my way to check on Wick and see if Coils had returned. Private Zunnert's mount managed to get airborne when the Kraken appeared. Moon Ash, tethered, never stood a chance. Wick suffered a broken wing when the wave struck, but had fended off the enemy's spears. I rubbed my hands together. There hadn't even been time to clean up after digging, but the grand wizard had seen me covered in worse than sweat and dirt.

Belinda the Cursed told me Outpost 4 in ages past had welcomed visitors from across the world. They'd met and dined here, plotted and schemed here, maybe even forged their ultimate destruction here. I guessed it wouldn't be long before the fate of Keesee might be decided within this building.

The troglodyte stopped halfway to the door where Lilly stood while I continued on. "Lilly," I said. "The grand wizard wishes to speak with me?"

Lilly nodded and knocked on the door before opening it. "Flank Hawk is here, Grand Wizard."

From deep inside the room I heard Grand Wizard Seelain say, "He may enter."

I stepped past Lilly and through the wooden door bearing a bronze three letter inscription just below eye-level. They were part of some sort of series, as most of the doors had them, probably numbers.

Upon entering, there was a small room on the left with tiled floor and walls. A fancy polished white wash basin, chamber pot and wash tub took up most of the space. Straight ahead was a square room with a desk and a bed. The bed was more than a cot but far less than what the palace in Keesee offered its guests. My charge sat in an armed leather chair next to the desk, wearing clean robes. Her hair was damp and her eyes retained some of the tell-tale redness of tears. Her staff rested across her legs.

She looked up to Enchanter Jonas standing next to her. "Go with our scout, and check on Wick." She handed him a wooden whistle. "Attempt once again to call back Coils. Return in thirty minutes."

Enchanter Jonas stepped around me and closed the door as he left. I stood silently, waiting for Grand Wizard Seelain to speak. She turned her head and gazed through a doorway that led to an identical adjoining room. Captain Bray lay asleep on the bed, his chest gently lifting the maroon-colored blankets.

"The corpsman gave him a medicine to help him sleep," Grand Wizard Seelain said.

The regal tone once again resonated in her voice, but to me it hung hollow. More than once I'd seen that look of defeat, of despair in an officer's eyes. Even though she was my charge, my superior, I had to risk stepping beyond my station.

"Grand Wizard, war brings horrors. It promises death."

She glared at me a second, then stood. "You do not understand, Mercenary. Leave me."

"I do understand," I said, ignoring her order and meeting her gaze. "I've watched others die in my place. Die so that I might continue. My actions, my decisions led to..." I stopped, thinking of my cousin Guzzy's death. Pops Weasel, Short Two Blades, Piyetten, Roos. Faces, memories flashed through my thoughts—soldiers and mercenaries, friends and comrades. Now buried, or burned, or eaten by beasts of the enemy. Some raised as zombies to march against me. Facing them—their lifeless eyes, silent, intent on killing me.

She must have seen the anguish and regret across my face. She stepped closer and rested a hand on my shoulder. I stood straight. At attention. "Duty calls upon me," I said. "It calls upon you."

"Duty. Is that your answer, Flank Hawk? Your wisdom?"

"It's what gets me through, Grand Wizard."

"Through what?"

"The next day. To the next battle." I shrugged. "Through the nightmares."

Wizard Seelain gestured to a chair off to the right, facing hers. "Please, sit."

I waited until she sat, and then I leaned my spear against the wall and sat.

"Which do you fear more, Flank Hawk, failure or death?"

I had a feeling it was a question she was facing, so I thought carefully before I spoke. "I fear death. I dread failure."

She stared at the floor a moment, as if counting the floor tapestry's threads. "You would sacrifice your life to save mine, out of a sense of duty?"

"Yes," I said. "And loyalty. And because your life is worth more than mine."

"Is it?"

"It is a fact, Grand Wizard. Who can bring more destruction down upon the enemy? You, an accomplished air wizard? Or me, a simple mercenary, and neophyte healer? Which of us can do more to save those I love, the king and his people I have pledged to serve and defend?"

"You brought destruction down upon the Necromancer King. Destroyed his factory city."

"I played a part, Grand Wizard. I did not do it alone. Some of them died." I met her gaze. "Like Private Zunnert did today."

"I ordered Captain Bray to land because I sensed a water wizard. I desired for us to remain hidden, but I fell into their trap. That ill-conceived action cost lives. Not only Private Zunnert's, but those defending this outpost. It cost us our mounts."

I answered, "But what did it cost the enemy?"

"Each additional day—even if our mission meets with success—equates to additional lives lost."

"And you'd bear responsibility for those deaths?" When she nodded, I said, "Then consider that even if we do retrieve the Blood Sword, it may not turn the tide. We may still lose."

She sighed. "I now begin to comprehend the weight of sorrow and regret carried by Reveron, his brother and father. Intellectually I understood, but now their words, and their silence hold meaning."

She ran her fingers over several of the shallow runes carved into her staff.

"When I am unsure what to do, Grand Wizard, I think upon what Major Jadd might do. Rely on your knowledge of Prince Reveron, and what he would do."

I saw her begin to stand and I hurried to stand as well.

She smiled. "Thank you for your counsel, my mercenary friend."

"You're welcome, Grand Wizard."

"We meet with the Colonel of the West's men within the hour." She gestured to the room where Captain Bray slept. "Go and clean the dirt and grime from battle as best you can in that time." Before I could object, she added, "I shall be on guard and safe until the scout and enchanter return."

The warm brown fungus in the wooden bowl reminded me of oatmeal. At least the consistency and texture did. The taste? It didn't taste good, or really taste bad. It had no taste. But it was filling. Our host named it *Olgresh*, and it was a staple food grown by the troglodytes in caves tunneled deep underground.

I couldn't complain. Although Captain Bray had loosed our supply bags while rising to battle the Kraken, the contents we could find were still laid out to dry. Seawater had ruined most of what little food we carried. Our host even pretended to ignore Enchanter Jonas as he cast a quick poison detection spell over Grand Wizard Seelain's *Olgresh* and water.

We sat at a long rectangular table in padded, high-backed chairs. Grand Wizard Seelain sat on one end of the table with me to her right and Enchanter Jonas to her left. Lilly stood guard near the door that led to a main hallway. A row of blue-tinted windows lined the east wall, facing the ocean. None were broken. If the Kraken returned we'd be about eye-level with the beast.

The flat feet of the female trog servants slapped on the polished wooden floor as they moved about, serving us. They wore tan sackcloth garments that hung like night robes. Their faces remained as plain and emotionless as their dress. Like the male troglodytes, they didn't have hair on their heads, but their eyebrows were longer and curved an inch or so down from the brow to just above their cheeks.

Across the table sat a big troglodyte. His eyes glowed and light emanated from his throat when he opened his mouth to eat or speak. Even a glimmer of light streamed out of his broad nostrils. Inside the troglodyte was a lamenting soul named Janice Welson. I knew her and she knew me. She'd tried to possess me—wrest the Blood Sword from me the first time I'd entered the Colonel of the West's Outpost 4.

I held no ill will for the troglodyte, but the lamenting soul inside, I neither cared for, nor trusted. But the soul inhabiting, or possessing the trog, was currently the Warden of Outpost 4.

"Thus," said Grand Wizard Seelain after taking a sip of spring water from a narrow glass, taller but identical in shape to mine and that of Enchanter Jonas, "one of your kind, while they may enter a physical creature's body, can only heal one that has been bonded with shortly after the physical creature's birth."

Lamenting souls were floating balls of light. They could expand and contract, but usually remained about two feet across. The best I could figure is that they're spirits of people, transformed and surviving from the time of First Civilization's fall. They gathered and lived in ancient structures that also survived the fall. Their magic and knowledge, coupled with troglodyte physical strength and ability, maintained the ancient the skyscraper that sometime over the centuries became Outpost 4.

Lamenting souls, Major Jadd called them wandering souls, existed elsewhere. Once at night I'd flown over the ancient city of Milan while serving as Major Jadd's aft-guard. There, I saw a high-walled castle filled with such souls, flickering and filling its windows and walkways like tiny stars in the night.

The big trog, or really Janice Welson, nodded, as did the corpsman sitting to her left. "That is why Captain Bray's leg cannot be healed except through time and his own body's strength." The trog's voice was deep and gravely.

It surprised me that so many of the Colonel of the West's men spoke our tongue. It made me think that the Colonel had expected our arrival at Outpost 4. Even if it was so, there appeared to be a lot of things he hadn't anticipated.

"And because of the attack fended off the night before our arrival," Grand Wizard Seelain said, "you are unable to contact the Colonel or even other outposts using a cableless telegraph."

Lieutenant Niven, a rifle soldier sitting to the right of Janice Welson, said, "Destruction of the communication gear appears to have been an object of the strike. We do not have here technical skill or tools and materials to repair it."

That meant that none of the Colonel's aircraft could be called to carry us to his fortress buried inside a huge mountain a thousand miles to the west. The last message sent by Outpost 4 was during the first attack to the outpost where the now destroyed attack helicopter came from. And the flying machine's shorter range cableless telegraph equipment was now smashed as well.

Grand Wizard Seelain said, "The Colonel of the West is at war. And we are allies."

Lieutenant Niven pushed his empty wooden bowl aside and shook his head. "We are at war, and we have some enemies in common. That does not make us allies."

The trog holding Janice Welson leaned forward, his eyes glowed brighter, a silvery blue. "That may be an inaccurate statement, Lieutenant."

The trog stared at me. I stared back, into the trog's glowing eyes, at Janice Welson.

Then its gazed dropped to my breastplate and the lamenting soul, through the trog, said, "It may be that Corradin the Conjurer's demon horde wasn't entirely successful. A small part of Tyegerial may have escaped their grasp."

"No," said the lieutenant. "You saw it the same as me. The warden destroyed many of the horde before they broke and bound him, and took him down into the abyss. They held us, my men, at bay, snuffed out any shining soul that challenged them."

"Yes," Janice Welson said. "Even with your mortal eyes you witnessed the angel's essence drawn from his flesh."

The lieutenant said with a measured steadiness in his voice as he recalled the recent event, "I saw and felt the gate to the abyss—to his imprisonment—open and close. Nothing remained but the husk of his immortal flesh."

"They took my brother as well," said Janice Welson. "That I shall never forget."

The two black spots in the grass, I thought. And the feathers, one of which Enchanter Jonas picked up. I found it hard to imagine anything besting the fallen angel. But wasn't that what demons were? It must have been a horrific battle. It must have made our battle against the Kraken look small. And they hadn't destroyed the fallen angel. They'd taken his bound spirit down into their domain.

I began to wonder if Jonas still had the feather he picked up when the lamenting spirit said, "Enchanter, the angel's wing feather you carry in your satchel. Will you retrieve it and hand it to the mercenary?"

While I pondered how the lamenting soul knew Jonas had a feather, the enchanter asked, "Might I ask the purpose of your request?"

"An effort to confirm a belief."

"Possibly another time," Wizard Seelain said. "Let us return to the topic at hand."

Janice Welson ignored Grand Wizard Seelain. "Mercenary, you bear a gift from Belinda Iceheart?"

"We bear more than one gift from the Colonel of the West's daughter," I said, "as it is our goal to return to his mountain fortress."

"As has been stated," said Janice Welson, "we cannot communicate with Colonel Ibrahim. Nor can we communicate with other outposts except through runner. For the time being."

Grand Wizard Seelain signaled for Lilly to approach the table. "Demonstrate your rod."

Lilly pulled the rod from its sheath in her pocket and dropped it on the table. As always, it fell pointing west.

"This is a gift from the one you name Belinda Iceheart," Wizard Seelain said. "We believe it points unerringly toward Colonel Ibrahim's stronghold. We also have maps in crystals that Enchanter Jonas can summon that show the way in a limited fashion. Even so, we would request a guide."

The lamenting soul remained silent.

"Even if we are not allies," Wizard Seelain said, "we do share the same enemies. What we hope to achieve through cooperation with your master will bring strife and possible ruin to at least one of our mutual enemies."

The big troglodyte and Lieutenant Niven exchanged a quick glance.

"We have no guides to offer," the rifleman officer said. "None that have traversed the overland path you intend to take. But my men and I will share with you what little knowledge we have of the land, terrain, plants and animals, beasts and creatures you may encounter. As well as the locations of several outposts along your anticipated path."

The big troglodyte stood. "In the last day we lost many of my kind and nearly a third of the troglodytes that assist us in maintaining this outpost. Even so, as your companion the serpent master will be unable to travel for some time and must remain with us while recovering, I will offer one to accompany you in his place."

Grand Wizard Seelain stood. Enchanter Jonas and I did the same, as did the corpsman and Lieutenant Niven. "Your generosity and faith in our cause is much appreciated," said Grand Wizard Seelain.

Without another word the lamenting soul left the big troglodyte and shot into a grated vent in the ceiling, taking its light with it. The loss left the trog looking miserable and empty as he slumped back into the chair.

CHAPTER 23

"I'll be sure that Wick is well cared for," Captain Bray assured me.

He sat on a padded chair in Outpost 4's lobby with his broken leg elevated and sealed in a plaster tube running from his thigh down past his ankle. The corpsman said it would immobilize the leg better than a splint and speed proper healing. I'd used what healing magic I had, repairing some of the damaged blood vessels before they'd put the cast on. The corpsman guessed I'd cut the healing time down by maybe a week. Still, the serpent cavalryman wouldn't be on his feet for eight weeks. The mission couldn't wait. Maybe if I were a better healer.

"Thank you," I told Bray. "Wick's taken to the roost they set up inside…what did they call it?"

"Parking Garage," Bray said. He remained sharp despite the pain medication they gave him. "Lieutenant Niven thinks he might have heard Coils last night while on patrol, so Private Zunnert's mount may eventually return."

"That would be good," I said. If we returned to Outpost 4 with the Blood Sword, two wyvern mounts would allow two riders to return to Keesee. Unless we could find another way. "Maybe in a week they can lure him in with a carcass."

"I'll worry about that," Bray said. "You've got more than enough to keep you occupied."

He was right. Without him or Zunnert, much more fell to me—and Lilly. I knew she was ready for it. Jonas wasn't one to shirk responsibility either.

The Colonel's men didn't have horses or other beasts to speed our journey or carry any of our gear, but they offered a troglodyte named Ormb. On the far side of the lobby he stood encircled by nine other troglodytes, one of which contained a lamenting soul. I guessed it was Ormb's family saying good bye.

I saw that they'd taken Ormb's shovel and replaced the blade with a narrow steel spear tip which he held with pride.

He looked young but had reached his full height. He spoke Sea Spittle, and wasn't yet skilled in construction or maintenance, which was probably why they selected him to accompany us and to bear some of our gear. They'd dressed him in a loose-fitting brown shirt with a hood that could be drawn over his head to shield him from the sun. Both it and the pants were made of a tightly woven fabric that caught and reflected bits of light, and from somewhere they'd found a pair of sandals for his flat feet. He looked uncomfortable in them but they were better than nothing and better than boots which were bound to cause blisters. Even the sandals properly tied with lacing up his calf might slow us down initially.

Grand Wizard Seelain entered the lobby from a wide hallway. She was speaking with Janice Welson shining within the big troglodyte.

Grand Wizard Seelain had dismissed me from guarding her. She told me to remain with Captain Bray and put him at ease. She probably sensed the growing dislike that emerged between the leading lamenting soul and me. Both Lilly and Enchanter Jonas remained with Wizard Seelain so there was little to be gained by arguing, other than to insult our scout and enchanter's abilities.

"You take care of yourself," I said to Captain Bray and shook his hand.

"I will," he said. "Once they get the communication equipment fixed I'll be sure they alert the other outposts and the Colonel of the West."

He didn't add the fall back plan. If he didn't hear from us or we didn't return by early November, he would return to Keesee and report what he knew. I thought about the cold of Greenland. November might be waiting too long.

"Grand Wizard," Captain Bray said, nodding once.

"Captain, heal swiftly," she replied and rested a hand on his shoulder. "Be ready upon our return."

"I shall," he said, and noted the sheathed hunting knife on the wizard's belt. "And I will keep Private Zunnert's sword for our return."

Ormb came to stand next to the trog containing Janice Welson.

Wizard Seelain turned to me. "Flank Hawk, see to our gear with Lilly and Ormb."

I nodded and looked up at the young trog. "With me," I said in Sea Spittle.

The three of us went through several halls and out a back steel door to where Lieutenant Niven and another solider stood next to our gear. Lilly took up a smaller saddlebag whose straps had been cut and adjusted. I took my wooden-framed backpack that the lieutenant had helped me lash together. Ormb shouldered one similar to mine, yet nearly twice the size. Between us we split the food, water and camping gear, including two halves of an a-frame tent. Enchanter Jonas was to carry a satchel of supplies, his bedroll and would shoulder my crossbow, while Wizard Seelain would carry her satchel, a coil of rope and her bedroll.

Grand Wizard Seelain and Enchanter Jonas came out alone just after we finished loading up.

"Good luck," Lieutenant Niven said to me while Lilly and the other soldier helped Wizard Seelain and Enchanter Jonas with their gear. "May your journey meet with success."

"And may our enemies suffer defeat wherever both you and we encounter them."

He stepped back and saluted Grand Wizard Seelain. His fellow soldier did as well. She nodded and said, "Both I, and King Tobias through me, thank you for your courage and assistance."

Then she turned to me. "Flank Hawk?"

"Everyone ready?" I said. In Sea Spittle, I asked Ormb, "You ready?"

All nodded.

"Scout," I said, "lead the way."

Even though it wasn't necessary, Lilly dropped the brass rod. As always, it landed pointing west.

I fell in line behind Lilly and followed as she led us past Private Zunnert's grave and into a stand of maples, their seeds spiraling down in the early morning breeze. Grand Wizard Seelain walked just behind me with Jonas following and Ormb bringing up the rear.

"I prefer the smell of the trees to that of the ocean," I said over my shoulder to Wizard Seelain.

She laughed lightly. "As do I, Flank Hawk."

The first few days proved to be easy travel over relatively flat land that sloped up toward a range of ash and spruce-covered mountains. Once we reached them, our pace slowed as we wound our way up and down the rock-strewn slopes. The mountains weren't as large or steep as some I'd travelled over, but every day meant further advances of Fendra Jolain's forces toward Keesee. I knew King Tobias and all his allies would fight hard, but the odds were against them. Time was against us.

Lilly's keen hearing helped us avoid a number of dangerous encounters, including stumbling into a giant bear-like sloth. The beast stood over twenty feet tall when on its hind legs.

Often, when I took the lead or during rests, Grand Wizard Seelain spent time with Lilly. She explained the way the royal court worked and how to get along with noblemen and women, or at least be tolerated by them. Lilly took care of setting up and tearing down their tent, caring for and cleaning with wizard's garments, and braiding the wizard's long, near translucent white hair.

When Lilly wasn't with the grand wizard, she spent time showing Enchanter Jonas how to use a sling he'd gotten from one of the bazooka soldiers. The leather that formed it came from scraps cut from the tack of Wizard Seelain's fallen mount.

I spent time with Ormb, teaching him how to use his spear. He quickly learned to mimic all of the blocks, and thrusts and slashing attacks, but struggled to employ them while practice fighting. Ormb was quiet, easy going, and didn't complain when his sandals initially caused some blistering. His rubbery gray skin seemed to heal and callous nearly over night.

Even more valuable than having Ormb's strong back to bear much of our gear was having an enchanter and a wizard along while hunting. It allowed us to live off the land as we traveled and lighten our load. Grand Wizard Seelain collapsed the air around speckled wild turkeys we came across. At night Enchanter Jonas sent a ray of light into the eyes of a local deer species and wild spotted goats. That made them easy targets for my crossbow.

Ormb did eat a lot but didn't favor meat. He collected fungus growing on rotting logs and mushrooms and ate as we travelled. Lilly said half of it was poisonous, but Ormb ate every bit he came across without ill effect. And together Ormb and Lilly were also able to collect a variety of roots and greens that we added to the small stew pot.

On our fifth day after leaving Outpost 4, Enchanter Jonas helped me spot and kill a goat to supply food for the next day's travel. He grabbed the end of the rope I'd tossed over a high tree limb and used while gutting the goat, and helped me hoist it farther up, near the limb.

"Why build a separate fire and prepare the goat away from our camp?" Jonas asked. "And why leave the carcass dangling from that branch over night?"

"It's safer," I said, tying the rope to a sturdy sapling.

"Vastly more work," he replied. "We didn't do it before."

"We used to have a dragon. Any predator that'd smell our meat would smell the dragon. Not many predators'll mess with a dragon. Not even dire wolves."

"Lieutenant Niven said there were some wolves in these mountains, but no dire wolves. And we have a fire in our camp."

"They talked about a lot of other dangerous beasts that roam these mountains and beyond," I said.

Even as I finished my statement, a rustling through the branches and fallen leaves caught our attention. Grunting and deep snorting breaths followed, approaching from downhill. I grabbed my spear while Jonas cocked my crossbow and set a quarrel. We both stepped closer to the small fire used to light our work gutting the goat.

A bear ambled out of the dark woods into the edge of our firelight, sniffing and eyeing us warily. It was black with splotches of brown over its muzzle and easily weighed more than Jonas and me together.

It sniffed again and walked over toward the pile of goat innards that I hadn't buried yet.

"I see what you mean," whispered Jonas. "What should we do?"

"Back away," I replied. "Slowly."

Just as we took our first step away from the fire the bear stiffened and looked around. Alert as it was, the bear never saw the rugged spear lance out of the darkness and take it through the ribs. The hurled spear was little more than a twelve-foot limb big around as my bicep. It'd been cleared of bark and its sharpened tip emerged through the ribs by over a foot on the side opposite where it entered.

The stunned bear spun about, half snarling, half groaning as it attempted to run despite the shaft driven through it. I looked to our right, the direction the spear came from. *Whumping* footsteps sounded as a figure big as an ogre trotted out from the darkness and slammed a huge club down on the dying bear.

"Mountain troll," whispered Jonas. "What do we do?"

I looked at the monster as it stood over the dead bear and turned its black-eyed gaze upon us. It was over twice the height of a man but its shoulders were far broader and a light coating of hair covered everything except its face, hands and feet. It wore an assortment of crudely sewn firs over its shoulders and around its waist.

I stood straight with spear held ready but not pointed at the troll. "The bear is yours," I said in Sea Spittle. I pointed with my spear up at the goat. "The goat too."

The troll's gaze followed to where my spear pointed. It reached up, unable to touch but sniffed and examined the carcass. Then it smiled, showing double rows of pointed teeth. Everything on the mountain troll's face seemed pointed. Its ears, its long nose. Even its chin.

"But leave the rope," I said, and walked over to the sapling and untied the rope holding the goat just above the troll's reach.

The troll made a repeated retching sound as it yanked loose the rope tied around the legs of the goat carcass.

"It's laughing," said Jonas, just loud enough so I could hear. "That is good?"

"Let's hope so," I said.

The troll threw aside the rope and placed a foot on the fallen bear before tugging his spear free. Then the troll skewered the goat on the spear tip and grabbed the bear by the hind legs. It laughed again before dragging the bear beyond the firelight. It faced us with a nasty grin until it was gone in the darkness.

After a moment Jonas asked, "Why didn't it kill us too?"

"It was so quiet," I said. "Who knows how long it was out there watching us."

"Maybe it was the fire?"

I shook my head. "Maybe it saw your magic." I thought a moment. "And maybe it had enough food for its stomach tonight, and didn't want to risk injury."

Jonas said, "We should get back to camp."

"I agree. Double watches tonight."

"I am not sure I will be able to sleep, Flank Hawk."

I wondered if I would be able to as well.

We made it out of the mountains without seeing another bear or mountain troll. Our march westward carried us through some flat lands before encountering a rising hilly region.

Enchanter Jonas stepped up next to Grand Wizard Seelain and kept pace with her. "I have been reviewing our route in my mind," he said loud enough for me to hear. "If I am correct, there should be an outpost in this region. The river we forded yesterday. And those hillsides Lilly pointed out earlier today. If we reach a river by tonight, we are close to one of the Colonel's outposts.

"Summon a map at our next rest," I said, using as few words as possible. Lilly kept a fast pace like Grand Wizard Seelain requested. With my load talking wasn't easy.

Enchanter Jonas fell back to his place in our march westward until our break an hour later. Lilly had selected the shade of a lonely willow tree near a small brook flowing through a flowering meadow.

Having taken a long drink from the brook, I splashed water over my sweaty face and hair. Ormb did the same, except he lacked hair on his scalp.

White moths outnumbered the blue and purple butterflies fluttering around the red and orange wildflowers. While they were pretty to look at, I preferred a stiff breeze that would keep the biting flies down. It seemed early for such biting pests to be out, but I'd never traveled through this region before. The waxy oil from some leaves Lilly found helped, but not enough to keep them completely off my sweaty skin.

Grand Wizard Seelain sat with her back to the tree with her eyes closed. "The fragrance reminds me of the North Garden. Do you not agree, Lilly?"

Lilly shrugged. "I saw rabbits here. Thought the enchanter might want to test his sling skills."

Jonas had his sling with several smooth stones laid out so I knew he was thinking along the same lines as Lilly. He'd already arranged the leaded crystals on a blanket spread over the meadow grass, each wrapped in a triangular linen cloth. Each had red symbols stitched into the white cloth and each crystal held a different aerial-view image Imperial Seer Lochelle had drawn from my memory. The flight aboard the Colonel of the West's *Osprey* from Outpost 4 to his mountain stronghold had taken less than a day. We'd be lucky if our trek took less than a month and a half. Still, it'd be far worse without the crystal images giving us a view of upcoming terrain and Lilly's skill and brass rod keeping us on course.

Enchanter Jonas selected one crystal and returned the rest to the padded leather pouch he kept stowed in his satchel. He carefully removed the polished crystal, examined it and then placed it on the triangular wrap spread on the blanket. After a few deep breaths to focus his concentration, the enchanter spoke several words and summoned the image held within the crystal.

The table-top sized image showed the local terrain from an elevation far higher than a serpent cavalryman would normally view. That made details harder to pick out. Even so, Enchanter Jonas pointed to a black spot. "The new growth from a previous year's fire Scout Lilly observed and reported." He pointed a little further east. "The river we crossed before making camp last night." His finger moved westward, just to the edge of the crystal's image. "We are here and this is the next river we must cross."

The next river appeared broader than the last. I hated crossing rivers. Finding a place to ford or cutting and lashing several logs together to carry our supplies as we hung on and swam across. Once, Lilly had shifted into her muskrat form to help each of us individually cross a deep and fast moving river.

Grand Wizard Seelain pointed a short distance northward on the map. "There, along the river. It appears to be a rectangular structure."

Lieutenant Niven said there would be an outpost along a river that would be near our direct line of travel. I guessed it was about a four hour march from where we sat to the river, and another three north along the river to the outpost, if Enchanter Jonas correctly identified our current location.

"I do not believe Colonel Ibrahim's men would be immediately hostile toward us," Grand Wizard Seelain said. "What do you think, Flank Hawk?"

"They may know an easy place to cross," I said. "They might have communication with Outpost Four and maybe with the Colonel."

I explained the discussion in Sea Spittle to Ormb. He nodded.

Grand Wizard Seelain said, "Lilly, forge our path northwest so that we might strike the river a short distance south of the outpost.

Lilly stood and examined the hilly region. "Okay," she said with concern in her voice.

Wizard Seelain smiled. "I know what I ask makes your task even more difficult. Yet, you have proven yourself equal to any of the king's scouts."

Lilly smiled back. "With Flank Hawk's help, we'll get us there."

Ormb carefully handed Lilly's spyglass back to Grand Wizard Seelain. From our distant hillside view we all saw the same thing. A burned wooden fort whose gate had been battered down and several places along its torched walls had been breached. No movement from inside except for crows whose black feathers matched what building walls remained standing. An occasional vulture rose into the air or circled before landing within.

"Lilly and I will go down first and look around," I said. "Continue watching the surrounding area. The victors might've left observers behind."

Grand Wizard Seelain opened her mouth to object but said nothing. She handed Enchanter Jonas the spyglass and adjusted her grip on her white staff instead.

Jonas set the spyglass aside and offered me my crossbow and quarrels. I weighed having my crossbow cocked and ready against carrying my spear. "You keep it," I said, wishing I was handier with a sword. If there was something big inside, my spear would be needed. "Lilly has her bow."

I led the way around the hill and down, stopping behind cover of trees or rock outcroppings to watch and listen. The fort stood about fifty yards from the river. The water looked deep and fast. A rope bridge consisting of two lines, one about five feet above the other, spanned the river. Cords spaced every twenty feet or so secured the top rope to the bottom and a large post rising twenty feet above the river's center kept it from dipping too low between the sturdy oaks that anchored each end. I wondered why it hadn't been cut or burned. Maybe the enemy wanted it intact. There was also a small wooden dock near the bridge extending five yards into the river with several posts for securing boats. None were present.

"Anything, Lilly?"

While I scanned the area once more she sniffed the air, then closed her eyes and listened. "Nothing, Flank Hawk. Just rotting flesh. Human. Maybe horse."

"Sunset's in an hour," I said and donned my helmet. "Let's get this over with."

Lilly nocked an arrow and covered me with her bow as I raced across the eighty yards of open ground. I leaned against the wall near the fallen gate. Both halves were splintered with bits of dirt clinging to some of the edges. Earth elemental, I thought.

Lilly sprinted up next to me. I stepped inside, sending several crows to flight. A few others *cawed* and hopped off the bodies scattered across the packed earth courtyard. Beyond the bodies and angry crows, very little of the main building remained. No more than a few blackened supports and beams set in a stone foundation covered in soot and ash.

Lilly came up next to me, her nose scrunched and a look of disgust on her face. I'd seen and smelled battlefields much worse. Lilly had seen at least one.

"Stay against the wall," I said. "Cover me."

"It's okay," she said, half holding her breath. "There's nothing in here but dead bodies."

"Then watch outside."

"Nahh," she said.

I went up to the nearest body. Shiny green flies swarmed about it as I prodded with my spear tip. Not a lot of flesh remained beneath the mottled green uniform. White squirming maggots crawled inside the chest cavity, so I figured the battle took place at least three days ago. No more than five. I avoided looking at the fallen soldier's face. The rifle nearby looked like a sledgehammer had been taken to it, but the shattered rifle and the uniform said he was one of the Colonel's men. There were twenty or so more of the

Colonel's fallen men scattered about. Probably the remains of more in the central burned-out building.

"I bet some wizard summoned a fire spirit that burned this place," Lilly said. "Guns wouldn't do much against it."

"Wizard Seelain might be able to tell for sure. I think it's safe to signal her down."

Lilly walked past the body I was examining and pointed. "What's that over there?"

I started to say, "A horse," but stopped.

She walked over to it, scaring away two stubborn crows. "It's got a human top half attached to a horse body."

She was right. The way the spine from the human torso merged with that of the horse half said so.

"Jonas will wanna see this for sure," Lilly said.

"Are you sure, Lilly?"

She looked about. "It does smell downright awful." Then she caught my grin. "You're right. He's pretty tough for a city enchanter."

The most nerve-wracking part was crossing the rope bridge. It offered a perfect opportunity for an enemy to strike. Forces divided with at least one of us helpless on the bridge.

The attack never came and we travelled well past sunset to put distance between us and the destroyed outpost. We set up camp just inside the edge of a thick woods with no fire to draw attention. Ormb stood watch while the rest of us huddled close and discussed what we'd seen.

"Do you think the centaurs were the ones that attacked?" asked Lilly. She called them centaurs because Enchanter Jonas named them that and Lieutenant Niven had mentioned scattered herds of them could be found on the other side of the mountains.

Since the lieutenant had called them herds, I figured they were animals. He didn't say they were allies with the Colonel of the West. He didn't name them as enemies either. There was just so much he'd said in such a short amount of time.

"I know very little about them," said Enchanter Jonas. "Only what I read years ago."

"What do you recall?" asked Wizard Seelain.

"They form tribes based on a dominant stallion. Their study of magic parallels that of goblins, having shamans, witches, and occasional wizards. Unlike goblins, they perform enchanter magic. I do not recall reading that their social structure breeds vile cruelty like that of goblins." He rubbed his temples with his middle fingers. "My attention focused on what the books said about their enchanter magic. They mostly discussed weather prediction, crossing over to seer abilities.

"Their kind has not been seen on the Main Continent in centuries."

Heavy rain had destroyed the prints and signs of battle both inside and outside the fort. It frustrated me. Zunnert would have seen what I couldn't. "So they could have summoned the elementals that attacked the outpost?"

"It is possible," said Jonas. "Whoever it was didn't leave much behind."

"What concerns me," said Grand Wizard Seelain, "is that the Colonel of the West is at war, not only on the coast but inland as well. We know not with whom."

"Maybe allies of our enemies," I said, thinking of Uplersh, Fendra Jolain, Corradin the Conjurer, and the Necromancer King. If so, it might bolster our request for the Blood Sword's return.

"I met the Colonel of the West," said Lilly. "He seemed pretty smart and powerful to me. You think so too, Flank Hawk?"

I nodded.

Lilly pulled her knees close. "Doesn't look like he's winning."

"Not knowing all who raise war upon him makes our need to travel unobserved even more pressing," said Wizard Seelain.

CHAPTER 24

Grand Wizard Seelain announced to me, "I have decided that both you and Ormb will not stand as part of watch tonight. You both appear exhausted."

"That centaur is still shadowing us," I said flatly. I was tired but I'd endured worse. I took a bite of the goat we'd killed and cooked last night. The meat was hard and chewy, and lessened the bitterness of the dandelion greens Lilly had gathered.

Grand Wizard Seelain's statement frustrated my attempt to enjoy our noon meal. Lilly had selected the bank of a slow-moving stream at the base of a lightly wooded hillside to stop and eat. She sat to my right, cooling her feet in the clear water. Grand Wizard Seelain sat to my left with her boots off and cooling her feet as well. I hadn't sat down yet. Lilly and Wizard Seelain enjoyed the dandelion greens and roots far more than I did. Jonas stood too, leaning against a gray boulder big enough to alter the stream's path. He absolutely detested dandelions, and reminded us every time Lilly gathered them, and that he didn't like dandelion wine either. So he stuck to just eating the goat meat.

Ormb stood watch fifty paces up hill, enjoying his handful of greens supplemented by some toadstools he'd gathered. Grand Wizard Seelain speaking his name in conversation caught his attention.

"I think it's the same one," said Lilly. "Three days now. I'd like to ambush it, but it's too good." She splashed the water with her foot. "Better than me."

"The question is," Jonas said, "why is it following us?" He stepped away from the boulder. "We don't know if it is an enemy of the Colonel. It may only be curious."

"Three days is more than curious," I said.

"It ain't following," said Lilly. "It knows the area and keeps ahead of us, like it knows where we're going."

I handed Lilly the rest of my dandelion greens. "Our direction is always west. That makes it pretty easy. We could throw it off by cutting north or south."

"It's faster than us," Lilly said. "And I'm not fully sure it's the same one."

Wizard Seelain looked over her shoulder, up at me. "The three of us will overlap our watches. You may deny your exhaustion, Flank Hawk, but you cannot hide it."

"Maybe you could send a whirlwind elemental after it," Lilly said to

Seelain. "That'd give Flank Hawk less to worry on. He'd sleep better."

I was about to tell Lilly I slept well enough when she jumped to her feet. At the same time Ormb dropped his sack of toad stools and picked up his spear. "Something coming," he warned.

I didn't have to translate. Wizard Seelain began pulling on her boots while Lilly closed her eyes and listened.

"What is it?" asked Jonas. "Centaurs or another one of those thrice-sized boars?"

"Shhh," I said as Lilly opened her eyes and sniffed the air.

"On the hills," she said. "Both sides of the stream." She looked at Wizard Seelain and me. "Smell on the air is a little like wyvern."

Reptiles, I thought, but not dragon. Wyverns hunted in packs or swarms or whatever they're called. "On the ground, not flying?" I asked Lilly.

She nodded. Ormb did too.

The stream was too shallow. The boulder Jonas stood next to wasn't big enough to cover our back. "High ground," I said, grabbing my pack. Better to close with one line of their encirclement than be hit from both sides at once. "Ormb, follow. Watch our back," I said in Sea Spittle.

Jonas was cocking my crossbow. "You stick near Seelain," I said to him, donning my helmet and moving up the hill. Lilly walked five paces to my left. With my helmet on I relied on her senses even more. "How many?" I asked her. She shrugged.

"Those trees," I said and pointed, "near the crest." A small hollow in them gave us a place to stand back to back, covering all sides. The trees around would break up a unified attack. There was one gap in them, but some of Wizard Seelain's spellcraft needed room.

Before we made it halfway there, two creatures crossed over the top of the hill, followed by a third. They looked like a cross between an ostrich and a crocodile—the worst aspects of each. With long, tooth-filled snouts and three-clawed hands, they stood on muscular hind legs made for running and leaping. They searched the hillside, leaning forward, bobbing, counterbalanced by long tails that tapered to a whip's point. Their scales glistened brown with green stripes. A line of dull yellow feathers ran down their necks and backs with tufts of short brighter yellow ones sprouting from each elbow. The creatures weren't nearly as big as wyverns, but if they stood up straight, they'd be eye to eye with Ormb.

The spine feathers stood upright when they spotted us. One puffed its chest and let out a call. It sounded like a honking goose accented with a scratchy growl. I signaled everyone to stop as four more joined the three among the tall ash trees near the top of the hill.

"Deinonychus," said Jonas. "Ground raptors. Pack hunters."

"We're in trouble," Lilly said, warily searching the lightly wooded terrain behind us.

Jonas came up next to me. "I watched three of them shred an equal number of dire wolves in the Circus Pits. Different color, same beasts."

Worry crept into Lilly's voice as she said, "And this time we don't have Zunnert or Bray and his dragon."

"No," I said. "We have a grand wizard." I dropped my pack and gripped my spear. "Take the fight to them before they surround and fall upon us."

The big ground raptor raised its snout and called out again. A pair of replies echoed from the hillside behind us, across the stream.

Seelain raised her staff, beginning a spell as Jonas aimed my crossbow. "They leap and disembowel with the sickle talons on their feet," he warned. Lilly nocked an arrow to her bowstring.

"Ormb," I said, "with me." He dropped his pack and grunted in reply.

At the *twang*s of my crossbow and Lilly's short bow, Ormb and I raced uphill. "Follow and ward Seelain," I shouted over my shoulder. "If she falls we all die."

Lilly's shot went wide, sticking in a tree next to a wary raptor that leapt back. Jonas had better luck, his quarrel taking one low in the thigh. Lilly shouted something I couldn't hear as Wizard Seelain's spell ended with a small thunder clap. She'd destroyed a sphere of air around the biggest raptor, allowing the outside pressure centered on her target to slam inward. The concussive force caused the big raptor to shudder once and crumple with blood flowing from its eyes, nose and ear holes on the sides of its feather-crested head.

"We must break their line," I shouted to no one in particular. "Break their fight."

Ormb kept pace with me, shaking his spear over his head and bellowing out threats in his own tongue. He hurled a bucket-sized rock high into the trees above the raptors, distracting them as it clattered off branches on its way to the ground.

The loss of their leader unnerved the raptors and I thought we'd route them until a dozen, snarling and waving their claws, joined them from behind. With leaps and clawed feet digging into the root-covered rocky ground the reinforced raptor pack charged us.

Lilly yelled, "A bunch are coming up behind us!"

At the same time Grand Wizard Seelain ordered, "Ormb, Flank Hawk, DOWN!"

I repeated, "Down!" in Sea Spittle as I dropped flat, preparing to grab Ormb's leg and trip him. No need. He hit the ground a half second after me. Maybe he knew what an air wizard could do.

Our action only encouraged the closing raptors, now less than twenty yards away. Just as the front six leapt with hooked foot claws extended, Seelain's spell slammed into them. The torrential wall of wind hurled the nearest six backwards, flinging them over the rocky ground and tumbling into their brethren. Even though I held the ground tight, the spell wind scooted me forward several feet.

Knocked down and pelted by sticks and debris, the confused raptors were momentarily vulnerable. Ormb and I leapt to our feet and raced among them, slashing and stabbing with our spears. I shouted, "Seelain, ward your flank!"

I knew that last spell took a lot out of Seelain. I only hoped fewer than we faced now were coming up the hill at them from behind.

Within seconds the ground raptors were back on their feet, snapping their jaws just beyond the reach of our spears. They began extending their line to encircle me and Ormb, cutting us off from Seelain and the others. We'd only had time to kill or wound six. Four others suffering from Seelain's spellcraft hobbled and limped, but their teeth and claws still posed danger.

Most predators backed off from prey with a vicious bite. These didn't seem to care that we'd bloodied them—that it wasn't worth the flesh they'd feed upon even if they won.

The clap of Seelain's spellcraft and Lilly's shout, "Back, against the trees," spurred me to action.

"With me," I told Ormb as he jabbed his spear at the nearest raptors, shouting and trying to keep them at bay. "Back. Not too fast."

I didn't want to turn and run. The raptors moved faster. But the hillside was riddled with roots and rocks, making each step treacherous. Snapping and snarling threats, flexing their claws, the pack looked ready to attack. To my right I spotted two raptors flanking us. Ormb blocked my view, but I guessed the same was happening on our left.

I swiped wide with my spear, using the motion to drive back the emboldened raptors while risking a quick glance over my shoulder. I wanted to avoid backing into a tree, and hoped to see what was happening with Lilly and Seelain. Even before I completed the maneuver, one raptor launched at me with its hind claws extended. A second drove in low, its jaws open wide.

Ormb slammed the butt of his spear into the leaping one's throat. I pivoted, causing the second to miss my leg by inches and nailed it with a sharp spear thrust to the neck just behind its jawbone.

Ormb's target landed on its back, stunned and gagging while mine, mortally wounded, thrashed and kicked wildly. But the two downed raptors separated us. We couldn't support each other when the rest of the pack came at us from all sides like gore crows to a carcass.

I fended off one raptor before a second knocked me back on top of the thrashing, dying one. The attacking raptor came down and tried to tear me open with its curved hind claw, scraping across my breastplate. I rolled away and took a kick to the helmet, but came up with sword in hand, slashing wildly. I connected with scaled flesh.

Then a blast like a crashing ocean wave—but made of wind—slammed into me, sending me airborne and tumbling into a crooked oak. I climbed to my knees, still gripping my sword and slashed at the nearest scaled body, both of us disoriented and struggling to stand.

An echoing horn sound reverberated in my ears. Those ground raptors that could stand looked about, snorting in alarm. I stabbed at the nearest but missed. Ormb stood twenty feet away, bloody and leaning against a small maple with his right fist raised, ready to strike. The uninjured raptors snarled and stood between us and their injured pack members, those that could stand and move. The nearest looked about warily before backing away and trotting over the crest of the hill, supporting the limping and injured as best they could.

Lilly raced up to me. She held her blood-covered dagger ready and looked about. "You okay, Flank Hawk?" She didn't wait for me to answer. "You hear that?"

I waved to Ormb. He wiped blood dripping over his brow and nodded. "Hear what?" I asked and searched for Seelain. Her second wind spell broke the raptor pack's will to fight. "Grand Wizard," I called.

Wizard Seelain stood, partially hidden by a tree and a fallen raptor. She looked okay. "Flank Hawk, come here!"

"There's that horn call again," Lilly said. "It's close."

With a sneer across his bloody face, Ormb drove his spear through the eye of a hissing raptor trying to stand despite a broken leg.

"Wizard Seelain needs me," I said to Lilly while looking at the hillside across the steam where the deep horn sounded again. It wasn't coming closer. At least not yet. "Check Ormb's wounds," I said, and added, "Be ready."

I sheathed my sword, picked up my spear and ran downhill to where Grand Wizard Seelain knelt. Three dead raptors lay sprawled further down the hill and one near the stream. Two others lay near her. One with Enchanter Jonas's rapier jutting from its throat.

Blood covered Grand Wizard Seelain's hands. Urgency hung in her voice. "Make haste, Flank Hawk. Help me."

I removed my helmet and searched the distant hillside and listened for danger as I ran to Wizard Seelain's side. She knelt over Jonas who lay pale and unconscious. She'd tied a tourniquet high on his thigh before wrapping his cloak tightly around his left leg. Blood had already soaked through it. Blood covered both of her hands, one holding the twisted tourniquet tight, the other pressed down over the wound on the enchanter's hip.

"His leg has been torn open to the bone," Wizard Seelain said. "From hip to thigh. What can you do?"

Lilly was already leading Ormb down toward us. I met the grand wizard's gaze and then looked around again. I might have enough spell strength to halt the bleeding, maybe. But the effort would weaken me. "The source of the horn call?" I asked. "Danger may still be nearby."

"Enchanter Jonas will bleed to death if you do not act immediately,"

Wizard Seelain said. "Flank Hawk, he interposed himself between the deinonychus and me."

Conflicting duty tore at me. I might be able to save Jonas—but what of Seelain's safety and survival or our mission? Would my strength and spear be needed? "Jonas did it to save you," I said. "The ground raptors may return. What sounds the horn? A foe? They may have set the ground raptors upon us."

"Heal him," Grand Wizard Seelain ordered, increasing pressure on Jonas's wound even as blood continued seeping from it.

Looking up at Lilly, I asked, "Ormb?"

"Scalp wound. Bloody but not bad. Help him, Flank Hawk. We'll be okay."

I asked Wizard Seelain, "Have you exhausted your spell strength?"

"I have not," she said. "Now. Every moment lessens the enchanter's chance of survival."

I nodded and pulled out my pouch holding the white oak bark. "Lilly, bind Ormb's wound quickly and remain alert." I examined Jonas's leg more closely. "No, Lilly, wait!"

I looked up at Ormb. "Watch and warn," I told him. "Lilly, help me first. I need to spread the bark but don't want him to lose more blood." I lifted Seelain's left hand for a fraction of a second and stuffed some bark into the unbound part of the wound. "Keep pressure on until I finish."

Lilly and I worked quickly. "You can save him, Flank Hawk. I'll help Ormb."

I nodded and took a deep breath before beginning the spell chant, focusing on the energies I needed to harness. I couldn't heal Jonas's wounds, but I might stop the bleeding long enough to give him a chance.

The maelstrom of energies swirled around my head and in my mind. I sensed the enchanter's wound. No major arteries cut. I directed an energy ribbon along his leg and then harnessed a second, sending it under Seelain's hands.

Although the ribbons I sought were easier to find and to grasp, I struggled. Weakened. My chanting began to falter. I refocused and selected a long one, silvery-gray, vibrant and strong. Peeling it from its path, I sent the ribbon along the sliced flesh, binding it with the powdery bark, healing some severed vessels, closing off others.

Sharp pain shot through my head. Burned behind my eyes. A fragment, more, I thought. It might make the difference. Life for Jonas—death for me…maybe neither—maybe both. My thoughts became jumbled. Chant…focus…take hold…small one…into the flesh…done.

Back out before I am lost.

The pain increased, the maelstrom faded.

I was lying down. Seelain cradled my head, saying something to me. I struggled to stave off the gray—stay awake. But all I could hear was the horn, fading. And a second one answering it.

CHAPTER 25

Greasy fish, burnt and sooty. The odor invaded my dreams, summoned memories of the One-Eyed Pelican, Major Jadd's favorite tavern. A run-down, rat-infested dive whose cooking caused my stomach to churn. The only thing edible besides the stale bread was the fish soup. Fish chunks floating in red and greasy broth.

I drifted out of the dream to take in a smell that was real, as was the nearby crackling fire. Instead of the dream pub's rafters lined with rats scampering to and fro, a tent—our tent sheltered me. And sleeping next to me under a blanket was Enchanter Jonas. His face was pale and his breathing shallow, but he was alive.

And so was I, but with an aching head added to by a throbbing pain behind my eyes. I sat up slowly while the battle against the ground raptors filled my thoughts. I gripped my sword. My spear must have been outside.

The odor of cold sweat, mine and Jonas's mingled with the aroma of cooking meat outside. Was it fish? Maybe from the stream. I heard water flowing against rocks, and Grand Wizard Seelain talking quietly with Ormb attempting to reply.

"You gotta practice being a better healer, Flank Hawk," Lilly said as she lifted the tent flap and showed me a big smile.

From what I could see, it was a few hours until dark. "Is that fish cooking?"

My question seemed to surprise her. "No. But I'm glad you're okay." The smile fled her face. "Really, I'm serious about your healing, Flank Hawk." She leaned over Jonas and listened to his breathing. "Grand Wizard Seelain said trying too hard—doing too much—could kill you."

Had it been that close that Wizard Seelain was worried? I rubbed my forehead. Lilly had a point. More than once people around me got hurt really bad. But what did Lilly and Wizard Seelain expect? We're at war, in the wilderness, and I'm a neophyte healer. I know *one* spell. And not very well.

Lilly stared at me. "How's your head?"

"Throbbing inside like a bullfrog filling his throat."

"You asked about food. Are you hungry?"

"Not really. The smell reminded me of a place Major Jadd likes to eat at."

She laughed. "The One-Eyed Pelican. Road Toad told me about it."

I smiled. "Don't go there, even if he invites you."

"You've told me that more than once." Lilly looked over her shoulder. "Can you walk?"

"Yeah," I said, starting to crawl out of the tent.

"Can you think straight?" Lilly asked, moving in front of me.

"Yeah. My head hurts but I think so."

"Okay," she said and pointed in the direction of the fire. "Grand Wizard Seelain and Ormb could use your help."

Near the fire Ormb and Grand Wizard Seelain stood, speaking to a centaur.

The horns, I thought, getting to my feet. My spear leaned against a sapling that they'd secured a tent line to. I took my spear. Ormb or Lilly had cleaned it.

Lilly said, "His name's Cloud Chaser, we think. Ormb can talk to him in Sea Spittle. But nobody but you can talk to Ormb. Mostly."

"Mostly? What happened, Lilly?"

Ormb turned a spit that held one of the raptor's legs over the fire. I recognized it by the dangling claw. Grand Wizard Seelain and the centaur looked up the hill, toward me and Lilly.

The centaur had the body of a muscular brown horse with black hooves and tail. He stood about seventeen hands high. But where a horse's neck and head should've risen out of the shoulders, the torso, arms and head of a man was attached. The man's skin was dark and his hair matched the color of his tail. Leather straps secured saddlebags just behind his withers. Paint or tattoos covered parts of the centaur's face and body, and a copper horn hung by a cord over his human shoulder. Leaning against a nearby tree rested a long spear. It had a broad metal head much like my boar spear but it was decorated with white feathers and lacked a crossbar.

"Three of them showed up a few minutes after you passed out," Lilly said as we began walking toward the fire. "Like I said, we think his name's Cloud Chaser. I think he's the one that's been following us."

"Why? Are they allies with the Colonel?"

Lilly shrugged. "Not enemies, we don't think. He tried a language that sounded like the Colonel's soldiers spoke among themselves. Grand Wizard Seelain agreed." Lilly shook her head. "If it was, he didn't speak it too good."

After a deep breath I followed Lilly to the fire. There was little breeze, so the smoke drifted up into the trees. About fifty yards away I saw the boulder Enchanter Jonas had leaned against just before the ground raptors attacked. On the far side of the stream, over the hill, I noted the sound of gore crows feeding.

The fishy odor of the cooking raptor leg sent a shudder through me. How close had it come to them feeding upon us?

The centaur's eyes studied me. They were dark and filled with confidence.

"Grand Wizard," I said, standing at attention with my spear.

"How are you, Flank Hawk?"

"Uninjured," I said. After a pause where she scrutinized me, I added, "My head aches something terrible."

"I can imagine," she said and gestured toward the centaur. "Lilly may have told you, this is Cloud Chaser. We suffer a language barrier." Then she gestured to our trog companion. "Ormb can speak with him, but he is unable to adequately translate what he learns to us."

Ormb had picked up some of our tongue over the past two weeks, but not enough to make a difference. "You fought well," I told Ormb in Sea Spittle.

He stepped back from the fire, stood straight and grinned. "You did, too."

I looked up and met the centaur's gaze. It was paint on his face, not tattoos. Three black horizontal stripes under his left eye and one finger-width vertical stripe ran down his right cheek. A similar pattern was painted on his chest.

"I'm gonna check on Jonas again," Lilly said, "and then return to watch." When Wizard Seelain nodded, Lilly hurried back up the hill.

The centaur held his right forearm across his chest and stamped the ground with his front left hoof. "I am Cloud Runner," he said. "You speak Trade like Ormb."

"I do," I said, deciding not to waste time or words. "Are you allies with the Colonel of the West?"

"The Undying Mountain Chief Toward the Setting Sun that Ormb serves," Cloud Runner said, glancing over at the trog. "Our peoples are friends. He calls us to battle at his side. Our tribes gather."

The centaur pointed at me and Wizard Seelain, and then up the hill. "Do you answer the Undying Mountain Chief's call?"

I translated for Grand Wizard Seelain and corrected her interpretation of the centaur's name. "What would you like me to tell him?"

She replied, "Cloud Runner sent two of his tribe to bring help. I did not know your condition and Enchanter Jonas is unable to travel. I believe we need their assistance. Just tell him the truth."

"We come from across the big ocean," I said to Cloud Runner, and pointed east, back across the stream. "We battle common enemies of the Colonel of the West. The Undying Mountain Chief. I have negotiated with him once before and we journey to seek his counsel and assistance again."

"You are a warrior. Are these your words or the wizard's words?"

It shouldn't have surprised me that Cloud Runner knew Seelain was a wizard. Her staff suggested it, or maybe Ormb had told the centaur. But that she *was* a wizard seemed to matter to him. "Grand Wizard Seelain leads our mission. They are my words because they are the same as her words, because they are the truth."

"I know of Ormb's people. They serve the Undying Chief of the Mountain. What he said is identical brother to what you said. You ask for help. To my chief, I will add my words to your words."

"Thank you," I said.

"Ormb told me you are a skilled warrior." Cloud Runner gestured from himself toward me as he said, "My people help you." Then he gestured from me back to himself. "You help my people."

Two hours before dawn centaurs bearing torches approached the camp. Lilly'd just roused me from a deep sleep to stand my watch, so I met them along with Cloud Runner while Lilly awoke Ormb and Wizard Seelain.

After we'd been introduced to the party's leader, a shaman named River Runs Down who also spoke Sea Spittle, they entered the camp. The shaman wasn't the smallest of the centaurs, but he was the oldest, with streaks of gray throughout his hair and tail. His paint markings were the only ones to include red.

Enchanter Jonas was awake, occasionally groaning despite the brew of tea laced with extract from leaves Cloud Runner had given us. It was stronger medicine than we carried. Wizard Seelain had held off any attempt to sew closed his leg wound once Cloud Runner sent for assistance as she believed they had a healer among them. If necessary, once there was enough sunlight, it could be done. She hoped by then I'd have regained some ability to stem bleeding should it be necessary.

After a quick exchange between Cloud Runner and River Runs Down, the shaman asked to see Jonas and examine his wound. He carefully knelt down as Grand Wizard Seelain and I undid the clean wrapping.

"Infection is there," said River Runs Down after examining Enchanter Jonas's leg. He was probably right. Despite Grand Wizard Seelain and Lilly's efforts to clean and dress it, the redness around the wound didn't appear healthy. "We must take him to our healer."

"Aren't you a healer?" I asked him. Goblin shamans had healing spells.

"Not for this," he said, running his rune-carved spear above the length of Jonas's wound. "Star Before Moon has the strength."

I explained to Wizard Seelain and Lilly what the shaman said, allowing Jonas to overhear. Then I asked River Runs Down, "How far is your healer?"

"One day gallop, bearing your wounded spell man."

The shaman must have sensed Jonas's magical abilities. I am sure he sensed my frustration. "Didn't those sent by Cloud Runner tell you how injured our man was?"

"They did," he said with confidence. "Chief Fleet Hoof sent me."

"He cannot travel that far," I interrupted. "Even by stretcher."

River Runs Down stood and crossed his arms. "I can prepare him. We rest now."

He said something to Cloud Runner in their own tongue. Then the shaman addressed me again. "Tell the white-haired spell woman, at sunrise we will go."

The next morning, using some herbs combined with spells, River Runs Down put Enchanter Jonas into a deep sleep. The shaman appeared surprised how quickly his spells took effect. The shaman must not have known that enchanters had less resistance to spellcraft.

It was more than a deep sleep. The enchanter's breathing had slowed to one breath a minute and his heart beat one time compared to my heart's six.

We made good time riding on the centaurs' backs. It was difficult to see ahead, around the human part of the centaurs. It was also uncomfortable without saddles and stirrups. Blankets helped and it was better than trying to keep up running alongside. Four of the centaurs bore Jonas on a stretcher between them. I rode ahead upon Cloud Runner. River Runs Down bore Grand Wizard Seelain, while Bear Chaser carried Lilly. They even had a massive warrior that stood nineteen hands, enabling Ormb to ride. That centaur was aptly named Strong Back.

The terrain remained hilly, mainly wooded with scattered meadows and glens. Large furry animals that looked to be half horse and half sheep wandered the area. The adults stood four or five hands taller than Strong Back. Cloud Runner named them llamas, and said they were protected by his people and a main source of food and leather. He said they also hunted the giant, tusked boars, as did the ground raptors. As well-armed and fierce as the raptors were, going up against a giant boar had to be dangerous. I wondered how the centaurs did it. I'd only seen them armed with spears.

As we neared the centaur tribe's home camp, which they named the Ground of Our Ancestors, we passed by grottos and deep overhangs cut into cliff sides. Grand Wizard Seelain said they were cut into the stone over the centuries by the small streams that criss-crossed the area.

I'd spotted several outposts along the way. Lilly caught sight of two I missed. The last one sounded a horn. A few minutes later a dozen centaur warriors joined us as we approached their home camp established under a massive overhang. Cloud Runner blew his horn, announcing our arrival. We passed through a thick stand of pines backed by a high split rail fence. They'd added sharpened wooden shafts, dug in and pointing outward, to make it a difficult barrier to breach.

Female centaurs, slightly smaller than the males, galloped down well-beaten paths to welcome the returning warriors. Unlike the males, their arm-length hair grew both from their head and down along their human torso's spine. Colt-sized children raced after them.

The females wore colorful chest wraps with lacing that allowed their straight black hair to flow in the wind as they ran. All of the females wore necklaces of beads and fancy stones, including the young girls or fillies. I guessed the red, green, blue, black and yellow striped designs and the necklaces had some cultural meaning, just as the feathers on the weapons carried by the males did. It reminded me of the purple and gold that soldiers of Keesee wore and carried into battle.

Their encampment appeared permanent with circles of tents of varying depths evenly spaced in the cleared area around the overhang. The tents were tall A-frame structures made of leather hides stretched across wooden poles. Central fires smoldered in each tent circle and appeared abandoned for the moment. The overhang looked to be the public area with permanent wooden structures built underneath it. Above, along the rim, I spotted two sentries.

Dozens of dogs joined the return celebration. Brown, with narrow snouts and white-tipped tails, lean and built for speed, they leapt and yelped for several moments before racing off to whatever they'd been doing before.

A female centaur rode up next to Cloud Runner, smiled at him and greeted me. She was a brown-eyed beauty who rivaled just about any woman I'd ever seen. My thinking struck me as odd. A year ago a horse-human crossbreed would have been a strange creature—a beast or monster, no different than an ogre or dragon. Maybe because they were potential allies. Or maybe life experiences, including befriending Lilly, had changed my view.

We continued up the hardened paths wide enough for three horses to gallop abreast. I wanted to dismount and walk but wasn't given the chance. I knew my legs would be stiff and sore at first.

Grand Wizard Seelain was riding next to me so I said to her, "I'd prefer to meet their chief standing on my own two feet."

"My thoughts are similar," she said.

I rested my hand on Cloud Runner's shoulder. "We would prefer to walk the rest of the way."

Cloud Runner signaled for the procession to halt while we climbed down. I looked back and said to Cloud Runner, "I bet even Strong Back is happy to give up his rider."

Cloud Runner looked over his shoulder and laughed. "I agree, Flank Hawk."

I was right. It took about five minutes for our legs to loosen up. Lilly, Ormb and I watched as Grand Wizard Seelain checked on Jonas. The enchanter remained in a deep sleep and only a small amount of blood had stained his newest wrap.

"I feel more than strong enough to heal any re-injury caused by the ride," I told Wizard Seelain.

"The enchanter appears stable for now," she said. "Offer your assistance after we meet and speak with the healer."

The four centaurs returned to their place around Jonas.

"Want us to carry him?" Lilly asked.

"They bore him this far," Wizard Seelain said. "If they choose, let them finish."

As we started the final distance into the encampment, Lilly said, "I sure hope some of them speak Mainland or Crusader."

I smiled back over my shoulder at her. "Me too."

The lodge was dark inside, lit only by a central fire that was more coals than flames. It made the two-story log cabin uncomfortably warm inside. Before the meeting we'd been given food and water, and the chance to wash up, only to be soaked with new sweat.

The packed-earth floor had a wooden ramp leading to a second tier that overlooked the ground floor's center. The second tier had small slit windows just below where the roof angled upward like a squat steeple.

"I bet this was hard for them to build," Lilly whispered to me. She stood on my left. Grand Wizard Seelain stood to my right and Ormb stood behind me. They'd placed Enchanter Jonas on the floor to Wizard Seelain's right.

Three dozen male centaurs lined the walls behind us, standing between leaning posts and facing in toward the fire. An equal number of female centaurs on the second tier edged up to the railing between similar posts. On the opposite side of the fire stood Fleet Hoof. He appeared middle aged with red striping painted on his face and chest. To his right stood the shaman, River Runs Down, and to his left stood Cloud Runner with feathered spear in hand.

The chief held his right arm across his chest and stamped with his left front hoof. "Travelers in need, welcome to the Ground of Our Ancestors." Although the words were oddly accented, he spoke in Mainland. That greatly relieved me.

A smile crossed Grand Wizard Seelain's face as she bowed her head slightly. "We thank you, Chief Fleet Hoof, and your people for assisting us in our time of need. I am Grand Wizard Seelain, on a mission in service of King Tobias of Keesee from across the Great Ocean. These are my companions." She gestured toward us in order of naming. "Flank Hawk, my guide and protector. Lilly, our scout. Ormb, our bearer and emissary from Outpost Four to the Colonel of the West. And this, our injured companion, is Enchanter Jonas, counselor and advisor in the ways of magic."

Chief Fleet Hoof stood silent for a moment and then said, "Cloud Runner, Warrior of First Rank, has told me of you and your mission. We will assist you, but for this boon, I request of you a service you and your companions are better suited for than my people."

Well, I thought. Fleet Hoof gets right to the point.

Wizard Seelain asked in a pleasant yet even voice, "What boon do you offer and what service do you request?"

The chief signaled to the tier above and a female centaur backed away from the railing and made her way down the ramp.

"Star Before Moon will cure your counselor of his wounds." He waited for the young centaur to move between himself and River Runs Down. She was the centaur who'd greeted me along the path to the camp. Despite my weak ability, had she identified me as a fellow healer? Even though she appeared young, it made me wonder how powerful she was. Maybe it was her magic that made her appear so attractive. But I didn't sense magic like I did with Enchanter Thereese's enamor spell back in the King's Palace.

Fleet Hoof's voice pulled me back from my thoughts.

"I and my warriors answer the call of the Undying Mountain Chief Toward the Setting Sun. We will bear you swiftly to that gathering. If one of the Undying Mountain Chief's flying chariots is not there to take you to him, six of my warriors will bear you swiftly to the home of the Undying Mountain Chief."

Fleet Hoof offered exactly what we needed. Faster travel and guides, and strength in numbers that assured a safer journey.

That was the good news. But knowing bad news was to follow reminded me of my father's saying: Now it's time for the ogre to grin.

Fleet Hoof continued speaking Mainland. Even so, he not only addressed us as he spoke, but seemed to be reinforcing what all the others in the lodge knew. "A blood devouring creature has invaded the Ground of Our Ancestors." He made a sign with two hooked fingers. "It stalks the night. Those of our people it feeds upon fall ill and weak. Those it tries to remake into its kind cannot be. They die. When it cannot feed upon the people, it feeds upon the llamas, killing them."

My thoughts began to form on a vampire, especially when Fleet Hoof said, "We hunt it with silver and fire, and blessed spears and darts. My people, as we are, cannot reach it."

He then switched his focus on me, on us. "We have tracked it. Attempted to bury it within its daylight lair. It is cunning and the caves are many and offer endless escape.

"We have seen the creature take the form of both a two-legged woman and a black-winged bat.

"The service we ask of you is to enter this creature's lair and end its life. So that my people may live and prosper."

Fleet Hoof crossed his arms and said no more. River Runs Down and Cloud Runner crossed their arms as well. Star Before Moon stared down at Enchanter Jonas before meeting each of our gazes.

Grand Wizard Seelain asked, "Is this creature of which you speak a vampire? Or a lycanthrope?"

The second possible foe Wizard Seelain mentioned hadn't occurred to me. I'd heard horrid tales of vampires that sometimes stalked the cities. I'd rather face a lycanthrope, any lycanthrope.

Fleet Hoof leaned close and consulted with his shaman. "We do not know what a vampire creature is. What you name a lycanthrope, we also name werebeast."

I wanted to see Lilly's reaction, but at the same time didn't. I chose the latter.

"Fleet Hoof's request seems equitable," Wizard Seelain said. "His people can provide what we need. We can act where his people cannot."

I stared out between the tent flaps made of llama hide and drank cool water from a wooden cup. The sun was near setting and warriors of the centaur tribe had already scattered throughout their territory. In addition to their spears, they carried an atlatl, a carved stick with a hook at the end that enabled them to throw their narrow four-foot javelins at impressive speeds and distances. Lilly had pointed out that their javelin tips were silver.

The centaurs were spreading out before nightfall to spot and track the lycanthrope back to its cave in anticipation of our hunt.

Wizard Seelain was right. Our mission's success depended on the aid the centaurs could provide. And from their view, we would be able to enter the caves and root out the werebat. Something they couldn't do.

"Are we sure there's only one?" asked Lilly. "Ever heard of a cave with only *one* bat?"

They'd brought Enchanter Jonas out of his sleep. He lay flat on a cushion of llama pelts. "I can provide light within the cave," he said, struggling to keep his voice even despite the pain racing through his leg. The medicine was wearing off.

Lilly shook her head and stared up at the high cross pole supporting the tent. "Anyone here ever been in a cave?"

"I believe Ormb has," I said.

Lilly crossed her arms and huffed out a deep breath but didn't say anything.

"Look," I said, "if we don't slay this werebat, then Fleet Hoof will have to leave more warriors behind to defend his women, children and livestock. If we help, maybe that'll count for something when Grand Wizard Seelain negotiates with the Colonel of the West. Action on our part will enable more centaur warriors to aid the Colonel of the West in his war."

"The caves may be narrow and twisting," said Wizard Seelain. "We may not have access to Ormb's subterranean skills and knowledge."

"Whatever we decide," I said to Wizard Seelain, "you're not going underground." She started to protest but I cut her off. "What spells can you summon underground—in a narrow, twisting cave?"

Lilly reminded us, "Their healer said she'd heal Enchanter Jonas whether we went or not."

"What are our chances to make it the rest of the way to the Colonel overland?" I asked. "We may not cross paths with allies of the Colonel next time we run into trouble."

"They were following us," Lilly argued. "Your friend Cloud Runner only showed up to help *after* the fight."

"They didn't know if we were enemies or not," I said. "Even if they haven't said it, they probably feared us being attacked by that werebat if we entered their lands." Wizard Seelain nodded even as I finished my thought. "The last thing they need is more werebats."

"And that's just what you're volunteering to be if you go after it," Lilly said.

"River Runs Down said he and their blacksmith could add silver to my sword's blade." I patted my boot sheath. "Like my dirk."

"How good are you with a sword?"

"Competent," I said. Lilly rolled her eyes.

"You're not going after it alone," I said to her. "Enchanter Jonas already said that next to werewolves, werebats are probably the most vicious."

"I can be pretty vicious."

Grand Wizard Seelain placed a hand on Lilly's shoulder. "You will go. It is not the full moon, so in your muskrat form, you will have greater control. Flank Hawk will need your senses and ability to fight in tight quarters."

Before anyone could say anything else, she added, "Enchanter Jonas, you will use your spell strength to create glowing ropes to supplement their torchlight. If something goes wrong, I may need you to accompany me."

"You will *not* come after us," I said. If we failed, I suspected Fleet Hoof would still take Grand Wizard Seelain and Enchanter Jonas to where allies of the Colonel were gathering.

"If you fail, Flank Hawk," Wizard Seelain said, "you shall not have a say in the matter."

That made me even more determined. I gripped my spear and looked through the tent flaps again, watching two puppies playing tug-of-war with a scrap of leather.

Lilly asked, "What about Ormb?" The trog had sat quietly through our debate.

"It is up to him," Grand Wizard Seelain said. "But for the sake of Keesee and our people, we have no choice."

I finished the water in my cup and set it on one of the tent's leaning posts. "Let's go get Enchanter Jonas healed then."

CHAPTER 26

Lilly walked next to me through the trees in the predawn light. I hadn't slept well, wondering if they'd be able to track the werebat back to its lair. Lilly's warning about where there was one werebat there was probably more hung heavy in my thoughts and dreams.

Cloud Runner set the pace ahead of us with Ormb trailing by several strides. Behind him River Runs Down and Enchanter Jonas came next, followed by Grand Wizard Seelain and Fleet Hoof.

Lilly asked me, "Aren't you glad you're not a healer like Star Before Moon is?"

I nodded, remembering the healing ceremony. Inside Star Before Moon's tent Ormb and I held Enchanter Jonas on his stretcher in front of her. The healer's tent was larger than a centaur family's tent, but I didn't think she had a mate or children, or foals. Like the inside of the few centaur tents I'd seen, it was sparse of decorations and possessions, other than things like pelts to be worked, sewing equipment, and wooden dishes.

River Runs Down and Strong Back had stood on either side of Star Before Moon. She chanted, closing her eyes. Her words were like a song with a repetitive rhythm that might lull an alert sentry to sleep. Then she placed her right hand on Jonas's leg, and ran it the length of his red and infected wound. Already sweat from fever had afflicted him.

Jonas flinched but didn't cry out. But, as his wound faded, Star Before Moon did cry out. Her piercing shriek startled me. Her chant ended, she broke out in a sweat and River Runs Down and Strong Back leaned against her and held her up.

Lilly saw it first on her. She stepped close and whispered for me to look. The centaur healer's left rear leg bore a wound mirroring Enchanter Jonas's. He was unconscious. The centaur healer was nearly unconscious, her eyes rolling up in her head as she began chanting again, faster with an alternating rhythm. River Runs Down chanted too, helping her keep focused.

After a moment, a female centaur came in and directed us to carry the healed enchanter out. I gave my half of the stretcher to Lilly and stayed in case my healing skills were needed. I doubted they would be, but it seemed like the right thing to do.

It was hard to stand and watch Star Before Moon in pain, struggling. It took a half hour for her to complete the healing ceremony, the healing spell fixing her leg and breaking the infection and fever. Time seemed to stretch much longer than the half hour.

The entire time it took for Star Before Moon to recover I thought about Grand Wizard Seelain watching me struggle, suffer and fall unconscious while I strove to heal Enchanter Jonas. She had to endure without being able to help, knowing that both of us might die in her arms.

A change in direction that took us steeply downhill brought me back to the present, pushing my thoughts on healing and the centaur ceremony from my mind.

Cloud Runner began leading us along a shallow stream. Long-legged insects skittered across the water in the slow moving elbow turns while minnows darted between the rocks for deeper parts.

I rested my left hand on the pommel of my sword while stepping over a log lying across a narrow section of the stream. My sword was better now, at least for slaying lycanthropes. After the healing ceremony, I'd watched River Runs Down's magic assist the tribe's hammering blacksmith infuse silver taken from the tips of several long javelins into my sword's blade.

It wasn't magical, and wouldn't hold an edge as well as it once had, but Lilly assured me she wouldn't want to be cut by my sword's remade blade.

"Thinking about your fancy sword?" Lilly asked.

Her question shook me out of my thoughts, reminding me she'd asked a different question a moment before. "Thinking about a lot of things," I said.

"They seem kind of primitive," Lilly said. "Living mostly in tents and all. But like with magic and blacksmithing and growing things, they know an awful lot."

I nodded again, recalling the impressive apple and peach orchards we'd walked through on the way to where they'd tracked the werebat. Following a bat, even a large one, though the night was an impressive feat. The only person I ever knew who might've been able to do it was Private Shaws, one of the king's infiltration soldiers. He was dead now. I wondered if I would soon be the same. I wondered if Enchanter Jonas or Grand Wizard Seelain would someday be thinking back about me in a similar way.

"You ain't talking much," Lilly said. "Maybe I should talk to Ormb."

"Sorry," I said.

"All I can say is that Colonel better help us after all we've gone through."

"You've met him, Lilly. I don't think our struggles will concern him much."

"Yeah," she said. "Ain't he like a couple thousand years old?"

I nodded. "You saw where he came from."

"We're just a blink of an eye to him." She smiled. "I bet he'll remember you, Flank Hawk."

"I don't know why," I said. "But I bet his gargoyle assistant remembers you. Not many care to tangle with stone creatures."

"You scared, Flank Hawk?" she whispered.

I shrugged, then nodded. I'd faced worse than a werebat, much worse.

But not in the dark, in a cave, not knowing where it—or they—might come at us from. How I felt didn't matter. It had to be done. Every day meant more gains by Fendra Jolain's forces. And more dying by ours.

Cloud Runner pointed downstream where the creek widened just before curving underneath an eighty or ninety foot cliff face. Where the cliff's base met the stream, two oval holes emerged with their bottom lips just below the stream's surface. Spread several feet apart in the limestone, one was about three feet wide and the other closer to four. They were dark, like a pair of mismatched eyes staring out from a flat, moss-speckled skull buried in the rock.

The patter of raindrops on leaves began.

Cloud Runner whispered, "In there." Then he pointed near the cliff top. "Several fissures, maybe connected."

I handed my spear to Strong Back and said to Cloud Runner, "Help me remove my armor."

Grand Wizard Seelain was whispering into Lilly's ear. Lilly nodded and began removing her clothes. Then she stepped up next to me. "Remember, I go in first. I can find it."

I nodded as they took my breast and backplate and set it against a tree. "Don't try to take it yourself," I said, reminding her of our plan. "One on one it'll tear you up."

"They'll probably tear us both up."

"They only saw one?" I asked Cloud Runner.

He said, "Yes," and signaled for me to step close. With two fingers he spread black lines on my cheeks. Horizontal on the left and vertical on the right.

I didn't know what it meant and at that moment didn't really care. Grand Wizard Seelain handed me my helmet. I slid it on and buckled it tight under my chin.

"Be careful," she said.

I checked my gauntlets, making sure they were pulled on tight as possible. "Did you tell Lilly that?"

"I told her to listen to you." Seelain made sure my dirk in its sheath was secure on my right forearm. I figured crawling through a narrow cave, if I needed the dirk, I might not be able to reach my boot. The grand wizard took my leather-clad hands in her pale white ones. "I have no illusions that either of you will heed my words."

"Did you say something to Ormb?"

She frowned, and started to say, "You know he is unab—"

She stopped when she saw my smile. "I'll tell him for you," I said.

I looked around. Lilly crouched behind several bushes. I knew what she was doing—allowing to happen. Enchanter Jonas was just completing his spell upon two leather cords. Sweat rolled down his face, mixing with rain drops as he chanted the last words.

He tied one leather cord around Ormb's left wrist and tied the other to mine. "Yours will begin glowing in five minutes," he said to me. "Its illumination will increase for ten minutes and then fade away over ten more minutes. Ormb's will begin in twenty minutes and last for twenty, just like yours.

"Thank you," I said, and then explained what Enchanter Jonas said to Ormb.

"I wish I could be of more assistance. I could go in Ormb's place."

"No," I said and glanced down at the nearby, staring black holes. "I'm not sure how far Ormb will even be able to follow." I gripped the enchanter's shoulders. "Ward the grand wizard well in my absence."

"Make it a short absence."

With that, Lilly, in her beast form, came up next to me. The centaurs watched her with both hesitation and curiosity. I stroked her dark brown fur and stared down into the dark muskrat eyes. "Take it slow," I said.

She bowed her head once and began making her way through the trees down toward the stream. I signaled to Ormb, "Let's go. Oh, and Grand Wizard Seelain said for you to be careful."

The trog grinned and turned to wave back at Seelain before extending his weapon back toward her as a sort of salute.

The centaurs had provided him three of their silver-tipped javelins, which he'd lashed together. His job was to watch our rear, offer advice, and make sure anything that got past us didn't get past him.

A stiff breeze brought dark storm clouds over our heads and the light rain became a downpour. I followed Lilly while checking my sword in its scabbard. Ormb strode close behind me. Lilly's muskrat form sniffed at both entrances before selecting the larger one, scuttling in and disappearing in the shadowy darkness. I crouched, ducked my head and followed her in. After crawling on hands and knees for several yards, an opening to my left came into view. Scant light from the second smaller hole showed that the two had merged before jutting upward. Lilly was already climbing up into that deeper darkness. The crevice started wide but quickly narrowed, making me feel like a cockroach climbing up a corroded scabbard.

The walls were damp and dark and my sword's scabbard scraped along the side as I pressed my back against the wall, looking up into the darkness. I guessed I'd only gone about fifteen feet up. There was no way Ormb would fit.

I didn't want to warn the enemy, but my noisy climbing probably already had. "Wait, Lilly," I whispered.

Finally, Jonas's cord tied to my wrist began to glow. Lilly was already fifteen feet above me, still climbing. Only fifteen feet—she probably had gone slow.

"Ormb," I whispered downward. "Too narrow for you." He nodded and removed his cord, tossing it up to me. Reaching down between my legs I caught it on the second try. Then I climbed, trying to find purchase with my boots while grasping and clinging to cracks and small fissures in the gritty stone. Bits from Lilly's climb sprinkled down on my face. A rancid, acidic smell hung in the quiet air. It reminded me of rats, but stronger.

A larger opening, making me think of a merging vein, spilled into the shaft we climbed. The vein was wet, beginning to trickle with water. Still, it gave me good enough purchase to continue my climb. Ormb would have fun looking up.

A female voice from somewhere above yelled. It wasn't Lilly's. Even if she had been in human form it was too shrill. It sounded muffled, and in a language I didn't understand. Some of the words might've been like what the Colonel's men spoke but the distance and cave's distortion made it difficult to know for sure. Although Ormb might know, he was too far away to ask. Even as the shouting ended, it reminded me of an angry bird threatening a cat nearing its nest.

In my experience, cats usually backed off from a really belligerent bird. We couldn't back off. Also, in my experience, even if pressed, a cat usually won but didn't come away unscathed.

Lilly's climbing pace picked up even as the shaft narrowed, making it hard for me to bend my knees unless I turned them sideways. Uncomfortable. And using my arms to climb became more tiring and difficult. I placed my right hand between my chest and the wall, holding myself in place while I found better footing. Holding up my left hand I allowed the cord's glow to illuminate the tunnel above. I could just barely see Lilly's black scaled tail dangling downward as she climbed, using her four feet for purchase at every angle possible, sometimes using her back for support just as I did.

She was waiting. Why? Was she close to the werebat's lair?

"Take it," I said, climbing fast as I could. "Don't wait for me." The shouting meant the werebat wasn't in its beast form—at least not yet. Unless it had weapons, Lilly had the advantage.

Then I heard clattering, rock striking off rock, and Lilly squeal. She shifted and skidded back for a second before bursting upward, climbing again. Several flat rocks clattered past her, one glancing off my helmet and tumbling off my shoulder. "Rocks!" I shouted down to Ormb. First in Mainland—on accident, then in Sea Spittle.

Two more rocks about the size of plates but twice as thick fell. They must've hit Lilly, because there wasn't much room in the shaft, and they struck me with less force than they could have. My steel helmet deflected and my padded armor absorbed the impacts.

The second cord began to glow. I hadn't even noticed the first had begun to fade.

We pressed upward, past another vein opening, this one dry, and then Lilly slipped forward and from my sight. I recognized her murmuring squeal matched by ear-piercing screeching. Scraping and the sound of tumbling and tussling against the rocks followed. The werebat had shifted to beast form!

My arms were weary but I climbed, almost slipping twice, reaching a ledge that opened onto a shelf. It was like an internal section of the hill had split, dropped about three feet, and then settled.

The first thing I spotted was a ball of tumbling fur, black and brown rolling away. Screeching filled my ears. Then a black creature, the size of a cat, winged and bounding like a squirrel came at me as I scrambled to get my feet in place to thrust myself onto the shelf. Shining eyes, dark and red caught the glowing light. Exposed teeth, fangs darted into my face. Whether tooth or claw, something drew blood across my cheek and forehead before I could knock it away. I stumbled back, almost losing my footing.

It came back at me like a magnet to iron. At the last second I ducked my head. It struck my helmet, biting and clawing madly. I grabbed it—slammed it on the rock, once, twice. It bit through my gauntlet. I threw it back into the darkness, away from me. It came on again. This time I slashed out with my dirk as it leapt. It squealed in pain like a shrill dog whistle and flopped about, bleeding.

I took the chance to thrust with my legs and roll onto the ledge just before the werebat fell upon me. Fetid breath and long fangs assaulted me. I dug my head into its shoulder to protect my face and neck, and kicked over, rolling us away from the ledge. It was fast and stronger than me, and slick with blood. Blood! Was it mine, Lilly's or the werebat's?

Our rolling ended with it on top of me. I drove my dirk through the werebeast's shredded wings and into its ribs. It bit down into my shoulder. No stinging pain arose from the wound. Only numbness.

I strained to pry its head from my shoulder and couldn't. I stabbed again, but its hand—claw—grasped my wrist. I stopped trying to pry its head away and instead sought out its eyes with my thumb and drove it deep into the vulnerable socket.

That worked. It rolled off of me and backed away, seeking shadows and darkness. Hunched over I drew my sword and crawled after it. It stared back at me with its one good eye and released a wailing screech, causing pain in my ears and head. I shouted back, I don't know what, and launched myself at it just as it bunched to attack me.

It knocked aside my sword thrust, but I expected that—bait to give me an opening. When the werebeast came down on me with fangs bared I fell back and drove my dirk up, into its jaw and twisted. The werebat tumbled and thrashed. I kicked it off me and sent a sharp sword thrust into its side. Not deep, but I twisted and turned the blade. It rolled over and I scrambled on top of the dying beast. I sent my dirk's blade deep into its remaining eye.

It was dead—just quivering limbs.

I looked about and spotted another set of dark red eyes, watching me from their narrow corner of darkness. The second infant werebat squealed and ran on all fours for the shaft. I caught it with a hack of my silver-edged sword and finished it with a second stroke.

I searched the cave area again, trying to catch my breath. Sharp, acid feces, fir, blood and sweat all taken in. No more enemies, so I crawled over to the pile of fur that had to be Lilly.

My own blood dripped into my left eye, but I still felt no pain from the cut above it. Not in my shoulder either, although blood seeped into my padded armor. The scratches on my cheeks, those stung.

Bites and scratches scarred Lilly's face, shoulder and side. Bare skin showed where fur had been torn from her body.

I'd sent her against the werebat alone. She weakened it so that I could finish it. Now, I had to get help for her. I could try a spell to stop her bleeding, but first I needed to get help.

Leaning over to the ledge I shouted down the shaft to Ormb. "Send Jonas up here. With rope." I added, "Hurry!"

CHAPTER 27

It was my turn next on the table. It consisted of llama pelts supported by two poles lashed between leaning posts within the healer's tent. Star Before Moon had refused to heal Lilly and risk taking the werebat wounds into herself. She'd refused to heal me for the same reason.

Outside the caves, River Runs Down had stopped our bleeding with a paste of yellow mud, honey and herb juices. He said the spit of the werebat numbed pain and kept a wound's blood flowing. They didn't drink from fangs like a vampire, but pierced a vein or artery and drank the blood that flowed from it.

The bites inflicted during our battle hadn't been so delicate.

After being bandaged in her human form and helped down, Lilly sat and struggled to remain awake. Exhausted from battle, loss of blood, and returning to her human form so quickly had sapped her strength. Fortunately, reverting to her human form had initiated healing of her deepest bites and scratches.

After climbing onto the table with Cloud Runner's assistance, I watched Lilly's eyes flutter and slowly close. She slumped over, to the ground near the tent wall, at the hooves of Star Before Moon.

My padded armor had protected my shoulder except for two puncture wounds where the nearly inch-long fangs had bitten through. One of the infant lycanthropes had slashed me just above my eyelid with its teeth despite my helmet. I was lucky. I hadn't lost an eye.

As River Runs Down chanted while casting a spell over me, I wondered about my luck. Being bitten by a lycanthrope in beast form wasn't good.

Enchanter Jonas stood by Wizard Seelain and both observed. During the fight Jonas had been waiting just outside the cave entrance. He was up into the cavern with a coil of rope so fast I hadn't had a chance to begin a healing spell. He'd admitted using a little magic to assist his climb.

I waited, watching River Runs Down. He hadn't struck me as a man prone to smiling, but I was hoping he'd grin wide with good news. Although I wasn't sure exactly what his spell limits were, he knew a lot. His enchantments helped his blacksmith, he could cast healing spells to close cuts, and now he sought to know if werebeast blood flowed within me. Whatever he said, either way, I'd believe him.

River Runs Down frowned. In Sea Spittle, he said, "Flank Hawk. Over your chest, you wear a charm. You must remove it."

His request surprised me, but I did as he asked and removed the acorn-sized crystal holding the fallen angel's blood. Enchanter Jonas took it by the chain made of paired silver links and River Runs Down continued as if he'd never stopped.

Less than a minute later, he ran his hand over my body, slowing over my face and wounded shoulder, and my heart. "The spirit of what you call a lycanthrope is within you," he said, folding his arms across his chest. "Your spirit is fighting it. Refusing to share your camp's fire, your heart." Then, to Fleet Hoof, Cloud Runner and Star Before Moon, who'd been watching in the background, he spoke in his own tongue. I guessed he repeated what he'd told me because their eyes, filling with sorrow and defeat, met mine.

Even though I fully expected to hear the news, I didn't know what to say.

Wizard Seelain stepped forward. "What did he say, Flank Hawk?"

I suspected she knew, but I told her anyway.

She took my right hand and squeezed it. "Ask him which is stronger, Flank Hawk. If your spirit can vanquish it."

I asked River Runs Down. He continued to frown. "Your spirit is strong. Your healing ability acts as a shield in the fight, but it is a small shield."

He signaled for Jonas to give me back the necklace. "Your charm nips and distracts the beast's spirit." He shook his head. "Come the round moon, when it is at full strength, those three will not be enough."

I thought back. Four days before the ground raptor attack. A full moon. Lilly had changed—she had no choice. And soon, neither would I.

I didn't have to tell Wizard Seelain the answer. She looked up and away, blinking, trying to hold back tears.

River Runs Down placed his hand on my shoulder. "Your spirit is strong, Flank Hawk. Even nights of the round moon, the beast's spirit will dominate the fire, but will not be able to drive your spirit out."

Blood and evil, I thought, remembering the red eyes in the cave. What will happen to me? Who will I be—what will I become? I let go of Grand Wizard Seelain's hand. She tried to take it again. I balled it into a fist and pulled it away and sat up.

"Can your magic help me fight it?" I asked the centaur shaman. It was a selfish question. It might mean abandoning Grand Wizard Seelain, and the cause to retrieve the Blood Sword. But would I even be safe around her?

River Runs Down shook his head." I have no magic to help." He backed away. "I could not help my own people. We cannot survive such a merging of spirits and they now run with the herd of our ancestors."

CHAPTER 28

Getting used to riding on a centaur's back without stirrups or a saddle took less time than I thought it would. A rope around the centaur's human waist helped. Grand Wizard Seelain, Lilly, Enchanter Jonas and I each rode on three different centaurs during a day's travel so we wouldn't wear any one down. Ormb, because of his size, required five.

We were now in open grassland where I thought centaurs would be more at home, but they seemed to be more nervous and alert. We stopped for lunch. My meal consisted of dried llama meat wrapped in flat bread. The centaurs always supplemented their meals of whatever they offered me and my companions with large amounts of leaves or grass. It made sense as they were half horse. They also ate while on the run, snatching a handful of leaves or grass from a tall thatch as they tirelessly galloped along.

Fleet Hoof led a little over two hundred centaur warriors of his tribe northwest toward a place where the Colonel of the West's forces were supposed to gather. About eighty male warriors, most of the females, and all the colts and fillies remained at the camp, the Ground of Their Ancestors. River Runs Down remained there as well. Fleet Hoof said they needed a leader and protection in his absence. He believed The Undying Mountain Chief Toward the Setting Sun would have plenty of shamans to call upon. Thirty female centaurs, including Star Before Moon, along with two dozen hunting dogs, brown, lean, and built for running great distances, came with us as well.

I sat down in the deep grass fifty yards past the outer sentry. Halfway through my meal I heard someone approaching. It wasn't the thudding hooves of a centaur. I didn't bother to turn and see who it was. I wasn't in the mood for talking, or even silent company.

Lilly sat down next to me. It wasn't going to be silent company.

"Wizard Seelain said to give you some quiet time," Lilly said, looking at me even though I stared ahead. "She said you'd talk when you're ready. She doesn't know you like me."

I didn't say it, but Lilly didn't really know me—especially now.

"I bet you're scared, Flank Hawk." She pulled and twisted a few strands of grass around her finger. "Wondering what's going to happen to you. To your life." She twisted the grass so tight her finger began to turn red. "If you'll even be you."

After a few breaths, she asked, "Are you counting days until the full moon?"

"Don't you?" I asked.

She flashed a grin. "Got ya to talk at least."

"I talk," I said.

"When? The last person you actually said more than two words to was that centaur shaman before we left. What'd he tell you?"

"You know what he told me." I got up and began walking.

Lilly followed. "Why don't you talk to me? I'm your friend. I know more than anybody what's going on inside you."

"You don't." I stopped and turned on her. "I feel it growing each night. Getting stronger. At first I thought River Runs Down was wrong—that I could beat it."

"You still might," Lilly said. "If you beat it the first full moon, it'll die inside you. It needs to emerge the first full moon to survive."

"I know that, Lilly." I shook my head. "It's in my dreams. I dream of blood, Lilly. I think about it—all day. Crave it." I turned away from her again. "It makes me sick." I stood and began walking away from her again. "I don't want it, but it's what I'll be. Forever."

"You're planning on leaving us, aren't you? The night of the full moon. Or before."

I didn't say anything, but that was my plan. I couldn't risk being around anyone. Not then, maybe not ever.

"You can beat it," Lilly said.

Lilly was a lycanthrope. I'd never heard of anyone afflicted ever subduing their beast. "I'd only have to beat it once. Have you ever seen anyone defeat their beast?"

"No," she said. "But I've only seen two bitten ever fight it." She latched onto my arm and turned me around. "But they were not strong like you. You've fought the Blood Sword when it tried to possess you. You fought that lamenting soul when it entered you and tried to make you give up the sword."

"But I only won because I had help. Roos's saint-blessed saber and the threat of the Blood Sword."

"That must've taught you something, Flank Hawk. You're tougher now, and a healer. And you have that amulet. Maybe this is what Belinda the Cursed gave it to you for."

"I'm not much of a healer and I don't think Iceheart has much concern for me."

"We're going to see the Colonel of the West. He's lived for thousands of years. I bet he could help, if he wanted to. Or if we make it back to Outpost Four before the full moon maybe one of the lamenting souls could get inside and help you fight? Then you'd have help like before."

Just then, Enchanter Jonas came running up to us. "Flank Hawk, Wizard Seelain and Chief Fleet Hoof want you with them right now. And bring your crossbow."

High above us circled a hawk. I'd seen a hawk circling yesterday and the day before, but didn't think much of it. Was it the same one?

"Are you certain it is the animal familiar of an enemy?" Grand Wizard Seelain asked Fleet Hoof.

"I believe so. River Runs Down could tell me for sure." He looked skyward and moved his arms in a pattern much like a flag man signaling distant troops. "I have warned it off twice today and yesterday. Friends of my people would recognize the message."

He spoke in his own language with Cloud Runner and two other Warriors of First Rank and then said to Wizard Seelain, "Through it our enemies know our location, direction and speed of travel. The hawk flies higher than our spears and darts can reach. If it is within your power, kill it."

Wizard Seelain touched the quarrel on my ready crossbow with a spell. I took aim, knowing that the weak air elemental summoned would guide my quarrel far beyond its normal range.

With a *thwunk* the quarrel raced four hundred yards skyward and found its mark. The hawk staggered in flight, then fell.

Cloud Runner sent one of the dogs to retrieve the fallen bird. It was larger than most hawks I'd seen, brown with a speckled feather chest and red feathers making up the tail and long feathers in its wings. My quarrel had pierced it through the chest, killing it within seconds.

Fleet Hoof offered Grand Wizard Seelain one of the feathers. She declined, but I took the red one he offered me and tied it to my boar spear like the centaur warriors did.

Enchanter Jonas said, "Some witch out there is hurt and undoubtedly angry."

I shrugged, not feeling much of anything. Even knowing that bringing down the hawk increased our safety—that of Grand Wizard Seelain—didn't seem important. That thought bothered me.

Fleet Hoof changed our direction of travel more toward the west. Even so, by late afternoon an enemy force appeared arrayed for battle across a hillside, blocking our path. About a hundred pikemen, actually satyrs bearing twelve-foot pikes, lined their front rank. I'd only seen a satyr once and these resembled him, manlike and burly with goat horns and legs.

They wore no clothes, and had only a leather strap over their hairy chests supporting their sword belt. All of the curved scabbards, however, appeared empty. Behind them at least four hundred human foot soldiers stood ready. Half wore chainmail armor with swords and shields. The rest wore leather with rings sewn into it. They bore axes or spears and lacked helmets. Behind them stood a hundred unarmored long bowmen. All of the soldiers held neat lines and appeared disciplined, except for the satyrs.

I handed Lilly back her spyglass. She'd already lent it to Fleet Hoof and Cloud Runner. She handed it to Grand Wizard Seelain. Enchanter Jonas stood further back, eyes focused nowhere, but concentrating on something. A spell.

Centaur scouts reported another hundred reserve soldiers and about eighty horse-mounted cavalry on the hill's far side. Whoever they were outnumbered us four to one. We could turn back and outrun them. We could circle around and make it to Fleet Hoof's destination by adding no more than a day.

The dogs had settled down, with only an occasional snarl or warning yelp. They wouldn't be much help in a battle. The centaurs stood ready, gathered mainly in family groups. Against the soldiers on the hill, man for man, I'd put my coin on a centaur. But the enemy outnumbered them, outnumbered us. Organized and disciplined meant trained soldiers.

Fleet Hoof signaled me over, to join his Warriors of First Rank. "You have faced enemies like these?"

I nodded. "Except for satyrs."

"Share your knowledge with me. With my warriors."

"They'll slaughter you if you charge them," I said, giving my honest opinion as I would to any superior officer who requested it. "The archers are long bowmen. They can reach three-hundred yards. From the hilltop, even farther. Farther than your javelins, even with the atlatl."

Fleet Hoof listened and translated my words for his warriors. They either didn't like or didn't agree with my words.

"The pikemen look to be the least trained," I continued. "But charging forward, those warriors that survive the archers? At least twenty more will be lost to pikes. They'll break your charge and then the foot soldiers will carve up those of you that remain. They look to be trained and know their business."

I waited for Fleet Hoof to translate.

"Your shields are hardened leather and small. They won't protect your entire body from a rain of arrows. Your javelins will hurt them, but you cannot afford to exchange fire with the bowmen."

I shook my head. "Add the reserves on the other side of the hill. They are too many. Retreat and go around." I stepped back when I finished. I could've used a word other than 'retreat' but I felt it better to be direct.

Fleet Hoof shared and considered what I had to say. He and his warriors were discussing the situation when one of his council pointed toward the hill. A man and a woman emerged from the pikemen and were walking toward us. She had a white cloth tied to the top of her gnarled staff.

Lilly came to stand next to me. "Enchanter Jonas says they got a seer or a witch." She looked back and then ahead. "Pretty strong. Are we going to fight them?"

"I don't know."

Fleet Hoof said something to his warriors and then turned to me. "Join me, Flank Hawk, as I go to listen to their words."

That surprised met. I met Cloud Runner's gaze. It was his place. He nodded, solemnly. "I will," I said to Fleet Hoof. To Lilly I said, "Ward Wizard Seelain."

Lilly met my gaze. "I will, Flank Hawk."

Fleet Hoof waited until Lilly returned to Wizard Seelain standing among the centaurs. "You honor me," he said.

One of the female centaurs affixed a pale gray cloth to my spear before I moved to Fleet Hoof's right and walked forward with him. I guess they didn't have anything white. I know I didn't.

"The woman is a witch," he said quietly. "She does not know you, and your blood crystal charm will trouble her."

"And her familiar's feather on my spear will unsettle her." I knew very little about witches, other than some of their spellcraft mimicked that of enchanters, sorcerers and seers.

I observed the two as our distance closed. The man was tall, probably having seen fifty summers guessing by the gray in his thick red mustache. He wore breastplate similar to mine, scarred from many battles. His hand rested heavily on the pommel of his broad sword. He looked more like a mercenary than a long serving officer of some military force.

The witch's flowing black hair showed no sign of gray, but as we got closer, her green eyes revealed the wisdom of age. A spring green shawl wrapped over her shoulders stood in contrast to her gray blouse, black tunic and tattered skirt. It appeared she'd attempted to mend the skirt dozens of times and then gave up. Walking through the deep grass demonstrated the futility.

They were sizing up Cloud Runner and me as well. What they decided upon remained hidden behind calm, confident eyes.

We stopped ten feet away. Fleet Hoof waited for them to speak. The mercenary soldier did, in Sea Spittle. "You are Fleet Hoof, Centaur Chief of the Ohio Valley." It wasn't a question, and I was fast learning Sea Spittle to be a language widespread, far beyond sailors.

"I am chief of my people," Fleet Hoof replied, folding his arms. "And you are?"

I felt a bristling of magic, not quite like what Grand Wizard Seelain gave off when she was angry. It was more like what I'd felt when in the presence of Imperial Seer Lochelle, but weaker. The witch was concentrating on Fleet Hoof. Whatever it was—a spell, came from her.

Before the mercenary could answer I tipped my spear toward the witch and said, "Like my feather, witch?"

My question caught Fleet Hoof and the mercenary off guard, but the witch kept staring at Fleet Hoof, rubbing her index finger over runes on her staff. I didn't know what she was up to, but it wasn't good, so I spit across the distance, striking her on the cheek. "I asked if you liked my feather."

The mercenary reached with his sword hand for his blade but the witch touched him and said, "No," and focused a wicked smile on me. Her teeth were white and straight, but somehow cruel.

Fleet Hoof sighed even as I felt a wave of magic roll over me and into me. She squinted at my chest, where the amulet hung under my breastplate. I summoned my own healing magic, a thread of energy, not knowing what to do other than send its warmth across my skin in an effort to block her magical probing. Doing so without preparation stung behind my eyes, but it was worth it.

She laughed, but I smiled back at her, knowing I'd foiled her effort on Fleet Hoof.

"You," she said, pointing. "You slew my hawk. Whether it comes to battle or not, whether you survive or not, I shall lay a curse upon you—"

I cut her off. "Can't you see, witch, that I am already cursed?" I stared at her, while inside dropping the barrier I held between me and the werebeast—letting some of it surface.

Once, Roos had looked upon Lilly, seeing her aura and naming it as gray. I imagined the witch, if she could see such, saw black. Although her eyes didn't widen, her pupils did, then narrowed.

Whatever she saw, blood of a fallen angel, mercenary, healer—and dark werebeast—I pointed back and said, "Whether it comes to battle or not, I'll taste your blood, witch."

"When I finish with your frail enchanter and discover what secret he is hiding, we shall see which of us tastes the other's blood."

"Enough!" the mercenary said.

The witch frowned and glared at me as the drop of my spit slid like a tear down her cheek.

"Fleet Hoof," the mercenary continued. "I am Major Wex. I lead the forces under the banner of the Pantheon of Sky Color Gods."

I'd never heard of such gods, but Fleet Hoof must have. I focused my attention on the witch while he and the major spoke.

"Where are their colors?" Fleet Hoof asked.

"They will be unfurled if it comes to battle. So know this…" Major Wex paused while placing his hands on his hips. "You may choose the side of the victors and join us.

"You may engage us in battle and be destroyed. We will then march to the Camp of Your Ancestors and destroy it after slaying your people there.

"You may retreat back to your lands and await our victory. You will then be marched upon and destroyed along with the Camp of Your Ancestors.

"You may flee us to join the enemy, whereupon we will march to your lands and slay your people there and destroy the Camp of Your Ancestors. We will then join in the battle, where you will be slain with the rest of the enemy."

He folded his arms and said, "Decide."

Fleet Hoof replied without hesitation, "Reveal the colors of your masters so that we may trample them with your blood."

There were no more words between Fleet Hoof and Major Wex. The witch flashed a wicked grin my direction while the major smiled, satisfied and confident of his impending victory.

We took several steps back before turning to return to our lines. They did the same.

As we strode back, I focused on driving the beast back into its corner. Sealing it in. When calm returned to my face Fleet Hoof said, "My people resist magic well. The witch is strong. You saw and acted and risked much."

I nodded and tugged the gray cloth from my spear. I wanted to ask what she'd tried to do and what he thought I risked, but instead said, "Wex wants this fight. He doesn't intend to lose much more than the satyrs."

"He is hiding an additional strength," Fleet Hoof agreed. "Will your grand wizard stand with us?"

I didn't see that we had a choice. If the centaurs engaged in battle, how could we do otherwise? "I believe she will."

"That is one of our hidden strengths."

"What's the other?"

"The satyrs will stand to war with us."

CHAPTER 29

At the top of the hill four flags flapped in the breeze, green, blue, orange and purple. To reach and trample those flags I rode into battle behind a thundering line of male centaurs. The three female centaurs armed with staves and slings carried me, Seelain and Lilly in the hoof-thundering wake. Ormb and the rest of the females, along with the hunting dogs, remained behind, circled around Enchanter Jonas as he fought a losing magical struggle against the witch. His only hope: We kill the witch before she killed him. That was the plan.

From my right, Seelain shouted, "There's a wizard among them!"

The enemy archers drew back on their bows. Wizard Seelain saw it and raised her staff. The hail of arrows arced toward us while magic bristled about Seelain as she loosed her spell.

All arrows but a few to the far east and west angled down and stuck the grass short of our charging formation. Fleet Hoof shouted encouragement to his line of centaurs backed by a cluster formed to drive a wedge through the enemy forces.

A ball of flame shot up from the hill's far side, confirming a fire wizard's presence. Grand Wizard Seelain's counter spell scattered the flaming ball before its fire lanced down into us. But that allowed the second volley of arrows to reach us unhindered. Some steel-headed shafts bit into the grass or leather shields held high. Others found centaur warrior chests, arms and flanks. Wounding some, dropping others.

My centaur mount, Raven Shadow, leapt over a fallen warrior as we closed.

At fifty yards the centaurs cocked back their atlatls and hurled their darts among the enemy on the hillside. As the enemy ducked behind shields, dodged or fell, Fleet Hoof and his warriors closed to less than twenty five yards. The satyrs held their wall of pikes ready, glinting in the sun. Behind them, men with swords drawn stood ready. Some looked prepared to step forward and strike any pikemen that fled or faltered.

Fleet Hoof held more faith in his fellow woodland brethren than I did.

Fifteen yards. Ten yards. Five—as one the satyr line dropped flat to the ground, taking their pikes with them. Shouting wild battle cries, Fleet Hoof and his warriors leapt over the satyrs and drove into the swordsmen defending the hill's base.

We followed them into the line, close behind the driving wedge and among the enemy and satyrs, hoping to avoid arrow fire. The satyrs abandoned their pikes and dashed into the fray, taking up fallen swords and axes against our foe.

I shouted to Lilly and Seelain, "Dismount!" Our mounts knew the signal and came to a stop. Mounted combat weakened Seelain's concentration and made us obvious targets.

Sword and axe armed soldiers waded through the ragged centaur line and came at us. Lilly downed one with her sling before drawing her dagger. Seelain dropped another with a swift concussion of collapsing air. Raven Shadow missed a parry and suffered a slash to her arm before being decapitated by the soldier's backswing. I leapt over her still kicking fallen body and took that man in the throat. Shouting curses, I fought wildly to draw the enemy to me.

A satyr wielding two axes fought at my back. We parried and blocked more than attacked but it gave Seelain the space she needed.

The centaur warriors drove the enemy back. The black stripe-painted warriors fought, pivoting and slicing with their spears, kicking and crushing heads and chests with their hooves. The enemy held the weight of numbers but not determination nor strength.

The battle seemed to halt when a flaming elemental spirit crested the hilltop and raced down into the raging battle. Like a ten-foot torch, scorching the earth, burning and blistering friend or foe as it passed, it closed on Fleet Hoof and his knot of centaurs wreaking the most destruction.

From the sky a whirling air elemental descended upon the fire spirit. Seelain's creature shredded the flames but suffered and slowed as its foe ignited anew and fought back.

Spears and swords clashed and sang again, drawing blood. The satyr at my back fell and I was pushed back, dropping to one knee, after ducking a sword thrust but taking a hammering axe blow to my side that *clanged* off my armor.

I spun, bringing my spear around while trying to catch my breath. A buzzing shadow flowed between me and the axe-wielding soldier. I squinted as several insects pelted my helmet and face, but followed through on my sweeping strike. My spear's blade caught the axe-wielder below the knee, slicing through his leggings and into muscle and tendon.

A quick spear thrust into his chest dropped him.

"Flank Hawk!"

Still fighting for breath from the axe blow, I stood and turned to see Lilly slapping at a black mass of hornets swarming over Grand Wizard Seelain. I sidestepped and ducked under a centaur kicking her back hooves into a wounded swordsman. What could *I* do? Fire or water was all I could think of and I had access to neither.

Twisting wind knocked Lilly back and engulfed Wizard Seelain. The elemental stripped and caught up the hornets from Seelain's body and whisked them skyward. Showing rising red welts on her face and hands, Wizard Seelain held her staff and refocused her effort to snuff out the fire elemental.

I looked up the hill. She'd held control of her elemental while casting a second spell—a feat I'd never seen before. And both while being bitten and stung. I spun back again to see remnants of the female centaurs that had been with Jonas racing our way. Horse-mounted cavalry in pursuit. The outnumbered female centaurs looked battered and scared. I shouted to Fleet Hoof, Cloud Runner—any Warrior of Rank, "Look to the rear!" I ran to put myself between Seelain and the charging cavalry. "We've been flanked!"

Lilly was at my side as a few dogs followed the female centaurs galloping past us. "Jonas!" Lilly shouted. "Where's Jonas?"

A series of three or four muted thunderclaps sounded from behind, up on the hill. I didn't dare turn to look. Instead I grabbed Lilly by the shoulder and pushed her back. "Ward Seelain!" was all I said and charged forward. Strong Back and another centaur angled in from my right to meet the closing enemy along with me, one that numbered least fifty riders armed with maces and swords.

We'd hardly slow them but, if I could take a lead horse, I could cause several that followed to stumble.

Their leader raised a hand and barked an order. Their charge slowed. They stared beyond me for a few seconds and then turned on the order of their leader and retreated.

I couldn't believe it, and watched for a moment before turning to see what the horsemen had seen.

Except for the scorched path through the grass, there was no sign of the fire elemental. Not even smoke. Fleet Hoof stood atop the hill with the impaled head of Major Wex held high upon his spear.

Closer to me, Lilly had her arms around Grand Wizard Seelain, holding her up.

"She's okay!" Lilly shouted, waving and pointing back to where the female centaurs had been attacked. "Get Jonas. He might need help."

I hesitated until Wizard Seelain looked up and tipped her staff, signaling she was okay. Spear in hand, I trotted back the three hundred yards, even as a few male and female centaurs galloped around and ahead of me. My side hurt where I'd been hit. Probably a bruise, and I'd have to hammer out the dent in my armor. But no blood, nothing permanent.

As I got closer, I saw the carnage. Twenty of the female centaurs were down. A few lay moaning and bleeding, but most were dead. Stabbed, trampled, legs broken and twisted. A centaur knelt with a tearful eye next to one of the dogs. Its side slashed open with entrails spread across the ground. Even mortally wounded, the dog managed a weak tail wag and struggled to raise its head to lick its master's hand. The centaur whispered a word, covered his canine's eyes and ended the misery with a quick dagger thrust.

"Jonas!" I called, then shouted his name again. Strong Back, who was kneeling and tending to a fallen female looked up at me and pointed. Next to two fallen females lay Jonas's body. Just beyond him, a battered and bleeding Ormb shoved a fallen horse off his legs and climbed unsteadily to his feet.

Closing the distance between us, I asked, "Ormb, are you okay?"

He spit and wiped blood from his mouth. "I am," he said and sat down next to Jonas.

The enchanter lay in a heap, like he'd collapsed of exhaustion. He was pale and a dampness that must have been sweat covered his body. There were no wounds and no breathing. I checked his eyes and listened for a heartbeat. He'd died with his rapier in its scabbard. The witch's spellcraft had gotten him.

For some reason I ran my hand over his hair to smooth it. Then picked him up and began carrying him back to Seelain and Lilly. I left my spear. It didn't seem important. I found myself mumbling, "Jonas, this is why enchanters hide their ability."

Ormb came up next to me and kept pace, resting a hand on my shoulder.

Lilly saw me and who I carried, and ran toward us. She looked back at Wizard Seelain who leaned on the shoulder of a satyr. Seelain waved for Lilly to go ahead to us.

Even though she knew it, Lilly asked, "Is he dead?"

I nodded and held him for her to see. She touched his cheek and turned away. "I knew it, but only half believed," she said, grief-stricken. Her voice shifted to anger. "Belinda, that cursed hag, knew it too—when she gave me the rod." She turned back to me. "Jonas knew it, too. Said it was possible, but wouldn't admit the hag was right."

"Maybe," I replied, not affirming either of Lilly's declarations. "The only promise war offers, the only one it can keep, is death." With that I swallowed hard, some of my grief beginning to spark toward anger. "Come on, Lilly. We're needed."

"Where's your spear?"

I ignored her question. Next to Fleet Hoof, Cloud Runner prodded the witch forward, toward the satyr and Grand Wizard Seelain. Along with Major Wex's head on his spear, Fleet Hoof carried the witch's broken staff.

I handed Jonas to Lilly. "Carry him."

She and Ormb followed me as I strode to reach Wizard Seelain before Fleet Hoof did.

They'd gagged the witch with a rag, a muddy strip torn from the purple flag tied tightly across her mouth. The witch walked with her hands behind her back, probably tied as well. A bleeding knot from a blow to her forehead was the witch's only apparent injury.

I stopped next to Wizard Seelain. She looked weary, and in pain from the red welts on her face and hands inflicted by the hornets. She leaned on her staff but stood on her own. I didn't need to tell her Jonas's fate. With anger in her voice, she ordered, "Deal with the witch, Flank Hawk."

Cloud Runner brought the witch to stand in front of me. Her eyes looked just behind me to where Lilly stood, still holding Jonas. A glimmer of joy crept across her face.

Fleet Hoof asked, "Do you have anything to say to the witch?"

"Remove her gag," I said and signaled Lilly to come up next to me.

This surprised both Fleet Hoof and Cloud Runner. They knew as well as I did that it was within the witch's power to utter a curse upon any one of us. It would cost her, but I guessed if the satyrs got a hold of her, they'd inflict worse than death upon her. Urges of blood rage boiled up within me. Was I picking on the urges of the surviving satyrs that stared at us from a short distance away or was it the werebest stoking my emotions?

When I stared hard at the two centaurs and nodded, Cloud Runner did as I asked and untied the mud-stained gag.

The witch's eyes held wicked mirth as she spit out the balled wad of cloth they'd stuffed in her mouth. Before the ball hit the grass, I drew Jonas's rapier from its scabbard and slashed its tip across her throat.

Surprise filled her eyes even as blood began to flow. It wasn't a deep cut, but enough to keep her from uttering a spell or curse. Reflexively she tried to bring her hands to her throat, but couldn't. I thrust the rapier into her chest, just above her right breast, and then again, above her left.

Anger filled the witch's eyes as she fell to her knees. I licked the end of the rapier, tasting her blood before spitting it in her face. The warm, salty taste further excited the beast that has risen within me.

My boot to her chest knocked the witch on her back. I ignored her gurgling breath, her struggle for air as blood filled her lungs.

I also ignored the darkness within me, striving to stir up increased fury. With gritted teeth, I forced the beast within me back, separating its urgings from my thoughts. Jonas might have wanted me to avenge his death, but not in such a cruel, bloody manner.

I took a step back. "We have a brave friend to lay to rest," I said to Fleet Hoof after taking a deep breath. "You have many of the same."

CHAPTER 30

We rode northwest, away from the centaur funeral pyre and the grave of Lesser Enchanter Jonas. Lilly carried his rapier. She said he once told her he didn't think it right for such a magnificent weapon to rust in the ground before its time. Instead, we buried the ashes of the witch's staff at his feet and Ormb placed his weapon of three javelins lashed together at Jonas's side, the silver tips still bloodstained from combat. Cloud Runner even painted the enchanter's face with a warrior's black stripes.

Over the past two years I'd lost scores of comrades, but Jonas's death hit me harder than most. A quiet city fellow, out of his element yet ever willing to step forward. He'd stood with me against the Necromancer King's goblins and ogres, even when his weapons appeared too frail. Together we'd survived a powerful sorcerer's attack.

I pondered what Lilly'd said about Jonas's impending death. Was there anything he or we could've done? Or was he fated to die here, so far from home? Did Jonas have a wife and children like Private Zunnert? A sweetheart, a mother and father awaiting his return?

As much as his death left a hole in me, it struck Lilly harder. Was I so focused on Grand Wizard Seelain's safety that I'd become blind to life's bonds being forged around me? And without Jonas at Seelain's side, it'd be harder to separate from her when the full moon came. When the beast gaining strength within me emerged to claim its portion of my life…

Grand Wizard Seelain's eyes revealed her grieving, but she'd hardened since our last loss. Maybe it was that she'd fought so hard—couldn't have done more. I glanced over at her, a distant gaze on her face, holding the saddle horn tight. We all rode on saddles taken from enemy mounts to make travel easier on us and the centaurs' backs. Because of Wizard Seelain's lingering spell fatigue, she didn't object when we strapped her into the saddle on Mud Splasher's back.

We rode past the surviving satyrs driving the captured enemy supply wagons. They were piled high with armor, swords, axes and shields scavenged from the battlefield. Even boots. Strung behind by a line of rope plodded five enemy survivors destined for interrogation, followed by slave labor, or maybe death. I didn't know. Fleet Hoof had put all the others, wounded or otherwise, to a quick death.

Only eighty of Fleet Hoof's warriors survived. Half of those suffered wounds that inhibited travel. They remained near the battlefield with Star

Before Moon, to be healed. I didn't know if they and the surviving females would follow us or return to their home camp.

We waved to Fleet Hoof and his warriors escorting the wagons.

"Two days hard travel for us," Cloud Runner told me over his shoulder. "It will take them five."

We raced ahead to report our battle to the Colonel's gathering leaders. Strong Back, bearing Ormb set the pace. I, on Cloud Runner, followed ahead of Wizard Seelain and her mount. Lilly on Rock Hammer brought up our rear.

Cloud Runner signaled the rider upon the winged horse circling above us. He called it a pegasus. Until it came close enough to see clearly I'd thought it was a griffin.

After two more hours of travel over sparsely wooded terrain a mule-mounted patrol intercepted us. Mules weren't as fast as horses, but they were more rugged with greater endurance. The soldiers, wearing wide-brimmed hats and mottled green uniforms, looked equally rugged. They carried long-barreled revolvers and curved sabers.

Cloud Runner exchanged words with the patrol's officer while the rest looked us over with hard, unfriendly eyes. The only one they managed to intimidate was Ormb. Finally the officer turned and pointed, giving Cloud Runner directions, or instructions, or both.

Within an hour we approached the Colonel's mustering camp established near the shore of a great blue lake.

"Look," Lilly said to me and pointed to three tall buildings that resembled Outpost 4's skyscraper. They stood only about half as tall but appeared far more squat and expansive. "Maybe they have lamenting souls there that can help you, Flank Hawk."

I shrugged, trying not to get my hopes up.

The distant buildings did impress me, but not as much as the gathering military force we rode through on our way to the ancient structures.

"How big is his army?" Lilly asked, looking at a heavy wooden rail where over thirty winged horses had been tethered.

I breathed in the odors of campfire ashes, horses, sweating men and oil on steel. I smelled blood too, from somewhere. The beast stirred deep inside me. I tucked it back into its dark corner.

"At least twenty-five thousand," I guessed. That didn't include the freemen and women supporting the camp: cooks, blacksmiths, porters, animal handlers, tailors and so many more. Then there were the beasts. Great gray, tusked elephants, some moving logs, others pulling wagons or cannons or artillery pieces. Wooden kennels holding short-snouted war dogs with collars bearing studded spikes. Even a gray-scaled dragon with sturdy wings whose head appeared more bovine than reptilian, including long curved horns.

We'd learned from Cloud Runner that the Pantheon of Sky Color Gods included five colors. Fleet Hoof's warriors had trampled only four at the top of the hill. Cloud Runner said, "With the red flag missing, the Undying Mountain Chief Toward the Setting Sun must have slain the Red Sky God and placed her head on his war spear."

What we'd seen of the war waged against the Colonel of the West caused me to believe, like Keesee, he was on the defensive—maybe losing. What Cloud Runner said, and the huge force surrounding us, made me think how the Sky Color Gods might have made a big mistake picking this fight.

"Those are trucks," I told Wizard Seelain as five of them rumbled past us with growling engines. Their flatbeds each held two machine guns mounted on tripods. She'd seen similar guns recovered from the Necromancer King's crashed Stukas, and knew what firepower they held.

Tents and shanties organized in rectangles, with packed dirt and gravel roads graded to allow rain water to run off without muddying them, emphasized that someone maintained organization over the growing army. Our presence seemed swallowed up.

As we neared the brick buildings, stationed guards challenged us. Cloud Runner's password and explanation always enabled our continued passage.

A rhythmic growl approaching from the west filled the cloudy sky. Lilly spotted it first. "Look, Flank Hawk. The *Osprey*. Remember it?"

How could I have forgotten the flying machine? It had carried Lilly, Roos and me from Outpost 4 to the Colonel of the West's mountain.

Wizard Seelain watched the propellers mounted on the wings rotate upward as the craft slowed and landed on the shortest building's roof. She adjusted her cloak. "It may be that we have arrived at the appropriate time."

Two guards escorted us through the wide hallways. They were armed only with sabers but struck me as knowing how to use them. They even let us keep our weapons.

Our steps fell into rhythm with theirs, boots clomping on the stone floor and echoing off the brick walls, the bottom third painted gray and the upper part a dingy white. High above tubes of light hummed. They bathed the hallway and ancient-looking wooden doors an odd color.

"I hate those lights," Lilly whispered to me. "They're like flickering candles that can't make up their mind on staying lit."

I didn't notice any flickering. But maybe in fourteen days I'd sense what Lilly did. Ormb seemed to be enjoying the stroll down the hallway. He'd even taken off his sandals. If I listened close and ignored the boot-clapping, I could hear his flat feet slapping against the cold mosaic-tiled floor.

Most of the doors had windows set into them bearing lettering formed by black or white paint. The script used for the ancient symbols looked a lot different from what I'd seen at Outpost 4, but I recognized some of them as being the same.

We turned and then continued down an even wider hallway until we came to a set of double glass doors with metal frames. Two guards stood at attention outside of them. Upon our approach, the left guard pulled open one of the glass doors and went inside. He spoke to a woman with long red hair working behind a desk piled with papers. She nodded, stood, and straightened her green uniform before going over to knock on a set of solid double oak doors a half dozen paces behind her desk. She opened one of the dark stained doors a crack and stuck her head in.

"I haven't seen any lamenting souls," Lilly whispered in my ear. "You should ask Ormb if he senses any."

"Grand Wizard Seelain will ask when the time is right," I whispered back. Lilly gave me a sharp look so I added, "I'll ask Ormb when we get the chance."

The red-headed woman turned and signaled for us to enter. She carried a curved dagger on her left hip, so she must've been a soldier.

One of our escorts said to Wizard Seelain in Mainland, "A good day to you, Madam Wizard." They both then turned sharply and walked back down the hall. The guard remaining in the hallway opened a glass door for us.

I noticed dark ink stains on the red-headed soldier's hand as she signaled us toward her. Up close I could see dark circles and crow's feet around her eyes. In Mainland she said, "The warden has set aside time in his schedule to meet with you. Go on in. I'll close the door behind."

I moved ahead of Grand Wizard Seelain before she could object and stepped through the half-open door. I didn't expect trouble but, recalling my memory of meeting the fallen angel, Warden of Outpost 4, I wasn't about to take any chances.

I didn't really know what to expect but what I saw wasn't close.

Eight lanterns with downward reflective hoods hung by bronze chains halfway down the forty-foot ceiling. Wooden shelves lined with hundreds of square slots covered the right and left walls to a height just below the lanterns. One or more rolled scrolls filled nearly every slot.

The far end of the room held a large rectangular pedestal with the narrow end facing us. Upon the red granite block, etched with black scenes of buildings, trees and battles, rested a fearsome beast. Most of it was lion, except for the head of a red-bearded, straight-nosed man. Wavy red hair flowed back from his head and face, almost like a lion's mane. The fur on its body appeared more of a yellowish tan than anything else. The creature rested on the six-foot high pedestal with great forepaws extending just over the edge and watched us enter. Its golden eyes held my gaze. If it stood, the beast's shoulders would be above my raised arm and hand.

Six people were in the room. The first two were soldiers, guessing by their sabers, mottled green uniforms, and holstered revolvers. The others were young women, beautiful, with long red hair that fell past their waist. They wore white, sleeveless silk gowns that reached only a little further down than their hair. Emerald paint surrounded their already green eyes.

Wizard Seelain, standing to my left whispered to Lilly on her right, "A sphinx."

Two women carefully pushed a tall table bearing a map with markers designating military forces from in front of the sphinx while it ordered in a deep, purring voice, "Captain Elder, see to my orders. General Agnatious, stand aside while I attend to this matter."

Both men saluted. The taller one strode to the right of the pedestal and down a stairwell set into the floor. The general turned sharply and strode to a place along the right wall and studied the map on the table while rubbing his fingers across his broad chin.

The tallest of the red-headed women took a scroll from a table near the stairwell and stood at the head of the pedestal before lifting the unrolled sheet above her head for the sphinx to read. The fourth woman lifted a long-handled fan and hurried to the rear of the pedestal. There she climbed a staircase set alongside and began to gently fan the lion-like beast to the slow rhythm of the bushy tail tip slowing moving from side to side next to her.

The room was quiet, except for the sphinx's deep breaths. Ormb stood behind Wizard Seelain, more still and silent than Wizard Seelain and me. Lilly fidgeted, placing her hands inside her blue wool jacket's pockets and watched the two women who'd moved the table and now stood near a ladder along the left wall. They appeared poised to climb the polished metal rungs and retrieve one of the high-placed scrolls.

After another moment the sphinx fixed its golden eyes on us. "You may approach."

As we did, the tall woman hurried to her place near a ladder along the right-hand wall.

Wizard Seelain gripped her white staff in her right hand and bowed her head slightly. Lilly and I bowed once as well, a little longer and more deeply than Wizard Seelain. From behind, I guessed Ormb did the same.

"Welcome to Outpost One," the sphinx said. "Your stay will be short. Word of your journey reached me from Outpost Four and Colonel Ibrahim requests your presence as soon as it can be arranged. The *Osprey* will convey you to him."

At some unseen signal, the women near the ladders moved to open the wooden doors behind us.

"It departs within the hour."

Wizard Seelain said in low but firm voice, "Warden of Outpost One, if I may request another moment of your time?"

"I have read the report of your engagement," the warden replied, examining his paw. "Assistance by pegasi has been dispatched to aid what remains of the Ohio Valley Centaur Tribe." Then his voice blended with a growl. "Your audience is at an end."

At some other unseen signal, even before the warden finished his statement, the fanning woman and scroll-holding woman hurried to return the map table to its former position.

Lilly stepped forward. Grand Wizard Seelain placed a hand on Lilly's shoulder, but she shrugged it off.

"Lilly," I said between clenched teeth. "Let Wizard Seelain—"

Without turning back to me she said, "No! This is important."

Both Wizard Seelain and I stepped up next to Lilly as she continued. "Warden of Outpost One, we're allies. I don't know if you read about what Flank Hawk did, but because of him, Chief Fleet Hoof had two hundred instead of one hundred warriors when we wiped out that army fighting for the Pantheon of Sky Color Gods. Your enemy. Our enemy. Without the two hundred, we'd have lost. They'd be still out there, and you wouldn't have any centaurs coming.

"Maybe compared to the thousands you already got around your outpost here, those enemies we killed and those centaurs that survived that are gonna show up to fight with you ain't much. But if you treat all your allies fighting for you like they're nobody—and Grand Wizard Seelain ain't nobody and neither is Flank Hawk—who'll..."

Lilly stopped and took a deep breath. It surprised me that the sphinx, although looking at her with fuming eyes, let her keep talking.

Lilly held her hands out to her sides. "Why will anybody wanna fight hard for you?"

The warden smiled, but his eyes remained hard. "Thank you for the impromptu speech on leadership, Scout. I am aware of what Grand Wizard Seelain contains and represents. I know of Flank Hawk and his exploits. I even know of you, Scout Lilly." The sphinx flexed his claws. "My sources say you were willing to fight Dr. Mindebee to defend the honor of your mercenary companion."

It was true. Both Roos and I had to hold Lilly back from the gargoyle.

"Wouldn't you, for a friend?" Lilly asked.

General Agnatious stood at attention, stone faced, while the servant women backed up against the scroll shelves.

The warden stood and stared down at us. At Lilly. "Mindebee *is* my friend."

That statement surprised me. Maybe Lilly too. Seelain and I stood closer to her. Ormb closed in behind us.

"Grand Wizard Seelain follows court etiquette," Lilly said. "Flank Hawk is tied to duty. So neither feels it right to ask. So I will."

The sphinx sat on its haunches. "Of what will you ask?"

"If there's a lamenting soul that can help Flank Hawk. See, he got bit by a werebat when—"

The warden raised a paw and swiped left to right. It wasn't an aggressive move but it stopped Lilly's words. Maybe it was magical. If so, I didn't feel it.

"Centaur Warrior Cloud Runner has already petitioned for assistance on Flank Hawk's behalf."

That surprised me. Lilly and Seelain too. We'd stood with Cloud Runner and reported our encounter and travels before we went separate ways. That was less than two hours ago.

Lilly looked at the floor, walls and ceiling. "You must have lamenting souls around here, like Outpost Four does. So, can you get one to help Flank Hawk get rid of the beast growing in him?"

The warden shook his head. Both Seelain and I grabbed Lilly as a smile crossed the warden's bearded face. It wasn't a cruel smile or a mirth-filled smile. It settled into a smile of understanding.

"A lamenting soul cannot oust the beast, nor can one assist your friend in the task."

"Why not?" Lilly asked, still tense and leaning forward.

The beast within me felt the stirring of Lilly's beast. "Lilly," I warned.

"Lycanthropy," the warden said. "Both curse and disease, at least when applied to your mercenary friend. Just as the soul can influence the mind and body, so can the mind and body taint the soul. The beast is rooted in his mind and body. Not within his soul. Thus, other than moral support, the lamenting soul cannot be of assistance when the final struggle ensues. Even if he had foreknowledge, a lamenting soul's intrusion would hinder your mercenary friend's battle against his inner beast rather than assist it. I know of no magic to assist your friend."

Lilly let out a deep breath. Her shoulders sagged. Color returned to the servant women's faces. Only the general remained at attention.

"It's alright," I whispered to Lilly as Grand Wizard Seelain said, "I thank you on behalf of myself and my companions for your thoughtful concern and insight, Warden of Outpost One."

"*O Fortuna*," the warden said to Lilly. "Dr. Mindebee has seen and learned much over the centuries. If your friend mercenary can be assisted in his coming struggle, Mindebee may have knowledge of such a way. If you ask and he first denies your friend assistance, Scout Lilly, ask him to translate *O Fortuna* by Carl Orff. That may stir his stone heart."

With that, the servant women once again began to move the map table to its former position. The others opened the doors behind us.

In a dismissive voice the Warden of Outpost 1 said, "Now, your audience is at an end." To me the tone sounded forced.

Ormb turned away from me and got sick again, filling his fourth sack. He'd never flown on a dragon's back, let alone inside one of the Colonel of the West's flying machines.

"At least we're not on the *Hercules*," said Lilly to Grand Wizard Seelain. "That was a lot bumpier."

Grand Wizard Seelain said, "I wonder what it would have been like to fly in one of the Necromancer King's Stukas?" She leaned back in the canvas bench seat mounted along the *Osprey*'s side wall. "Similar to a riding a wyvern," she decided. "Far faster, however. Less wind and exposure to the cold air, even at higher attained altitudes."

We'd been seated aft near the *Osprey*'s loading ramp for the four hour trip. Wooden crates strapped down and covered in netting were piled between us and the other eight passengers. With the engine noise and us speaking in Mainland—except when I talked to Ormb—it was as if we were alone.

Despite the belts holding me in place, I reached up and patted Ormb on the shoulder. "It's okay. Flying isn't for you. First time I was in a boat I got sick over the side."

He tied off the top of the last sack and set it next to the others, as far away from us as he could reach. "No water up here to carry it away."

I ignored the acidic odor. There were far worse smells to endure.

"When you're done being nice to Ormb," Lilly said, "you could always say 'thank you' to me."

"Didn't Grand Wizard Seelain teach you court etiquette?" I replied. "The warden looked pretty mad. How'd you know he wasn't going to attack, or at least deny our request?"

Lilly grinned. "The Colonel of the West is like King Tobias. Who'd dare not to send somebody the king requested because they asked a question out of turn?"

Grand Wizard Seelain patted Lilly on the leg and smiled.

"You met that Colonel," Lilly said. "Even if you were tough as that sphinx looks, would you want to explain it to him?"

I shook my head. "But he could have just sent us and not you, Lilly." I didn't really believe my argument. Lilly didn't either. "Thanks," I said.

She looked away but couldn't suppress a gleeful smile. "You'd do the same for me."

I wanted to tell her I hoped she never crossed paths with the Warden of Outpost 1 again. Instead I said, "Lilly, the proper words are, 'You're welcome.'"

CHAPTER 31

Upon landing at the airfield a waiting truck carried us up the winding road leading to Mountain Base 1. Two huge barns that looked like barrels half buried in the ground kept hidden from our view whatever other flying machines that the Colonel had. The tarp covering the truck bed where we rode kept us dry from the steady rain. It also limited our field of vision to the rear where half of the tarp had been tied back above the gate.

"This truck sounds like a muffled panzer," Grand Wizard Seelain commented, sitting on the vibrating wooden bench.

Sergeant Arnolds, a blue-eyed man with calloused hands sitting across from her and next to Ormb asked, "A panzer?"

"One of the Necromancer King's steel battle wagons," I said. "He learned how to build them from damned souls from before First Civilization's fall. They carry machine guns and a big cannon that rotates to find a target. And they reload from inside. Not from the muzzle like the Crusader cannons."

"How did you fight them?" he asked.

"With earth elementals," I said. "How are the winged horses, pegasi used in combat?"

"Mainly scouts and messengers."

"Are they faster than griffins?"

He looked out the back of the truck. "I can't really say."

After that he listened to us talk but didn't say anything until we needed to put on blindfolds when we neared the entrance to Mountain Base 1. He was probably under orders. Lilly had started to talk about our plans, but caught on when I switched topics to my liking to ford rivers more than her, especially in the rain.

After about fifteen minutes with blindfolds on, the truck stopped and waited while a gate creaked open. A few minutes after passing through, echoing sounds hinted that we'd entered a tunnel. Less than a minute later the sergeant helped us out of the truck and announced, "I'll take your blindfolds now."

We stood in a tall corridor that reminded me of the coal mine near Pine Ridge. But this tunnel was at least twenty feet high, carved from stone, demonstrating expert workmanship. Tubular glowing lights like those at Outpost 1 lit the area.

Lilly looked up and around. "These lights are more like Outpost Four's.

They don't flicker."

"This way," the sergeant said, directing us through a metal door. Two soldiers dressed in solid green with holstered pistols on their belts followed where Sergeant Arnolds led us, through a maze of halls, doors, and stairs.

Finally we stopped in front of a room whose door slid open. Stepping into it, I asked Lilly, "Remember this?"

She nodded as the closet-sized room began going down, like a bucket lowering into a well.

Although she'd had plenty of time to prepare, I stood close to Wizard Seelain, knowing she didn't like being underground.

The door slid open and we stepped out into a hallway that resembled the top levels of Outpost 4, but without tapestries on the floor. We passed no one the entire time and I was pretty sure it was intentional—just like the last time Lilly and I walked the same halls. The Colonel of the West was at war, so his mountain fortress might have been sparsely manned, and that was why we passed no one.

Upon reaching the third door down on the right, one of the guards following us pulled out a flat key held by a sturdy chain around his neck. He unlocked and opened the door and flicked a switch upward, causing a set of overhead tubes to light up. Inside the square room was a rectangular oak table. Four padded chairs lined the side closest to us. On the opposite side sat a single chair. Three of the walls were painted olive green. The wall opposite had a door like the one we'd entered through. The forth wall, to the left, was actually a large mirror.

"Remember this room, Flank Hawk?"

I nodded to Lilly.

Before leaving, the escorting guard said, "Major Parks will be with you shortly to interview you. Then you'll be escorted to a meeting with Colonel Ibrahim."

Lilly sat down and folded her arms across her chest. "This whole big mountain and we get put in the same room."

Wizard Seelain laid her staff on the table and sat down next to Lilly. "Maybe Colonel Ibrahim is a creature of habit. Why alter successful patterns developed over time?"

"It makes you predictable," I said.

Wizard Seelain ran her fingers across the smooth table. "Maybe he trusts us."

Lilly got up but then changed her mind and sat back down. "I don't think so. He blindfolded us. Even Ormb."

"Well," I said, "his wireless telegraph communications are back up. Word got to him from Outpost Four about us, so he probably knows why we're here." I got up and walked around the table once. "That should speed things along."

We all sat silently for a few minutes. In Sea Spittle, I asked Ormb, "Have you ever been in one of those falling rooms?"

He nodded. "Chains and cables looped through pulleys powered by ancient motors raise and lower them."

"I prefer stairs," I said.

"We don't use the lift at Outpost Four very often."

Someone knocked twice and then opened the door. A lean man wearing a solid green uniform nearly the color of the walls, with a darker green ribbon hanging down from his collar, stepped in. We all stood.

"Good afternoon," he said in Mainland. "I am Major Parks." He offered us his hand to shake. Wizard Seelain did first, then me, Lilly and Ormb.

Before we sat the major said, "Ormb will be leaving us as it is my understanding he is not fluent in your language. He will be interviewed separately."

Then he turned to Ormb and said something in their common tongue. Ormb stood and said to me, "I hope to see you before you leave."

"I hope so as well."

Lilly hugged Ormb before he could turn to grab his spear leaning against the wall. The big trog returned the embrace and whispered something down into her ear.

Although the reasoning offered made sense, separating Ormb from us made sense for other reasons. That made me suspicious.

Major Parks began the interview by asking how the war with the Necromancer King had been going before the forces of Fendra Jolain began their invasion. Then he focused on Fendra Jolain's invasion and Keesee's plans for defense. Grand Wizard Seelain answered all of his questions, in greater detail than I would have, but leaving out specifics about troop numbers and disposition. Most of what she said was certain to be out of date anyway.

Then he asked about our journey. Here she provided exacting detail, even asking Lilly and me to fill in where her memory was lacking. Wizard Seelain covered the deaths of Private Zunnert and Enchanter Jonas without faltering. Lilly teared up a little when Jonas was discussed, but only for a moment.

Major Parks asked probing questions but wrote nothing down. I suspected that someone was listening in, somehow recording what Grand Wizard Seelain said. Normally she was more reserved in sharing details. I guessed she was under orders from King Tobias. Maybe the king believed the Blood Sword was the key to any hope of preserving his kingdom against conquest.

The war approaching Keesee seemed so distant. Maybe they already fought on Keeseean soil. My mind drifted, wondering what Major Jadd was doing. If he was still alive. If he, at this moment, might be wondering about me, about us.

When the interview came to an end, someone knocked at the door. Two soldiers stepped in, one male and the other female. After they saluted Major Parks, the female said to us, "We are here to escort you to facilities where you may clean up and prepare for dinner with Colonel Ibrahim."

The meal served us didn't appear to be anything special. We stood in a rations line behind several other soldiers and had food ladled onto a large rectangular partitioned plate. Although the plate was brown, it was made neither of wood nor of metal. Some sort of hardened wax was my guess. The chunks of chicken with thick broth and some sort of bread cooked with it slopped over the plate's central partition. Another cook placed a blue-tinted glass cup filled with apple cider into the round slot in a corner of the plate.

Major Parks led us through the line while Colonel Ibrahim followed, being given the same meal as his soldiers and us.

Long wooden tables and benches filled the mess hall, enough for two hundred soldiers to eat at once. Only twenty-five or thirty were there, seated in groups of five or six.

I spotted one table near the far wall with a white pedestal placed next to it. I figured that was where Major Parks was leading us. The Colonel stopped at the end of the serving line to address a concern with one of the cooks.

"These lights don't flicker," Lilly said. "You think it's magic, or ancient knowledge like the Necromancer King used, that makes them work?"

I didn't know if she was asking me or Grand Wizard Seelain. Maybe she wanted Major Parks to answer. When nobody did, I asked the major, "Where is Ormb?"

"He is being introduced to the troglodyte clan. To my understanding, he is young and lacks construction and maintenance skills, yet he is intelligent and his travel and combat experience will ensure status among his kind."

He gestured to a seat near where I'd set my spear on a rack along with the rifles of other soldiers in the mess hall. Grand Wizard Seelain walked with her staff while Lilly carried both hers and Seelain's food plates.

I stopped next to the round pedestal at the end of our table. "Will Dr. Mindebee be joining us?"

Major Parks gestured for us to sit on the bench along the wall-side of the table. "I believe he will."

Lilly let out a small hissing breath so I set my plate nearest the pedestal. "I'll sit next to him then."

Wizard Seelain leaned her staff against the wall and stood between Lilly and myself while we waited for Colonel Ibrahim to catch up.

The Colonel appeared just past middle age. He wore an olive green jacket over a light green collared shirt with a black ribbon knotted at his throat. He walked with a straight back, alert and without expression—just like countless officers I'd seen. But the Colonel of the West was a greater elf, an immortal blood. He'd walked the earth for nearly 3000 years.

Lilly made a point of tasting Grand Wizard Seelain's food and drink for poison before he reached the table. Seelain lifted a hand to stop her but changed her mind, knowing Lilly would object. Lilly was right and it was better to move forward than draw attention to it.

At the Colonel's invitation we all sat. He bowed his head, as did Major Parks, and said a silent prayer. When he looked up he said, "This is a humble meal, lacking the splendor of a distinguished visitor's banquet. But it is nutritious." He took a gray cloth napkin and placed it on his lap. "Whether I eat alone or with my officers, or occasionally among the enlisted men, I partake in the same food as they do."

Grand Wizard Seelain said, "You honor us by your presence and we expect no better than what you share with your soldiers."

He nodded and gazed across the table at Lilly. "Scout, you look as if you have a question."

Lilly hesitated but finally spoke after being urged by Wizard Seelain. "After all the years you've lived, doesn't it get boring to eat? I mean, this food smells *really* good. But how many times have you eaten it?"

"Many things have lost their luster, Scout." He spoke as if lecturing a newly recruited soldier, but in a friendly manner. "I encounter very few new or unique experiences." His voice softened as he pointed with his spoon to the food on his plate. "This chicken and dumplings is my mother's recipe. As always, the cook won't get it exactly right. Nobody but my mother could, except my grandmother."

He put a bite in his mouth, chewed and swallowed. "Although I think of them whenever this meal is prepared, I haven't shared this information with anyone in three generations."

Lilly's eyes widened. "Who was the last person you told about this?"

"A cook. A corporal named McCombs. He thought the recipe called for too much salt."

I took a bite of the chicken and dumplings. I'd never had it before. It was good and not too salty. Out of the corner of my eye I watched the Colonel eat. It was hard to reconcile the fact that he was a powerful immortal being. Some thought him equal to, if not a god. Yet he had his cooks prepare a meal that reminded him of his centuries upon centuries-dead mother.

Was he using guile to put us at ease when we should be on our guard?

We ate in silence for a few moments. After taking a long drink, the Colonel commented, "Grand Wizard, I am quite impressed."

Wizard Seelain smiled politely. "How so, if I may ask?"

"You appear much more at ease underground than any of my air wizards."

"I consider you to be an ally," she said. "Even so, I trust Flank Hawk to stand between me and any threat that presents itself. If Lilly were not at his side, she would be at my back."

"Loyalty and courage are admirable traits in those that serve."

"They are, in those that are served as well."

"Grand Wizard?" he said.

"Yes," she replied. The pleasant look fled her face. Prickling energy shot out, surrounding her.

The Colonel of the West frowned. "You attempt to deceive?"

As Wizard Seelain's magical energy flared, she stood and reached back, summoning her staff to her hand. Then several things happened at once.

Lilly flipped her plate into Major Parks's face and leapt over the table at him. He was quick and fended her off with one hand and went for his holstered pistol with the other. I stood, knocking back our bench and pulled my short sword even as the stone floor flowed up my boots, holding me in place.

Only Colonel Ibrahim remained seated.

Grand Wizard Seelain screamed, clutched her chest and struggled to conjure a spell. Gunshots went off and bit into the plaster ceiling as Lilly and Parks went to the floor. I leaned forward and hacked down with my sword while stone climbed and encased me up to my hips. Soldiers and cooks were on their feet. Some went for their rifles. Others leapt and climbed over tables to get to us.

The Colonel snuffed out Wizard Seelain's spell and caught my sword's blade in his left hand like a stone vice.

Lilly shouted, "Flank Hawk!"

Major Parks stood over her with his pistol pointed at her head. Her hands and feet sunk into the floor. There was nothing I could do for her. The encasing stone held me like a stump to the floor and the Colonel held my sword tight. Wizard Seelain held her staff between herself and the Colonel and his closing soldiers. With no other options, I grabbed my cup of cider and smashed the lip against the gray stone holding me before flinging the jagged mass into the Colonel's face.

The cider vaporized into steam before reaching him and the glass melted to blobs. They struck and rolled off his face and uniform like beads of water on waxed wood.

Wizard Seelain said, "There has been a misunderstanding."

Without looking the Colonel ordered the soldiers behind him. "Stand down."

The stone stopped climbing just beneath my shoulders. I felt fortunate that I wore breastplate or the encasing stone might've prevented me from inhaling a fresh breath.

"Even allies have been known to have disagreements," the Colonel said and nodded at Major Parks who then holstered his pistol.

"It appears I missed something." The fast spoken words echoed through the still tense mess hall. Lilly, still stuck in the stone of the floor, groaned. She recognized the gargoyle's gritty voice—that of Dr. Mindebee.

With a leap and flourish of long arms and claws, the gray stone creature landed on the pedestal. He wore a white jacket with slits in the back to keep free his folded bat-like wings. He had the build of a stout stone baboon with a grotesque tusked face and pointed ears.

"Now is not the time," Colonel Ibrahim said to the grinning gargoyle. "We will reconvene shortly in the conference room adjacent to your laboratory. See that it is ready."

The gargoyle nodded then looked at me and my extended sword arm. "A thrust attack might have served you better, Mercenary." He was probably right, but I doubt any sword attack would have succeeded.

Before anything else could be said to him, the gargoyle leapt down and shot away using all four limbs.

"Return to your meals," Colonel Ibrahim said to his men who watched us warily.

Wizard Seelain thrust the butt of her staff against the stone covering my left boot, causing it to crack. Strain of concentration showed as she did the same to the stone shell covering my other boot. With a few muttered spell words she smacked the stone covering my back, cracking it as well. A strike to my chest caused most of the remaining stone encasement to fall away. I'd have wagered a lot of coin that the Colonel assisted Seelain's effort. Even if it was true, neither would ever acknowledge or admit to it.

Lilly was already walking around the table to get away from Major Parks. He stood, ignoring remnants of Lilly's meal on his chin and uniform and waiting for orders.

"See to it that cider, bread and cheese are delivered to Dr. Mindebee's conference room." The Colonel then turned to us. "Retrieve your spear, Mercenary. Grand Wizard." His voice carried an odd inflection, an almost questioning tone when he spoke her name. "Please accompany me so that we might sort this out and move forward in solidifying our alliance."

Upon the oval oak table around which we sat rested the Blood Sword. I'd carried it long enough to recognize it by the hint of malevolence radiating from it, even sheathed. The ruby in the long sword's pommel was blood red. Fitting.

The blade harbored an evil soul, one that strove to possess the wielder. And any man, goblin, ogre or giant that the blade cut, died. Blood flowed from even the smallest wound while a foul illness spread throughout the body, causing sickly bruising and bleeding from the eyes, nose and ears.

The death its touch inflicted was as horrifying as it was painful. And we'd travelled and risked much so that it might be returned to the hand of Tobias, King of Keesee.

I didn't exactly understand what had happened between Colonel Ibrahim and Grand Wizard Seelain. Apparently a small ward created by Imperial Seer Lochelle and Supreme Enchantress Thulease had been hidden under Wizard Seelain's skin, above her sternum. Colonel Ibrahim was using some sort of detection spell and Grand Wizard Seelain wasn't being fully honest. About what, I wasn't sure. She thought she was warded. He was offended and I got encased in stone up to my armpits.

Politically, they patched things up despite the Colonel of the West saying, "Remember, we may be allies but that does not mean we are equals." Grand Wizard Seelain verbally agreed to an alliance on behalf of King Tobias between the Colonel of the West and the Kingdom of Keesee. Dr. Mindebee scribed two copies of the half page treaty for Grand Wizard Seelain and Colonel Ibrahim to sign.

From that moment forward it was Keesee, the Reunited Kingdom and the Colonel of the West allied against Fendra Jolain, Uplersh, the Necromancer King, the Pantheon of Sky Color Gods and the Az-Texas Empire, whoever they were. I didn't know if all of those standing against us were allies, but Keesee only had to directly worry about the first three. That was more than enough.

Against that, the Blood Sword seemed inadequate.

"I cannot spare my *Hercules*," the Colonel said. "Not even to get you to Outpost Four."

I looked to Grand Wizard Seelain. She nodded, so I asked, "What about winged horses?"

"They do not have the endurance. They might be able to get you from outpost to outpost, but the ocean crossing is out of the question."

Grand Wizard Seelain asked, "You said Belinda Iceheart was now at Outpost Four? Could she transport us across the Western Ocean as she did for Flank Hawk and Lilly?"

The Colonel shook his head. "By now, Jolain has healed the Kraken. If her ally Uplersh doesn't attempt to intercept you personally, she could easily send her tentacled attack dog."

"She fears the Blood Sword's return that much?"

"If she were wise, Grand Wizard, she would."

Dr. Mindebee leaned close to whisper into the Colonel's ear.

"That might work," Colonel Ibrahim said to his friend and advisor. "Grand Wizard, do you believe your serpent skills are up to handling a gray dragon?"

"While I have trained upon and flown red dragons and wyverns," she said, "I am not as skilled in handling and in combat as a true Keeseean serpent cavalryman."

She rested her right hand on my shoulder and her left on Lilly's. "Although both of my companions are experienced aft-guards."

Dr. Mindebee rolled up one copy of the treaty, slipped it into a brass scroll case and handed it across the table to Grand Wizard Seelain. "Colonel Ibrahim, I will deliver our copy of the treaty to Archivist Parmer."

"Very good, Doctor." Colonel Ibrahim stood and met Wizard Seelain's eyes before handing me the sheathed Blood Sword. I stood and took it.

Having the Blood Sword in my possession once again distracted me from what was being said. It was an evil sword and I wondered how King Tobias intended to use it. Its touch even managed to stir the beast lurking deep within me, bringing to my mind images of blood. I gritted my teeth, forced the thoughts from my mind and returned my attention to what was going on around me.

The Colonel examined the watch on his left wrist. "Grand Wizard, if you hope to be on your return journey tomorrow morning, we must be quick to visit my dragon master and his stables. We will select a mount and allow you and your companions ample time to familiarize yourselves with the beast and its handling. We have only two hours before the sun sets."

Grand Wizard Seelain asked, "Can it be accomplished so quickly?"

"Gray dragons are herbivores and much more docile than the reds you are familiar with."

"Before we go," Wizard Seelain said, "there is another matter." She went on to explain how and why I'd been bitten by a werebat, what River Runs Down had said, and that the Warden of Outpost 1 suggested that if anyone might have a solution that would give me a chance, it would be Dr. Mindebee.

Colonel Ibrahim crossed his arms while she spoke and then rubbed the fingers of his right hand back and forth across his chin. "What do you think, Mindebee?"

The gargoyle sat on his pedestal perch with arms wrapped around his knees and glared at me. I tried not to look too hopeful. Instead I strapped the Blood Sword across my back.

Lilly blurted out, "Translate *O Fortuna* by Carl Orff before you say 'no' to Flank Hawk."

The Colonel's eyebrows rose and Dr. Mindebee clenched his eyes shut. "It may take time," the gargoyle said after a moment. "Would you delay your return on the small chance I might find a possible solution to the mercenary's dilemma—one that may be prone to failure?"

"No," I said the same time Grand Wizard Seelain said, "Yes."

She turned to me. "Flank Hawk, your experience and your spear may be vital during our return journey with the Blood Sword. For the sake of our kingdom, I cannot risk failure. I cannot risk losing you."

I thought of the dire wolves and the sirens, and nodded.

Dr. Mindebee hopped down from his perch and signaled me to follow him. "I believe there is a case history of a San Diego priest who resisted the bite of a wereboar. If I can find it in the records, we shall know if there is any hope for you before midnight."

I don't know why Dr. Mindebee wanted me to go with him. I just sat in his laboratory while he stared into a box with a glass side where strange green glowing script appeared as he tapped his fingers on a board ink-marked with similar letters.

Glowing tube lights, twice as many as needed, lit the large rectangular room. Black tables lined walls where various boxes, cylinders and devices infested with wires sat partly pieced together. Scrolls bearing lined drawings with symbols sat next to most of what Dr. Mindebee called 'his projects.' He'd let me wander around, if I promised not to touch anything. I'd finished my third go round an hour ago.

Dr. Mindebee scribbled something on a small piece of paper and called to one of his assistants, Betty. The tall blond wore a very short blue dress that only reached halfway down her thighs, and matching blue knee-high boots with tall heels.

He handed her the paper and the two books she had brought to him a half hour before. "Bring that volume to me and have Veronica re-shelve these." Veronica was Dr. Mindebee's other assistant, identically tall but with long black hair and a short red dress and boots.

When Betty closed the door behind her, Dr. Mindebee turned away from his box. "The files on this system are not complete, but who has time to maintain, let alone upgrade it?" He swept his hand around, gesturing to the wire-filled boxes and cylinders. "Earth and fire wizards with the skills to do what is necessary are almost as rare as soldiers bright enough to be trained as technicians. Ibrahim expects miracles from me."

I looked at him blankly and nodded in agreement.

"Do you think my assistants are more alluring than Vincent Stansil's?"

"Who?" I asked.

He grimaced at me. "The sphinx. Warden of Outpost One. Betty and Veronica—those are not their real names." He scratched his nose adjusted his white jacket. "Are they more attractive than Stansil's assistants?"

"Yes," I said. "As I think back, Betty and Veronica are a lot better looking."

Sitting on his pedestal near his box, he raised an eyebrow and then squinted. "Are you lying?"

"No," I said. "Your assistants are not identical and smile more."

"Stansil always was and remains an arrogant ass. I know him from way back when the world first fell apart. The wave changed him just like it did me."

I recalled what Colonel Ibrahim had shown me of First Civilization's fall. How and why everything changed while collapsing I didn't understand and never would. "Why did you agree to help me when you have so much else to do? You don't even like me, or Lilly. Probably not Grand Wizard Seelain either."

The gargoyle rocked on his pedestal. Then he spun and looked away from me. "I was a scientist once. A human once. I remain the former, but am not the latter. You have a beast in you, just as I have a beast in me."

From behind I could see him hug his knees tightly.

"I cannot be separated from mine. I fight it every day and I would not wish such upon anybody. Even you, Mercenary. Even you.

"That ass, Stansil. *O Fortuna*, translating that song from Latin. A language ancient even before I was born. When I was human. It reminds me of fate. My fate, and if I can cheat the fate that works against you..."

We sat in unmoving silence until Betty returned with yet another dusty tome.

She placed it on the table next to Dr. Mindebee and returned to her seat across from him. After a moment the gargoyle stirred and opened the leather-bound book containing brittle, yellowed pages. He signaled for Veronica who carefully turned the pages for him, something he couldn't do without his stone fingers damaging the ancient book.

After searching several pages he directed her, this time in his own tongue, and she flipped to the middle of the tome and searched for a particular page. After a moment of reading, he stood high, flapped his wings and opened his mouth wide like a yawn, showing his tusks and pointed teeth.

He dismissed Betty and reread the passage.

"Mercenary, you may have a chance."

I sat up and listened. His voice held an excitement that gave me hope.

"A protestant pastor, Mercenary. The one horribly bitten by a wereboar and certain to become a lycanthrope, I told you about. He was close to a saint, from what the case study says. He was also friends with an alchemist. The alchemist convinced him to ingest silver nitrate prior to the night of the full moon. Lycanthropes don't interact well with silver, you know."

I nodded. "I know."

Dr. Mindebee sat and rubbed his chin. "The centaur shaman said Tyegerial's blood pendant is adversely affecting the beast within you. You are a healer, whose magic is resisting the beast. Those two elements combined might equal the faith of the priest. A blood pendant derived from an angel that *hadn't* fallen would virtually guarantee success. Unfortunately for you, in this context Tyegerial qualifies as fallen."

He shook his head while unfolding and refolding his wings. "Silver nitrate in your blood might weaken the beast enough for you to defeat it come the full moon, Mercenary."

He reread the page in the book again and wrote some notes on a piece of paper. "I am confident the infirmary maintains what you need in its inventory."

CHAPTER 32

Colonel Ibrahim handed Grand Wizard Seelain a steel scroll tube with a screw-on cap. "This is for King Tobias, to be opened within the confines of his palace. Anywhere else will destroy the contents."

What was in the tube, I didn't know. I doubted Grand Wizard Seelain knew what words it held as well. Security. We had a long and dangerous trip ahead of us. We, or it, could fall into the wrong hands.

Lilly looked around and handed a guard the torch we'd used while checking the gray dragon's tack. Although it was the same size and basic build as a red dragon, the gray dragon's horned head reminded me more of a bull than a reptilian serpent. It ate any and all vegetable matter with horse-like incisors and molars, and the splay-hooves on its hind feet emphasized that it wasn't a predator. That didn't mean the broad-winged beast was defenseless. Its three-foot curved horns were sharp and it had the ability to spout streams of scalding steam more than its body length, head to tail. That was only half the reach of a red dragon's fiery breath, but more than enough to fend off sirens and griffins.

Grand Wizard Seelain climbed onto her saddle first. I followed with Lilly after me, taking the rear-facing aft-guard position. We strapped our legs firmly to the saddle and checked our parachute straps before the stablemaster handed the reins to Grand Wizard Seelain.

"Take care of Balooga," the stablemaster said. He spoke awkwardly, like he'd memorized how to say the phrase in Mainland. "She a steady, a faithful mount."

"I will," Grand Wizard Seelain replied. "Thank you." The stablemaster nodded as if he understood Seelain's reply.

Grand Wizard Seelain then turned and looked down at Colonel Ibrahim who stood five or six paces back. "Thank you for your hospitality and gift, Colonel. May you earn great victories over your enemies, which are now our enemies."

I checked the straps securing the Blood Sword in place and patted the saddlebag holding three vials of silver nitrate. I met Dr. Mindebee's gaze and nodded. He yawned wide, fully exposing his tusks, and then returned the nod.

The Colonel of the West stood straight with arms at his side. "God Speed and take it to our common foes."

With that, Grand Wizard Seelain commanded, "Up," in the language of the Colonel of the West's men, one of twenty-eight verbal commands she'd memorized.

The gray dragon galloped several strides, snapped open her wings, and leapt into the air. Powerful flaps of the dragon's wings carried us skyward, toward the rising sun.

Lilly's second brass rod, a new one given to her by one of the Colonel's enchanters, guided us from outpost to outpost. The route to Outpost 4 wasn't direct. We flew east as we crossed the large continent, and then angled south before going generally east again. The final leg carried us northeast. Each night I watched the moon and counted the nights until it would rise full.

We saw signs of civilization through trading boats on rivers and learned of cities from our hosts where we slept. The rustic outposts offered us food, shelter and hospitality. Most were smaller than the overrun one we'd passed through before meeting Cloud Runner and his centaur tribe. After each stop a band of runes around Lilly's brass rod faded as we made our way toward the Western Ocean and Outpost 4.

Chesapeake Bay and the skyscraper along its shore finally came into view several hours past noon on the eleventh day after departing Mountain Base 1.

Grand Wizard Seelain shouted over her shoulder, "It will be good to see Captain Bray once again."

Lilly and I shouted agreement.

We circled the skyscraper twice before Wizard Seelain brought Balooga down near the tree where we'd buried Private Zunnert. Guards stationed atop the building waved and shouted. The broken glass and damage had largely been repaired. Along the pier Lilly and I both spotted the *Sunset Siren*, Belinda the Cursed's single-masted sloop.

Captain Bray had taken Coils and Wick to scout the area with one of the soldiers. It disappointed me as I'd been looking forward to reuniting with Wick, but it was good to learn that both the captain and Wick were in condition to travel and that Coils had returned.

A captain we didn't recognize escorted us into the parking garage where the wyverns roosted. Colonel Ibrahim had sent word by wireless telegraph to expect our arrival so they had a stable prepared for Balooga.

Then the captain escorted us into the skyscraper to meet with the new Warden of Outpost 4. Belinda the Cursed, the old crone with her white hair and glowing cobalt blue eyes, met us in a hallway leading into a suite of rooms on the third level. Her nails painted blood-red showed against her pale skin as she leaned heavily on her rune-carved staff. I knew it was an act, as did Lilly. Maybe it was habit that she walked in such a manner. Maybe like the Colonel of the West, her father, she too followed centuries old routines.

"Grand Wizard," she said in the tired voice of an old woman.

"Mercenary Flank Hawk and Scout Lilly, join me." She turned and hobbled back into her suite.

The large entry room had pale blue walls and plush, dark blue couches and chairs set around a squat, ornately carved table.

"Leave your spear at the door, Mercenary, and unstrap the blade you carry across your back. Keep it next to you if you choose."

Of course, Belinda the Cursed, also known to many as Iceheart, recalled my cautious nature. Having not even reached twenty-five summers, had I fallen into predictability as well?

I'd witnessed Belinda Iceheart's control over both air and water. As powerful as Grand Wizard Seelain was, I believed the hag's strength surpassed hers. The name Iceheart fit. I'd heard it said her blood was poison. Any man daring to spend a night in her bed would age, wither and die before sunrise.

Belinda Iceheart sat in one of the blue chairs. Grand Wizard Seelain selected one across from her. Lilly and I shared a couch. A young private came in and served us tea and a sour round fruit that I never learned the name of.

After sipping from her white cup decorated with purple flowers, Belinda Iceheart asked with a friendly smile, or one as friendly as her face could muster, "Tell me of your travels."

As we were now allies, Grand Wizard Seelain told of our journey, beginning with our experience in the Reunited Kingdom, our scrape with sirens and dire wolves, the battle against the Kraken and ground raptors, our visit with the centaurs, the werebat, and battle against the forces of the Pantheon of Sky Color Gods. She even told briefly of our meeting with the Warden of Outpost 1 and our visit to Mountain Base 1. Our return journey to Outpost 4 had little excitement, but Grand Wizard Seelain included that, too.

I guess she figured any information on the isolated outposts would be welcome. By beginning with our first destination, the Reunited Kingdom, Wizard Seelain didn't tell of our encounter with Madame Creeanne.

After Lilly had tasted the tea, Wizard Seelain took a sip from her own cup, then asked, "Tell us, Belinda Iceheart, how you came to be Warden of Outpost Four."

Belinda Iceheart sat back, glanced at Lilly, and fingered her staff as if pondering where to start or what to say. "I would have thought, Grand Wizard, your questions and concern might encompass the status of Keesee as your king falters in his attempt to stem the tide of soldiers thrown against his forces."

Using a courtly voice I sometimes heard her employ, Wizard Seelain replied, "I am deeply concerned about my king and his people. Yet, etiquette demands I honor the hostess, thus my question. Be that as it may, now that we are allies, our fates are linked and certainly your departure from Sint Malo to serve as the Warden here has its roots in the battle King Tobias wages against our common foes."

Belinda the Cursed smiled. It was a false one that didn't reach her eyes. They remained cold and hard.

"The tale is simple, Grand Wizard. Corradin the Conjurer, ruler of the open city of Sint Malo unleashed his demon sendings. They assailed me within Sint Malo, and fell upon Tyegerial, former Warden of this outpost."

She ran an index finger along her dark staff, following the runes carved into it. "Yes, the Conjurer has now openly allied himself with his father and the allies of his father." She smiled, and gazed unfocused above Grand Wizard Seelain's head. "I set traps for the Conjurer's summoned minions centuries ago in anticipation of that day. They failed to obliterate me and slew only a few of my people, while I banished each and every one of them. Even more, they failed in securing several items they sought."

Her eyes switched to me for a fraction of a second and then she continued speaking to Grand Wizard Seelain. "Tyegerial, being what he is, obliterated a score of the lesser sendings and two greater ones before they were able to bind and take him. Now that they have him, they find that they cannot obliterate him, and the Conjurer's surviving enthralled sendings must now expend much of their strength to keep the fallen angel bound."

Her lips creased into a cruel smile. "Not exactly what the Conjurer expected. Now poor Corradin must spend his own strength to hold his city in check, without threat of his leashed demons." She leaned back in her chair. "I made sure to apprise those who might resist his rule of the situation."

Although I could guess, I didn't fully understand what banished and bound meant for a demon or for a fallen angel. I figured obliterated meant their strength and essence to be utterly destroyed.

"And since I know you are curious, Grand Wizard, I shall share with you what I know of Keesee's struggle. The Crusaders of the Reunited Kingdom still press on through the Dead Woods in hopes of a final assault on General Mzali's fortress. The Crusader goal is to utterly defeat Mzali and obliterate him if they can, and his son in Sint Malo can no longer provide any relief."

Belinda Iceheart's gaze shifted from Wizard Seelain to Lilly and me. "Fanatical as the Crusaders are, they may succeed, although the sea goddess Uplersh has begun assaulting their oversea supply lines.

"However, Grand Wizard, Keesee herself will fall before the Necromancer King does. Paris-Imprimis has long since fallen. The Faxtinian Coalition and the Doran Confederacy are no more. Only two of the Lesser Kingdoms have held out. Fendra Jolain is massing her forces along the northern reaches of Keesee and Uplersh is preparing an amphibious invasion to be launched from the Southern Continent."

I knew the odds were against Keesee and her allies, but to hear it coming to pass knotted my stomach. Grand Wizard Seelain held a straight face but I knew the news was tearing her up inside.

Belinda Iceheart asked Grand Wizard Seelain, "Does your king know you carry the Blood Sword to him?"

Wizard Seelain nodded. "I sent word using split crystals upon securing it from the Colonel of the West. King Tobias knows its support is on the way."

"I am afraid, my guests, that you will have to delay your return journey by at least a day."

Grand Wizard Seelain set down her tea cup. "Why is that?"

"A hurricane, bearing powerful winds, rain and lighting, is off shore, coming up the coast. It will make landfall just south of here before nightfall and is likely to travel north, up the coast."

"Belinda Iceheart, do you believe it to be magical in nature?"

The crone shrugged and ate one of the small sour fruits. "We will know when it reaches us."

"If we depart immediately, do you believe we might outpace it?"

"If it were a normal storm, it might be possible. If it isn't...even its remnants could chase and overtake you up into Greenland."

Grand Wizard Seelain picked up one of the fruits, but politely handled it until Lilly smelled and tasted one. I was sure Belinda the Cursed knew why as she winked at Lilly and chuckled.

"May we then impose upon you until the storm passes or breaks?" Grand Wizard Seelain asked.

Belinda Iceheart reached forward and tossed me one of the sour fruits. "That you may, Grand Wizard, if sometime during your stay I may speak with your bodyguard. Alone."

CHAPTER 33

As predicted, the hurricane crashed ashore with lashing rain and wind gusts capable of sweeping a trog off his feet. Belinda Iceheart said it wasn't magical in origin but magic lent it additional energy and direction. Thus, it hammered Outpost 4 until near nightfall the next day, the night of the full moon.

I finished drinking the vial of silver nitrate as Dr. Mindebee had directed. It was the third, having taken one the night of our arrival at Outpost 4 and one the night before that. Belinda Iceheart held out her hand for the vial and smelled the remains of its contents. The action reminded me of the night I first met Belinda the Cursed, in the back room of an herb shop under renovation.

"So this is the gargoyle physicist's solution?"

I nodded and kept pace with her as we went down the concrete steps into the skyscraper's basement. I handed her the vial's top. "You can keep it."

"Of all the lycanthropes out there, Mercenary, you had to discover a werebat. They are the vilest of all. More vile than wereboars and the nastiest of werewolves."

"Thanks," I said.

"If someone hasn't told you—"

I interrupted her, "I already know."

"And your friend Lilly has prepared you?"

Lilly was outside awaiting the moon's rise. I thought it best to be inside, underground even, to put as much distance between me and the full moon as possible. Belinda Iceheart offered to accompany me. She said she couldn't be affected by a lycanthrope's bite and would make sure I was contained. I guessed she'd encase me in a block of ice—which was fine with me if I changed and couldn't control the beast.

First Mate, a sailor aboard the *Sunset Siren* who also held the same title as his name, once told me how a werewolf had become unruly the night of the full moon. Belinda Iceheart castrated him with a silver blade, froze him in a block of ice up to his neck, and pushed him overboard.

We reached the bottom of the stairwell and entered a large room with rows of support pillars and shadowy light cast from hanging lanterns. It wasn't quiet as teams of trogs worked the long levers of pumps. That only a few inches of water remained attested to their long hours of labor.

"You wanted to talk to me alone?" I asked. "You might want to do it before I change."

"You don't believe you will be able to resist, Mercenary?" She seemed surprised.

"I don't know. I feel it rising. It's like when you have the fever and need to vomit. The beast, it's struggling to come up like that from within me. It's getting stronger." I tried to keep worry from creeping into my voice.

She took one of the hanging lanterns and led me through a set of propped-open metal doors. The room held rows of crates temporarily stacked upon pallets elevated by stone blocks to keep them above the flood water. The muffled sounds of working trogs crept into the otherwise quiet room.

Belinda Iceheart pointed by tipping her staff. "That way, Mercenary. Up a few steps is a room that once held a backup generator. The Colonel needed it elsewhere."

I felt naked without my armor. I wore my boots, breeches and a cotton shirt. I kept my sword as well, for what it was worth. Inside the low, rectangular room were two wooden chairs, along with a small round table. Upon it sat a bottle of wine, two wooden cups and three tall candles set in a triangular holder.

One chair sat next to the table in the center of the room. The other chair sat along the far wall. Lying on the floor next to the far chair was a manacle attached to a heavy chain set into the wall. The manacle appeared to be coated in silver.

"If you prefer, consider it a bit of ankle jewelry," Iceheart said.

"I thought you might use a block of ice to encase me."

"If it comes to that, I will. This might work out better for you."

I walked over and sat down. She tossed me a lock. "Those are a nice pair of boots. You might consider removing them."

"Good thing I mended the holes in my socks."

"You might remove them too. The rest…we'll replace if necessary."

"You want my sword?"

She shook her head and poured wine into the two cups while I placed the manacle around my left ankle and clicked the lock in place. "It's getting close," I said.

She hobbled over and handed me a cup and returned to her seat. She then lit the three candles before turning the lantern's wick down.

"Why did you give me the blood charm?" I asked. "Grand Wizard Seelain said because of it, the demons cannot fully destroy the fallen angel. If they try he'll be reduced for a time, but escape their grasp and slowly rebuild his strength. Is that why?"

She rested her staff across her legs. Her eyes glowed their cobalt blue. "No, Mercenary."

"The charm was what Corradin the Conjurer sent his demons against you to find? That's why you gave it to me?"

"No, Mercenary. But it worked out that way."

My mind began to race, not about the blood charm, but about blood. Images of its warmth in my mouth and throat. My arms—wings stretching, carrying me aloft in search of it. I shook my head and concentrated. "Then why?"

"Do you know about seers?"

I nodded. Took a drink and thought. "They see into the truth of things. Can predict the future. Can see the past and into people's minds and thoughts."

"Close enough," she said.

"You knew I'd get bitten by a werebeast and gave me the blood charm to help me fight it?"

She laughed. It wasn't cruel or mocking, more amused. "No, Mercenary."

"Tell me, then," I said, my voice beginning to shake. "Maybe I'll remember in the morning."

"Because, Mercenary, you're a player on the board. A pawn. Fendra Jolain's seers know that. They sought to track you and your movements, and thus know your king's plans." She took another drink. "Your healing magic. When you summon it, direct it, you see the energy?"

"Ribbons," I said.

"Are they the same since you've worn the gray angel's blood?"

"No." I took another drink. My hand was shaking so I set the cup down on the floor next to my boots.

"His blood alters the pattern of energy around you. That, Mercenary, distorts their vision, gives the seers false divinations. Hides your travels and intent to return the Blood Sword to the hand of King Tobias."

I began shaking. I held my arms tight around me. I don't know if I was holding onto my humanity or holding the beast—stopping it from emerging.

I heard Belinda the Cursed say, "Know this, Mercenary. If you are outcast among your people, you'll have a place among mine." She turned up the lantern's wick, doubling the light in the gray-walled room. "Even so, Mercenary Flank Hawk, I am not fond of you and I suspect you abhor me. So vanquish it!"

From that moment on, until the full moon rose, we sat in silence. Neither of us moved, except for me once, searching with my fingers to be sure the fallen angel's blood charm was still in its place under my shirt, against my chest.

I felt the moon's pull, seeking to draw me outside, to stand and soak in its silvery light. Release the strength and energy it offered. And I shook my head, gritted my teeth and squeezed myself tight. Waited…each closing minute, the beast waiting to pounce and drive my humanity—drive me into that dark corner I'd confined it to these past weeks.

Then the moment came. It burst out from within, like an angry wildcat prodded from a box with a red-hot poker. My blood roiled and boiled in my veins. It wasn't like Lilly said it would be. So much pain—for both of us. Still, it came at me, through me clawing for sky, lusting for blood. We both cried out, my scream, harsh. Its, shrill and piercing.

I met it with force of will, like a man wrestling a wild boar to the ground, barring its way, searching for purchase and strength to stop it. And its tusks—no claws—rent my skin, prickling energy surging into my bones, muscle and skin. Again, acid pain—every inch, every fiber of me. Waves of fits and shaking, convulsing me upon the floor. My shackled leg straining, burning.

Despite the agony my skin rippled, my teeth grew pointed—sharp.

I reached out, to the healing energy I knew, sending my confused mind diving into the energy maelstrom. Clutching, sending ribbons I recognized into my skin, muscle and bone. Into my teeth.

Wild energy strands I didn't recognize retreated, not many but a few, making my second foray easier. Despite this, my skull throbbed, my mind whirled, the ribbons reached my body randomly. No focus or reason.

The werebeast lashed out, rolled over upon me, pressed me down. I grabbed its throat with bleeding hands, its fur, brittle and patchy, like it was afflicted with mange. We rolled over and over, fire in our veins, stinging acid in our muscles, grinding into the depths of our bones, collapsing our lungs, seizing our heart. Graying, then blackening our mind—our mind.

"NO!" My mind! My heart!

I snapped shut the beast's box and assailed it with ribbons of healing energy. Shearing its claws, its hold on me. I bled, and it bled, but its blood poured out, sickly, steaming. Its brittle fur fell away. Crackling, it became a husk, dried, crumbling…into dust.

I lay still on the floor, among the wooden chair's shattered pieces, in my own sweat, yellow vomit and my blood, gasping for air, for light, for strength, for hope.

A voice behind cobalt eyes broke through the ringing in my ears. "Impressive, Mercenary. Impressive."

I grabbed and held onto those words, slipping, falling into blackness, clutching words of hope.

CHAPTER 34

I awoke to the sun's rays shining through one of Outpost 4's rectangular windows.

From her bedside seat Lilly grabbed my hand. "You're awake! Just a minute."

She shot up and ran to the nearby door, opened it and shouted down the hall. "Tell Grand Wizard Seelain he's awake!"

The ceiling in the room was white with amber walls that matched the bed covers. A plush brown chair and a wooden desk with matching chair, the one Lilly had been seated upon, made up most of the room's contents.

And there was an emptiness in me. Nothing lurking in the shadows. It felt wonderful.

Lilly sat back down beside me. "See, you did it, Flank Hawk."

I started to speak but my throat was dry. Dry and sore. Every muscle in my arms, legs and back ached like I'd hauled enough field stones to build five miles of fence wall. Lilly handed me a cup of water she'd poured from a pitcher resting on a table beside the bed.

I struggled to suppress a groan as I slowly sat up before taking a drink. The cool water soothed my throat just a bit. "Thanks." Even after the water, my voice came out hoarse.

"You really messed yourself up," Lilly said and pointed to my face.

I ran my fingers across my face, finding ridges along my cheeks and chin.

"Scratched yourself up pretty good, but Belinda the Cursed has a rogue healer here with her. Not much better than you, but she healed you some." Lilly offered me more water. When I shook my head she set the cup down. "That stuff the gargoyle gave you. Belinda the Cursed said it was poison, only a lot more poisonous to the werebat in you than to you."

"I thought Dr. Mindebee said it came from their infirmary. When did she tell you this?"

Lilly shrugged. "Never trusted that gargoyle."

"You didn't trust Belinda Iceheart to go with me last night—the full moon was *last* night, right?"

Lilly shrugged again. "Yeah, it's about three hours before sunset." Her eyes brightened. "Hey, Captain Bray gave me a lesson on how to use Jonas's rapier. He doesn't know much really, but a lot more than you." She grinned and broke into a laugh. Then she became serious and leaned close, her voice dropping to a whisper. "I figured something else out. Grand Wizard Seelain colors her hair white."

I just stared at Lilly for a second.

She nodded in earnest. "I think she's tougher than a grand wizard. She has this small tin of white pasty stuff. White as a cloud. I seen her use it a couple of times since we left Keesee. Combs it into her hair. I bet the Colonel of the West knew it or figured it out, or something." She sat back. "I don't know, but something almost got me and you killed."

I was having trouble following Lilly's line of thought, but knew she was trying to talk fast. Grand Wizard Seelain's voice reached the open door to my room from somewhere down the hallway. We spent a few seconds in silence as several notions crossed my mind. In battle alongside the centaurs, Grand Wizard Seelain had cast more spells in succession, stronger spells than I thought she could. She even kept control of an elemental while casting another pretty powerful spell. I'd never seen a wizard do that before.

Maybe Lilly was right, at least with Grand Wizard Seelain hiding her ability. The more powerful in her element Seelain became, the more it took color from her hair. Her eyes didn't match, but had the one healed from near destruction become lighter blue over the past year?

I took Lilly's hand. "Don't tell anyone," I whispered. It was easier to whisper than talk anyway. "If you're right, she must have a reason."

Lilly nodded and looked toward the door. A second later, Grand Wizard Seelain strode into the room, followed by Captain Bray and a hunched over Belinda Iceheart. The serpent cavalryman showed no sign of his leg injury, not even a limp. Strapped to his back he carried the Blood Sword, lashed securely in its scabbard by a leather cord.

Grand Wizard Seelain's eyes sparkled and she couldn't suppress a wide grin. "How are you doing, Flank Hawk?"

"It's gone."

"So I have been told and you have just confirmed it."

Belinda Iceheart remained by the door, but Captain Bray came up to my bedside opposite Grand Wizard Seelain. He rested a hand on my shoulder. "I guess Lilly's right. You're tougher than an ogre's toenails."

Lilly said, "I didn't say *anything* about an ogre's toenails."

My laugh turned into a hoarse cough, which hurt my whole body. Wizard Seelain handed me the cup of water from the table. I took a drink and handed the cup back to her.

"Just don't teach Lilly too much about sword play," I told Bray.

"Afraid she'll best me, or you?"

Lilly folder her arms in a fake pout. "If the king offers me a boon again, for getting his sword, I'm going to ask for rapier lessons. Then you both'll really be in trouble."

I smiled at Lilly's statement, but inside I wondered if King Tobias would have any arms instructors left by the time we returned. Even more dire thoughts reflected upon the question: If we won the war.

Grand Wizard Seelain's smile faded. She must have sensed my dark thoughts. "Flank Hawk, we shall allow you to rest and regain your strength."

"I'll be ready to leave tomorrow morning," I promised her.

She rested a hand on the covers over my leg. "Belinda Iceheart's people are cleaning and mending your armor. Lilly has seen to your crossbow. Captain Bray has sharpened and oiled your spear, sword and dirk and has seen that Wick is prepared for the last leg of our journey."

I took the cup of water back from Wizard Seelain and finished what it still contained, then stared at the Blood Sword's red ruby set in the pommel sticking above Captain Bray's shoulder. "Thank you," I said and set the cup on the table before lying back down. My hand came to rest on the blood charm under the white cotton shirt someone had slipped on me.

Everyone quietly stepped out of the room except for Belinda Iceheart. She hobbled up and stood next to my bed and refilled the cup from the pitcher. Her aged hand poured steadily.

She stood for a moment, silent.

Even though it was getting harder to talk I said, "Thank you. For last night."

"Anyone could have sat in there with you, Mercenary."

I shook my head. "You summoned some of the energy ribbons away, making it easier for me."

"You noticed that?" the crone said thoughtfully, adjusting the grip on her staff. "You know, Mercenary, with the right training, and if you gave up the spear and sword, you just might have the aptitude to become a respectable rogue healer."

I shrugged and looked out the window. "It's not who I am, or want to be."

She laughed—more like a cackle and not filled with mirth.

I reached for the cup and took another drink, knowing I'd regret continuing to talk, but I thought it'd be worth it. I probably would never get another chance to ask a question that'd been bothering me. "You've lived a long time. You've seen a lot of people age and die while you go on." I took another drink. "How do you deal with it? How do you treat them as this happens?"

"Thinking about your lycanthrope friend, are you?"

I nodded, knowing that Lilly would become an old woman before I reached thirty-five summers. I thought about First Mate, Belinda Iceheart's trusted sailor aboard her ship.

"You have posed a question few ever consider," Belinda the Cursed said. She sat down in the chair and ran her fingers along the runes in her staff. "How to describe it…"

After moment of thought she said, "Have you ever had a faithful dog?"

I nodded, thinking back to Old Chip. He'd died three summers ago.

"Do not take this the wrong way, Mercenary, but this is the best relevant comparison I can come up with. You know First Mate. I think of him far more highly than any animal. He's served me for many years, just as a faithful dog. I have watched him learn, mature and come into his own, and now he is beginning to show his years. Unlike an animal, he is cognizant of it happening, but accepts it. Once he cannot do what I expect of him, I will replace him."

"Just like that?" I asked.

"The *Sunset Siren* needs a competent and able first mate. What would you have me do, Mercenary? With your lycanthrope friend, remember life is never equal, never fair, and continued life is never certain. Treat her as you do now until age changes the relationship, then move on." She raised a hand before I could object. "Don't forget her, but allow your friend her life cycle. For you, visit her. Let her know when she passes, you'll remember her.

"First Mate has seen in my cabin. There, scribed on the wall, are the marks of all first mates who have served aboard the *Sunset Siren*, including his that he placed there." She stood and started hobbling toward the door. "In your line of work, Mercenary, the mortality rate makes it a moot concern."

I cleared my throat and said, "You think I abhor you, Belinda Iceheart. I don't."

She half turned to face me, her cobalt eyes glowing despite the light in the room.

"I just don't fully trust you."

She smiled a crooked smile and pointed back at me. "Wise, Mercenary. You can trust me as long as our purposes are not crossed." She turned and began making her way out of the room but stopped in the doorway. "The Blood Sword, Mercenary. My father handed it over into your care. See that it is used to achieve our goals."

She closed the door before I could ask what she meant. It didn't matter. Iceheart wouldn't have answered anyway.

Stiff and sore as I was, it felt good to have my legs strapped to my saddle again. I patted Wick on his neck. My wyvern mount spread his wings and cawed quietly. Maybe he was happy to serve as my mount once again.

The troops at Outpost 4 would miss having the wyvern support for their scouting missions. Although they had six horses for scouting and over fifty riflemen, five bazooka teams, and five mortar teams, I got the idea they still felt vulnerable to attack. The major in charge of day-to-day operations appeared to think highly of the mortars. I wasn't so sure the miniature artillery would be much help in a fight, but I'd never seen it in action. If I hadn't seen the bazooka team fire on the Kraken, I probably wouldn't think much of them either.

The plan was for Wizard Seelain on Balooga to lead most of the time, allowing me on Wick and Bray on Coils to draft. Lilly would serve as Seelain's aft-guard. I think Grand Wizard Seelain noticed, like me, how much smaller our team felt without Zunnert, Jonas, her wyvern mount, Moon Ash, and Bray's serpent mount, Flint Spitter. Balooga was a strong, steady mount but she was neither as impressive nor as dangerous as a red dragon.

I wondered if Major Jadd was still alive, still riding Flame Lance into battle. Hopefully I'd learn soon enough that he was.

Belinda Iceheart stood on a small balcony to see us off. First Mate stood next to her. Our launch point was close enough to the skyscraper that I saw the blue snake tattoo winding from the sailor's jaw, across the bridge of his nose, and circling around his left eye.

I waved farewell to him, wondering about his future. Would he survive the war? Would he ever go back to sea aboard the *Sunset Siren* before he was too old to serve as first mate? He waved back, maybe wondering if I'd survive the war.

Grand Wizard Seelain shouted, "We depart to carry woe to our enemies!" With that Balooga galloped several strides before spreading her wings and leaping into the air. Wick released a screeching *caw* and spread his wings, leaping and flapping skyward in pursuit with Coils flying close, taking position on our right.

It was a beautiful, clear morning to fly, like most during the course of our return trip. The weather in Greenland and Iceland was warmer. We'd learned our lesson about wolves and although they approached our camp, with dragon and wyverns, a campfire and a grand wizard, they moved on to easier prey.

We flew at night to the Faroe Islands and established cold camps in an effort to escape the eyes of the enemy. Once, we heard the distant song of the sirens, so Bray and I stuffed our ears with wax. As with the wolves, nothing came of the threat.

Our day's rest at the estate of Luke Cromwell was a somber event. Only Luke and his son Thomas brought food and visited with us in the barn where we sheltered. Even then they warily eyed the stall where I'd stashed the Blood Sword under Wick's saddle.

Before leaving, Luke Cromwell had several of his servants deliver a padded rocking chair for his son. As Thomas rocked he told me of the war while Lilly and Grand Wizard Seelain slept and Captain Bray stood guard.

"It goes hard," he said. "We advance on the Necromancer King but suffer losses that grow difficult to replace. The one who names herself the Sea Goddess harasses our supply ships. She sends her serpents to attack our coastal fishing vessels. They pluck unwary men, women and even children from docks and shores adjacent to deep water."

Thomas, with his only hand, scratched the stump of his missing leg covered by the fold in his black pants. "There is a rumor that an emissary from the Colonel of the West has secretly visited the Parliament and that we are in communication with him. My father is close to some in the Parliament. He does not believe it is true."

"It could be," I said. "Colonel Ibrahim has wireless telegraph. His words can cross a continent larger than would be from here to well beyond the King's City in Keesee. Maybe he uses it to communicate with your leaders?"

"We had a night of demons not long after you departed us," Thomas said, changing the subject. "They left hundreds maimed, insane, or dead. But only one night, which baffled our leaders. Some demons were confronted and banished, or undone by our faithful, and our pastors and priests. Not all." He shrugged.

"Then there are your people. I do know that they have sent requests for assistance. For a while they were frequent and said to be urgent, bordering on desperate."

I asked, "Your people didn't send aid?"

He shrugged. "Our leaders pray and decide, and deny direct assistance against the one who names herself the Goddess of Healing. The opportunity to bring down the Corpse Lord, rid the world of him forever is at hand. For if we do not, he will grow strong again and bring his wrath upon both of our peoples."

The calm way he explained the choice of his people made me angry. "How long before the Goddess of Healing, once she consolidates her power over the Mainland, will be strong enough to challenge your people, even without the support of her ally, the Necromancer King?"

"If he is not undone, how fast could he rebuild an army of walking corpses from the land's battlefields? Faster than both Keesee and the Reunited Kingdom could rebuild their armies?"

I thought about it a second, but Thomas answered before I had come to a conclusion. "It would take him several years. It will take us a generation. He must be defeated while he remains weak."

There was logic to what he said, and I found it hard to remain angry. Colonel Ibrahim didn't think the Crusaders could launch a final assault on the Necromancer King's stronghold before Keesee fell. I wasn't so sure. Men like Roos and Thomas? I'd seen Crusader companies in battle. Maybe the Colonel of the West didn't know the Crusaders like I did.

When I didn't say anything for a moment Thomas asked, "Do you believe the evil sword you carry can change the course of the war?"

It was my turn to shrug. "I've been told it's like a great chess game and the Blood Sword is a piece that will be added to the board on King Tobias's side." I pulled my dirk from its boot sheath and checked the fireweed resin on it. "I've also been told I'm a pawn in the game."

Thomas frowned but didn't say anything.

I spent the rest of the afternoon telling Thomas about our journey before going to catch a few hours sleep. The last thing he told me was something to share with Lilly. "A cancer took Sister Ruth from us twelve days ago," he said. "Her soul is now with her brother Paul's and is at peace in the presence of our Lord."

The final part of our journey from the Reunited Kingdom to the King's City held the greatest risk of allowing the enemy to learn the Blood Sword was soon to be again in King Tobias's hand. Flying by night we spotted the large enemy encampments by their cooking fires. Even small campfires revealed themselves as the enemy. What Keeseean or resistance force would risk fire revealing their presence?

During daylight, while resting, we spotted or heard an occasional griffin with riders overhead. Isolated and abandoned farms with surviving barns, or secluded wooded areas offered us shelter from enemy eyes. Only once a small ground patrol stumbled upon us. The surprised mercenary scouts wearing red and white, the colors of Fendra Jolain, didn't have a chance. We weighted their four bodies down with stones in a nearby pond. Before we did I pointed out a black tattoo on the forearm of one of the mercenaries. A tiger with dagger-like canine teeth. He was a Long-Tooth, sworn enemies of the Sun-Fox Brotherhood to which both Major Jadd and Prince Reveron belonged. After that we loosed three of the horses, hiding their saddles and tack in deep brush, and allowed our wyverns to feed on the bulk of the fourth that suffered a broken leg during our ambush.

Even upon reaching Keeseean lands we traveled in secret. That we were able to do so, both in Fendra Jolain controlled territory and within Keesee, indicated the war was being hard-fought and inflicting high casualties on both sides. But Keesee, having already suffered heavy losses battling the Necromancer King's invasion could less afford them. Fendra Jolain knew this.

We came within sight of the King's City an hour before dawn. Grand Wizard Seelain angled us inland from our oversea line of flight. No one challenged us, not a serpent rider upon a dragon. Not a wyvern rider. Several small boats patrolled the coastline and the city walls appeared to have an ample watch, but nothing in the air. An unsettling experience that hinted at how bad things were.

We flew over the outer wall toward the palace. "Have your wyverns call out," ordered Wizard Seelain. "They may not recognize a gray dragon's call."

Captain Bray and I complied and our mounts each let out a screeching cry as we approached the palace. Movement atop the nearest barbican brought a manned ballista to my attention. We circled until an armed squad of soldiers with torches entered the courtyard to await our landing.

Bray landed first, followed by Grand Wizard Seelain. I brought Wick down last.

"Flank Hawk!" someone shouted. It wasn't quite a man's voice but I recognized it.

"Rin," I said, tossing Wick's reins down to him. I was just as surprised to see him as he was to see me. I climbed down off Wick.

"I thought you were long dead. Nobody saw you or Wick in a long time and nobody knew where either of you were."

"Hold him steady," I said to Rin while I unstrapped my spear, followed by the Blood Sword, its hilt and scabbard wrapped in worn canvas.

"Your mom thinks you're dead, but your dad keeps telling her you're not. Katchia just cries whenever they talk about it."

His words surprised me. "You know my parents and my little sister?" Our home in Pine Ridge was gone and my family moved to the King's City, but nowhere near Rin's home. My father worked in the king's royal stables caring for horses, not serpents. "How?"

A sadness fell across Rin's face.

Soldiers shouted and moved around us. One climbed into Wick's saddle. Another was climbing into Grand Wizard Seelain's saddle on Balooga. Lilly told him, "You fly her. I'll tell you the commands. They're in the Colonel of the West's tongue."

"Don't tell my parents, anyone I'm alive," I said to Rin. "That you've seen me, Lilly or Grand Wizard Seelain. Not yet." After I said it, I realized my words weren't necessary. Even if Rin didn't realize he shouldn't say anything, an officer would order him to silence—under sentence of death.

Rin handed the reins up to Wick's rider. "I won't."

"I have to go, Rin." Grand Wizard Seelain turned back to look for me. She had her staff in one hand and the metal scroll tube from Colonel Ibrahim in the other. I gripped my spear in my right hand and the wrapped scabbard holding the Blood Sword in my left. "Though unexpected, Rin, I'm happy you were the first to greet me upon my return."

CHAPTER 35

The chief of the night watch roused King Tobias from his bed chamber moments after our return. Guards escorted us down to Imperial Seer Lochelle's rune-scribed octagonal chamber where the king joined us, along with Seer Lochelle, and a dark-haired and mustached colonel I didn't recognize. After bowing and courtly greetings Grand Wizard Seelain returned the Blood Sword to the king by placing it, and the scroll case containing a message from Colonel Ibrahim, on the floor before his chair.

I realized he'd been awakened at an early hour and had taken little time to dress and prepare before arriving at the seer's candle-lit chamber, but he didn't look well. His gaunt and wrinkle-creased face left him looking as if he'd aged a decade since our departure. His voice and manner remained regal but he lacked the fierce, confident sparkle in his eyes. The two escorting guards held more determination in their eyes than did King Tobias.

Imperial Seer Lochelle stood to the king's right. It was harder to tell if she looked haggard and worn down as her face and sightless white eyes always carried that appearance.

Grand Wizard Seelain then gave King Tobias the highlights of our journey, focusing on our meeting with the Colonel of the West and the war being waged on the far side of the Western Ocean.

We stood quietly for several minutes after Wizard Seelain finished speaking. Then the king said to one of his guards, "Take the scroll tube to the first interrogation room. Have Master Enchantress Merkle examine the case and its contents. If she has concerns, instruct her to await Supreme Enchantress Thulease."

After the guard left with the scroll case, the king turned his gaze to me. "Mercenary, did you draw to verify that the sword at my feet is indeed the Blood Sword?"

I stepped forward. "The Colonel of the West held the sword drawn before us before giving it to Grand Wizard Seelain to return to you. Prior to our departing Mountain Base One, I examined the sword and drew it a third of the way from its scabbard. The etchings matched what I remembered it having. The same evil spirit contained within the blade stirred."

In a neutral tone he asked, "You did not fully draw and examine it?"

"I did not, my king."

Silence in the chamber followed my answer. Even now, the king must have felt the evil within the sword lying before him. Those who'd wielded it couldn't otherwise.

The king looked to the seer standing next to him. "Lochelle?"

"It is the sword."

King Tobias smoothed his mustache with his forefinger and then rubbed his beard. "Colonel Eckstein, summon my war council to meet here in Lochelle's chamber three hours after dawn. See to it that the mounts are gone from the city before sunrise."

"The gray dragon and two wyverns in question are already beyond the city limits," Colonel Eckstein said. "They shall be housed in the vacant serpent stables at Lady Mitchell's estate. Upon your release here I will summon those members of the council that can be reached and arrive by the appointed hour."

The king replied, "See to it that Seelain's scout returns to my palace, seen only by the most loyal of eyes." Then he turned his gaze to me. "Mercenary, you will be debriefed, then confined to whatever accommodations Imperial Seer Lochelle sees fit. You will have contact only with those I or Seer Lochelle approve until I have decided upon a course of action. Now, go with Colonel Eckstein."

King Tobias sat back in his chair. "Seelain and Captain Bray, remain with me."

I endured a three hour debriefing where I told my story to a lieutenant younger than me. He asked narrow-scoped questions while a scribe wrote down the important points in my answers. Afterwards one of the king's guards escorted me up one flight of stairs. There I was given a room with a small bed, square table holding a lantern, a wooden chair and no windows.

"I will see that a meal is brought to you," the guard said.

"Thank you," I replied. "A wash basin and towels would be much appreciated."

"I'll see what I can do," he said, and left.

I sat in the chair and dozed off until the guard returned with a bowl, pitcher of water, cake of soap and two small towels. "Your meal will be here within a half hour, Mercenary Flank Hawk."

"I appreciate it," I said. The guard was young. Although polished and well maintained, his breastplate appeared older than him. I doubted he'd worn it when the steel received its permanent dents and scars. It seemed odd that a guard would deliver wash water. Being so tired, it took me a moment to realize they wouldn't send a maid. The king didn't want anybody to see me. "Do you have a moment to answer a few questions?"

"I do not," he said. "I have many duties yet awaiting my attention."

I nodded and gestured toward the water and towels. "I know you went out of your way to provide me this small comfort."

"I don't mind." He looked like he wanted to say more, but instead turned and left, closing the door behind him.

A few minutes after washing up and dressing again, a knock sounded on the door. It was Rin, with a tray of sliced ham, bread and a crock filled with weak cider.

I smiled as I took the tray from him and set it on the table. He stood in the doorway, still wearing his stable-work clothes and a sheathed dagger hanging from his belt. "Not only do you care for serpents, but you work in the kitchen as well?" I asked, and signaled for him to enter.

He pulled the door closed behind him. "Our king musta figured I'd already seen you. 'Sides, there's not many people in the palace like there used to be." He looked around the room. "Never been in this part of the palace. I'm good at following directions."

"Care to share a meal with me?"

"Sure," he said. "I know not to ask you any questions cuz you can't answer them anyhow."

I pointed to the chair for him and pulled the table along the bed so I could sit and eat. "But I can ask you questions."

"I don't know much." He sat down. "Our king's losing the war. Everybody knows it but doesn't talk much about it. There's just too many of them. Not enough of us."

"Is the prince still alive?"

"Which one?"

"Prince Reveron," I said, suddenly more worried.

"I think so. I saw both princes a couple weeks ago. Saw Major Jadd too. Figure you wanta know that. But there ain't many dragons left that can fly."

I prepared sandwiches and didn't interrupt Rin—just let him talk. It seemed like he needed to.

"Some alchemist figured out how to get the crippled ones, there ain't any healers that can fix them much, he got them to lay eggs outta their season. I think he's married to one of our king's advisors. There's this really tall, I mean really tall girl that asked me about you once. And your dad and mom think about you a lot. Your sister too. They don't say it much, but they think about your other sister too."

That's when I interrupted him. "How do you know so much about my family?"

That sadness fell over his face again. "The Long-Tooths killed my family. Woulda killed me too if I'd been home that night they broke in. Tried to kill your family too, but your dad knows how to use an axe. Learned it in the militia he said—but you know that. So our king had us moved inta the palace. I stay with them cuz our king thought it'd be a good thing."

"Why?" I asked. I could see why my family might be a target of assassins, but why Rin's?

"Payback cuz I helped you get the grand wizard t'the palace that one day, and a bunch of them got killed. Somebody told the Long-Tooths I'd helped.

They was all over the city. Our king's hunted them mostly out, or they're hiding and waiting for us to lose."

"I'm sorry, Rin."

He shrugged and looked away. "Ain't your fault. You told me not t'go with you. I cried a lot after it happened, but not anymore. I figure it's war and when they get here, reach the city," he said, resting his hand on his dagger's pommel, "I'll pay'em back for what they did."

He looked up at me for a second. "You don't have t'say anything. I can see it on your face. Our king's got a plan t'win."

He slid his hand away from his dagger when I handed him his sandwich, looking a little sad. "Your dad says I'm his adopted son and I give him the coin I get for caring for what few wyverns and serpents there are left." He bit into the ham sandwich and said while chewing, "Guess that makes me and you brothers."

Time passed, allowing me to recover lost sleep and tend to my boots, armor and weapons. I didn't see Rin again, or Lilly or Grand Wizard Seelain. At night I was free to walk the short hallway and speak with the guards, mostly small talk but better than nothing. I did learn that King Tobias ordered torches, laced with some powder that made them burn green, lit along the top of the palace walls. The guards were young and had seen little if any combat. They didn't recognize the torches as a signal. I didn't reveal what I thought the torches were but wondered who the king might be sending a signal to within the city. Early the next morning it struck me. The Colonel of the West had some way of watching things from the sky. The green torches were a signal to him.

By the morning of the third day confined to my room I began to wonder if the king and Imperial Seer Lochelle had forgotten about me. That was until a guard arrived to help me don my armor. He then gave me my orders, to report to the entry of Imperial Seer Lochelle's chamber to serve as Grand Wizard Seelain's personal guard.

While waiting outside the seer's chamber, I watched Supreme Enchanter Thulease lead a line of six enchanters past me. I knew they were enchanters because each wore a version of a black mask that covered each face below the eyes. The last in line was her daughter, Thereese. Her leg that I broke during the assassination attempt had apparently healed as she strode without a limp. I couldn't tell for sure because of her floor-length olive dress, but the young enchantress must've been wearing heeled boots because she appeared noticeably taller than the last time I'd seen her.

As I looked up to her face our eyes met. Her eyes betrayed a smile and a redness filled her ears. I nodded and then looked straight ahead as if on sentry duty. I wondered if she'd tested and advanced from apprentice to journeyman enchanter.

Next came Colonel Isar, Commander of Keesee's m'unicorn cavalry. She now bore a deep scar above the left eye of her tight, leathery face and a bandaged stump where her left hand had once been. She nodded to me. "Mercenary Flank Hawk."

I stood at attention and replied, "Colonel Isar." Since I remained a mercenary and wasn't a member of the Keeseean military, saluting wasn't appropriate.

Less than a moment later Prince Halgadin, accompanied by Colonel Eckstein, appeared down the hallway and made his way toward the chamber. The crown prince looked more like his father than did his younger brother, Prince Reveron. Prince Halgadin's light brown hair hung straight to just below the ear. His chain-mesh armor showed signs of mending and battle as did the worn grip of his long sword. He'd stuffed the folded leather riding gloves of a serpent cavalryman into his broad belt. His brown eyes looked ahead and both men ignored me as I stood at attention and bowed my head as they passed.

A minute later Prince Reveron, dressed much as his brother, escorted Grand Wizard Seelain down the hall. She carried her staff and wore sky blue robes, and looked much refreshed. Both could hardly contain their smiles. I guessed the prince had only recently returned from the battlefield.

Behind them strode Major Jadd. His pock-marked face looked more stern than usual. He shifted left to take his place directly behind Prince Reveron so that I might take mine as personal guard behind Grand Wizard Seelain.

I knew bad blood existed between Major Jadd and Prince Halgadin going back to a time when Jadd disobeyed an order from the crown prince. That got Jadd exiled, resulting in his taking up the life of a mercenary, and picking up the mercenary name Road Toad along the way. War and strife changes much. Jadd's action years ago set into motion events that eventually benefitted relations between the Reunited Kingdom and Keesee. That played a part in King Tobias rescinding Jadd's exile and returning him to his former station as a serpent cavalryman.

It wasn't hard to guess that both Major Jadd and Prince Halgadin weren't excited about being in the same room together. I wasn't sure if Jadd was attending the council meeting because the king requested it or because Prince Reveron, long-time friend of Jadd who'd once served as the prince's mentor, insisted upon it.

I decided it didn't matter as I walked behind Grand Wizard Seelain, next to my friend and mentor, and followed Wizard Seelain, stepping over the poured gold line in the entry door's threshold.

Seven lanterns hung from the domed ceiling centered on the table in the middle of the room. They shed just enough light to reveal the intricate runes etched into the walls and support columns. Imperial Seer Lochelle sat on her tall stool at the head of the oval table. Stringy brown hair hid her face as she silently gazed down at the table. This time she wore only two jeweled rings on her right hand.

Lesser Seer B'down stood along the wall to the left of the door. His gray robes lacked the intricate stitching that lined the imperial seer's.

I moved to stand behind Grand Wizard Seelain as she took a seat next to Colonel Isar. Prince Reveron took his seat on the other side of Isar, to her right and to Seer Lochelle's left. A seat remained open to the seer's right, which I knew was the king's. To the right of that open chair sat Prince Halgadin with Colonel Eckstein standing along the wall several paces behind him. There was another open chair and then one occupied by Supreme Enchanter Thulease. That left a chair open around the oval table between the supreme enchantress and Grand Wizard Seelain.

Behind the supreme enchantress stood her daughter. Both wore their hair in an identical tight ball on the top of their head. The remaining enchanters stood to the left of the doorway along the wall. All but two were women. There weren't any stools for the attendants, enchanters or Seer B'down. We'd be standing for the entire meeting. There wasn't even a scribe set off along the wall.

Master Wizard Golt entered next. His dark skin matched his brown robes. As always his feet remained bare. I'd fought in pitch battle alongside the earth wizard and a powerful elemental he'd summoned. He sat down in the seat nearest the door, between Enchantress Thulease and Wizard Seelain, exchanging brief greetings with both.

Five minutes passed. Except for Prince Reveron and Colonel Isar's whispered exchange, no one else spoke.

Everyone around the table stood, the enchanters removed their masks, and all in the room bowed as King Tobias entered, followed by General Ellis. The king's bearded face looked less weary as his piercing blue eyes scanned the chamber. He carried what appeared to be a staff wrapped in a white silk cloth. General Ellis removed the king's red cape, more clearly revealing the royal purple and gold colors of King Tobias's silk garments—and the Blood Sword hanging at his side in a jewel-encrusted scabbard.

King Tobias strode around the table and took his place next to Imperial Seer Lochelle. "Seal the chamber," he said in a stern voice as he set the wrapped staff on the table.

Seer B'down closed the doors and uttered a spell to raise the power of the runes, warding the room from outside magics.

General Ellis, the king's most experienced field general, made his way back to the open seat between the crown prince and Enchantress Thulease. Once the hawkish general stood at attention with his bearded chin thrust forward, King Tobias sat down and said, "Be seated."

After clearing his throat King Tobias continued. "I have not called you here for the purpose of determining our next course of action to preserve the kingdom. By lighting the green torches, I signaled the Colonel of the West and set a plan into motion which will bring this war to an end. You are here to participate in seeing to this plan's successful implementation."

He looked to Enchantress Thulease, Prince Halgadin and Seer Lochelle. "Some around this table I have consulted with, and appreciate their offered advice. For the others, I lacked the time to await your arrival. Tides of oceans flow to their own appointed schedule, and thus, we are tied to that. To await an additional month for the opportune time for our allies, the Reunited Kingdom and the Colonel of the West, to play their part, would mean a weaker Keesee and us less able to see to *our* part." He paused and looked around the table. "Our part to ensure the final blow is struck."

He stood and drew the Blood Sword, and placed it on the table. Its blood-red ruby set in the pommel began to glow, pulsing like a heartbeat. Even Imperial Seer Lochelle raised her head to fix her sightless eyes on the malevolent blade. Its cold, sickly evil filled the room, every corner, every flicker of light and every black shadow.

"This weapon shall find its appointed place, buried in the chest of Fendra Jolain. There, stilling forever, her immortal heart."

I'd seen the Blood Sword in action. It was formidable. I'd personally slain a giant wielding the blade. But slaying a giant was nothing compared to a goddess. My mind flashed back to our confrontation with the Colonel of the West in his dining hall. Lilly, Grand Wizard Seelain and I were only feet away from him. He'd defeated us without even rising from his seat. Fendra Jolain was sure to have hundreds of troops defending her. Healers had personal guards that made me look like a boy wielding a warped wooden sword. What kind of guards would be protecting her? Beyond men and women, images of the Kraken and the sphinx came to mind.

The foreboding evil sense drained from the room as the king slammed the Blood Sword back into its scabbard. My attention returned to the conversation around the table as King Tobias placed the sheathed Blood Sword back on the table. Without pausing he carefully removed the cloth from the staff he'd brought to the War Council meeting.

"Now that I have your attention and you know what is at stake, I will reveal how we might accomplish our objective." He held up the staff for all to see. It was twice as thick as a quarter staff, pure white at its core but with six narrow brown, rune-carved rods set into it. A steel shod enclosed its base. It was capped by a smooth circular knob that appeared to be silver. The metallic sphere also appeared to have depth, as when peering into a bottomless shaft, no matter the direction the staff was held or turned.

"This is the Shard Staff," King Tobias announced, "the second of three ancient weapons of power wielded by my ancestors and passed down to me, as it will be to the heir to the throne after I am gone."

King Tobias walked around the table, past Prince Halgadin and General

Ellis and stopped behind Supreme Enchanter Thulease. She stood and turned.

"You, Thulease, shall carry the Shard Staff into battle." I couldn't see her face as she bowed slightly, still a head taller than the king. "Enchantress, you will divide the staff's shards among the collection of enchanters in this room. Instruct them in their use and powers, as well as their limitations and concomitant risks."

He handed her the staff. "That I shall do, my king," she said and raised her head. The silver knob's depth appeared to writhe and spin, so much so that I looked down because it made me sway, unbalanced on my feet. I wasn't the only one to avert my eyes. General Ellis and Colonel Eckstein did as well before the king handed the enchantress the silk cloth.

As King Tobias returned to his seat the enchantress wrapped the staff with what appeared to be a practiced hand. She settled back into her seat a second after the king sat, but she kept hold of the Shard Staff in her right hand.

"We shall bring one more surprise to the assault." The king's gaze fell to the enchantress once again.

From her robes she produced what looked like a foot-long stick, but wrapped in dark paper with a long wick sticking out of one end. She placed it on the table. "My husband has constructed with guidance from our Crusader allies, a number of these. They provided the fuses. When lit the fire slowly travels along the fuse into the heart of the device, whereupon it explodes with both a flash and a respectable concussive force. It is similar to the design the Crusaders use aboard their ships. They call those devices that dwarf this," she said placing her hand on the stick, "depth charges. They detonate those underwater, killing, wounding or driving off sea serpents and other marine creatures controlled by the sea goddess." She rolled the stick several inches to her left. "These devices are fairly reliable but employing them carries risk."

Seer Lochelle slid her right hand forward on the table. King Tobias acknowledged her and she asked, "Major Jadd, you have something to add?"

Everyone turned his way. He stepped forward. "I have seen these dynamite sticks employed. I've seen them blow the limbs off of wielders before they threw them. I would also recommend wrapping nails around each stick. It will make them more effective." He then returned to his place.

The king said, "Thank you for your input, Major Jadd. You will have three days to work with Master Alchemist Butlir to master the use of the dynamite sticks, as you call them, and train a selected group of others in their use."

King Tobias cleared his throat. "Three days from today, the assault party will depart. Half of the remaining serpents will participate in the raid, to be led by Prince Halgadin. As many wyvern scouts as can be managed will accompany, including two newly trained female mounts.

"The rest of the serpents I am immediately releasing to you, General

Ellis. I understand your frustration in being recalled here instead of preparing for my ordered offensive. You needed to know what is at stake and why, and why I am releasing all reserve troops to the effort. Launch the attack as soon as you return and press forward with all the cunning and vigor you can muster.

"Everyone at this table knows moving to the attack alone cannot bring us victory and will only hasten the inevitable. I am destined to lose this war unless this plan succeeds." The king rubbed his chin before speaking to the entire table, the entire room. "Word of the offensive will reach Fendra Jolain three or four days before our assault on the Capital of the Vinchie Empire. It will cause confusion and draw troops away. It will make the move of our allies appear more tactically sound."

He nodded to Prince Halgadin who signaled behind him. Colonel Eckstein stepped forward and handed the prince the metal scroll tube carried to Keesee by Wizard Seelain and delivered to the king. The prince opened it and removed several of the papers. "I do not know how the Colonel of the West obtained these detailed drawings of the city or even the layout of Jolain's fortress. But I have studied them and with advice will formulate a plan of attack before we must depart."

The prince pointed to a spot on one of the papers. With the poor lighting and from my angle, I was unable to see details. "On the morning eleven days hence, at high tide, an amphibious force made up of Crusaders and troops from the Colonel of the West will land and assault the capital city. Jolain cannot allow them to establish a beachhead and will send all she has to repel them. At noon that same day we must make our assault and do as my father asks."

He sat back, looked across the table at Prince Reveron, and slid the Blood Sword across the table to him. "If we fail in this task, Brother, the war is lost and all of Keesee falls."

CHAPTER 36

It turned out to be a good thing I got plenty of rest. The training and combat practice during the three days before departure proved grueling.

Handling Wick in practice flights, teaming with fifteen other male wyverns and their scouts proved challenging. Six of the riders had only two days of training on wyverns before we started. Although the new scouts were strong with a sword and expert horse cavalrymen, that didn't translate well to handling a wyvern. They'd do okay if it didn't come to aerial combat.

The two female wyverns added difficulty for the other riders and me. The dominant females intimidated Wick and the other male wyverns. Wick was prone to following their lead despite my commands and despite my dirk coated with fireweed resin. That was okay, up to a point. The males bonding to the females was important to the mission once we arrived at New Lisbon's harbor and began our assault on Fendra Jolain's hilltop fortress. Some called it her Main Temple, but to me it was a fortress.

We all knew the title of fortress was accurate, not only from the layout provided by Colonel Ibrahim, but also through visual images Imperial Seer Lochelle drew from memories of imprisoned healers. But the images were fleeting and blurry. The most powerful healers knew the inner rooms resisted Seer Lochelle's spells.

We viewed these images in groups of five. My team included Grand Wizard Seelain, Sergeant Drux, two wyvern scouts and Lilly. I was happy to see Lilly. Grand Wizard Seelain insisted she be part of the assault team. I *wasn't* excited to see images of ogres in heavy armor with spiked shields, but I worried more about the dragon-like creature with five heads. Seer Lochelle named the beast a hydra and said they don't breathe fire or acid like dragons. That was one encouraging aspect. The other thing I noticed was that the creature didn't always appear in the images outside the main worship chamber.

I said to Drux, "If that hydra must be fought, I hope by the time we arrive it's been sent down to the shore against the Crusaders."

He laughed. "Not a charitable thought, but I agree."

Lilly said, "*Someone's* gonna have to kill it." Wizard Seelain nodded in agreement.

Imperial Seer Lochelle said, "Yours is not the only group that has uttered concern. Those that enter I feel *will* face this beast.

Sergeant Drux pointed to each of us around Seer Lochelle's viewing table. "I count five here." He grinned wide, stretching the deep scar across the right side of his chin. "That's one head for each of us."

Seer Lochelle stepped forward and frowned at him, as did Wizard Seelain. Lilly's jaw just dropped and the two wyvern scouts looked at each other. I had to agree. The seer's spell chamber didn't seem the place for humor.

Drux held his hands out, shrugged, and said with eyebrows raised, "Sorry."

Forty minutes before sunset we prepared for departure. The plan was to fly out over the Tyrrhenian Sea, northward. Upon darkness we'd double back and travel south. Upon reaching the Southern Continent, we'd travel east and then north for the final leg of our journey leading up to the assault.

Eighteen wyverns, including two females, four red dragons and two black dragons were all the mounts we had. Each wyvern could carry only one rider. The reds carried three on top and two slung underneath. The blacks only two on top and one slung beneath. That meant only forty-four of us against the fortress. Actually fewer, as the serpent cavalryman would remain on their dragons to intercept reinforcements to the temple fortress and watch, should the goddess attempt to escape on foot or in the air. The two m'unicorn cavalrywomen turned wyvern scouts riding the scorpion-tailed females would lead the flock of dismounted males into the sky to drive off griffin reinforcements. That meant thirty-six against the fortress and its defenders. Of that, Prince Halgadin was to let his aft-guard take his dragon so he could hold the entrance with seven while the rest, twenty-eight under Prince Reveron, carried the assault to the worship chamber, where the princes believed Fendra Jolain would take refuge. That was twenty-eight *if* we all survived the journey.

Of the forty-four, I knew Lilly, Jadd, Drux, Wizard Seelain and Prince Reveron, Wizard Golt and Enchantress Thulease and Jotey, a top crossbowman from Pine Ridge. I knew who Prince Halgadin was, but he ignored me. Maybe it was because I was the only mercenary. He ignored Lilly too, which was fine with her.

I did overhear the crown prince tell Major Jadd that his service to the kingdom made up for his past wrong, but to not disobey another order. Major Jadd agreed and they shook hands.

I told Lilly and we agreed that war and desperate situations caused most soldiers to forget bad blood. We both thought better of Prince Halgadin for what he had done.

Besides Earth Wizard Golt, Air Wizards Seelain and Prince Reveron, and Enchantress Thulease, we had a lesser fire wizard named Bruneene who looked more like a bookish city dweller than Jonas, and an earth wizard, Greater Wizard Clarissa. Her name didn't match her pillar-like frame. One of the former m'unicorn riders had some air wizard ability, probably apprentice level, and we had a gray-haired rogue healer named Zandie.

Sergeant Drux had served with the rogue and said she wasn't overly powerful but made me look like an amateur—which I pointed out to him, I actually was.

Eight spellcasters. More than Keesee could afford to lose, but somehow it felt like not nearly enough for the task. And thirty-six of us who had to count on steel, strength and our wits. Even with the dragons and wyverns, no matter how I looked at it, against a goddess in her city we were overmatched.

Maybe the Crusaders would come in great numbers. Maybe the Colonel of the West sent a war machine that would make a difference. Right, and Maybe Drux and Lilly would stop annoying each other by trying to get the last word in on any conversation between them. That annoyed me too since their words usually edged towards heated ones.

Our small force, the best the Kingdom of Keesee could muster, took off on our mounts into the sky without ceremony. I looked back, wishing for the chance to say good-bye to my mother, father and younger sister, and wondering if the future held a reunion with my older sister, Raina.

During the long nights traveling, I wondered if Raina had changed. What she looked like, who she'd become, and what I'd say if we crossed paths. Was she the enemy? Would she see me as the enemy?

The topic came up during the assault team's sixth daytime camp where I drew sentry duty with Crossbowman Jotey.

The earth wizards had raised a rock-filled sand dune to block any ground-level view of our camp established next to large rock outcropping that offered shade from the sun's scorching heat. There wasn't much for Lieutenant Jotey and me to see but a desolate brown and gray landscape. It was the first time Jotey and I got the chance to say more than a few words to each other.

"Still getting used to you being called Flank Hawk," Jotey said. He was six summers older than me and I'd known him my whole life. He was thin and smart, and a skilled huntsman, especially with a crossbow. I had been the second best crossbowman in Pine Ridge—when it still existed. He'd been the best by far.

I shaded my eyes, peeking my head around a rock atop the dune and scanning the barren landscape. "Took me some getting used to."

"Seen quite a bit since the Necromancer King's zombies overran Pine Ridge, haven't ya?"

I nodded. "Seen plenty of things I'd like to forget. Bet you have too."

"The prince and Grand Wizard think a lot of you. Treat you pretty well."

"I've served them since just after the war started." I looked back to where Prince Halgadin was tending to his red dragon. "You must've done something right to be a lieutenant and picked by the prince to be here."

He shrugged. "Just east of some wizard's tower, I think his name was

Phebeus. He'd painted it so that at a distance it blended in with the landscape. Mostly stunted trees and shrubs. Anyway, the enemy was charging and my company broke. I didn't." He looked up at the clear blue sky. "A griffin with rider was diving down on me. I waited with my crossbow. When it got ready to strike—opened its beak I shot right through to the back of its throat. Stepped aside as it and the rider crashed and tumbled by, reloaded and took aim at the nearest cavalryman's horse. Shot it in the neck and sent them tumbling too."

He shrugged. "Prince Halgadin's dragon snatched me up seconds before the cavalry line's lances impaled me. Never saw it coming."

I looked over the lip of the dune and scanned the countryside. "That's pretty brave, if you ask me."

"Not really," he said. "My company was on foot. There were three hundred of them on horse against our thirty. I decided to die facing the enemy rather than take a lance through my back. Guess that's why the prince made me an officer. Picked me for this venture."

He took his turn to peek over the dune's lip and scan the countryside. "Think we have a chance?"

"Chance for what?" I asked. "Winning the war?"

"Just surviving," he said. "I mean we're led by some powerful people here. But against a goddess? Don't get me wrong. I'll fight hard as anybody."

"At least you get to stay with the crown prince. I'll be going in."

"That's not what I meant, Kri—Flank Hawk."

"I know," I said. "I've been up against it before. Prince Reveron and Grand Wizard Seelain, if anybody can do it, they can. And Prince Halgadin, nobody's better with a sword."

Jotey nodded. "I heard you've held it, the sword the young prince carries. Think that blade can do the job?"

I wasn't sure, but said, "Yes, I think so." Then I took my turn to check the nearby terrain.

"Where's your crossbow?" he asked.

"Too much weight for little purpose," I said. "My spear or it? Spear'll be needed more. Gave my crossbow to Rin. Told him to give it to Dad eight days after we left."

"Thinking you might not come back?"

I shrugged and thought about Private Zunnert. Wizard Seelain told me the king promised to personally give the sword and hunting knife we'd carried back to Zunnert's son and daughter. I imagined on the same day Rin gave my crossbow to my dad.

"Think there'll be any kingdom to come back to?" When I didn't say anything he asked, "Why didn't they send back at least one wyvern rider to warn of the army massing on the Southern Continent? With all those ships gathered, it won't be long before they invade from the south."

"Word's been sent back," I said.

I knew Supreme Enchanter Thulease did it using the Shard Staff because Grand Wizard Seelain told me so. The effort took a lot out of the enchantress too. Wizard Seelain explained that energy from the staff's shards is meant to flow to the staff wielder, not the other way. When I asked her why we didn't have all the remaining dragons with us, at least to carry more soldiers if our mission was so vital, she said that the main reason Enchantress Thulease is with us is to hide our final approach. Even with the assistance of the Shard Staff, hiding six dragons in flight will be difficult.

Other than the fact that word had been sent back, I didn't share any more of what Wizard Seelain told me with Jotey.

My gaze fell back to the tall enchantress sitting with her legs crossed in the shade of a small rock overhang. The Shard Staff's core, white and missing the six rods I'd originally seen set into it when King Tobias revealed the weapon, rested on her lap. Her hands held it and I knew she was casting a spell, or rather keeping one active. Wizard Seelain told me that when we rested the enchantress cast a spell of reluctance. Anybody passing by would be disinclined, she said, to look our direction. Until that moment, I hadn't realized how much the grand wizard was telling me about what was going on.

In any case, I didn't share with Jotey what the supreme enchantress was doing either. It wasn't that I didn't trust him; it was just that Wizard Seelain trusted me with information probably not meant for me to know. "Your wife and daughters are in the King's City?" I asked.

He shook his head. "They're with my father and my sister in a refugee farming village a hundred miles south of the King's City." He scanned the sky again. "You probably shouldn't have let me know word was sent back."

I shrugged and searched the countryside again. "Just don't say anything."

"I won't." Jotey shifted his position and peeked over the dune's lip. "Takes a load off of my mind, knowing the king can act and my family might yet survive."

Rumors said that Fendra Jolain's forces executed all captured soldiers and randomly slew civilians, including women and children. Jadd told me they only killed civilians they somehow deemed too loyal to the local lord or ruler. Maybe that was true, and maybe it was a method of intimidation to keep control amid the chaos of a war. The less trouble they had, the fewer troops they needed left behind to maintain order.

Jotey asked, "Where do you think your sister Raina is? Think she'll be in the capital city—in the temple even?"

I knew Jotey cared about my sister. He was one of the few my father considered an acceptable suitor before Fendra Jolain's people came and dragged her away. "I hope she's not," I said.

He patted me on the shoulder. "Yeah, me too."

CHAPTER 37

Our approach to New Lisbon was going without a hitch and for some reason that made me even more nervous. We flew concealed by low cloud cover. My position in the flight below and ahead of the dragons made it impossible for me to ask Wizard Seelain or any other spellcasters about the clouds. I'd have bet a lot of coin that they were the remnants of a magically summoned storm to wreak havoc with ships approaching shore and to disrupt the Crusader amphibious landing—if they made it.

We pressed on, guided by deep-throated calls from the female wyverns leading us and the male responses. The calls and replies weren't loud enough to travel far, but strong enough for the flock to keep its formation despite the surrounding gray that looked and felt like heavy morning lake fog, only thicker.

Flying blind is never easy, especially into combat. After what seemed like an eternity, we heard the distant booming of cannon fire soon followed by the crack of gunfire—including ripping volley fire which signaled the Crusaders had arrived. The calls between the wyverns intensified. Wick became tense, shifting his head from side to side, searching through the gray clouds. Just before we broke from the low cloud cover I heard the fast *whump-whump-whump-whump* from at least one of the Colonel of the West's flying machines.

Wick and the other wyverns shifted to blend with the gray sky above, hiding our appearance. A sharp *caw* warned the dragons flying behind and above that the clouds ceased covering our approach.

So much of our success depended on surprise. As the dragons emerged Supreme Enchantress Thulease's demonstrated the primary reason for her presence wielding the Shard Staff. She called upon her spell strength and that of the shard holders. I knew it was supposed to happen but as I looked up and back at the trailing dragons, they disappeared seconds after emerging from the cloud bank.

Grand Wizard Seelain explained it as warping or bending light so that anyone below the dragons and their riders would see only the sky above, in this case the gray clouds. It gave us our one chance to reach Fendra Jolain's main temple undetected.

We were over the water, approaching New Lisbon's ocean port within the enormous bay. Smoke rose from the battle in the water, along the shore and a few spots within the city, one that rivaled the size of the King's City in

Keesee.

Upon a signal from one of the scouts riding a female wyvern, we slowed to allow the dragons to overtake us before rising several hundred yards to our assigned position above them. While doing this I gave commands to Wick, causing him to tip left and then right so that I might see the sea battle below as we adjusted our path to come in straight over the city, giving Enchantress Thulease's magic its best angle to work.

Ships filled the enemy harbor, mostly Crusader with a few enemy war galleys racing in from some patrol to defend the besieged port. Unless the wooden ships driven by wind-filled sails had wizards and other magics they wouldn't stand long against the steel-hulled, steam-driven vessels manned by Crusader crews. Not only were the ships of the Reunited Kingdom faster and more maneuverable, but cannon and gunfire were more effective than catapults throwing burning pitch, or arrows and hurled spears.

But Fendra Jolain's war galleys weren't the main Crusader concern. At least a dozen of the steam-driven ships drifted on fire or capsized. Around them swam mermaids and mermen, seizing and drowning Crusader sailors. At least thirty Crusader warships remained afloat, with an equal number of flat-bottomed cargo ships having run aground before lowering ramps to disgorge soldiers and equipment to seize the port and fight their way into the city.

To protect the landing, those surviving thirty warships maneuvered and fought. Several ignored the naval melee and fired their cannons into the city in support of the ground troops battling to expand their toehold. All the while, minions of the Sea Goddess Uplersh—giant snake-like sea serpents spewing venom, great long-tentacled squids entangling paddlewheels and propellers while snatching men from decks, and even a massive sea turtle rising up underneath smaller Crusader vessels to capsize them, fought to break our allies. The Crusaders fought back with saber and muzzle-loader, with cannons and exploding depth charges, raising geysers of blood and broken bodies.

I wondered if the Kraken had seen battle below, then driven off—or maybe, like the galleys racing to the fight, was soon to arrive. Certainly minions of Uplersh had detected the naval force before it arrived, giving time for her serpents and other beasts to harass the ships along the way while preparing a defense, and also sending ample warning for their ally, Fendra Jolain, to prepare.

On the piers and close in to shore, summoned water elemental spirits, standing waves or whip-like snake forms the size of serpents, lashed out at Crusaders, engulfing and dragging them into the sea. Crusader priests and holy men holding crosses before them drove back the magical creatures, shattering the binding magic wherever their words and prayers reached those that didn't retreat quickly enough.

Companies of Crusader riflemen pressed forward, past collapsed shops and burning warehouses. Cannons wheeled into position by man-force supported the drive. I even spotted a squad of green-clad soldiers with small machine guns and bazookas flanking enemy light infantry and archers racing to reinforce weakened lines to prevent a breakout. At the same time, behind an eight-foot wall of earth and stone moving like an ocean wave down a wide cobbled street, marched what looked to be heavy infantry followed by crossbowmen, all under the cover of steel shields held over their heads.

The salty smell of ocean mixed with the odors of smoke, gunpowder and burning flesh as we moved overland. Bodies of fallen Crusaders littered the piers and shore with medics moving among them, searching for those yet alive. Initially there were fewer fallen to be seen among the enemy, until I saw a line of wagons loaded with wounded winding through the city. But just as I saw it, bursts of light and explosions rained down upon the wagons and the horses pulling them. I immediately thought back to the mortar teams stationed at Outpost 1, and Captain Bray's later explanation of their use and effectiveness. Attacking wounded struck me as methodically cruel and not how I thought of Crusaders. But, if they didn't finish the job, Fendra Jolain's healers would have the wounded back in the battle within hours.

The helicopter hovering ahead and above us must've been using wireless telegraph to direct the mortar fire. That must have been how selected structures, such as a massive stable burning with dead griffins lying about, had been targeted and destroyed. Griffins wouldn't be effective against Crusader guns. Dead griffins floating along the shore and scattered on roofs and streets indicated the enemy had learned that through a hard lesson. Better for us. Better for Wick after we landed at the temple.

We passed under the helicopter. I wondered if the enemy knew its tactical purpose and if they'd tried to destroy the Colonel's flying machine. The swivel-mounted machine guns manned from door-sized openings on each side could fend off griffins. The Colonel of the West and his men were smart and battle-hardened. Unlike the Crusaders, they used magic and probably had air wizards inside the helicopter, further defending it.

I thought for a moment about the size of the Reunited Kingdom's landing force. It wasn't powerful enough to take the city, but the destructive force and pressing effort to advance into the city disguised its primary purpose as a diversion for our assault. Maybe they'd decided that this was a decisive moment, not only for the survival of Keesee, but the Reunited Kingdom's long-term survival as well.

The riders on the female wyverns led us upward to our position above the dragons as we flew over the city toward the hilltop where Fendra Jolain's main temple sat. I again directed Wick to tip and swerve slightly in his flight so I could look below at the dragons flying in a tight formation clustered around the red bearing Supreme Enchanter Thulease. The dragons appeared to be flying above a pocket of air that waved and shimmered like I sometimes saw above heated metals at a blacksmith's shop.

Our hilltop target, a triangular building with grand entrance steps covered by a slate roof supported by massive pillars, was easy to spot. Large bladders, that reminded me of a hot air balloon I'd once seen in Pine Ridge as a child, flew high above the temple, tethered in place by long cords. I didn't know their purpose. Maybe a way to signal defenders by releasing one or groups of balloons? Varying in color would have allowed more complex messages signaled, but they were all tan, without even flags attached to the cords. It didn't matter. The fifteen balloons were too wide spread above and around the temple to affect dragons or wyverns approaching.

Even as we came on, armored enemy soldiers marched below us toward the harbor. If the sharpest-eyed ones among them took a moment to look up and examine the skies, they might've spotted hints of movement—and discerned the wyverns in flight far above. But they weren't concerned about what appeared to be a near empty sky. The Colonel's flying machine, and a second that had just lifted off of a large Crusader vessel rearmed for battle, certainly loomed foremost in their thoughts. Maybe the rising helicopter carried the team that was to collapse the underground escape route from the main temple. Jadd told me that was the responsibility of the Colonel's men.

From our elevation I could see beyond New Lisbon's far wall. Less than ten miles away a formation of at least eight thousand soldiers marched toward the city.

There was about to be a lot more dying, especially on our side. If our assault succeeded, how many of the assault team would survive—and would the Crusaders know it? Would there be any mounts on which to make an escape? If we failed in our mission or failed to retreat by air even if we succeeded, the enemy would certainly capture the Blood Sword. The harbor was too far away with too many soldiers between us and the battling Crusaders.

There wasn't time to ponder my—our—possible fate further as the dragons below broke formation and became visible to the temple's defenders.

CHAPTER 38

The Healing Goddess Fendra Jolain's main temple appeared to be a fortress, built from interlocking granite blocks twice the size of hay bales. The enormous triangular structure sat alone atop a steep hill overlooking the city. Wide steps carved into the hillside wound their way up to the temple, terminating in a slate-roofed granite landing with rows of thick pillars that led up to a pair of arched double doors, oak monstrosities reinforced by steel bands. A lowered portcullis made up of a latticework of barbed wrought iron bars protected the oak entry doors.

One red dragon landed, breathing gouts of flame between the pillars leading to the main entrance. Flesh burned and men guarding the entrance screamed. Two other fire-breathing reds swung around to the triangle point opposite the main entrance to sweep clean the two high balconies on the opposing walls near the point. Each dragon carried an earth wizard whose task was to seal the steel doors certain to have slammed shut when we were spotted. The objective was to hinder any escape efforts through those doors.

Major Jadd on Flame Lance swept in to clear the roof of defenders while one black cleared the stairway up the hill and the other, Prince Reveron's, flew top cover. All the while, the wyverns spiraled down and landed in the gardens near the temple. Once dismounted the wyverns returned to the sky and the dragons were to land to drop their loads of weapons and men, including aft-guards, so that we might make the assault. Because of this, Prince Reveron bearing the Blood Sword flew as aft-guard on his mount, as did Prince Halgadin so that he might command the rear defense and hold the entrance.

While descending upon Wick, I saw Jadd bring Flame Lance around one of the balloon cables to scatter the squad defending the roof. He banked sharply left and then right, avoiding two ballista-launched spears. Then an air wizard flung her spell, driving back both Flame Lance and his fiery breath while tearing into the dragon's leathery wings.

Flame Lance flapped wildly, struggling to maintain control so that he might land. Wyverns scattered as the dragon came down hard in the gardens. The top-cover black dragon descended, bringing air wizards Seelain and Prince Reveron to the fight. I dismounted Wick, removed his reins and pulled my spear from its sheath. I slapped him, encouraging my mount to take flight where the dominant female wyverns screeched, calling the males to them.

Small thunderclaps sounded above the temple and Prince Reveron's black dragon spewed a stream of acid before rising back into the sky, circling while awaiting a place in the temple garden to land.

I caught a glimpse of Major Jadd and his injured mount. They'd landed hard but looked okay as I ran and took my place next to Enchantress Thulease. I was assigned to ward her until the rest of my team, Wizard Seelain, Sergeant Drux, Lilly and two wyvern scouts, Lieutenant Krogeman and Corporal Otis were ready. Krogeman and Otis waited for Drux, Lilly and Wizard Seelain to dismount from their dragons and form up next to our assigned spot, a support pillar. It stood third deep on the left-hand side, nearest the marble walkway leading up to the main doors. My initial separation seemed an arrangement that encouraged confusion going into battle, but the supreme enchantress wanted me at her side before entering. I took it as an honor. She trusted me to ward her until the two infiltration soldiers dismounted from their dragons and made it to her side.

But the assault couldn't wait while the dragons and earth wizards finished their tasks. I moved to the enchantress's right as she strode up the steps and past the fallen enemy that had been dropped by dragon's fire. The burned flesh gave off a horrible odor. Enchantress Thulease clutched the end of her green robe's sleeve and held it across her nose and mouth as she passed by the bodies.

Movement from one of the fallen caught my eye, causing me to hesitate in my stride. I swung my spear toward the fallen soldier. His hand flexed and curled into a fist. With all the charred flesh, he should've been dead. Images of zombies rising raced foremost in my thoughts. Fendra Jolain was the Necromancer King's ally. It could be a necromancer's magic animating the dead.

Enchantress Thulease stopped. "What is it, Flank Hawk?"

There was little time. Already teams had formed around the entrance, awaiting Enchantress Thulease. Her spellcraft was needed to raise the portcullis.

"The dead moves," I said, realizing I didn't have any salt to use against zombies. "Necromancy."

Her eyes widened then narrowed.

The body twitched and then groaned. I stabbed it through the neck, causing the body to bleed.

"Not necromancy," said the enchantress. "Healing magic."

Several other torched bodies began moving. My heart sank. It had to be healing power radiating from Fendra Jolain herself. No healer that I'd heard of could heal so many, hurt to the point of death, and from a distance.

"They're healing!" I shouted, and pointed to a waiting team of wyvern riders nearby. "Decapitate the downed enemy or they'll rise and threaten our rear. Inform those that pass through and warn Prince Halgadin before following us in."

I wasn't in the chain of command and they hesitated until Enchantress

Thulease stepped toward them and ordered, "Do as he says!" Although we wouldn't have landed if the enchantress hadn't detected the healing goddess's presence, the rapid healings made it clear to everyone.

The scouts sprang into action. Enchantress Thulease clutched the Shard Staff, her face twisted in sickening disgust. As we raced forward I guessed she'd never been in combat, at least not filled with such carnage. I imagined my face held the same look the first time I faced a hoard of rotting zombies.

Half of the assault team stood behind the pillars facing the portcullis. Several had just finished hacking off the heads of the enemy. Their grim faces showed they weren't happy about doing it.

I turned quickly to see Major Jadd leading Flame Lance between the pillars toward the main entrance. Deep down I felt his sadness. Unable to fly, even if we succeeded his mount wouldn't escape.

The supreme enchantress raised the Shard Staff and began uttering a spell. Immediately a flash that could only have been lightning shot from the portcullis right at the enchantress. Somehow she deflected the blue-white bolt upward, into the slate roof. Gray fragments, some the size of plates fell upon the men behind us.

The warding spell's crackling energy left the scent of a thunderstorm and my hair standing on end. It had knocked the enchantress to her knees. She looked about momentarily confused, her eyes wide and hair frayed. I offered my hand. "Enchantress, are you okay?"

She looked up at me for half a second and took my hand. "I am," she said and stood with my help and that of the Shard Staff. Again she raised it and began her spell. Others sheltered behind pillars or backed away. I remained at her side, unsure if it was the wise thing to do. At that moment she needed my support, my confidence—at least that's what I told myself.

The portcullis' latticework of barbed wrought iron bars began to shimmer with silver sparkles. Metallic clicks and clangs followed. The enchantress raised her right hand and the bars began to slowly rise, then stopped.

Tremors ran along Enchantress Thulease's right arm and hand, sweat dripped down her temple. The sparkling faded, then intensified.

Scraping claws on stone and deep, sulfury breathing told me Major Jadd and his serpent mount waited behind us. "Stand ready team," Jadd said.

The iron gate slammed upward, out of sight. A brief metallic grinding sound followed. Enchanter Thulease took a deep breath. "I have fused the chains and gears. It shan't fall until well after our task is complete."

I didn't know if she was talking to me or someone else. Maybe Major Jadd. He came up to stand on her left, holding the reins to Flame Lance in his right hand. We watched a team of soldiers race forward and place bundles of dynamite sticks against the arched double doors. Waiting behind the men stood two torchbearers.

"I sense powerful magic behind those doors," warned Enchantress Thulease. "Even with the Shard Staff..." Her voice trailed off.

Enchantress Thulease's two infiltration soldiers trotted up behind her. One said to me, "You're relieved."

Jadd said to her. "I'll lead Flame Lance in first. His strength and breath should counter any magic."

The dynamite placing team ran back from the door. The torchbearers looked over their shoulder to the enchantress.

"I'm with you," I said to Jadd.

"No," Jadd, said to me. "You ward Seelain." Then he shouted. "Change in plan. As soon as the doors go down and the enchantress drops her spell, throw the dynamite in. Flame Lance and I will then lead the way."

Enchantress Thulease nodded to the torchbearers. They lit the dynamite fuses and ran to the side. Even though the enchantress erected a spell to focus the blast against the wooden doors, most stepped further back and looked away. I grabbed a shield lying near a fallen enemy and stepped behind the enchantress as she chanted. "Here," I said to Jadd. Our eyes met, probably for the last time.

"Thanks," he said, taking the shield. "Follow me in with Seelain. As always, you'll have my back."

I turned and trotted the short distance to my assigned pillar. Above the enchantress's chanting and just before the dynamite blasts, I heard Jadd say to his serpent mount, "Ready, Flame Lance."

I made it back to Seelain, who stood with a hand on Drux's shoulder. Jadd's aft-guard stood with a snarl across his scarred face, leaning forward with halberd ready. Lilly met my gaze, her broad-bladed dagger already covered in blood. She knew Jadd's chances too.

The dynamite bundles exploded against the doors. Enchantress Thulease's magical barrier redirected all the blast force back against the tall doors, knocking them askew. The enchantress shouted sharp spell words while thrusting the Shard Staff forward. The doors creaked, then toppled.

Thulease slumped as the two infiltration soldiers that relieved me pulled her from Flame Lance's path through the open doorway.

Four soldiers rushed forward with dynamite sticks wrapped in nails and each threw a pair of the explosive sticks with fuse-wicks burning into the room beyond the doorway.

Blasts from the detonating explosives echoed. I don't know if cries of surprise or pain, or even shouted orders followed because Major Jadd, holding shield and reins, led Flame Lance roaring through the open doorway. I worried that the enemy might kill the dragon in the doorway and block our passage. Maybe this was why no dragon had originally been sent to accompany us. More likely every dragon was needed to give us time to complete our task. Plus, fighting next to a dragon in the heat of battle—it matters little to the beast's flailing tail, wings and claws whose side you're on.

The torchbearers stood along each side of the entryway. Four soldiers with large shields passed by them and lit the wick-fuses of two dynamite sticks bound together and wrapped in nails. Sheltering behind the shields they followed Flame Lance in.

That signaled our moment. Grand Wizard Seelain said to our team, "We go!"

We were the second team through the door with Prince Reveron's team behind us. I felt the Blood Sword's sickening evil. Fendra Jolain couldn't miss it.

We sprinted into the worship hall that took up the entire base of the triangular structure. The hall was lit by a combination of slit windows and lanterns suspended by long chains reaching halfway down from the forty-five foot ceiling. The south face where we entered had a level above us supported by stout square pillars. The layout I'd seen said the upper level contained fifteen rows of benches elevated like arena seating. Enough benches to seat over a thousand worshipers filled the main floor. Two tiers of balcony seats with white tapestry displaying red crosses hanging down ran along the east and west walls. Along the north wall was a ten-step dais topped with a huge white-cushioned throne encrusted with oval rubies. A bare white marble altar sat at the base of the dais.

Hundreds of bodies broken by dynamite explosions and dragon fire lay scattered among the shattered benches, some aflame from the dragon's breath. Most of the fallen were dressed more like worshipers than soldiers—singed, bloody clothing, without helmets, armor, or shields. About thirty still standing chased after Flame Lance with clubs, knives and bare fists.

Fists against a dragon told me they were fanatical worshippers.

Archers lined the balconies, raining arrows down on the dragon while soldiers that had survived flame and explosion-flung nails surged forward from the east and west walls. Two of our teams split to meet them.

Most concerning to me was the defenders of the alcove which held the only door leading to the Sacred Chamber beyond, where Fendra Jolain was expected to be. Eight armored ogres, hulking twelve-foot brutes, stood ready with spiked clubs, large shields and steel helmets that hid all but their yellow eyes and their single short upturned horns rising from their sloped foreheads. Behind the ogre vanguard stood a steel statue towering a man's height above the biggest ogre. The shining metal man with golden beard and blue sapphire eyes was adorned in a leather vest and breeches and was armed with an iron javelin and sheathed sword.

The statue was alive, just like a gargoyle. Jadd led Flame Lance forward, crashing through the remaining benches near the altar, commanding his serpent mount to spread fire upon the ogres fanning out before charging forward.

"We take the archers along the west wall first," shouted Seelain above the din as they shifted their aim from the dragon toward us. A series of claps sounded along the balcony as Seelain collapsed air around the archers. They crumpled from sight.

Lilly pointed to a spiral staircase leading up to the balconies.

"Krogeman, Otis, with Lilly," I ordered. "Finish them before they heal."

Wizard Seelain spun and repeated her spell against the east balcony archers. Prince Reveron ordered two of his men to deal with the newly fallen archers. Another team climbed stairs up to the upper level to deal with defenders felled by dynamite.

Around us the lesser wounded fanatics among the benches began stirring. Drux and I stood close to Seelain, watching for possible threats, preparing to take the fight to the ogres and support Jadd. Flame Lance bellowed, the steel statue's javelin having been hurled deep into the serpent's shoulder. The dragon charged forward, slapping aside surviving fanatics with his tail while spewing flames again as the steel giant drew its sword.

Prince Reveron came up to Wizard Seelain. "Golt will be here momentarily," he said. "Can one of his summoned elementals bring down that golem?"

"I believe not," said Seelain.

Several white-robed healers appeared from behind the dais and began healing the flame-burned ogres as the golem and dragon clashed. I couldn't see Major Jadd but saw Flame Lance bite down on the golem's sword arm, breaking teeth while holding the weapon at bay. Even so, the steel giant began smashing his left fist down on Flame Lance's head and snout.

Prince Reveron shouted over his shoulder, "Thulease, bring the golem down! Seelain, when the fire wizard enters, have him set fire to the benches!" He raised the Blood Sword high, filling the chamber with its malevolent emanations, and charged down the path Flame Lance had cleared. "Flank Hawk, Drux, with me."

The prince's orders overrode my duty to ward Wizard Seelain, so Drux and I followed the prince and three sword-armed soldiers warding him.

The white-robed Lain healers had three of the five burned ogres back up and ready for battle. At the same time three of the uninjured brutes fell upon Flame Lance with their clubs, driving spikes into the shoulders and sides of the dragon already in its death throes, its skull having been pummeled and crushed.

Jadd, with two arrows protruding from his left leg and one from his back limped up behind one of the unwary armored ogres and drove his sword's blade between metal plates sewn into the heavy leather shirt, piercing skin and kidney. The ogre bellowed and spun about, slamming his shield into the hobbled Jadd. My friend flew back, losing his sword as he landed among a pile of fanatic worshipers smashed and broken by Flame Lance before the serpent fell. They'd heal and rise. Jadd didn't move. He wouldn't.

I had no idea how Thulease could take down the golem, now signaling with his steel hand for us to approach. "Come to your death, little prince," the statue said, his echoing voice reminding me of metallic thunder. I hoped the enchantress could stop the steel giant. I wasn't sure we'd even be able to handle the armored ogres turning to face us, let alone the metal titan.

Lilly, Krogeman and Otis ran across the tops of benches, closing in from the left. A dozen soldiers from the right charged toward the ogres as well. But until they reached us, it was Prince Reveron and five warriors, counting me and Drux, against the golem and six ogres, with two more healed and getting to their feet.

I leapt over Flame Lance's quivering tail and shouted a challenge to the ogre Jadd had stuck with his sword. It snarled, standing battle ready with club held high. I'd fought ogres before. They're faster than their size suggests and the armor this one wore didn't appear to slow him much. My goal was to keep the brute busy and off the prince until the Blood Sword's strength could be turned on my chosen foe—and Thulease completed her magic.

I jabbed with my spear and jumped back to avoid my foe's spiked club. He grinned and stepped forward, driving me back with heavy swings. I cut to the left, not wanting to be forced back into the benches and bodies where I'd trip or lose my footing. My cut and pivot put me back to back with Drux who shouted, "Down!"

I ducked and rolled, evading a club from behind, but had to keep scrambling as my foe pursued me, stomping down with his iron-shod boots, trying to crush me. I got to my feet only to get slammed by his shield. I landed a dozen feet back among the stirring zealots, just short of where Jadd fell. The fact that I hadn't been at his side during a critical moment cut deep to my core, but there wasn't time to fret over that.

A thunderous *clap* of air collapsing said Seelain's spell strength was with us. Deep, agonized bellowing announced the Blood Sword had scored a victim as I got to my feet with spear ready. My shoulder hurt but wasn't broken.

Crackling flames began to rise in the hall behind me while the ogre stomped forward with club held ready to finish me. "*Goll grull awk!*" I taunted in the Foul Tongue, shouting a phrase I learned from Jadd the first night we met in battle against the Necromancer King's ogres and zombies.

The ogre stood erect and snarled at the insult. I laughed and poked my spear against his shield. Cries of pain—fanatics caught in the fire—arose behind me. The stench of death already filled the hall and it was going to get worse. I understood the prince's order. They'd heal and be at our back, but the act sounded cruel. Then my mind flashed to Keesee burning and Rin's family killed. War was ugly no matter the side you fought on.

I blocked out the sounds of suffering as best I could while ducking my foe's roundhouse swing, feeling the wind of his club. The attack left the hulking brute off balance, giving me an opening. I attacked and came back with his blood on my spear having scored a shallow neck wound just below his helmet's reach. My foe's backswing drove me back several steps, but this time he kept his shield between us. He didn't see Lilly shoot in from his left, stabbing her dagger deep behind his knee before leaping way.

A second ogre's bellow joined the first. The Blood Sword struck flesh again.

Otis came to Drux's aid, the aft-guard having blinded his foe in one eye but losing his halberd in the process. Armed with swords, they came at their ogre from opposite sides.

As my foe turned to confront who'd wounded his leg, Krogeman slashed with his long sword, striking armor and not scoring blood. Three on one, we had a chance if we could take advantage of his wounds before they healed.

Then, leaping over the altar, the golem landed hard and began striding down the central isle. The action shook the floor and rattled my teeth. It distracted our foe and Lilly took advantage of it, charging in and stabbing the bleeding leg again, cutting tendons and crippling our foe. He swiped at her while I jabbed my spear into his face. My weapon found only helmet. Krogeman's sword pierced leather and bit into the ogre's thigh. The soldier caught the furious ogre's shield smash as the brute stumbled to one knee. The strike sent Krogeman reeling back, but it was a weak blow and he recovered.

I shouted, "Krogeman, behind you!"

The wyvern scout spun and dodged, but not fast enough. An ogre's club slammed down on his shoulder, driving him to the floor like a sledge hammer smashing down on a stool. From behind the victorious ogre, the Blood Sword flashed, biting through armor and into the ogre's side. I didn't have time to watch as my crippled foe lunged forward, swiping at me with his club.

The swing was too low to duck. I leapt, but it caught my boot, causing me to land hard on my already hurting shoulder. The crippled ogre came on, crawling toward me as I rolled over and scrambled to my feet, trying to raise my spear. The wound on his neck had already closed. If he got a hold of me it'd be over.

Lilly leapt onto the ogre's back and stabbed down, but there was little her dagger could do to stop the brute. A crossbow's quarrel sped by my shoulder and buried itself deep in the ogre's right eye. My foe hesitated in his pursuit to pluck the shaft from his eye. I stabbed with all I had but failed to pierce his mailed gauntlet.

Drux knocked me aside, beyond the ogre's reach. Lilly shied away as Prince Reveron closed, thrusting the Blood Sword deep into the besieged ogre's ribs. He withdrew the foul blade and slashed again, catching the ogre across the forearm as the brute spun to confront the prince and two other warriors bringing their swords to bear. The Blood Sword's second wound wasn't deep, but any cut from the Blood Sword was fatal. Death had already begun creeping through his veins and arteries.

Even with a single eye the crippled ogre recognized the Blood Sword and his fate—the same as his fallen brothers, each writhing on the floor, blood flowing from nose, eyes and every wound. At least from this distance, Fendra Jolain's magic wasn't equal to the Blood Sword's malevolence.

I stepped wide around the dying ogre and ran to Krogeman. Dead. I looked about. Lilly was dragging Jadd's body away from the spreading flames.

Listening for breathing upon her ear, she shouted, "He's alive!" How she could determine that through the rising smoke and screams, I had no idea, but I believed her. "Can you heal him?" Looking down, I shook my head. Blood trickled from his nose and mouth, indicating pierced lungs, plus the arrows and the twisted angle his right arm hung. There was no way.

I thought of our rogue healer. "Zandie might," I said, and scanned the worship hall for her. My eyes centered on the steel golem amid benches and flames, battling to get past Wizard Golt's earth elemental and reach Enchantress Thulease whose magic was undoing him.

Prince Reveron ordered me, "Flank Hawk, heal your shoulder if you can. Drux, gather those who are left." Maybe the way I struggled to hold my spear told him of my injury.

The prince was experienced and battle hardened, and knew better than I that Supreme Enchantress Thulease and Master Wizard Golt must survive for us to reach and confront Fendra Jolain, and there wasn't anything he, or I or any of us could do to help.

CHAPTER 39

The earth spirit summoned by Wizard Golt manifested itself as a fifteen foot jumble of compacted earth and stone. It resembled a faceless ogre, but larger. As powerful as the elemental was, it faced a steel foe greater in size and strength. Both combatants crushed bodies of fanatics underfoot and ignored flames reaching their calves as they hammered each other with fists and sword.

Sharp metallic bellows echoed throughout the hall as the two grappled and fought. The steel golem's luster was gone, his exterior pitted with rust. Dents showed wherever the elemental's fist struck. The golem's sword again clove deep into dirt and stone. Beyond, Thulease and Golt focused their magic, defended by Seelain, Prince Halgadin and several of his men.

That the crown prince had abandoned the outer defense could've been good news or bad.

The numbing ache in my shoulder reminded me of Prince Reveron's order. Jotey came up next to me. I realized then it was his quarrel that struck the ogre's eye at a critical moment. He said, "I'll ward while you conjure your spell."

"Thanks," I said and hurriedly knelt before reaching out into the energy maelstrom. The ribbons I sought were quick at hand, easily summoned and directed. Less than a minute later my shoulder was better. I stood and realized I'd tapped into the magical flow the goddess showered upon her followers, allowing them to heal. Maybe I *could* heal Jadd.

Lilly ran up to Drux who knelt over Major Jadd. "I can't find her," she said.

I took a step toward them when Jotey shouted, "Raina!"

My sister? I turned to follow the marksman's gaze. She wore white robes stained in blood. Her wavy brown hair was longer and she was heavier than when I last saw her—but Jotey was right. It was my Raina. She stood with her hands on a fallen ogre's back—trying to heal the one that nearly killed me. Prince Reveron saw her too. Raising the Blood Sword, he strode toward my sister.

I raced to intercept him.

Raina stared up as the prince neared her. She made no move to evade. Rather she spat at him.

I shouted, "Prince, NO!"

Even as Prince Reveron hesitated, Raina lunged at him with fists raised. He swung the Blood Sword down. I extended my spear, deflecting the blow and followed with a kick that caught Raina in the stomach. I stood between them. "Please don't, Prince. She's my sister!"

Raina stood up straight as I removed my helmet. Jotey came to stand next to me.

"It's me, Raina," I said. "Krish." There was so much going on. Fire, screams, the golem pressing his attack, making his way toward Thulease and Golt. There just wasn't time to explain.

Her face twisted in anger as she looked past me and pointed. "That sword's evil. He's evil."

"Deal with her, Flank Hawk," Prince Reveron ordered and turned to join two soldiers exploring behind the dais.

"Raina, you know me," I said. "You know Jotey. Join us, help us." I pointed. "Heal Major Jadd, my friend."

She picked up a discarded sword and inexpertly raised it above her head. "Get out of my way, Krish."

I had no choice; the Blood Sword would do worse than kill her. "I'm sorry, Sister," I said and attacked with my boar spear, slicing her fingers and knocking the sword from her hands. She staggered back and I followed, smashing her in the face with the butt of my spear. Stunned, nose bleeding and broken, she cried out my name. I slammed the spear shaft across her temple, knocking her to her knees. Each blow saving her, and killing a part of me.

She held her arms protectively over her head, crying.

"I'm sorry," I said, holding back my own tears and kicking her in the stomach, telling myself it was better than her dying at the prince's hand. When she brought her arms down, I hit her again with shaft of my spear, knocking her unconscious.

That wasn't enough. She'd heal and be up again if I didn't do more. I raised my spear but Jotey grabbed my arm. "Here," he said, handing me my helmet. "I'll finish what has to be done."

"She'll heal fast," I said, realizing my words weren't necessary even as I uttered them. "Tear part of her robes to bind her." Because my first impulse was violence to save my sister, Jotey must've seen my despair and spun me to face the battle between the golem and elemental. I watched but felt only a hollowness inside me.

The elemental tore the left arm from the golem's shoulder. Rust poured from the golem's gaping wound like sand from a bucket. The doomed golem didn't give up. A final sword blow clove into an already gapping wedge that sheared his foe from shoulder to hip, breaking the magic that bound the summoned elemental spirit to the rock and dirt in which it manifested.

The rusted golem dropped its sword and stumbled to its knees before collapsing across the pile of stone and dirt.

All seemed quiet. No bellows or screams of pain. Enchantress Thulease fell to her knees. Wizard Seelain caught the Shard Staff and wrapped an arm around the enchantress. Prince Halgadin began shouting orders as did Prince Reveron.

"We have little time to act," called the crown prince, leading several men and Wizard Golt past the fallen titans. Wizard Seelain helped Thulease to her feet and they followed at a slower pace.

Lilly rushed up to me, despair in her voice. "Our healer's dead. There's no one to heal Jadd."

I started to say "I can" but Drux took me by the arm. "Let's go," he said to me and the other survivors. "The final challenge awaits us through the doors beyond." He pointed and led us past the dead ogre vanguard, the crushed head of Jadd's mount, and around the dais. "Reinforcements come. Time is against us."

Drux was Jadd's aft-guard and Sun-Fox Brother. Maybe Jadd had a better chance of survival being left behind. There wasn't time to argue.

One of Prince Halgadin's men dropped a backpack filled with dynamite sticks next to the tall wooden doors ornately carved to show scenes of stars, waterfalls and unicorns. Two men with hammers and chisels chipped out places for two other soldiers to place the dynamite. Greater Earth Wizard Clarissa assisted with minor spells. I guessed she was saving her spell strength for the battle to come.

Prince Halgadin came up behind us. "Quickly. The serpents are nearly spent and thousands of troops are scaling the hillside like ants to reach us."

Prince Reveron moved about, organizing us. There were only twenty-one of us left, counting the two princes, Wizard Seelain, two earth wizards, and Enchanter Thulease.

Jotey whispered in my ear, "Griffins got past the dragons. Killed a bunch of us before we stopped them. That's where we lost our healer and our fire wizard got hurt bad."

"Griffins are tough," I said. "Worse than ogres. Thanks for—"

He put a hand on my shoulder and interrupted me. "Say no more, Krish. Let's just get through this."

Prince Reveron came up to us. "Jotey, you hang back with your crossbow. Lilly, you ward Seelain. Drux, Flank Hawk, with me."

I gripped Lilly's hand before following the prince to the right side of the doors. She went to the left to stand in front of Grand Wizard Seelain. Enchantress Thulease was next to her. Despite the tall enchantress's determined look, tears streamed down her face.

"As soon as the doors go down," Prince Halgadin said, "Team One will enter and throw lit dynamite at targets of opportunity. I'll lead Team Two in along with the wizards, then Reveron's Team Three goes in. My brother *must* reach Jolain with the Blood Sword. Nothing else matters."

Prince Reveron drew the Blood Sword and nodded. Its evil pulsed against my skin, setting goose bumps upon it. I hoped it affected the goddess the same way.

We all stepped back around the dais as Jotey and Otis quickly set torches to the emplaced dynamite's wick-fuses.

Prince Reveron looked to me and Drux. "Flank Hawk, Sun-Fox Brother, this is the moment. Let us not fail our king and people."

"I'm with you to the end, Prince," I said.

Drux said, "It's about time someone showed that—"

I don't know what Drux said, if he ever finished, because at that moment deafening explosions toppled the doors to the Fendra Jolain's Sacred Chamber.

Four dynamite throwers lit their sticks and ran forward behind steel shields. Prince Halgadin's team charged forward, the spellcasters on their heels. Drux and I flanked Prince Reveron as he followed.

CHAPTER 40

The goddess Fendra Jolain sat reclined upon a white-cushioned récamier atop a ten-step dais in her Sacred Chamber's far corner. Two lean servants in red robes waved long-poled feathered fans over her, one stood at the récamier's curved headboard and the other at the scrolled footboard. The Goddess of Healing's sheer sleeveless gown, pure white with a wide belt of rose-red silk tied loosely around her waist, accented her curvaceous beauty.

To the dais' left and right, winding stairs led up to balconies whose steel doors stood wide open, letting in sunlight. The thirty bronze lanterns set in sconces further lit the polished floor and walls filled with engraved scenes of trees, birds and woodland creatures. The single archer standing in each balcony's doorway worried me far less than the fact that the doors were open—that the goddess didn't fear our dragons.

An array of defenders at the bottom of the dais steps stood ready. The most fearsome was the green-scaled hydra the size of a black dragon. Each of the reptilian beast's five heads at the end of long serpentine necks hissed, bearing toothy maws dripping inky venom. Two leather-clad ogres held tight to thick chains, keeping the battle-hungry beast from charging us. A curved line of twenty armored soldiers stood at attention in front of the hydra and ogres. Each held a drawn broadsword and round shield that bore a black-lined drawing of a long-toothed tiger's head upon a red field. Their steel helmets resembled a yawning tiger with onyx eyes and oversized canines protecting the soldier's temples.

One step ahead of them, nearer to us, stood two women in white robes who could've been twins. One, easily identify by her fiery red hair that hung in long curls and ruddy skin, was a fire wizard. The other, with brown hair and swarthy skin was obviously an earth wizard. The fire wizard held a flaming staff in her right hand while the earth wizard clutched a craggy stone staff in her left.

Fendra Jolain's dais was nestled in the far north corner of the triangular chamber. In the chamber's center rested an oval pool fed by a fountain in the form of a marble mermaid statue pouring water from an ocean shell. Except for wooden benches lining the east and west walls, the chamber's polished marble floor was empty.

The thrown dynamite sticks made it only half way across the triangular shaped room. The fire wizard's fist-sized bolts of flame intercepted and engulfed the sticks, causing them to flash and fizzle above the shallow pool without exploding.

Fendra Jolain rose to her feet. Her face was beautiful beyond compare with unblemished skin and deep almond eyes framed by wavy raven-black hair which draped over her shoulders and extended down past her hips. The goddess towered over the servants who'd stopped fanning and looked up to her adoringly.

She spread her arms wide, her left hand holding a staff crafted from three pearl-white shafts twisted as if braided into one. "Princes of Keesee," the goddess said in an alluring voice that reminded me of a siren's song.

Prince Halgadin didn't stop to hear the goddess's words. He didn't even break stride. Instead he pointed his sword at the goddess, shouting, "Forward!"

Even though we were outnumbered, facing a goddess able to heal her defenders at will, fresh wizards and a five-headed venomous beast, King Tobias's plan to surprise our foes must've worked. Deep down, I never thought we'd make it this far. Getting Prince Reveron and the Blood Sword to the top of the dais was all that mattered now.

Adding my voice to the rising battle cries around me, I shouted, "For Keesee!"

Undaunted by our brash bravery, the followers of Fendra Jolain raced forward to join battle. The earth wizard stepped forward first and stomped her bare foot against the polished stone floor, creating a leading wave of lava. The arc of molten rock rolled towards us, cresting four feet in height. The fire wizard snuffed out two more hurled dynamite sticks before causing the flames held by our torchbearers to race down the wood and engulf their arms and bodies. They screamed and fell to the ground, rolling to smother the flames. Exploding dynamite threw the bodies of both men into the air. Jotey was the only one near enough to be knocked to the ground.

Our wizards countered. Master Wizard Golt called for Prince Halgadin to halt before creating a four-foot rift in the floor.

When the ogres released the hydra, Earth Wizard Clarissa softened the stone in front of the beast and then solidified the morass after the beast's clawed front feet sank into it.

Wizard Seelain summoned a whirlwind that knocked a balcony archer aside before it raced down and swept up the enemy earth wizard and carried her toward us.

The lava wave rolled forward, swallowing the pool in a fount of steam as it passed.

The other archer dropped with one of Jotey's quarrels buried in his chest, but not before loosing his own arrow, piercing wizard Clarissa's throat. The archer dropped to his knees before yanking the quarrel from his chest. Within seconds blood from the wound stopped flowing and he nocked another arrow.

Somehow the earth wizard broke free from Wizard Seelain's whirlwind, but her flight's momentum carried her toward us, falling among Halgadin's waiting warriors. Their swords came down upon her. Evens so, Fendra Jolain chanted words and the wizard's body healed as fast as swords could strike. A severed arm even began flowing back to the body.

Prince Halgadin severed the wizard's head and kicked it into Golt's crevice just as the lava flowed into it. The healing goddess shouted a curse, but there wasn't time for Halgadin or his men to listen as they clashed with the long-tooth warriors following on the heels of the wave.

Although the lava hardened, it was still frying-pan hot. Halgadin and his men threw back the Long-Tooths, knocking many down onto the scorching surface after the enemy had leapt over it.

Drained as she was, Wizard Seelain was barely able to summon the spell strength to knock aside an arrow targeted at her. Lilly held up a discarded shield, deflecting a second arrow aimed at Seelain. I felt for Prince Reveron as he charged past his fiancé. It was tough for me too, knowing she was vulnerable. But Prince Reveron's brother had carved a gap in the enemy line so that the Blood Sword might pass through.

A flame bolt shot past on our left. Enchantress Thulease cried out briefly.

There wasn't time to look back. Prince Reveron slashed with the Blood Sword, drawing blood from two Long-Tooths. I knocked one back onto the hot floor before he could fully rise. Drux did better, hacking off a sword arm as we passed through the Long-Tooth line.

We had to be fast. The enemy's wounds would heal. Ours wouldn't.

The Long-Tooths turned to pursue but Prince Halgadin's surviving men took them from behind. Prince Halgadin's sword parried and cut with amazing speed and precision. I'd never seen such skill and came to fully understand why Jadd once said it'd be foolish to cross swords with the crown prince.

The two ogres turned from chipping at the stone with their swords to free the hydra and strode forward to intercept us. The fire wizard turned her attention to Prince Reveron, the evil of his malevolent Blood Sword forging a path through a spell encouraging peace and calm that the healing goddess directed at him. I kept close to Prince Reveron to avoid the edges of the spell that tugged at me.

Was it wrong to follow close to evil to avoid peace and comfort? Maybe at another time I'd have been torn, but I again drew upon images of Keesee burning, the war Fendra Jolain waged against us as the aggressor—that she was an ally of the Necromancer King, his animated zombies, fallen family and fellow soldiers raised to march against us. To kill us.

In a war, there isn't always a side fully in the right battling against a side fully in the wrong. Just your side against the enemy's side.

We pounded across the stone floor, now rippled and still hot from the lava wave. Before we clashed with the ogres an arrow flew past, inches above the prince's head. Maybe he'd used air wizardry to make it miss, or maybe it was just luck. He ducked under the lead ogre's sword and slashed the brute across the leg before pivoting to stab him in the same leg.

The second ogre ignored us and fell upon the prince with wild abandon even as the first one turned, bellowing out in pain. Drux charged into the fray against the second ogre. I plunged my spear into the bleeding ogre's leg, causing it to collapse.

How long could Prince Halgadin keep the enemy off us? How long before Fendra Jolain's troops broke through the dragons and wyverns and stormed the temple? We didn't have time to stand and fight the ogres toe to toe.

After wounding the second ogre across the cheek and chin, Prince Reveron broke away.

I interposed myself between the bleeding brutes as the prince swung wide around the snapping hydra still trapped by Golt's spell and reached the dais steps.

Drux was down, but moving, shaking his head and grasping for his sword. Several of the hydra's heads hissed and strained their long necks to lock teeth onto the fallen warrior. Coming to his senses, Drux rolled several feet further out of reach.

Blood continued to flow from the second ogre's face wound, but Fendra Jolain's magic fought to stem the Blood Sword's deadly effects. I stabbed my spear into the brute's face. He slapped my weapon aside, forcing me back. Behind him, the crippled ogre crawled forward, sword in hand to reach the dais steps.

Otis leapt on the crippled ogre's back and drove his sword's blade between the brute's muscular shoulders, biting into the spine. The ogre collapsed on his chest, with arms and hands limp and unmoving.

I ducked a deliberate sword slash. My ogre foe kept me at bay, making his way to the steps. I had to stop him. Prince Reveron couldn't afford a foe at his back while confronting the goddess. A crossbow quarrel caught the ogre in its ear. He ignored it and pressed forward. I dodged his sword thrust and slashed with my spear tip, carving a shallow wound.

The cut didn't immediately heal while the flesh around the ogre's cheek wound festered pink. Blood began to pour from it.

From behind me Otis yelled, "Take'em, Flank Hawk."

The ogre ignored me and cocked his arm back, preparing to throw his sword up the dais at the prince in a desperate bid to help his goddess.

The two fan-bearing servants lay at the bottom of the dais, dying from bloody wounds inflicted by the prince's sword. Prince Reveron stood a step below the goddess, the Blood Sword's ruby flaring red being so near to the healing goddess. At least eight feet tall, she towered over him, raining down sharp blows with her white staff. Despite an arrow in his calf, Prince Reveron parried and deflected the goddess's attacks. He'd managed at least one successful strike as the goddess's white robe showed blood around a split in the fabric below her hip.

They exchanged words as they fought, but with the sounds of battle echoing in the chamber, what they said couldn't be heard but by them.

Even as I took the ogre in the chin, driving my spear into his throat up to the crossbar, he followed through with his throw. With a twist I yanked my spear free and leapt back to avoid the collapsing ogre. He didn't clutch at his throat as he fell. His eyes remained locked on the goddess. I turned in time to see his sword strike Prince Reveron across his calves.

The prince toppled back while taking a blow to the head from Fendra Jolain's staff. The Blood Sword flew from his hand and clattered down the dais steps. The prince lay unmoving where he fell, a dent creasing his steel helmet.

"NO!" I shouted and hurled my spear at the goddess. It pierced her robe and stuck in her chest. She pulled it free, clean of blood and smiled as she tossed the weapon aside. An arrow pierced her arm. Otis had killed a balcony archer. She ignored the shaft and stepped down, picking up the prince with ease.

Drux came up next to me, wheezing with blood dripping from his nose and mouth.

"Surrender, and he lives," the goddess announced. "Lay down your weapons."

"The sword," Drux whispered to me as the sounds of battle dropped off. "Fight her with me."

It didn't even look like Prince Reveron was alive, and Drux was in no condition to fight.

"Never!" shouted Prince Halgadin from the far end of the chamber.

"It matters not," Fendra Jolain said. "My worshipers are but moments away. Your king's gambit has failed and your lives are forfeit." With that she tossed Prince Reveron down the steps, to the awaiting hydra.

Wizard Seelain attempted a spell to save her fiancé, but she lacked the strength and only slowed his descent into the snapping, venomous jaws.

Regally the healing goddess descended the steps toward the Blood Sword.

I dove for it, but with a flick of her wrist, the sword lifted off the floor toward her hand.

Supreme Enchantress Thulease must've used the Shard Staff, shouting a spell that countered Fendra Jolain's. The Blood Sword fell and I caught it by the grip.

The ruby flared. I looked up and saw fear on the goddess's eyes as the evil spirit contained within the sword flowed into my arm. Memories of the time I wielded the Blood Sword, and its possession of me, must've inspired a similar look of fear spread across my face.

The evil soul contained within the sword felt stronger than before, but I knew how to hold it off. Summoning energy from the maelstrom around me I forged a barrier within my arm and forced the soul back. Maybe it was the abundance of energy radiated in the healing goddess's presence, or maybe it was the sword's desire for blood, but it didn't resist.

That also meant that facing the goddess, I could draw only upon my comparatively feeble sword skills.

"Flank Hawk!"

Drux's voice snapped me back to the situation at hand in time to roll aside and avoid the butt of Fendra Jolain's staff. It thudded against the floor. Without attempting to rise, I thrust upward, over my head, nicking the goddess's sandaled foot with the Blood Sword's blade.

I continued rolling away and the goddess followed with her staff ready to slam down upon me. There wasn't a chance to get to my feet. Drux dove at the goddess, grabbing her legs and tackling her. I lifted the Blood Sword as she landed on top of me. The blade's tip pierced her chest, slicing into her heart.

She rolled off of me, screaming. Her momentum swung me over on top of her. I held onto the Blood Sword and drove it deeper. Part of me carried on the fight, but most of it was the sword's savage hunger to kill.

Energies flared, magical. The goddess's hands clasped over mine, pushing away, struggling to withdraw the sword. I leaned in, forcing the hilt down, too afraid to look at her face. Too many times I'd seen the Blood Sword's power at work.

Otis leapt past us, attacking the second archer charging forward. Drux climbed to his feet and staggered forward, swinging down two-handed with his sword, chopping deep into the goddess's exposed throat.

Wild energies whipped around me, centered on and through the Blood Sword—like a lightning rod in a thunderstorm. The goddess fell limp, blood oozing from her chest and neck—from her fingernails as her hands slipped away from mine. Her beautiful skin, bruised with blood vessels, ruptured.

I stood and withdrew the Blood Sword. The ruby in its pommel glowed pink. The evil the sword held— the malevolence emitted—was gone. Replaced by calm, warmth. I stumbled back, my mind a jumble.

Prince Halgadin grabbed me by the shoulders. "Steady, Flank Hawk." He shouted over his shoulder, "We must go!"

Wizard Seelain was next to me, gripping my hand, sliding the Blood Sword into a scabbard.

Lilly held Drux, his arm wrapped over her shoulder. "The balcony," she said. "The Colonel's flying machine's out there."

I stared at Lilly, still trying to gather my thoughts and bearing.

"Don't you hear it, Flank Hawk?" Lilly turned away with Drux leaning heavily upon her. "Come on!"

I shook my head, to clear it.

"He's in shock." The voice was Road Toad—Major Jadd's.

Dreaming, now. That had to be it, I thought as Wizard Seelain led me like a child, up the stairs several steps behind my friend who carried my unconscious sister over his shoulder.

Angry shouts somewhere, distant behind me. Curses and arrows. One hit me, stung me. One hit Wizard Seelain too before Wizard Golt closed the metal door.

I faced a ladder—there were three, rope with wooden rungs—and climbed it up to the roof. Up there, three dragons and a handful of wyverns waited. And the Colonel's helicopter. Wizard Seelain pushed my head low as I stumbled under the wind of spinning blades before climbing past a machine gun and onto a canvas seat next to Enchantress Thulease. One of the Colonel's men threw a blanket over her shoulder and legs before buckling her in. Her eyes were wide and teary. She smelled like burned meat.

I watched Wizard Seelain's hands buckle me in place before I vomited, and everything turned gray.

EPILOGUE

I made my way into the Royal Stables, knowing my father would be working there. I found him brushing Little Thunder. The dark bay was one of the queen's favorite mounts. Maybe it was because he was sturdy and reliable. More likely the queen favored the pony because King Tobias refused to be seen with his wife riding upon such an ignoble mount.

The past year's strain showed in my father's narrow face, creased with more lines than I remembered. The gray that once touched only his temples had spread to all but the top of his head. There, remnants of brown remained.

He nodded to me and dismissed a stableboy, but kept brushing as I approached the stall. "Krish," he said, "it's done with?"

"It is," I said. The memorial service for Prince Reveron took most of the morning. I stood as Grand Wizard Seelain's personal guard during the ceremony. She hugged me after the ceremony ended, but said nothing. She hadn't said more than a few words to me since the prince's death, her fiancé's death, even during our return trip. Jadd had been the prince's mentor, and she shared her thoughts with him, and briefly spoke with Lilly. But not with me.

"Grand Wizard Seelain blames herself for the prince's death," I said. "It was me, Dad, who failed him." I didn't tell him she'd heal emotionally once she fully realized who was to blame. It was *me* who failed to stop the ogre's blade.

My father stepped out of the stall, took my helmet from under my arm, and set it on a nearby bench. He then helped me unbuckle my breast plate. I'd paid good coin to have both cleaned and polished, but their luster remained tarnished in my eyes.

He set my armor next to my helmet. "Does the king blame you?"

I shook my head. "I don't think so." Imperial Seer Lochelle would eventually piece everything together. "It depends on what Prince Halgadin thinks."

"I know the crown prince doesn't care much for your friend, Major Jadd."

Dad knew Jadd. He'd even had dinner with my family twice. I'd told my father a few things about my mercenary mentor's history with the crown prince. Besides, my dad picked up on stories about officers and nobles while working in the stables.

"I think they've settled some of their differences," I said.

My father went back to brushing Little Thunder. "You'll know where you stand if the king gives you another medal. If he does," he said, winking once, "you might hang on to it this time."

I smiled briefly. He was right. I grabbed a rag and some oil and began working it into the pony's saddle.

After a few minutes my father said, "A lot of you didn't come back. From both your missions." He patted Little Thunder's neck. "Was getting the Blood Sword back worth it?"

Although I couldn't freely talk about the mission to retrieve the Blood Sword or the raid against Fendra Jolain, he knew a little about them. Serpent handlers picked up on things. Serpent handlers considered themselves better than stablehands, but still they talked. And Rin heard things too, and shared them with Dad. If nothing else, they could count.

And, after today, the names of those who died during the raid on Fendra Jolain's temple would be widely known. Only seventeen of us made it back. Four of the enchanters holding a piece of the Shard Staff also died during the raid. It was the price paid for Enchantress Thulease's efforts. Her daughter and one other enchanter lay in a coma with only an ember of life burning within each of them.

"The war's not over," I said. "Most of the enemy's mercenaries demanded their coin and are returning to the Southern Continent. But the Long-Tooths haven't given up. Won't give up."

"Their morale's broken," my father said, picking up a comb. "Their goddess is dead."

I focused on inspecting the saddle's billet strap, not knowing what to say to my dad. I didn't think Fendra Jolain *was* dead. I held the Blood Sword for only a moment after pulling it from the fallen goddess, before Grand Wizard Seelain helped me sheath it, but its evil was gone. I knew that. She, the goddess's essence, was in the sword now.

The immortal bloods, the gods and goddesses, were at war, but they had rules. I didn't know what the rules were and didn't understand why they had them, but the Colonel knew and followed them. I'd learned that after bartering with him, trading the Blood Sword for a weapon to stop the Necromancer King.

I'd have bet a lot of my own coin that Colonel Ibrahim knew what would happen to Fendra Jolain if we succeeded. Maybe King Tobias knew as well.

If the ancient soul trapped in the Blood Sword brought suffering and death through the blade, what might Fendra Jolain do? Did the king know? If not, he'd certainly learn, but it might take a while. Supreme Enchantress Thulease's burns were healed. She was physically healthy but something inside her was broken. She'd done as ordered by Prince Halgadin. She brought down the steel golem, and through her—through the Shard Staff—sapped the lives of four enchanters to do it. The spell cast to keep the Blood Sword from reaching Fendra Jolain's hand summoned strength from her daughter and another enchanter, leaving them little more than a razor's edge from death.

I looked up to see my dad working, combing Little Thunder's mane. Five minutes must have passed.

"They're releasing your sister to mine and your mother's custody tonight," he said. "It'll be good to have her home again." He paused his combing. Little Thunder stomped once and he started up again. "It's been more than a few years and it's not our home in Pine Ridge."

The moment had come, the one I dreaded. My stomach knotted, but he had to know. I took a deep breath to steady myself. I met his eyes, but couldn't really see him through the welling tears. "Dad, I...I..."

He dropped the comb and moved to stand in front of me. "I know, Son," he said. "I know what happened. Jotey came by yesterday when he learned Raina was going to be sent home." Dad gripped my shoulders. "You did a hard thing—what had to be done. You loved her enough to not let her die."

There was a long silence before I wiped the tears. "She wouldn't speak to me on the way home. Wouldn't even look at me."

"You've been through a lot, Krish. She's been through a lot."

"You think she'll forgive me?"

He shrugged. "Even bound up, she healed your friend Major Jadd, didn't she?"

That was true. Raina awoke, lying bound next to Jadd. He was dying. And even though he was the enemy, she healed him, leaving herself open to vengeance, or his mercy.

My dad turned and went back to his work. "Allow her some time, Son."

I took a deep breath. Another anchor of guilt tied to my heart, but from this one I might someday be cut free.

"What're you going to do now?" he asked.

I didn't know. Prince Reveron was dead. Grand Wizard Seelain? Would she even need a personal guard now, and would she want me to serve as hers? King Tobias knew I was a neophyte healer. He trusted my loyalty and ability to complete missions, but not as much as Prince Reveron did. The prince and Grand Wizard Seelain had been my patrons, and I'd served as the king's pawn through them.

The war wasn't over, but I was tired of death. Weary of seeing those around me fall. I never set out to be a mercenary. The path opened before me and couldn't be avoided.

"I don't know, Dad." I shrugged and sighed. "I don't know."

"You'll figure it out, Son."

He then looked past my shoulder with a smile. I turned to see what he was looking at. Drux, Jadd and Lilly were walking down the line of stalls toward us. Jadd and Drux were still in their dress uniforms, but Lilly had changed out of her formal dress back into her green shirt and leather breeches.

Lilly nearly shouted, "Flank Hawk, we're going to the One-Eyed Pelican. You wanna come too?" She ran up and took my hand, not really giving me a choice.

"I'll see to your armor," my dad said. "Go and enjoy yourself."

"Have you ever eaten there?" I asked him.

Dad smiled a knowing smile even as Jadd crossed his arms and scowled. "Is there something I'm missing?" he asked.

Drux slapped Jadd on the shoulder. "Taste buds?"

"I'm getting the fish soup," Lilly said. "That's your favorite, isn't it, Flank Hawk?"

Jadd put a hand on my shoulder as we turned to go. "You may be right, Lilly," he said before I could reply. "I believe it's the only dish he's ever dined upon there."

THE END

ABOUT THE AUTHOR

Terry W. Ervin II is an English teacher who enjoys writing Fantasy and Science Fiction. He is an editor for *MindFlights*, a guest columnist for *Fiction Factor* and is the author of over two dozen short stories and articles. ***Blood Sword*** is the sequel to his debut novel, ***Flank Hawk***.

When Terry isn't writing or enjoying time with his wife and daughters, he can be found in his basement raising turtles. To contact Terry, or to learn more about his writing endeavors, visit his website at www.ervin-author.com.